THIS SPLINTERED SEA

Haley J Munroe

Madisson—
I'd go to the ends of the earth for you

CONTENT WARNING

Content warnings include:

- Death/grief
- Suicide ideation
- Sex
- Physical and emotional abuse
- Alcohol use
- Violence
- Swearing
- Blood/injuries
- Loss of a mother

Your mental health is important to me. If you have any questions regarding the content of this book, don't hesitate to reach out on Instagram (@haleyjmunroe).

Intercepted correspondence

from the late King Golan after

the fall of the Earth Court

Cordelia,

If you're reading this, Prince Barren is dead. Sarenia has fallen to King Caelus and the Sky Court, and the Princess of the Sea is missing.

You're our only hope.

1

I was a legend, a fable, the chorus of a shanty.

Altars built in my honor once sprinkled shorelines, but the pyres have since been smothered, the mortar crumbled to dust. Once, I was feared, worshipped. Powerful. A decade ago, I was the heir to the sea.

Now I'm a petty thief.

I weave through the crowd and slide a bracelet from a woman's wrist, the diamonds catching the dwindling sunlight as I pocket it between the folds of my dress. Bodies twirl around me, silked in shades of lilac and gold. I slink through and pin my gaze on a ruby ring—one size too large—perched on a hand.

I hold my breath, stilling my heart as I look in the opposite direction, and—

"Briar, there you are."

My blood freezes. I lower my hand and lock eyes with the man I've wanted to kill for the past decade.

I bow my head—not nearly as low as the others would, and force a smile to my face. "Caelus."

A looping melody weaves through the marble columns, pouring into the open-air balcony.

Caelus blocks my view, his lips pressed tight as he sets a hand on my shoulder, squeezing tighter than necessary. "What have I told you?"

"I apologize, Your Majesty." The words are like sand down my throat, pooling in my lungs. A title he never earned, but took. One that he forces me to use while others are around.

He nods. "That's better."

From the arched ceilings, chandeliers cast a soft glow over his blue eyes, emphasizing the way they wrinkle from his smug grin. His fingers weave through mine—unforgiving hands that would execute me if he knew who I am.

But it's been a decade, and not once has someone remembered me, nor recognized me. The Princess of the Sea, forgotten.

"You were looking for me?" I ache to peel his hand from mine, to widen the distance between us before he hears the jewels tapping in my pocket.

"Yes. It's about Sir Dyerson." He yanks me closer, breath brushing my neck as he tilts his chin toward a group of men across the ballroom. "I need you to figure out what he's hiding."

I hum. "Are you worried?"

"Not particularly. I assigned him to one of the territories we claimed last year, and he'd be foolish to attempt anything, but I'm concerned enough to want something against him. And I've heard whispers about his discontent about being assigned to the far reaches of the continent."

The exact blackmail Caelus wants balances on the tip of my tongue. I heard it earlier in the afternoon, from one of the visiting ladies. Dyerson doesn't want anyone to know about the loan he had to take out to keep his business. Or that his wife recently left and took the children with her.

But I swallow the information for now. Ten years ago I

managed to be hired as a royal courtesan, and it didn't take me long to make myself invaluable. Lips are loose when there's a beautiful woman involved, and Caelus knows that, craving the information I feed him in sips.

If I give it to him all at once, however, I give him more power than he already has.

I nod. "Consider it done."

His approving smile churns my stomach, and I clench my jaw. In the years I've overheard conversations within these walls, none of them have been useful. None about the war brewing in the sea, my mother—the queen, at the front.

"Is something the matter, Briar?"

Caelus trails a finger down the length of my spine. Behind him, I catch Queen Isolde staring, eyes narrowed at her husband's hand teasing the base of my spine.

I hold her gaze and smirk. "Of course not, Caelus."

His smile fades, and he lifts a hand, flicking a finger. A gust of wind rattles the windowpanes and shoots in through the balcony, whipping my hair around my head.

Queen Isolde doesn't flinch, despite the power being siphoned from her marrow to fuel his outburst. This stolen display of power.

"Don't forget how quickly I can return you to the streets," Caelus hisses in my ear.

Air wraps around my throat like fingers, digs into my skin, and squeezes just enough for my lungs to burn. They beg for a gasp of air, but I clench my hands into fists, my nails digging into my palm as I hold his gaze.

One wrong move, and he'll stay true to his word. I can't break my curse if I'm fired and banned from these halls.

I force a swallow and nod.

"Good." He releases his hold on me and retreats a step.

I bite into the flesh of my cheek and suck in a controlled breath through my nose until the haze in my vision clears. If I had my power, I'd drown him on dry land—crush him and his people under a blanket of water.

With the wind gone, my dress fans out, settling over the intricate grooves of the tiled floor—a mosaic of intertwined tree limbs. The Earth Court crest. One of the few things in this castle that remains unchanged since Caelus conquered Sarenia.

"Don't make me ask you again," he snarls, striding off.

In the far corner, Thea—caged against the wall by a man—catches my attention.

"Are you okay?" she mouths.

I nod, as I always do.

Her sapphire eyes contrast deep umber skin, and the opal beads in her braids tap against her waist as she flicks her gaze toward the balcony. The sun sinks lower with every second, and my chest squeezes.

If I don't leave soon, I'll be too late.

I lose myself in the crowd, scanning necks, wrists, fingers—any place I could slide off or unclasp a piece of jewelry, and get to work.

Within minutes, my pockets weigh down my dress, and sweat gathers at my brow. I wander toward the open balcony and slip a bracelet off the wrist of a woman as she passes me. Sliding it into my pocket, I give myself a brief reprieve—a stolen moment in the fresh air, free of the bodies packed into the ballroom.

On either end of the balcony, a curved staircase descends to the castle gardens. To the right, a mountain range casts half the castle in jagged shadows. But to the left, the city of Sarenia sprawls to the ocean, where boats bob against a maze of docks.

I brace myself against the rail and close my eyes, pressing my hands against the cold stone. A breath passes my lips, and I dive into myself, searching for a glimpse of my power—a sign it isn't fully gone.

I reach, grappling, but all I find are frayed strands of what was once an endless depth.

There's nothing.

My gut sours, and I blink my eyes open against the setting sun. I can almost hear the ocean's whisper, beckoning me like a lover. My breath hitches, and I turn back to the ballroom, straightening out the dress that wouldn't last a second at sea.

I reach into my pocket and press my fingertips into the sharp edges of the gems, tallying their size and worth. One of my most successful days.

The woman I passed on my way out clutches her wrist and glances around the floor, searching for a bracelet she won't find.

My cue to leave.

Tugging at my ear, I slip into the ballroom and stride past Thea. She nods and pushes away from the wall, weaving under the arm of the man as she strides toward Caelus, ready to distract him.

Keeping to the outskirts of the room, I sneak to the doorway as a man notices his ring missing. He turns to the waitstaff beside him, face ruddy as he accuses him of theft.

Shouts billow, echoing off the ceiling, and I yank a cloak at random from the closet, disappearing into the hallway. My heart races, but I force myself to keep my steps calm. This is the first time my thievery has been noticed during a ball.

The heavy oak doors swing shut, muffling the ballroom. I drape the cloak over my shoulders and button it at my throat, forcing my racing pulse to calm. The vacant hallway welcome me, and I stride past open windows framed with blue silk curtains billowing in the breeze.

Banners drape overhead, embroidered with a falcon pierced by a bolt of lightning—the Sky Court crest. The night I first walked beneath them sweeps into my memory, but ten years ago, they bore a towering tree. When they belonged to the Earth Court.

A decade ago, to this day, climbing roses and wisteria adorned these walls and wrapped around the window frames. A pianist played for hours while guests mingled, waiting for the wedding ceremony that never came.

The night I killed the man I was arranged to marry.

And the moment I slid my blade across his throat, I learned my mother made a deal with the goddess—promised my hand for reasons I have yet to discover. A pact she made in blood that, when I failed to fulfill, cursed me.

Stowing away the thoughts, I glide around the corner and stop in front of a mirror, tucking errant strands of brown hair into my hood. Leaning closer, I dab off my lipstick and wipe the blush from my cheeks.

"Such a pretty thief."

I gasp, whirling as a shadow emerges from the alcove and slinks into a sliver of sunlight.

Queen Isolde smiles, blue eyes so light the irises nearly blend with the whites. She tilts her head and studies me. "Care to tell me where you're taking those stolen jewels, courtesan?"

I smile. "Wouldn't you like to know."

Her eyes spark, and a hint of power swirls below the surface—what little is left of what she gives to Caelus. She steps closer, stopping an inch away, and my heart trips over itself.

She lifts a hand and drags her thumb over my bottom lip. "I hate it when he touches you like that."

I swallow. Before I respond, she crashes her mouth to mine. Weaving a hand to my nape, she tilts my head, and as she deepens the kiss, my pulse thrashes in my ears. I part her lips with mine, tracing my tongue against the sharp edge of her teeth.

She makes a noise, halfway between a sigh and a whimper, and I force myself to pull back. As much as I'd love to lose time with her, I don't have that luxury. Her chest expands on an inhale, breath ragged.

"Simply part of the job," I say, wiping a smear of my lipstick from her mouth. And that's what dragged me to her, too—at first. The promise of information, the temptation of revenge. It was Isolde, after all, who surrendered to Caelus and gave him rule over her court and her power.

Because of her, he controls the Sky Court, conquered the Earth, and is after the Sea.

I never thought I'd fall in love with her.

"It doesn't make it any easier," she says, straightening her bodice.

I tuck a blonde curl behind her ear. "Did he mention what he's announcing this evening at dinner?"

She shakes her head. "Nothing I don't already know, but all of his generals and governors are here, staying in the castle. Whatever it is, it has him worried. I can feel it."

Voices and footsteps sound from around the corner, and I stiffen, pressing my hand against the jewels in my pocket.

Isolde's eyes widen, but she presses a kiss to my temple and lifts my hood onto my head. "Go, before they catch you."

I gnaw on my lip. While still a queen, she's not permitted to roam the castle unaccompanied. Caelus insists it's for her safety, but we all know it's out of fear she'll somehow manage to escape his hold on her. And if it were truly for her safety, he wouldn't beat her every time she's caught.

And if he knew about her relationship with me, I'd be executed.

"Will you be okay?" I breathe, eyeing the turn in the corridor.

"Of course." Weaving around me, she gives one last smile and strides toward the hall. "I'll come up with a valid excuse."

I watch her turn the corner, hating that whatever she faces on the other side, she'll be doing it alone. But I swallow and take off down the opposite hall, my cloak billowing behind me as I weave to the side door.

There's one thing she said, her words churning—tumbling in my mind. If Caelus is worried about this upcoming announcement, it can only mean one thing—he's losing his grasp on control.

As I clear the final turn and push through the door, a stone settles in my stomach. If Caelus is desperate, there's no telling what he's capable of doing.

2

____

I weave through the streets of Sarenia, my footsteps light as I glance over my shoulder, searching the shadows in my wake, but no guards follow.

I tilt my head to the sky, letting my hood fall. Judging by the height of the sun, I have about an hour before high tide. Any longer, and I risk the pirates raising their anchors and leaving shore for several more weeks.

The streets bustle, bodies packed tight across the wide avenue. I skirt around a vendor tucked beneath a canvas tent. Overhead, a woman leans out the window of a worn brick building, hanging wet laundry on a line sagging over the alley.

I dip off the main street, onto the deserted path, and make my way to the docks.

The sun blinds me as I emerge from the alley. Salt air sprays over my skin, brine clinging to the ends of my hair, waves crashing in the distance.

My footsteps slow, and I sigh.

The ocean.

I close my eyes and tune out the world. My thoughts wander, and I'm aboard *The Twelfth Night*, the breeze teasing my hair, mist caressing my face. Waves crest, whitecaps lapping against the hull. My crew, raising the sails. Thea clinging to the mast, her smile a crescent moon.

Even after a decade, the phantom feeling of a deck swaying beneath my feet is more comfortable than the stillness of land.

A seagull screams, and I open my eyes, where there is no ship. No crew. Where the deck beneath my feet, the sea at my fingertips, and the power coursing through my veins is nothing but a faint memory.

Clouds roll in from the mountains and billow overhead, shadowing the sea-battered homes.

"Fuck," I murmur.

Caelus released his hold on the weather.

There's a brief intermission between the ball and dinner, but if I'm back too late, Thea will run out of excuses for my whereabouts.

Oil lanterns flicker to life, and the clouds darken, promising a storm. I throw the hood back over my head and break into a run, my feet splashing through shallow puddles.

I clear the last row of homes, and masts soar into the sky, teetering with the waves. Crews bustle around the ships, hurrying barrels and crates into hulls before the storm hits.

I lower my gaze from the well-kept ships of the Sky Court and follow the dock to the end, where the vessels fly flags with a skull.

Pirates were banned when Sarenia belonged to the Earth Court, but now Caelus employs them, paying a price worth trading their dignity for. They sail the seas, capturing enemies that outrun Caelus's aerial armada.

But I've met enough pirates to know they can be bribed.

I step in front of a man and slap a hand on the keg he's rolling toward the gangplank. "I'm looking for Cassio."

He pauses, raking his eyes over me. "And who should I say is asking for him?"

"Irene."

"Irene," he repeats, tasting the name one letter at a time.

"I don't have all day."

"A shame you aren't looking for me." A smile. "I've always liked the ones with sharp tongues."

My nostrils flare, and I narrow my eyes, leveling him with a glare. "If you don't stop talking, you'll be missing yours."

I slide my dagger out, far enough for the sinking sun to reflect off the polished metal. His smile falters, and he mutters a curse under his breath before disappearing up to the deck.

Ships groan against their ropes, and seagulls argue overhead, fighting over scraps one managed to pluck from the docks.

I toe the gangplank.

The first few weeks of the curse were tempting. Bottle of wine in hand, I'd sit on these docks, legs swinging over the edge, and stare at the ships, debating whether to end the agony of being landlocked.

All it would take is a step aboard a ship. A dive into the water. In a blink, I would die.

But when I found Thea working as a courtesan, the thought never crossed my mind again. I'd watch the world end before I leave her.

She must have disobeyed my orders and left the ship, running into the castle the night I was cursed. That's the only reasoning I can come up with as to why she's here and the rest of my crew isn't. If only I had asked them to follow me—like they wanted to—then I wouldn't be searching for them, hoping they're still alive.

"Irene."

Cassio appears on the deck, hands clasped behind his back as the sun glints off the sword strapped low around his waist and the silver rings embellishing his fingers.

A pang shoots through my chest at the leathery tan of his

skin. I have since paled without the relentless sun beating down on me, my freckles washed away like sand.

He smiles and leans an elbow on the rail. "To what do I owe this pleasure?"

"You know exactly why I'm here."

I cross my arms, and he stares at my pocket, narrowing his eyes. He drags his tongue across gold-capped teeth. "Always one for secrets, aren't you?"

"And the one with your payment."

He scoffs and glances over his shoulder. "Bring them up!"

I stiffen, holding my breath as a crew member leads a line of women out from below deck.

Four this time.

My heart pounds, hope twisting into the space between my ribs. Two more than last month.

Shapeless, threadbare dresses hang from their bodies, and canvas bags cover their heads, their wrists bound behind their backs.

I fist the fabric of my cloak. "They aren't your prisoners."

"Aye," Cassio says, "but I had to take precautions when they started fighting back. A shame, since their faces were so nice to look at."

He runs a finger over the shoulder of the one closest to him. She jerks back, muttering something indecipherable. I hold my breath and inch forward. That's something one of my crew members would do. They'd fight back.

"Remove the bags," I say, voice hardly more than a whisper.

Cassio turns to the pirate and nods. My pulse rattles in my ears, jaw clenched so tight it aches. In quick succession, he removes the sacks from their heads.

My stomach sinks.

I don't recognize them.

The pirate wraps his hand around the arm of the first and steps toward the gangplank, but Cassio blocks the path.

"I'll be collecting payment first."

I root my feet to the spot, firmly away from the gangplank. "Then come get it."

He cants his head, tilting the wide brim of his hat away from his face. "You're brave enough to steal fine jewelry and do business with pirates, yet too scared to step aboard my ship?"

I glance down at my nails. "Why would I want to step onto your poor excuse of a ship?"

"Careful, lass."

"If you'd rather me take my business elsewhere, I can find another pirate to work with."

The women shoot me a glare, and I can't blame them. I can only imagine where Cassio rescued them from—the treatment they received in one of Caelus's prisons.

Cassio stares at me, assessing.

I shrug and turn on my heel.

One step.

Two.

"Wait!"

I pause, smirking as Cassio steps onto the dock, each heavy footfall shaking the wood. I blindly reach into my pocket and grab a handful of jewels on the top, avoiding the valuable ones carefully arranged at the bottom.

"A little too desperate for my business now, aren't you, Cassio?"

I shove the jewelry against his chest and smirk at the way he scrambles, catching them before they drop through the slats.

Facing away from the royal ships, he sorts through each piece of jewelry and drops them into a velvet pouch. "This isn't enough." He pulls the drawstrings. "There's a bounty hunter out here searching ships, and I have some people I need to pay off to avoid her."

I shake my head. "Not my problem. This is all you're getting."

"Then you're only getting half the women."

I yank him by the collar of his shirt. His eyes shoot wide, and I lower my voice to a snarl. "I wonder what would happen if Caelus found an employed pirate exchanging prisoners for stolen jewels?"

He swallows. "You wouldn't dare."

Goosebumps spread down his neck, and I tilt my lips into a wicked grin, tightening my grip. "Prison? Torture? Perhaps he'd freeze your body inch by inch, until you're begging him to kill you."

He rips himself free and shoots a wary glance to the ships docked beside us. "You're a peach to work with, you know that?"

"I make you rich."

Ignoring my words, he ties the pouch to his belt. "Bring them down."

The pirate leads the first down, and the rest follow, their feet unsteady, eyes scanning the docks.

I nod at their wrists. "The rope."

Cassio pulls a pocketknife from his belt and shears away the rope. It drops to the deck, slides through the cracks, and the women rub at their raw wrists, their shoulders trembling.

"I'll see you in a few weeks," Cassio says, sauntering back to his ship.

I wait until he's out of sight then turn to the group of women. "Follow me. Don't walk too close, and don't speak. Don't attract any attention. Understood?"

Despite her untrusting eyes, the one closest to me nods, and the others follow her lead.

The bottom swell of the sun touches the horizon, clouds chasing after it, and the ships around us raise their anchors, eager to outrace the storm. I tug the edges of my cloak closer together and retrace my path away from the docks.

Weaving between buildings and alleys, I take a complicated

route toward the safe house, doubling back on myself just in case. Only when I'm a block away, do I glance over my shoulder and check on the others. From various distances, the four women stare back at me.

Ice spreads beneath my skin.

There's a fifth.

3

———————

I halt, and the women I rescued pause, glancing at me.

The closest furrows her brow. "What's wrong?"

An oil lamppost flickers to life, reflecting off a blade strapped to the stranger's waist, her features veiled by a hood pulled over her eyes.

I swallow and gauge the distance to the safe house. If I didn't have the others, I could outrun her, or at least throw her off my trail. But with them, I risk exposing the location.

"Take the next left," I whisper, wrapping a hand around my dagger. "Five doors down, there's a house with an orange awning. Knock three times and ask for Rita."

"But—"

"Go." I grit my teeth and push her forward, tilting my chin at the other three to follow. "Run."

They take off, darting down the adjacent alley. The woman stalking closer doesn't slow, nor does she chase after them. She lifts her head, enough for me to catch the smirk on her lips as tendrils of black hair come untucked from her collar.

"Don't split up on my accord," she says, an amused lilt to her voice.

I narrow my eyes, tightening my grip on the blade. "Can I help you?"

Her steps are silent as the distance between us shrinks. She scoffs. "How strange, offering help while your fingers dance on a weapon. I saw you with that pirate."

I stiffen.

She circles me like a beast would prey. "You wouldn't happen to be the reason why the castle is up in arms about stolen jewelry, would you?"

My chest tightens. "I have no idea what you're talking about."

"So you didn't just trade a handful of jewels for those women?"

I trace her movements, searching for a weakness, a single misstep, but she shifts into the light, far enough that I catch a glimpse of her eyes. A deep, honey-brown.

I shake my head. "You're mistaking me for someone else."

"Couldn't possibly forget a face like yours." There's a dare in her voice, and she comes to a stop, scanning me. "I'm sure they'd offer a handsome reward for you, wouldn't they?"

I lunge, shoving her against the alley wall, and pin my forearm against her throat. She brings an arm up, but I flick my dagger up and angle it against the artery in her neck. Those honey eyes widen, and I relish in it, waiting for her surprise to morph into fear.

But they relax, challenge me, and the fiery thrill racing through me fades.

I shove my arm against her windpipe, earning a wince. "If you so much as speak a word of this, you won't be alive long enough to see how much they'd pay."

She clicks her tongue. "Such harsh words from such a pretty mouth."

My grip falters.

She slams a fist into my side and knocks me off balance. I

stumble, throwing an arm out, but before I regain my footing, she twists and slams my back against the wall.

Forcing in a breath, I adjust the dagger in my grip, aim it toward her ribs, and—

She captures my wrist with a hand and squeezes until my dagger drops, clattering to the stone.

"You're getting ahead of yourself, love," she whispers, breath hot against my throat. "I never said I *would* turn you in, just that I could. But..."

Her words trail off as a breeze floats down the alley and parts my cloak, exposing the beading on my silk, castle-issued gown.

"A courtesan?" That tilted smirk returns, and her eyes meet mine. "It appears you're much more valuable than I thought."

I bare my teeth, and she drags a finger over my jaw.

"No need for that." Keeping me pinned to the wall, she inches back, far enough to slide her sword from its sheathe. I writhe, but she jerks the tip of the blade to the space over my heart.

"What do you want from me?" I say, pinning my gaze to her rather than the sword threatening to plunge into my chest. My breaths are too shallow, but if I pull in more air, the blade will pierce skin.

"You'll find out soon enough, I'm sure." Without lowering her blade, she sinks down and plucks my dagger from the ground. Straightening, she holds my eyes as she parts my cloak and finds the sheathe strapped to my thigh.

My chest tightens as she slides my blade into its holster.

She steps back. "I'll be seeing you again."

Before I can form a response, she strides down the alley. I push off the wall and train my gaze to the space between her shoulders, but stop short.

It wouldn't take much to catch her—weaving through the alleys until I intercept her path. But I'm losing time, and I need to get the jewels to Rita before she comes looking for me.

I grind my teeth together and watch the woman's shadow disappear around the corner, my wrist aching from where she held it against the wall.

Blowing out a breath, I turn and follow the worn, familiar steps to the safe house. I climb the short staircase, and before I have a chance to knock, the door swings open.

"Oh, thank goodness," Rita breathes, throwing her arms around me. "I was so worried."

She pulls back and frames my face with her hands, scanning me over a pair of thick glasses.

Warmth blooms in my chest, and I smile as I gently pry her hands from my face. "I'm always fine. You know that." I glance over her shoulder, into the warm light of the kitchen. "Are they?"

"Come see for yourself." Her eyes soften. "I have tea waiting for you."

I follow her through the doorway and into the kitchen where the four women sit around the large driftwood table. My heart aches for them—the sunken eyes, nails worn to jagged stubs, skin pale as they take careful bites of food Rita laid out for them.

"They're doing better than the last ones," Rita whispers. She sweeps across the threshold and removes the steaming kettle from the stovetop.

I watch as she pours the water into a mug, her frail hands sure and steady. She found me crying into the sand on one of those first blurry, drunken days and took me in. Just like she has for hundreds of others.

But it's been a decade since then, and time has worn on her. It has pressed wrinkles into the corners of her eyes and grey into her hair, and suddenly the woman who was like a mother to me is now a grandmother.

One of the women sets down her fork and stares at the wall behind me, tilting her head.

I lean against it and drag my fingertips over the painted mural. "Everyone who comes through here adds to it, each painting something new." A field of flowers. A brick house. A pair of clasped hands. "Dreams, if you will."

"They're beautiful," she breathes.

I pause over my own—waves cresting against the hull of a ship—and my throat thickens. Dropping my hand, I step away. "Feel free to add your own."

Something in my chest thaws at the smile that ghosts her lips. I don't know her name, and I never will. And she'll never know mine—not my real one anyway. It's safer that way.

I motion for Rita to follow me into the hallway. She nods, wiping her hands down the front of her apron.

Laughter floats down from the bedrooms upstairs, and I lower my voice as she joins me. "I need to get going."

Her eyes widen. "But you just got here."

"I know, but Caelus has something big he's announcing at dinner." I dig the remaining jewels out of my pocket and offer them to her. "This should be enough to last until I'm back."

She pockets them in her apron and takes my hand, giving it a squeeze. "This could last us years, and you know that. Keep yourself safe."

I glance over her shoulder into the kitchen where there's no noise but the clinking of silverware. I should teach them how to fight, how to protect themselves, but—

"We'll be fine," Rita says, pulling my gaze back to her.

I chew on my lip and nod. "I'll be back as soon as I can."

"I know."

She kisses my cheek and returns to the kitchen. I watch her go, memorizing her gait and the bounce of her coiled hair, just in case it's the last time. A swallow makes its way down my throat.

I should mention the woman I ran into and the threats she spewed. But that will only worry Rita.

I push myself outside, where rainfall pours from the sky, splashing onto rooftops and rolling down copper gutters. Sunset has long faded—flickering lanterns the only light spilling over the path.

Dinner will start any moment.

A vise seizes my heart. I've been gone too long.

4

My shoes click over the marble steps. Shedding my damp cloak, I throw it over one arm and keep to the edge of the staircase, half-hidden behind a group of women.

Bodies pack the castle, far busier than it was this afternoon, and my shoulders loosen. If I'm lucky, Caelus hasn't noticed my absence.

I push my damp hair out of my face and branch off at the landing, heading down the hallway to the living quarters I share with Thea. The door swings open beneath my touch, and I slide in, pressing it shut behind me.

A fire crackles in the hearth, drying the rain gathered at my hairline and the soaked hem of my gown.

"What took you so long?"

In the vanity mirror, Thea raises a brow and twists a tube of lipstick before dabbing crimson along her lips. I undo my braid and comb my fingers through my hair. It's damp, a mix of rainwater and ocean spray, but it'll do.

I shrug. "The usual heckling from Cassio, but you know how it goes."

Her gaze meets mine in the reflection, and she nods, giving a disapproving tilt of her lips. "I do, unfortunately."

I ignore the judgement in her tone and slip off my wet shoes, trading them out for a dry pair. "Was Caelus looking for me?"

"Not at all. He got caught up with a general, discussing the warfront."

My throat constricts. "Did they mention anything about Marina?"

I choose my words carefully, balancing them on the tip of the tongue, parsing out the word *queen*. My mother, the last one fighting. And, because of the curse, convinced I'm dead.

Thea shakes her head. "If they did, I wasn't close enough to hear." Her brow furrows. "Why?"

I school my face, wiping away the guilt that's eaten at my marrow for the last decade. "Curious, that's all."

Bypassing the two four-poster beds, I drape my cloak over the hearth and sink into the chair beside it, facing the sweeping view of the ocean out the window.

Thea's gaze follows me. "Don't you think you're being a bit reckless? You carry a weapon and lift jewels off anyone who gets close enough. Aren't you worried what Caelus will do if he finds out?"

I prop my chin on my hand. "He's not going to find out."

She scoffs. "What makes you so sure of yourself?"

A knot forms in my chest. I inhale a long breath and rest my feet on the low coffee table. "Thea?"

Her hands pause on the tube of lipstick, eyes meeting mine. "Yes?"

Here goes nothing.

"I am Briar, Princess of the Sea, Captain of *The Twelfth Night*. And you, Thea, are my first mate."

Her eyes glaze over.

"When I refused to marry Barren and killed him, Terra

cursed me. And you, too. I cannot touch the ocean or use my power, and you can't remember who we are. No one can."

She tilts her head, and a deep vertical line forms between her brows.

"The only way to break the curse is to captain a ship. Impossible, considering I can't board one, and Caelus forbids women from captaining."

She presses her eyes shut, and when they open, they're clear. Familiar. Angry. They widen, then narrow. Her nostrils flare, a muscle feathering in her jaw.

The countdown begins.

Five.

She stands from the stool and drops her tube of lipstick. It rolls under the bed, out of sight. "Briar, we have to get out of here. Where's the ship?"

Four.

"What if I become a captain somehow, then give the ship to you? We could make that work, right?"

Without waiting for an answer, she paces in front of the fireplace, nodding to herself. I can't do anything but watch. After doing this every day for nearly ten years, I know exactly how it plays out, but the repetition doesn't ease my guilt. If anything, it worsens the blame.

Three.

"I'm going to kill Caelus. He took advantage of your absence and started a war. He wants to take the sea. The *sea*. It doesn't belong to anyone, not even us." She glances down at her dress and fists the material with her hands. "What the fuck am I wearing?" Her gaze darts to me, and she grimaces. "Briar, why are we dressed like courtesans?"

A long pause, then her shoulders fall. "Where's the rest of the crew?"

Two.

I bite my lip as a tear rolls down my cheek.

She stiffens and covers her mouth with a hand. Her eyes pierce me, widening. "They took her. They—they took Celia."

A sob escapes her throat, guttural, and like I do every time, I look away. A coward, unable to face my own consequences.

One.

Her back stiffens, and the sob halts as if severed by a knife. She drops her hands to her sides and brushes the wrinkles out of her dress. Our gazes meet, and she smiles that familiar smile. But the light behind her eyes is gone, extinguished—any hint of our conversation wiped from her mind.

She's still in there, somewhere. Thea, the fearless woman I've spent my life beside, my trust tied to her in knots. But this Thea doesn't remember Celia—the love of her life, other half of herself.

The wrench in my chest turns another notch.

She glides back to the vanity and sinks onto the stool, searching through the drawers. "Have you seen my lipstick?"

"Here," I say, handing her mine.

Her fingers brush mine as she takes the tube. "I can always count on you."

I press my tongue into my cheek and nod, fighting the tears climbing up the back of my throat.

The storm outside clears. One moment, rain pelts the window. The next, stars twinkle in the cloudless sky. Our cue dinner is about to begin.

We leave our quarters and follow the crowd to the grand hall, skimming the edges of the room until we find out our assigned table with the rest of the royal courtesans. Guests take their seats while waiters sweep through the room, passing out glasses of wine.

Thea leans over. "Any idea what he's going to announce?"

I take a sip of wine and shrug. "He didn't tell me anything."

The crowd hushes as two armed guards flank the wooden

doors and pull them open, the hinges groaning under the weight.

"Please rise for His Majesty, King Caelus of the Sky Court."

Draining my glass, I rise to my feet and press my lips into a thin line. Treating him as a superior never fails to make my skin crawl.

He enters, his suit so powder blue it's nearly white, with a series of metal chains hanging from his lapels. Isolde follows in his wake, her crown of ice catching the light from the chandeliers, curls pinned away from her face.

I scan her for marks, bruises—any indication Caelus punished her for wandering the castle earlier this afternoon. But I know better. He ensures his beatings are lower than her collar, higher than her sleeves.

She lifts her attention from the runner, and our gazes meet. Her eyes soften, imperceptible to everyone else in the room, and my chest squeezes.

She's only ever whispered about her regret in the small hours of the morning—that if she could turn back time, she wouldn't surrender or allow Caelus to siphon her power. But it's too late, and the invisible chains linked to her wrists are clamped tight.

"Isolde," Caelus hisses under his breath.

She stiffens, and her gaze snaps back to the space at her feet. I splay open my palm, as though I'm reaching for something at the edge of the table. As Isolde passes, she swings her arm at the right moment.

Our hands brush.

The air thickens between us for a fraction of a heartbeat, and the tension in her shoulders eases, ironed out. I swallow, watching as they climb the steps to the dais. There's a slight limp to Isolde's right side, and my hands ball into fists.

She takes her spot on the throne beside his, her hands

clasped in her lap. Lifting her gaze to mine and barely moving her lips, she mouths, "I'm okay."

I bite the inside of my cheek.

Caelus turns to the crowd. "You may sit."

Chairs scrape against the floor, drowning out the murmurs that circulate through the room. I perch on the edge of my seat, my hands pressed against my knees as I scan the generals faces for any hint of what's happening at the warfront. But they're all staring at Caelus, waiting for his announcement.

Caelus clears his throat, adjusting his collar, and the room silences. "Today marks a decade of my rule, and during this time, we have seized dozens of territories in the name of the Sky Court. Across the continent, we have built an empire stronger than ever before." Low applause fills the room, and Caelus smiles. "To celebrate, I am holding a competition."

I hold my breath.

"The Gales will be no ordinary trials, but a series of three deadly tests. Most who sign up will lose their lives, but those who make it to the end will be judged by Terra herself. And whoever earns her blessing, will have a single wish granted."

I jerk forward in my seat, air rushing from my lungs as voices fill the ballroom. My gaze darts to Thea. "I should sign up."

She blinks. Once. Twice. Then bursts into laughter, the sound like bells. "That's ridiculous."

Gnawing on my lip, I study the way she so delicately holds the stem of her wineglass—the same hands that once gripped a rope as she swung between masts and hoisted sails. A memory she doesn't have.

I can win. For her, my court, and the crew I wronged.

A gust of wind shoots over our heads, hushing the voices, and Caelus lifts his chin. "If you choose to enter, enrollment will be held outside the castle gates until midnight."

Out the balcony, a flock of massive falcons soar over the city, dropping leaflets over the rooftops. They flutter down like snowflakes, and, even from here, I spot crowds gathering in the streets.

"Good luck to all those who enter."

Caelus lowers into his seat, and a servant sets a plate of steaming food in front of him. A flurry of waiters enters, each balancing trays on their palms.

This could be my only chance.

I lean closer to Thea. "Listen very carefully."

She stiffens, raising a brow. "Okay?"

"I need you to cover for me until I get back."

"Where are you going?"

I hesitate. If I tell her the truth, she'll try to stop me. "The restroom. I'm feeling unwell."

Her mouth pinches, and she glances at my stomach, unconvinced. "Maybe it was the wine you drank on an empty stomach."

"Yeah, maybe it was."

I slide out of my seat and slip through the front doors, nodding to the guards as I pass. I keep my footsteps calm and controlled, as any courtesan would when stepping out.

Gathering the skirt of my dress, I stride out of the grand hall and sprint toward the castle gates.

5

———————

Fresh air wafts over my face. In the center of the courtyard, a group crowds a table. Men, women, young, old. There's no orderly line—no direction. The flyers only fell from the sky moments ago, yet people are already fighting for a chance to gamble their lives.

I force a swallow and elbow through. Towering bodies crush in from every side, sweat cloying at my lungs. The noise dulls in my ears, heart pounding in my head. So many people. My chest constricts, and my heels slip over the uneven stones, but I keep my focus trained on the table and break through to the front.

The Sky Court guard raises a brow. "Can I help you?"

Bodies press into my back, and the jagged surface of the table digs into my hips and palms as I force myself to remain upright. "I'd like to sign up."

He straightens, frozen for a heartbeat, then barks a laugh. Within moments, others join in, their breath hot on the back of my neck.

My lip curls. "Is there a problem?"

His smile only grows. I burn his features into my mind—the

curve of his nose, the dark beads of his pupils, the arch of his lips.

I never forget a face.

"You're a courtesan." A scoff. "His Majesty's favorite, if I'm not mistaken."

There's a weight to his words—a judgment that paints a target on my back. Gazes bore into me, pressing closer.

"I'm failing to see your point," I bite out.

I snatch the quill, but before I ink my name onto the list, the guard slams my wrist into the table and pins it beneath his hand.

"You aren't allowed to enter."

I blow out a huff. "That's absurd. I have every right to—"

"No castle staff are permitted." He smiles, eyes dancing over me. "King's orders, darling."

"But—"

His free hand finds the pommel of the sword strapped to his waist. "Are you questioning the King?"

Registering the threat in his tone, I lower my eyes. I'm trained well enough to know I don't hold an advantage here— not with so many witnesses. "No."

If word got back to Caelus that I attacked a royal guard, I wouldn't live to morning.

And I refuse to die at the hand of a man rather than the embrace of the sea.

"Good. Move along, then."

Dropping the quill, I rip free from his grasp and push my way out of the crowd—past the pointed, lingering gazes clinging to me like moss.

I clench my jaw and slip into an empty, dark alley.

My feet ache, but I can't return into the castle. Not yet. Not with the only chance of freedom—the moment I've waited an entire decade for—ripped from my grasp.

The back door of a tavern swings open and slams into the

wall across from me. I slink into the shadows as two men appear, pulling another behind them. His head is bowed, legs limp, feet dragging over the floor. They murmur something unintelligible and roll him down the stairs.

He hits the ground with a thud, motionless.

The door slams shut, leaving his body bathed in the glow of an oil lantern. I step closer and furrow my brow. It's not a man after all, but a woman. Short, blonde hair spills from her collar, pooling into a puddle. I kneel beside her and press my fingers to her artery.

No heartbeat.

My breath catches. I reel back as thick, oily blood drips from a wound at her ribs and runs through the cracks in the gravel. There's a name sewn into the underside of her collar—Harriet Wells.

I lean closer and find a slip of paper peeking out from her clenched fist. Prying her fingers open, I retrieve it.

A list of names stares back at me—some illegible, some crossed out, and all with values scribbled beside them in the margins.

I scan her lifeless body. She must be the bounty hunter Cassio was talking about, the one he was so worried about avoiding. Returning my focus to the list, I scan the bottom, and my blood turns to ice.

Princess of the Sea.

Beneath that is a list of locations spanning every landmass and body of water, each crossed out, except for one. Sarenia.

My stomach roils, and I tear the paper into bits, scattering the remains into the puddle. Returning to the woman, I press my fingers to her throat, holding my breath while I check for her pulse again.

A minute passes with no heartbeat.

I sink onto my heels and ball my hands into fists. I only

wish she lived long enough for me to interrogate her about who's looking for me. Why she's scoured the world for me.

The only person I can think of is Caelus, but even then, he's never been concerned with trying to find me. Most people assume I'm dead.

Her hat falls off and sinks into the puddle. I ease it out, and water spills over the brim. I run my fingers over the worn edges and the folded sides sewn to the cap.

A pirate.

My heart thuds in my chest.

She would be allowed to enter The Gales.

Tilting my head, I scan her clothes—a tad oversized. They'd be long on me, but nothing a seamstress couldn't fix.

The puddle stills, and my reflection stares back. I'm cast in shadows, but I make out my blue eyes, long hair, and rounded cheekbones—so at odds with her short blonde hair and harsh features.

Nothing glamour can't alter.

I bolt upright and shake my head. No, it would be far too risky.

I retreat a step, and my foot sinks into water, soaking me to the ankle. A shout comes from the end of the alley, and a group of men stagger past, likely heading to a pub after adding their names to the list.

Their faces cloud my vision, and Caelus's smile haunts my thoughts—his every unwanted touch a brand on my skin. My hands grip the hat so hard they tremble, fingertips sinking into the worn leather.

This is my chance to break the curse.

Water drips from the gutter behind me, splashing to the cobblestones. For years, I've passed as a courtesan and spy, slipping right under the nose of the Sky Court.

If anything, I know how to remain hidden in plain sight.

My blood pumps faster, heating me from within. A serpentine smile tilts the corners of my mouth. I kneel down, my dress pooling in dirty rain water, and run my fingers over the cotton of her shirt.

I tug at the strings crisscrossing her collar. "You won't miss these clothes, will you?"

Standing, I arrange the pirate's hat in my palm and press it to the top of my head.

Perfect fit.

6

I slam the door shut and sink against it, tilting my head back. The pirate's clothes lay leaden in my arms, damp and reeking of spilled ale.

"Briar?"

I flinch and ball the clothes against my chest. "Thea? You should be at dinner."

"You were gone so long. I got worried, so I came to check on you." She eyes the clothes, the hat pinned beneath my arm, the water stains along the hem of my dress. A brow lifts. "Where have you been?"

I gnaw on the end of my thumbnail. In the years I've been stealing jewels, Thea never threatened to tell Caelus. Whether it's for the greater good, or because something deep in her soul recognizes mine, I'm unsure.

This—impersonating a pirate for a deadly competition— might be the final thing she cannot tolerate.

I glance at the clock, the minutes quickly ticking closer to midnight. Only one way to find out.

I swallow. "Thea?"

"Yes?"

"I need your help."

The groove between her brows deepens. "What is it?"

"Have you seen Marianne and Gemma?"

"Just a few moments ago, heading to their quarters. Why?"

I drag a hand down my face. The more people I pull in, the riskier it gets. But I have no other choice. "Can you get them, please?"

She steps closer, and the lantern's glow catches the side of her face. "Why do you need them?"

"I'll explain later. I promise."

She hesitates, but she must read the desperation in my eyes, and lets out a long, weighted sigh. "Okay, but I don't like this."

"Thank you," I breathe.

With a final assessing look, she crosses the room and slips through the servant's door tucked into the back.

I kick off my shoes and unbutton the back of my dress, letting it pool on the floor. Unlacing my corset, I yank it off and suck in a deep breath, my aching lungs expanding after being constricted all day.

I drag my gaze over the wrinkled clothing.

The dark alley concealed the stains marring the front of the shirt and the seams unraveling at the cuff of the pants. I grimace, but lift the shirt and thread it over my head. The sleeves billow around my wrists, ending in a fitted cuff. I fold down the collar, tightening the strings laced through the neckline.

I slip my legs into the pants and shove the shirt into the waistband. Nothing fits quite right, but Marianne can fix that. If she agrees to help.

The steady ticking of the clock fills the room, and I glance at the servant's door. Thea should be back by now.

Leaning over the loveseat, I snatch the hat and press it onto my head. Folded up on each side and forming a rounded point, it doesn't do much to hide my face. But with Gemma's help—

"What the fuck is this?"

I whirl. Thea stands, wide-eyed in the narrow servant's entrance with Marianne and Gemma peering over her shoulder. My stomach churns at the tone of her voice, the bite of her words.

Squaring my shoulders, I step toward her. "I'm entering the competition, but I can't as staff, so—"

She crosses the room and halts a foot away from me. Tugging on the loose strings of my collar, she huffs. "Have you completely lost it?" She shakes her head. "You're not entering this competition."

I lower my voice. "If I win, I get granted a wish."

"And what could you possibly want so bad you're willing to risk your life?"

I pinch my bottom lip between my fingers. Wishes are notoriously fickle, and if I don't ask for specifically what I need, it could backfire. Wish for my freedom, and I could touch the ocean again, but my power may not return. Ask for my power back, and I may still be landlocked.

In either scenario, I risk leaving Thea and my crew cursed.

I swallow, and just above a whisper, say, "A ship."

"A ship?" Her eyes search mine. "But you don't know how to sail a ship."

I press my tongue into my cheek. If only she knew. I pin her with a glare, my eyes blazing with the ferocity of a captain. *Her* captain. "I'm not asking for permission."

She folds her arms over her chest. For a heartbeat, I see my first mate and the fight brewing skin-deep. "You're out of your mind."

"Think about it. I won't have to work with Cassio anymore, and I won't have to be a courtesan. Neither would you. We could sail around the world and be free."

"I don't want to sail around the world."

My lip quirks. "I think you'll say differently when I win. And when I do, I'm naming you my first mate."

"This isn't a joke, Briar."

My mouth tilts into a full grin. "It certainly isn't."

Marianne steps around Thea, her long red hair burning like flames against her pale blue dress. The royal seamstress. She circles me, rubbing the thin fabric of my shirt between her fingers.

"You're asking us to commit treason." She props her chin in her hand. "What's stopping us from turning you in right now?"

My tongue turns to cotton, but I harden my gaze. "Have you forgotten about that friend of yours from the slums that I saved from execution? I'm cashing in the favor you owe me."

Her lips part, then close.

Gemma angles herself between her sister and me, her eyes narrowing as a glossy black sheet of hair falls over her face. "Did Caelus put you up to this? Test our loyalty and risk our power being stripped?"

"Gemma," Marianne whispers, setting a palm on her shoulder.

She brushes off the touch. "We can't trust anyone in this castle, Mar. She's his favorite. She'll turn us in, and—"

"I would never. I want to win to be free of him, and I can't do it without your help." I step closer and soften my voice. "Please."

Unflinching, Gemma glares at me—searching and assessing every plane of my face.

"Gemma," Marianne whispers. "She's telling the truth."

"How can you be sure?" Gemma says.

Marianne smiles at me. "It's in her eyes, the same look you get when you talk about freedom. We want the same thing." She looks to her sister and tilts her chin. "Show her, Gem."

"Are you sure you trust them?"

She nods. "I do."

Gemma releases a long breath and turns toward Thea and me. "If either of you mutter a word about this, I will kill you. Understand?"

Thea's eyes widen, and I nod. "You can trust us."

Gemma swallows and shuts her eyes. When she reopens them, the blue has vanished, replaced with a brown so dark it's nearly black. My breath catches, and I glance to Marianne. Like her sister's, her eyes morph to a warm brown.

"You're glamoured," I breathe.

Small changes, but enough to hide their identities.

Gemma nods. "We served King Golan until Sarenia fell. When Caelus took over, he pulled aside the staff who had power and executed them. We were young and, by some miracle, Marianne and I were never found, even as dozens of our friends and family lost their lives." Her voice wavers. "So, I've glamoured us ever since, and when we inquired about working in the castle, he hired us and gifted us with some of Isolde's power."

I run my teeth over my bottom lip.

If they knew who I really am—partly the reason their court fell into the hands of Caelus—they'd never help me. An ache spreads across my chest, and I swallow. "I'm sorry for your loss."

A shadow passes over her face, and the lantern lights the bob of her throat.

"We'll help however we can," Marianne says. Turning to Gemma, she nods. "You go first, then I'll do the alterations."

Gemma strides forward and removes my hat, setting it on the edge of the bed. She cups my head in her hands and turns it side to side. "My power weakens when I glamour someone this much, for this long."

I glance at Thea out of the corner of my eye. She sits on the edge of her bed and stares at the night sky through the window. She won't look at me, but I spot the tremble in her lip and the way her fingers shake in her lap. She's not angry—she's terrified.

But if she remembered who she was, I wouldn't be signing up alone.

"Close your eyes and picture who you want to look like," Gemma says. "The more detail, the better. Ready?"

I nod and close my eyes, picturing the bounty hunter with her blonde hair brushing her shoulders, the raised curve of her nose, the harsh arch of her cheekbones. She was taller, narrower. Squeezing my eyes shut, I hold the image in place, almost as if she were real and standing before me.

Not lying lifeless at the bottom of the channel I rolled her into.

"Good," Gemma whispers.

There's a prick of pressure, and her magic slides into me like a silk ribbon. It's not painful, but there's an unpleasant tug —followed by a shift of muscle and bone.

Her power migrates to the top of my head, and the weight of my hair lessens, reeled in strand by strand. The ribbons skate over the back of my scalp, sinking into my throat and shifting my jawline before traveling down my spine.

My bones grind as they're tugged apart, pushed closer. I grit my teeth against the pain, steadying my breaths as my body rearranges and takes on the shape of the woman in my head.

Then, as if it never existed, Gemma's power vanishes.

She drops her hands from my face. "All done."

I turn to the mirror, and my eyes widen at my reflection— the stranger staring back. Swallowing, I run my hand across my jaw. My eyelashes remain the same, but she lightened my eyes. They're no longer the exact color of the ocean, but an electric, cutting blue.

My hair, usually falling to the swell of my waist, now brushes the top of my shoulders, blonde and straight. I'm about half a foot taller than I was before, yet every movement is natural and familiar.

Gemma combs her fingers through my hair. "It only lasts a couple of hours, but if I can see you, I can maintain the glamour. However, if it fades completely, I'll have to touch you to place it again."

Marianne appears behind me, lip pinched between her teeth. "There's not much I need to do, but hold still."

Her gaze settles on my shirt, and the material shifts. Tightening, it hugs my torso, and the cuffs shorten until they rest comfortably at each wrist.

"A ship, huh?" She straightens the top over my shoulders and restitches the loose threads. "You could wish for anything in the world, and that's what you'd choose?"

She lowers her eyes to my pants, and in an instant, the waistband snaps in. The hem shortens until it kisses the tops of my boots.

"I want nothing but to feel the ocean air on my face. A deck beneath my feet." My chest tightens. This is the first time I've uttered those words to someone who will remember them. "If I win—"

"When you win," she says, holding my gaze. Her hair is a flash of red in the mirror as she turns away, and within moments, she's finished. "Ocean air sounds lovely. In fact, I think I'd love to sail around the world one day."

My chest warms, and she joins her sister at the foot of the bed.

"Briar," Thea says, her voice soft. Unsure.

"Yes?"

She rises and stops an arm's length away. "Dinner will be over any minute, so I'll go distract Caelus before he comes looking for you." She takes another step and pauses. "But, for the record, I think this is a stupid decision. You could be killed, or worse. So, for the sake of my sanity, please don't die."

I tuck a braid behind her ear. "This will change our lives. I promise."

Her gaze searches mine, like she can't quite trust my words. But I'd never lie to her.

"Good luck," she whispers.

Marianne hands me the pirate hat. "Go through the servant's doors. If the guards see a pirate running through the castle, you'll be arrested."

I stride to the small door nestled in the back of the room. Turning on my heel, I nod at the three of them. "Thank you. All of you. I don't know how I'll ever repay you."

Gemma pins me with a hard look. "Win, then we'll talk."

7

———

I wind through the corridors, ducking into the shadows whenever a lone servant scurries by, then exit through an unguarded side door.

I circle the castle and press myself against the wall, hiding in the shadows as I peer around the corner. Only one person remains at the table, bent over the roster and adding his name to the list.

From the balcony above, voices and the clink of silverware filter down, mixed with a low melody of string instruments.

Dinner is still going on, then. Likely extended, due to tonight's announcement.

The man at the table straightens and nods at the guard before striding away, his lips pressed in a thin line. His brown eyes meet mine, and I take in his ragged clothing and sunken cheeks. How many others will sign up, hoping they can wish themselves a better life? Escape the poverty Caelus forced them into?

I dip my chin in respect, and he trains his gaze on the path as he leaves the courtyard.

Swallowing the sour taste in my mouth, I tuck my hair

behind my ears and situate the hat on my head, unfamiliar with its weight. On an exhale, I turn the corner and stride to the table.

The guard assesses me and pulls out a pocket watch. "Looks like you'll be our final entry."

I fold my arms over my chest, as if it could stop my heart from racing. "It appears so."

He holds out the quill, an offering. Accepting it, I bend over the parchment lined with more names than I can count. My sleeve snags on the rough table as I scribble my stolen name onto the parchment.

Harriet Wells.

The moment I lift the tip of the quill, a chill runs up my arm, snakes around my elbow, and sinks into my chest.

"Congratulations, Harriet Wells," the guard says. "You are now bound to The Gales. I wish you the best of luck."

I let the quill roll from my hand and pull in a deep breath through my nose. At the end of the competition, I'll be free, dead, or bound to this curse forever.

Measured footsteps sound behind me, and the guard's gaze settles over my shoulder, his eyes narrowed. "Entries are closed."

"Good thing my name's already on the list, remember? Kressa Beaumont."

The hair on the back of my neck stands, and my stomach sinks. I know that voice.

Before I have a chance to turn, a fist grabs my hair and slams my temple against the table.

My vision swims. I go to stand, but my feet slip against the damp cobblestones as the wood digs into my ribs.

A face fills my vision. Honey eyes.

"You should be dead, Harriet," Kressa hisses.

Blood leaks from the gash on my cheekbone, spreading across the table. My heart slams against my chest, and I free my arm, swinging a fist toward her face. She dodges and yanks her sword from her belt.

Raising it over her head, she presses me farther against the table as the night sky twinkles off the metal blade. Then it comes down.

She swings it toward the base of my spine, aimed to paralyze and kill. A scream bottles in my throat, tears stinging my eyes.

Something shifts in the air. She releases a grunt, and her blade clatters to the ground, the sound echoing across the square. I force myself upright and whirl on her, pulling my dagger free from its sheathe.

My chest heaves, and hot blood drips from my chin, staining the white cotton of my shirt.

"Entrants can only kill each other in the arena," the guard says, bored—as if this isn't the first time competitors have made attempts on each other's lives.

"Where's my list?" Kressa growls, retrieving her blade.

I blink. "Your list?"

She pushes her hair out of her face and hedges a step closer, until our chests are a hands-breadth apart. "The list with my marks. The list you *stole*."

I swallow as her teeth form the final word. The woman I'm impersonating wasn't the bounty hunter, *she* is.

And she's searching for me. The Princess of the Sea.

"Perhaps you lost it." I tilt my chin and meet her glare.

"Arrive here the day after tomorrow at daybreak," the guard says, as he rolls up the roster and tucks it into his belt. "If you're late, or fail to attend, you're disqualified."

Neither of us budge, our teeth gritted. Kressa's hands curl into fists, and mine follow suit. We can't kill each other, but we can still do harm.

"Now," the guard yells, his hand resting on his blade.

Lighting flashes, distorting Kressa's features and emphasizing her smirk—the dimple it presses into her cheek. Her eyes dance over me, following the blood dripping down my jaw. "Don't worry, I'll be here."

She turns on her heel and props her sword over her shoulder. I watch her leave, until darkness engulfs her shadow and the guard brushes past me, into the belly of the castle.

Silence picks at my skin.

There should be laughter, silverware tapping, and music pouring from the balcony.

But my gaze trails up the trellises, over the gargoyles and marbled railing of the castle. The lights are off, the crowd gone.

I missed dinner.

8

———

I throw myself through the side door and slide along the narrow hallway, my pulse thrumming in my ears. If anyone saw a pirate sneak into the castle, the alarm will sound any moment.

Silence looms through the winding passageway, and flickering oil lamps light the way. My feet pound against the floor as I race through the corridors I know nearly as well as my ship.

I stop at my door and glance both ways, my hand resting on the iron handle. Pressing my ear to the door, I listen for any voices—Caelus in particular. But there are none. I release a breath and ease it open.

Quiet fills the room, save for the hinges groaning as I pull the door shut behind me. I pad across the space, toward the dressing room, and catch myself in the mirror.

A hard, sea-battered face stares back, my blue eyes nearly glowing in the dim light.

Loosening my belt, I slide it from my pants and drop it to the floor as I step into the closet. Billowing dresses line each side, and I shuck off the remainder of the clothes, discarding them in a pile.

I pull open the armoire tucked into the far end and rifle through the contents, settling on a tunic and leggings.

Something brushes my cheek, and I reach up as the strands of my hair unspool, lengthening past my shoulder blades. Shutting the armoire with a click, I sidestep to the thin mirror. The glamour wanes, slowly. My hair reaches my waist, but the harsh line of my jaw and unfamiliar eyes remain.

Thea's voice comes from the hallway, followed by a knock on the bedroom door—one that echoes through the room.

I freeze, and my stomach tightens. She has no reason to knock.

The door creaks.

"I'm not sure if she's back from visiting her uncle yet." Thea's voice floats through the bedroom, amplified. "He's fallen quite ill."

I backtrack, bumping into the armoire. Visiting my nonexistent uncle is a common excuse Thea uses for my sudden disappearances.

She's not alone.

The soft tap of her heels enters the room, followed by a pair of heavier feet. A sour taste fills my mouth.

"If she's gone like you say, you wouldn't mind me checking for her, right?"

Caelus.

My gaze darts to the pile of clothing I left on the floor. I drop to my knees and shove them beneath the row of courtesan dresses, but a whimper escapes my mouth. The dresses don't reach the floor, so the pirate's clothing pokes out like stuffing busting out of an armchair. But I can't open the armoire and risk making noise.

My chest tightens, a vise constricting my lungs.

"Well, Your Highness," Thea says, her voice even and controlled, "she's not here, but I'll be happy to send word when she—"

"I'll leave once I've looked everywhere."

My heart skips, and I search the closet, but there's nowhere to hide. I can't conceal myself within the dresses or slide into the armoire.

A shadow pauses in front of the closet door.

Caelus hums. "This is an interesting belt."

My stomach bottoms out.

"Sometimes my customers like to leave behind souvenirs," Thea says.

"A pirate?" The belt buckle clinks, as if he's turning it over in his hands. "You do know you're forbidden from doing business with pirates. Or do you not remember what happened to Allissa?"

My breath hitches, pulse kicking up a notch. Allissa was caught having a relationship with a pirate, and Caelus made her watch as he executed him. Then he beheaded her.

"Oh, that doesn't belong to a pirate," Thea says, a slight tremor to her voice. "It was a nobleman here earlier. I really should return it to—"

"The skull on the buckle says otherwise." He clicks his tongue. "But if it wasn't you doing business with a pirate, I'll have to assume it was Briar."

Thea falls silent, but her thoughts are loud. Screaming.

I shake my head. *No no no.* She's going to take the fall for me and admit to a crime she didn't commit.

I glance once more to the mirror. Harriet's face stares back —the glamour still solidly in place. I close my eyes and say goodbye to my ship, my crew, the sea.

Thea clears her throat. "I—"

"In here!" I shout. My breath catches. "I'm in here."

My voice is weak, as final as my death sentence.

Caelus inches the door open, his fingers curled around the edge. Bile creeps up my throat, and I back into the corner, as if the short distance could spare me from what's to come.

"Briar?"

The toe of his boot comes into view, and my heart pounds. I swallow and force my eyes open, gripping my hands together until they stop shaking. I'll surrender with dignity.

He pushes the door open, illuminating me in a glow of dancing firelight. His face is cast in shadows, features unreadable.

"What are you doing in the dark?"

I hold my hands out. "I can explain." But I catch a glimpse of myself in the mirror—my eyes their normal blue—and clamp my mouth shut.

Thea appears over his shoulder. "Briar, I'm so—oh."

"You missed dinner," Caelus says, venom laced in his voice. "How are you meant to work, courtesan, if you aren't present?"

I right myself, my head light and fuzzy. "I'm sorry. I received word that my uncle needed me, and I lost track of time. It won't happen again." I nod toward the belt clutched in his fist. "That's his. He collects odd items, and with his memory loss, he must have stuffed it into my satchel thinking it was his." I close the distance and pry it from his fingers. "I'll be sure to return it."

I angle myself between him and the clothes piled in the corner. Laying my palm against his chest, I guide him out of the closet and shut the door. Over his shoulder, I catch Thea's wide-eyed stare. I give her a nod, and she returns it, disappearing into the washroom.

Caelus covers my palm and smiles down at me, his canines sharp. Firelight dances off the pale blue of his eyes, turning the whites an eerie crimson. He squeezes my hand and digs his nails into my skin. "Since you weren't at dinner to speak with him, Dyerson is waiting for you in his room."

"Tonight? But it's so—"

"Or should I find someone better suited to do your job?"

I swallow and shake my head, my chest caving in on itself. "No. Give me a moment to freshen up, and I'll be there."

"Of course you will." His smile grows. "Because you do as you're told. You're mine, after all. Remember?"

He drops my hand, and I inhale a slow, centering breath. *I'm no one's but the sea,* I want to scream. But instead, I say, "Yes."

He leans in, as if he's going to press a kiss to my cheek, and whispers, "Yes, what?"

I grip the fabric of my tunic to stop myself from gouging his eyes out. His armada is killing my subjects at the war front—my mother the only thing keeping the massacre at bay.

Caelus is my enemy. I should be figuring out a way to kill him, not allowing him within an inch of me.

And yet.

"Yes, Your Highness."

"There you go," he breathes.

My stomach roils, but I clench my jaw and school my face. I will not show him the fear or discomfort he craves.

He pulls open the door, where a guard awaits with twin blades strapped high across his back. The second Caelus's heels clear the threshold, I shut the door and bolt the lock.

Thea emerges from the washroom, her hands wringing a towel. "I thought you were going to get caught."

I slide to the floor and hug my legs against my body. The cold floor seeps through my leggings as I rest my chin on my knees and sigh out a breath. "Me too."

"Don't you dare do that ever again."

I lift my gaze. "Do what?"

She kicks off her shoes and tucks them beneath the foot of her bed. Crossing the room, she slides down beside me and rests her head on my shoulder. "Don't you ever take the blame for me again. He would have killed you if he walked in and found you as a pirate."

"But if you were harmed, I wouldn't be able to live with myself."

I shudder. If I lost Thea, I'd lose the last thing keeping me from diving into the ocean and ending this torture.

She sighs. "You entered, didn't you?"

"Yes."

She pinches the bridge of her nose and shakes her head. "How are we going to pull this off?"

I smile against her hair. "We?"

"I don't condone this, but I won't let you do it on your own." She pauses for the span of five heartbeats, her silence heavy in the air. "I'm scared I'm going to lose you. I don't know how to explain it, but I feel like I've known you my entire life. Does that make sense?"

Tears gather in my eyes. "That makes more sense than anything." I take her hand and squeeze it. "Do you trust me?"

"To the ends of the earth."

A single tear travels down my cheek. After everything she's forgotten—our ship, Celia, me—she's never forgotten the words we promised each other the day she became my first mate.

I swallow. "To the ends of the earth."

9

———————

Years ago, when I told Caelus one of his governors was conspiring against him, I thought I had outgrown the role as a courtesan and earned a higher title. Perhaps I'd be made an advisor—get a seat on his counsel.

Instead, he assigned me to more men, more often. I've become known as the best, his favorite—the courtesan that only his most distinguished guests have the pleasure of being entertained by.

To Caelus, my importance isn't my mind, but what I could do with my body—how it can be used. *That* is the value he sees in me.

My fingers curl into a fist, and my silk sleeve slides to my elbow as I knock on the wooden door.

I hold my breath and count the seconds, each one ticking by without the sound of footsteps echoing from the other side. The tension in my shoulders unspools. If he doesn't answer, Caelus can't fault me, especially when I already have blackmail against Dyerson I can pacify him with.

Ten seconds drag by, and I sigh out a breath. He's asleep,

and I can go back to my quarters, crawl into bed, and wake to my last day before The Gales begin.

I turn away from the door and take a step down the hallway.

A lock slides out of place, echoing off the walls, and the door swings open.

"Ah, Briar. I was beginning to think you'd never come."

I freeze as his oily voice sends a shiver up my spine. They all breathe my name the same—as if they already know me. As if I'm a replica of every other woman they've came across. As if we're all one in the same.

They've seem to forgotten that, at one point in time, women ruled all four courts.

Painting a complacent smile onto my face, I face him. "Sir Dyerson, I apologize for my tardiness. I seem to be in high demand tonight, but I cleared my evening specifically for you."

Grey sprinkles his hairline, and the deep creases around his eyes adds at least thirty years to my twenty-eight. Over double my age.

In some ways, I pity him—this man who will forever wear an invisible collar, bending to the whims of whatever lord he serves, hoping for handouts he'll never receive.

I may pity him, but I'll give him no sympathy when he dies, unfulfilled.

"I'll make the time worth your while." He smiles as he steps to the side and gestures for me to enter the guest quarters.

Swallowing, I steel my spine and step across the threshold —onto the stone floor my feet have met far too often. The walls have stood witness to my charade for years, its windows like eyes upon me.

At the sight of the unmade bed, my stomach churns.

I dip my fingers into the hidden pocket of my slip and trace the small vial buried inside, allowing the comfort to wash over me.

As long as I have this, he can't hurt me.

The door shuts with a soft click, and Dyerson cuts across the room, lifting a short glass of brown liquor from a table. He settles onto a padded armchair and leans against its back.

He takes a long sip and slides his sleeve across his mouth. "At least I have you as compensation for how far I traveled to come here."

Like I'm a payment—a transaction. I grind my teeth and circle his chair, kneading his shoulders with my hands. I've been in this position more times than I can count, and the urge to snap their neck never fades.

"It must be difficult being so distinguished, yet having a territory so far away." I piece my words together carefully. Equal parts compliment and barb, enough for him to feel a tinge of insecurity. A hint of embarrassment.

"Indeed." He grabs one of my wrists and runs his thumb across the underside, directly over my veins. "It was no surprise that Caelus assigned his brother to govern the court's stronghold while he conquered Sarenia, but as a childhood friend, I thought I'd acquire one of the more established territories."

I lift a brow. "A childhood friend?"

There's very little about Caelus's personal life that he's shared with me. I know he comes from a generational line of wealthy business owners from the Sky Court—that he was an advisor of the crown before he manipulated Isolde and took it over.

But beyond that, I know nothing.

"We grew up as neighbors, went to university together. At one point, he was planning to ask for my sister's hand in marriage. Now though, it seems he's too powerful to care about old friends."

"Seems power has that effect on people." I slink around the chair and drag my hand across his shoulder, ignoring the way my own words tear at my chest.

"He won't be as smug if Callum decides he wants Atlas for himself."

My steps falter. "You think his brother would betray him? Take the capitol of the Sky Court?"

He shrugs and wraps his hands around my hips, pulling me onto his lap. His breath—already stained with liquor—skates over me. "Like you said, power can have that effect on people." He presses his face against my neck, hands roaming my waist. "And he's left Callum to his own devices for an entire decade."

I close my eyes and lean into him, as if I'm enjoying his touch rather than the value of his words. If he feels so comfortable discussing the possibility of treason, there must be some truth to it—others who feel the same. "Would Callum be a better ruler?"

I spear my fingers into his nape and encourage his lips to find the arch of my throat—a distraction as I slide my hand into my pocket.

"Surely more generous," he breathes against my skin.

Easing the vial out, I uncork it and pour the colorless and tasteless liquid into his glass.

Women aren't the only thing I barter jewels for.

And now, I've only added to the collection of information I have against him—knowledge I won't be sharing with Caelus. If Callum is indeed planning an uprising against his brother, I don't want Caelus to see it coming.

"You deserve nothing but the best," I whisper into his ear, leaning away as he presses a kiss to my jaw. I drag a finger under his collar and down his shirt buttons. "Go on, finish your drink and we'll get started."

He palms my hips and slides his hands farther down, cupping my ass. He pulls me closer. "I've already had enough tonight. Wouldn't want to drink too much, would I?"

My throat tightens, and a weight settles on my chest. There have been times, of course, where the men don't finish their drink after I pour the tonic in. Times I've blotted from my memory—forced myself to focus on the patterns of the painted ceiling rather than their hands on my body.

"Are you sure?" I tease, quirking the corner of my mouth. "This is the finest liquor on the continent, flown in monthly from Atlas."

He scoffs. "It tastes like every other whisky to me."

"But—"

His mouth covers mine, his lips dry, tongue eager as he weaves a hand into my hair. I tense, and my body goes rigid, screaming to get away. But I pin myself into place. If I step out of line, I'll be punished. Or worse, fired.

I force myself to melt against him and send my mind somewhere distant—on the shores of Delterran, the deck of my ship.

He grinds his hips upward, pressing his groin against me, and I clench my eyes shut. A moan escapes his mouth, and he dips a finger beneath the hem of my slip, sliding it up my bare thigh. "I can see why you're in such high demand."

I swallow, making my eyelids heavy as I offer him a smile. Glancing at his lips, I lift his glass from the table and offer it to him. "Some say I'm the best on the continent."

He takes the glass and places it back on the table as he pushes me from his lap and stands. "I can't wait to see why."

Cupping my face, he smothers me with his mouth and guides me toward the bed. My thoughts race, and as the back of my knees hit the mattress, a whimper escapes my mouth.

His grip on me tightens, taking the noise as a hint of pleasure, not panic. He lowers me down until the cotton sheets meet my back.

He climbs on top of me, settling his weight against my hips. I sink into the mattress, deeper, deeper—

A knock sounds at the door.

Dyerson presses his face into the crook of my neck and groans. "Who is it?"

The door creaks open, and he springs from the bed, adjusting his collar as a face peers through the crack.

Isolde.

Our eyes lock, and a silent conversation passes between us. There have been times in the past where she's risked sneaking out of her quarters to rescue me from the men I'm assigned to service. But this soon after she was caught?

A sour taste fills my mouth. She shouldn't be here.

"I apologize Sir Dyerson, but Briar is needed elsewhere."

"Right at this moment?" He doesn't glance my way as he crosses back to the armchair, lifts his glass, and drains it. "I was told she cleared her evening for me, and she hasn't even been here an hour."

Isolde dips her chin. "I assure you, this will not happen again."

I shove myself from the bed and straighten my slip, giving Dyerson an apologetic smile. "Until next time, Sir Dyerson."

Without waiting for him to convince me otherwise, I stride for Isolde. She holds the door open as I pass through, and swings it shut.

"Briar." She pulls me against her chest. "Are you okay?"

I settle into her space, breathing in the sweet lilac perfume I could recognize anywhere. Her warmth seeps into me—a balm to my nerves. "I am now, but what about Caelus? I would have been fine, but if he catches you—"

"I'll go back soon." She runs her hand down my hair, gently combing through the strands. "The staff said I had ten minutes to spare before he's meant to arrive at my room. Long enough to get here, knock on the door, and hurry back."

I press my eyes shut and listen to her steady heartbeat. This late, there's only a couple guards making rounds, but if any were to see her, they'd report it to Caelus immediately.

"Thank you." Pulling back, I drag my thumb over her cheekbone. "Tomorrow?"

She presses a kiss to my forehead. "Tomorrow."

Untangling herself, she glances down the hallway and strides in the direction of her quarters. I ache to follow—to lie down beside her and hold her close, bury my face into her hair. To protect her from Caelus.

But I can't.

Her shadow disappears around the corner, taking my heart with it.

10

"Wait," I say, breathless.

"For?" Isolde's eyes dance over me as she pulls me toward the conservatory. Milky, morning light spills through the stained-glass window and paints the room in watercolors.

I glance over my shoulder. "What if we're seen?"

These clandestine meetings of ours are usually spent in my quarters, away from prying eyes or curious ears. We never go anywhere else, not with the risk being so high.

She pauses and eases me closer, until the distance between us fades to nothing. The swell of her bottom lip brushes mine. "Oh, my Briar, who's around to see?"

My pulse skitters, and a swallow slowly makes its way down my throat. Behind us, the long hallway stands empty, save for a handful of marble busts. Every staff member is busy on the bottom floor, preparing for the opening of The Gales.

"He won't find out." Isolde lifts a hand, and a gentle breeze floats up my arm. It grazes the curve of my shoulder and travels across my collarbones. Her fingertips follow the path of her power. "Well?"

A shiver works up my spine, and warmth billows beneath my skin, spreading over my bones. I trail my hand over her waist and to the small of her back, reveling in the way her breath catches.

I hover my mouth over the shell of her ear. "By all means."

She sighs against my temple, and as she pulls away, her pupils widen, nearly blotting out her irises. A smirk plays on her face as she leads me into the conservatory.

Foliage swallows us.

Ferns curl overhead, their tendrils hanging over the entrance and tangling in my hair. Ivy climbs the latticed walls, passing behind broad-leaved plants.

Humidity clings to my skin, and Isolde banks right, luring me by the hand. She smiles over her shoulder—all mischief—as her hair bounces against her shoulder blades.

"Where are we going?" I whisper, my voice shrouded by the fountain bubbling in the corner.

A cloud passes overhead and throws a shadow over the conservatory. She comes to a stop beside a metal table surrounded by chairs. "Right here."

She guides me, pressing my lower back against the edge of the table. A lazy smile pulls at her lips as she dips her head and drags her nose up the slope of my neck.

My pulse flutters. Her touch shuffles my thoughts and makes it hard to remember the conversation I wanted to have with her—information that might save my life.

I anchor my arm around her waist, steadying myself. "Has Caelus mentioned anything about The Gales?"

The words are thick and oily on my tongue as her mouth brushes the hollow of my collarbone. I hate using her like this, but if anyone has insight of what to expect in the coming weeks, it's her.

She hums against my skin. "There's a lot he's not telling me." A kiss, pressed to the space below my ear. "He's been pacing his quarters, talking about how, if it were up to him, no one would survive."

"Why's that?"

"If everyone was dead, no one would be granted a wish."

I open my mouth, but she captures it with hers, pressing her body against mine. She eases me onto the table, her hands warm as they roam my body. My skirt hitches, and my legs wrap around her waist as she tilts my head back. Her kisses are hungry, wanting, and my body aches to give in—turn off my mind and fall into her.

"Anything else?" I breathe.

She pulls back and raises a brow. "Why are you so curious about it?"

My voice falters, but I manage a shrug. "Aren't you?"

A moment passes, and she drags her bottom lip between her teeth. "I suppose I am. Well, he mentioned this will become a running tradition—an offering of sorts that will celebrate his power and the coming unity of the courts. This year, apparently, The Gales will represent the sea."

"The sea?" My stomach churns. It's either Caelus making a mockery of my mother, or representation of the looming control he has over my home. But if any of the trials are on the water—

I won't last five minutes.

She nods, and on a low exhale, whispers, "I wanted to enter, but he wouldn't let me."

My hands freeze on her hips. "You, *what?*"

"Reckless, I know. Silly, considering most people would look at me and wonder what I could want, what I could possibly wish for." A huff. "He told me I'd be an immediate target—taken out by those who have a problem with the crown." Her eyes harden, offering a glimpse of the queen that once was. "But I want freedom enough to die for it."

My tongue is a lead weight as I study her face. Maybe if she knows I entered we could work together, her feeding me information and covering for me while I'm Harriet.

I bite down on my cheek. Isolde traded her dignity to cling to a fraction of her power when she surrendered to Caelus. She doesn't know that when I found out what she had done, I entered the castle with every intention to kill her.

But I trust her. We've spent nearly a decade together, and if we could earn our freedom, we'd have the rest of our lives.

She cups my face, her gaze soft as she brushes a finger over my cheekbone. "I'd give you freedom too, Briar. We'd be free, together."

Tears sting my eyes. "Isolde, there's something I need to tell you."

Her head tilts, and she nods for me to continue.

The air goes thin, and my heart pounds in my chest. If she disagrees with what I've done, there's no going back. "I—"

Greenery shifts behind her, and the hair on the back of my neck stands.

"You saw them go this way?"

Caelus.

Isolde's eyes shoot wide, and she throws herself away from the space between my thighs the same moment he rounds the corner.

I jump from the table and trip over my feet. Grappling for the edge of the table, I regain my balance and drop into a curtsy. "Your Highness." My voice is shaky, and my pulse goes still as I watch the blood drain from Isolde's face.

Caelus's eyes shift between us as two of his advisors appear behind him. His attention settles on Isolde, and although his hands rest clasped across his front, a muscle in his jaw tics. "You are excused."

Tears don't well into her eyes, but I catch the hitch of her chest—the way her fingertips tremble at her sides. She nods.

Gathering the skirt of her dress, she disappears the way we came, the sound of her footsteps fading into the distance.

My heart slams against my ribcage. He can't kill her. The power she provides him is too valuable, too important. But he can bring her close—make her wish she was dead.

Caelus nods to his advisors. "Be sure Isolde makes it back to her quarters."

A sour taste floods my mouth. A queen needs no keeper.

They leave us, and Caelus studies me, his face giving nothing away. My stomach twists into knots, forming a noose around my lungs. I smooth out the wrinkles coating the front of my dress, but there's nothing to be done about the undeniable flush to my cheeks.

He circles me, his hands clasped behind his back. "I need to speak with you."

My pulse sputters, and my breath is a solid weight in my throat, but there's no way he saw Isolde's lips on mine. If he had, I wouldn't be standing. "I'm listening."

Sunlight fills the conservatory, and a bead of sweat trails down my spine. He pulls out a chair, its feet dragging over the stone floor.

He must know I entered.

That's the only explanation for the line between his brows and the rigid set of his jaw. Either that, or he knows I'm withholding information about his brother's potential uprising.

My heart is a death knell in my ears. I trace my gaze over the weapons strapped to his body and gauge how quick I'd need to move to pull one off his waist. How deep I'd need to plunge it to pierce his heart.

"Isolde's power isn't enough to sustain me."

A stone settles in my gut. "What?"

"It's weakening. Depleting, actually. It's been over ten years that I've been siphoning her power, and soon it'll run out. And when it does, she'll die." There's no sympathy in his voice, only the bluntness of a man concerned more about losing power than the life tied to it. "Terra is requesting sacrifices to maintain the power, and we came to an agreement. The Gales. She offers a wish, I give her dozens of willing lives."

A hollow space widens in my core. The man who entered The Gales before me flashes through my mind—with his threadbare clothes and sunken cheeks. There were so many like him, seeking a chance to escape poverty. But if sacrificing them means keeping Isolde alive, I'd do it a hundred times over. I shift on my feet. "Why are you telling me all this?"

A slow, wicked grin spreads across his face. "Because I may be close to finding a way to separate my power from Terra. To have infinite power."

My jaw slackens. The humidity presses in, and sweat gathers along my hairline. "That's impossible."

"It's been done before."

"Only because the Fire Court queen gained her power from Serinos. The laws of the underworld work different from Terra's." I brace myself against the table. "And what came of that? She disappeared over fifty years ago, along with her court, because her power became uncontrollable."

"You're thinking too small, Briar. I don't want to link myself to Serinos." He taps a finger on the table. "I'd separate my power from the gods altogether. Become one myself."

My blood turns to ice.

"Think about it." His eyes grow distant. "Serinos rules the underworld, Terra the earth, but what about the heavens? I could become powerful enough to challenge Terra and the chokehold she's had on power. The Earth, Sky, and Sea would be mine."

I focus my breathing. *In. Out.* "How?"

His gaze returns to me, and his lips spread into a smile far too wide for his face. "I'm ironing out the logistics, but when I sort it out, I'll grant you whatever power you desire if you help me."

I clench my jaw until it aches. I want nothing from this man—nothing but to watch as he takes his final breath beneath my hands. "What do you want from me?"

"Like I said, it's still in the works. But you're smarter than you look, and with you by my side, there's nothing we couldn't accomplish."

He rises, dragging his fingertips along the metal table as he makes his way to me. I root myself to the spot, unwilling to back away.

"I want to see you at the welcome ceremony tomorrow," he says. "We're introducing the competitors."

A chill spreads over my skin, and my stomach flips. I can't be Briar and Harriet at the same time, and he'll notice if either are missing. I lower my gaze. "I have to visit my uncle tomorrow evening. He's unwell, as you know, and—"

"It wasn't a question, *courtesan*."

A swallow makes its way down my throat, and I nod.

He leans closer, his lips too close to my skin. "Very well, then. Tomorrow, at daybreak, the competitors arrive. With any luck, they'll all perish in the first competition, and I'll be done with it all. Terra says we have to hold a competition, not that anyone has to make it to the end."

His hot breath skates over my temple, and he presses closer, bringing the blade at his waist inches from my reach.

"You could be the most powerful woman in the world, if you help me. Think on it."

Biting down on my cheek, I hold in my retort. Whatever it is, I'd never help him defy Terra. And, when I win this competition, I'll already be the most powerful woman in the world.

His hand shifts and traces over my knee, roaming up my thigh. I grip the edge of the table and stop myself from squirming away.

I avoid his touch as much as possible, but unlike the men I'm assigned to entertain, I cannot pour tonic in all of Caelus's drinks. Nights with him are when I've mastered the art of removing my mind from my body. Turning myself into a shell.

But pinned against him like this, I can't pull away. I can't fight back. I can't risk him deciding I'm not valuable enough to keep around.

I close my eyes and grit my teeth.

Footsteps sound from my back, and Caelus sighs. He retreats, and I inhale a deep, cleansing breath.

An armada captain appears from around the corner. Medals crowd the front of his jacket, and metal caps adorn his shoulders, mimicking the wings of the falcons they fly. I clench my hand into a fist. How many of my people has he killed at sea? How many lives have ended at the blade strapped across his back?

"Updates from the warfront, Your Highness."

I hold my breath and scan his face. This is what I've been waiting for, why I've spent the last ten years hanging onto conversations—for a glimpse of news about my mother.

"Thank you," Caelus says. "Briar was just leaving."

My attention shoots to him. "Don't you think I should hear what he has to say? Maybe I could be of use."

"My dear." He chuckles, pressing his hand to the small of my back. "You're just a courtesan. No need to worry yourself with politics."

My molars grind together, but I hold back my argument. I brush the handle of his blade, only to know how easy it would be to unsheathe it.

"Yes, Your Highness," I grit out.

My mind whirs, and my inhales are shallow sips of air as I stumble out of the conservatory. If he has truly discovered a way to harness unlimited power, winning this competition will mean nothing. Saving Isolde would mean nothing.

If he becomes a god, I cannot stop him.

11

"Is he gone?" I whisper through the crack in the door.

Isolde's attendant nods, her eyes somewhere distant as she eases the door open. Lines of salt trail down her cheeks—dry tears. "It was awful."

I'm lucky all the attendants admire Isolde, otherwise I probably wouldn't get away with sneaking into her quarters so often.

If any of them have put it together that we're lovers, they pretend otherwise.

Out the window, moonlight reflects off the snowcapped mountains. It's been hours since Caelus caught Isolde with me, but this is the first time it's been safe for me to sneak into her quarters. My stomach clenches at the closed door leading to her bedroom. "Is she awake?"

"Barely. He suffocated her over and over again—stealing the air from her lungs until she was on the brink of passing out."

I waver, but steady myself and grind my teeth. He's beaten her plenty, but this is new—using her own power against her.

If he knew it was me, and not her attendant, that cleans her up after his punishments, he'd be sure I'm never seen again.

"How long will he be gone?"

The attendant inches closer to the servant's door, her hand eager on the doorknob. After what she's seen, she's probably desperate to get away. "An hour, at least."

With that, she slips through the hidden door and shuts it behind her with a soft click. Silence settles over the space, and a slight whimper comes from the bedroom.

I steel my spine. For years, Caelus has been carrying out the most horrific acts on Isolde, and I've learned I only make it worse if I cry when I see what he's done. I have to be strong, for her.

Blowing out a breath, I push open her bedroom door.

The iron tang of blood thickens the air. I swallow a gasp as I find her sitting on the mattress, her legs curled against her chest and head bowed against her knees.

Her back is to me, and I count the raw welts crisscrossing her shoulders and spine. Thick blood seeps from the deepest of the wounds and clots in her hair, turning the blonde curls a muddy brown.

She shudders a breath and straightens, wincing as the movement pulls her skin.

"Isolde." My voice is a whisper—one I'm unsure she heard as I cross the room and fall to my knees in front of her.

Her body is bare, save for the bruises marring her arms and peppering her legs. Marks that clothing will hide. She lifts her head, and her swollen, bloodshot eyes meet mine as she opens her mouth.

All that comes out is a hoarse wheeze.

I fight back tears. "Did he crush your vocal cords?"

She nods.

Bile rises up my throat. He's done that before, to stop her from screaming in pain after a handful of advisors overheard her cries for help. I ache to run back to my room, slide the dagger from under my mattress, and hunt Caelus down—peel the skin from his bones.

I reach up to brush her hair out of her face, but she flinches back, trembling. Her body is in shock, but if I don't clean her wounds, infection might take over. And while Caelus wouldn't let her die, he'd let her suffer.

But she's in no position to be standing.

I stand and lean against the mattress. "I'm going to pick you up, okay?"

A quiet sob wracks her shoulders, but she manages a weak nod. Careful not to press on any of the bruises, I slide one of my arms under her legs, and thread her arm across my shoulders.

I suck in a shallow breath and hesitate. I can't pick her up without pressing my arm against her welts, but I have no other choice. Weaving my arm around her back, I press lightly. Her mouth bursts open in a silent scream, fresh tears streaming down her face as I lift her and cradle her against my chest.

"I'm so sorry." My words are garbled through tears as her blood seeps down my arm and drips to the stone floor. The apology isn't so much for the agonizing pain I'm causing, but that she was caught in the conservatory in the first place.

I should have never agreed to it.

She clings to my neck, burying her face against my collarbone as I lean over the tub and start the water. It rushes out of the faucet, filling the basin to a lukewarm temperature, and I ease her in.

Her hands don't leave my neck. I lower to my knees beside her, and she presses her forehead to mine. She winces, and her breaths come out in shallow pants, but the tension eases from her shoulders, her body relaxing into the water.

"I'm here," I whisper, pressing myself from the edge of the tub.

I open the cabinet, grabbing a washrag and a bar of herbal soap I paid the healer for. It's seen far too many uses—worn down to a sliver—but it's medicinal and will help numb her pain and speed the healing process.

Turning back to Isolde, I cradle her chin with my hand and dip the rag in the water. Her lids are heavy, but her eyes meet mine, and a string of muddled words comes from her mouth.

"What was that?" I drag the rag over the back of her head, washing out the caked blood.

"You came."

My hand pauses at her temple. "Of course I did."

Her gaze softens, and she lifts her hand from the water, running her thumb across my palm. "Of course you did."

A shadow passes over her face, and even if she could elaborate, she doesn't need to. I've heard enough about her past to know that she's never had anyone she could rely on. Everyone she's ever known has taken advantage of her or used her for her power. Her mother, her brothers, Caelus.

Something shifts in my chest. It cracks—a hairline fissure in the wall I've built around my heart since I became cursed. I've never known a life where I haven't had my crew behind me, ready to support me in everything I do.

Isolde only has me.

I weave our fingers together. "I'll always come."

She closes her eyes, and despite the pain in her back, a smile pulls at her lips.

A comfortable silence settles between us, and I gently work the medicinal soap onto her skin. Her hands stop trembling, and I drain the tub, rinsing her with fresh water.

She opens her mouth, as if to speak, but I shake my head. "Save your strength."

Tears well in her eyes, but they're no longer ones borne from pain. They're open, trusting. Vulnerable. I offer her a hand, and she eases herself out of the tub. The welts on her back are still deep and swollen, but the soap has cleared the worst of it.

I pull a towel from the hook and wrap it around her, careful not to press too hard on her back and bruises. She melts into me, and I cup the back of her head, pressing her ear against my heartbeat. The way she held me when she saved me from Dyerson.

We stand for a moment, our breathing synced, steam curling off the curve of her shoulders. If I could, I'd pause time—make it so that we can exist in this moment together. Come tomorrow, when The Gales begins, everything will change.

I press a kiss to her forehead. "Let's get you to bed."

The rest of the words go unsaid. *Before Caelus comes back.*

Leading her into the bedroom, I fish an oversized shirt from her armoire and ease it onto her body. Exhaustion weighs at her eyelids, and wordlessly, she crawls onto the mattress and sinks her head onto a pillow.

Within moments, her breathing deepens.

I lean over the bed and comb her damp curls away from her face. Ten years ago, I had heard of the Sky Court's strength. How Queen Isolde ruled with insurmountable power—strength that intimidated even my mother. She was known to be fearless, unforgiving.

But here, asleep, she's fragile. Not weak—never weak. There's a peacefulness to her, one that I wish I could bottle and save for moments when she's on the brink of breaking.

A light knock comes from the door, and her attendant peers in. "Caelus will be back soon."

"Thank you." I trail my fingertips over Isolde's cheekbone and ease the sheets over her before leaving the room.

"Is she going to be okay?" the attendant says.

I nod, pulling the door to the bedroom shut. "She's strong."

"Strong enough to take the punishment for two."

My steps falter, and I freeze at the door leading into the hallway. "Excuse me?"

The attendant wrings her hands and shuffles on her feet, unable to meet my eyes. "When it started, Caelus said he was going to drag you in there with her, since he found you two together. But the queen insisted it was her who invited you there, so she begged him to spare you. She took her beating as well as yours."

Tears blur my vision as I glance at her closed bedroom door. I can't even begin to imagine the agony she faced over the last few hours, all for a handful of stolen kisses. She endured twice the pain, for me.

I can't tell her that I've entered The Gales. It's too much of a burden for her to carry—too high a risk of something like this happening again. If I'm caught, or anyone were to find out she was involved, Caelus would do unimaginable things to her.

I have to keep her safe, and I can't do that if she's constantly worried about me.

Swallowing, I wrap my hand around the doorknob and crack it open. "Check on her for me, please?"

"Of course, Briar."

Stepping into the hallway, I let out a shallow, rattled breath.

Tomorrow, The Gales begin. And if I die, there will be no one to take care of Isolde.

12

The grey, early morning sky churns, bloated with heavy clouds promising rain. Lightning crackles, dancing across the heavens, and a damp chill claws through my thin pirate shirt.

A clap of thunder shakes the ground, and a handful of the bodies gathered in the courtyard tilt their heads to the sky.

At a low balcony, Caelus observes us with an unamused smirk. Those around me avoid his gaze, but whether it's out of fear or respect, I'm unsure.

But not me. Not Harriet. I keep my unwavering gaze pinned on him.

He may wear the face of a predator, but I'm the hunter dressed in camouflage. I know his secrets and his weaknesses. When I win this competition, I'm going to laugh as I slowly drown him with my power. Revenge for ever thinking he could rule over me.

A gust shoots across the courtyard, blowing dirt and bits of rock. I throw my hand to my hat, holding it down as the courtyard silences.

"Welcome to The Gales," Caelus's voice booms over the

crowd, carried and amplified by wind. "As you know, I am hosting this competition to celebrate the considerable power Terra grants the Sky Court. Each of you are here in hopes of winning a single wish."

Eager faces smile up at him—falling for his lies when the odds of them leaving with their lives are slim. I cross my arms and swallow, my blonde hair falling into my eyes.

"Three trials will be held over the course of the next three weeks, and those left standing at the end will be judged by Terra herself."

Murmurs rise from the crowd, from those who have never seen Terra in the flesh. I've seen the goddess twice—one when she blessed me as the heir to the sea, and again when she cursed me. Other than that, she rests, indifferent to what we do on the surface.

Until now.

"As some of you are aware, you cannot kill each other unless you are in the arena."

I swallow and fight the urge to check over my shoulder—to avoid the possibility of meeting Kressa's glare somewhere in the crowd.

"You all will be residing within the castle during the length of the competition. You may come and go during the day, but come nightfall, anyone found outside the walls will be executed."

A lump forms in my throat, and feet shuffle around me, whispers circulating. Caelus only smiles and cocks a brow.

"Many of you will die competing for the prize, a handful will survive, but only one will win. Those of you who no longer wish to participate are free to leave now. This is your final chance."

Bodies weave around me, their heads hung low as they pour out of the courtyard. My feet don't falter.

Death doesn't scare me anymore.

But never again experiencing the thrill of sailing through a storm? Or never finding the rest of my crew? Now that, I'm terrified of.

Caelus surveys the thinned crowd and nods. "Remain still."

He lifts his hand, and a glittering tendril settles over the courtyard like a blanket. It sinks into my skin and forces itself down my lungs. It stings—not gentle like Gemma's power and not wild like my own. It's violent, like a pelting of hail.

It slithers into my chest cavity and pauses, as if noticing something out of place—or something familiar.

My dormant power.

Caelus stiffens. Eyes narrowed, he sweeps his gaze over the crowd, searching. My heart stutters, and sweat gathers on my palms. A muscle along his jaw feathers, and he turns, whispering into the ear of a guard beside him.

The guard nods, and Caelus returns his attention to the crowd. His power dissipates, lifting like an anvil from my stomach.

"Congratulations." His expression is as cold as the wind snapping at my face. "You are now bound to The Gales."

About fifty men and women remain in the courtyard, some whose faces are bright and unmarred by time. But there are others—their cheeks hollow, moth-eaten clothes hanging from their shoulders. The ones who lived in Sarenia before Caelus took control and forced from their homes.

A knot tightens in my chest. Caelus hosts these extravagant dinners and balls—entertains at any expense. Yet there are people unable to feed themselves. No place to call home.

My heart aches at the thought of the families they left to come here. The ones they may leave behind.

The lives I'll need to end if I want to win.

I blink, hard. My gaze settles on a group of pirates tucked into the far corner, eyeing me. Unwilling to look away, I search their faces, but I don't recognize any of them from Cassio's crew.

The wind shifts, and a shiver travels up the back of my neck, sending a jolt down my spine.

"Caelus?" a voice drawls—taunting and teasing out his name a letter at a time.

A fresh tremor shoots over my body, and every head swings in her direction, but I can't move. My feet are rooted to the spot.

At the balcony, Caelus's head swivels, and his gaze pins on the bounty hunter behind me. "Yes?"

"A shame you won't be joining us."

I raise my brows and finally turn. Leaning against a stone wall, cast in shadows, stands Kressa. Her hood is drawn over her head, but I catch the smug tilt to her lips.

He bares his teeth. "And why would I?"

She steps into the light, her smirk deepening as she shrugs off her hood. "Why? The chance at a wish."

"What could I possibly wish for?"

The air in the courtyard thickens, growing taut—the way a bowstring quivers before it's released.

"Power of your own, of course," Kressa says.

Lightning flashes through the sky, and a spear strikes the cobblestones at her feet, sending rocks shooting up. Those around her lurch back and shield their eyes. But Kressa doesn't so much as flinch.

"If I were you, *competitor,* I would reconsider how you speak to me."

A chuckle rumbles from her throat.

I scan her, trying and failing to find her prerogative—why she'd want to paint a larger target on her back.

But then I catch Caelus's knuckles blanching as he squeezes the marble railing. His eyes burn with a hatred so viscous, so fierce, I've only witnessed it a handful of times—moments before an execution.

It's not that he *won't* kill Kressa, or any of the rest of us for that matter.

He *can't*.

And somehow, she knew that enough to test it.

Caelus pulls his attention away from her and clears his throat. "Tonight, there will be a welcome ceremony, and your attendance is mandatory. If you are not present, it will be considered a forfeit of the competition, and you will be executed."

My throat bobs on a swallow. There's no room for error tonight. If I so much as time the glamour wrong, even for a minute, I'll expose myself.

"Guards will escort you to your quarters in the east wing. Staff will be at your rooms shortly with clothing that is more... suitable for tonight's ceremony." He glances at the men dressed in rags. "For the trials, you may wear whatever you wish. Good luck."

He spares a final, seething look at Kressa and turns on his heel, striding into the castle. The double doors slam behind him, rattling the glass panes.

Royal guards march into the courtyard, their gloved hands resting on the hilt of their swords. "Into two lines!"

Lingering behind, I survey the men and women I'm up against. I judge the gait of their steps and the breadth of their shoulders. The men lined up at the front, with their wide frames and clenched fists seem to be my biggest competition. But I know not to assume.

Sometimes the biggest threats aren't the most obvious.

A hand clamps down on my shoulder and jerks me back. My feet scramble as a man's brown eyes meet mine, and he leans forward, his hot breath skating over my face. "Tell me, pirate, how many innocent lives have you handed over to Caelus?"

I get a closer look at him—brown hair and a faint, jagged

scar running across the bridge of his nose.

My lip quirks. It's been ages since I was threatened in broad daylight, for all to see. "I'd take your hand off me, if I were you."

His mouth twists into a grimace. "I can't kill you, yet, but I can make you wish you were dead."

I bark a laugh.

His fist flies toward my jaw. I bank right, dodging it, but his elbow finds its mark at my temple and throws me back. Pain sears through my skull, but I grit my teeth as I grab his wrist, twisting it around his back.

Before he has a chance to regain his balance, I hook my arm around his throat and squeeze. Tight.

"Your question," I snarl, "about how many innocent people I've handed over to Caelus? The answer is none."

I loosen my hold and slam my foot into his back. He splays onto the ground and heaves, unable to suck in a full breath.

I wipe my hands on my pants and smile. "I look forward to doing this again."

Leaving him, I stride to the lines forming at the castle doors. Every competitor stares at me, some wide-eyed, others with a narrowed expression.

But there's a single one with her brow lifted, amused.

My skin crawls under her gaze.

I give her a wide berth as I join the opposite line and train my attention on the person in front of me.

"I see you've met Simon," Kressa says.

Without looking her way, I mumble, "It seems he met me."

She chuckles and mutters something under her breath that goes unheard as the guards lead us through the doorway.

We march up the grand staircase. Servants and nobles alike part for us, staring as we pass. Competitors gawk at the marble walls and the blue silks spilling over the banisters. Most of them have never entered the castle, or at least not since it's been under Sky Court possession. I'm the only competitor familiar with these halls, even if I shouldn't be.

Kressa's hand curls into a fist and reaches for a blade that isn't strapped to her waist.

We bottleneck at the landing, and I step out of line, kneeling down. I wait a moment before whispering, "Did you hear?"

I pull my laces from their perfectly tied knots and glance out the corner of my eye. Gemma and Thea huddle at the open window overlooking the balcony Caelus gave his announcement from.

Thea nods. "East wing?"

"Yes. And Marianne?"

"Pulled away to alter clothing for the competition," Gemma says, her hands flexing at her sides.

My face tightens as she reinforces the glamour.

"Thank you," I whisper.

"Pirate!"

A royal guard stands in the center of the hallway, waiting for me.

"Coming!" I straighten and tilt my chin at Thea and Gemma.

The guard shoots me a warning glare as I catch up, but he lacks the hardened demeanor the other guards wear like a badge. He's young, untested.

The kind whose loyalty may waver under the right circumstances.

"Sorry for holding you back." I send a smile his way and tuck a strand of blonde hair behind my ear. "What's your name?"

He spares me the smallest tilt of his lips, pressing a dimple into his brown skin. "Julian."

"Julian," I repeat, committing it to memory and tucking it away for later. "I'm Harriet, and..."

My words trail off, forgotten as we pass into the east wing—the only part of the castle untouched by the Sky Court's influence. The wing I have yet to explore.

The walls shine a brilliant gold, and servants scrub at the trees carved into the marble floor. Tattered tapestries hang along the walls, covered in different depictions of the seasons. And above our heads, a thorny blanket of twisting, barren vines cling to the ceiling.

I linger at the back and keep a watchful eye on Kressa and Simon, the latter rubbing his hand against his throat. My temple aches where he landed a blow, but I've had worse. And I won't let it happen again.

A guard steps forward. "Welcome to the east wing, where you'll find your assigned rooms. Report to the ballroom in four hours."

The group disperses. Alliances knit together as small groups branch off, whispering and glancing over their shoulders as they walk.

Ignoring them, I meander down the hall and pass a window offering a sweeping view of the mountain range, perpetually capped with a stubborn layer of snow.

Dragging my fingertips over the etched names in the plaques, I stop at a door tucked into the end of the hallway. I trace the indentations and the double consonant—my borrowed name.

Harriet Wells.

I push the door open.

It's humble compared to the quarters I share with Thea. A simple bed stands against the side wall, white sheets tucked in tight around the thin mattress.

An open doorway to a bathroom is opposite the bed, but it's the far corner I stride to. I stop beside the armoire and run my hand along the stone wall, fanning my fingers over the uneven surface.

Marianne went to endless lengths to ensure I got this room, even trading nighttime shifts with the housekeeping staff.

My fingers find the narrow seam. "There you are."

Scooping my fingertips around the edge, I ease the servant door open. A dark staircase greets me, the entrance lined with cobwebs and a thick layer of dust. Damp, musty air that hasn't been disturbed in years seeps into the bedroom.

I clear the cobwebs and peer down the steps into the dark. Without a source of light, it'll be impossible to navigate, but—

"What are you doing?"

I flinch back, scraping my face along the jagged opening. I reach for the dagger at my thigh, but my hand comes back empty. Weaponless.

My hand balls into a fist.

Leaning against the doorframe, Kressa taps her cheek. "You're bleeding."

I swipe at my face, and my fingers come back with a smear of blood. "Did you come here to defend Simon?" I wipe it off on my shirt. "Or are you wanting to know how I took him down so easy?"

"I'm wanting to know how you survived after I—" Her gaze finds the open doorway behind me. "What's that?"

"No idea." I ease the door shut, cringing as its hinges squeal. "It was open when I came in."

She crosses the room and stops in front of me, running a finger over the hairline fissure in the wall. Her breath skates over my neck as she whispers, "Interesting. Where does it go?"

Sunlight pools on her face, emphasizing a white scar arcing up her jaw and into her hairline. Our gazes lock, and over her shoulder, I catch the shadow of a man lingering in the hallway.

Simon.

I slide between her and the hidden door. "Get out of my room."

She doesn't step back. Her face hardens, and in a single

movement, she wraps her fist around my collar and shoves me against the wall. "Give me back my list."

"Sorry." I tilt my head back and smile at her down the bridge of my nose. "I tore it up and dropped it into a puddle."

A growl rumbles from her throat, and she reels back a fist, but a knock echoes through the room.

"Am I interrupting something?"

Thea. Her eyes narrow on Kressa, and she shoulders her way around Simon. "One scream from me, and I'll have every guard running this way."

Kressa's hand falls, and she takes a step back, adjusting the collar of her shirt. Without acknowledging Thea, she bares her teeth at me. "Can't wait for the first trial, pirate."

My stomach roils, but I school my face into indifference. The final line of her list flashes through my mind—the locations where she's searched for me, Briar, scribbled out.

Now she's at her final stop.

She shoves away from me and strides toward the door, ignoring Thea's searing gaze.

Gemma appears around the corner, clothes piled high on her arms. She spots Kressa and stiffens, pressing herself against the doorframe. Kressa furrows her brow, but shakes her head and sidesteps into the hallway, Simon following close behind.

Thea slams the door shut, nearly nipping the back of Kressa's boots, and secures the lock. "What's her problem?"

"She's a bounty hunter, and Harriet stole her list of marks. In fact, I'm pretty sure she stabbed Harriet." I sigh and relieve Gemma of the clothes, setting them on the mattress. "Long story short, she wants me dead."

"Her and fifty others," Gemma mumbles. She pushes her hair out of her face and scans me. "During the ceremony, Marianne and I will be at the back of the hall, waiting for the signal to meet in your room. Briar's room, not this one."

"And I'll keep Caelus occupied until the participants have

been announced and"—Thea gestures to my body—"you're ready to be Briar again."

"I'll only be Harriet for as long as necessary," I say. "Caelus will notice my absence much more than a single competitor."

I lead them to the servant's door tucked in the corner. "This is the easiest way for us to come in and out, but I haven't had a chance to explore it yet. I'm not entirely sure it's safe."

Gemma pulls it open and braces her arms on either side, peering in. "Marianne and I are both familiar with these passageways. The path to your room is relatively straightforward, so I'll show you another day."

"Thank you."

"Don't thank me yet." She looks over her shoulder at the bedroom door, her voice taut and shoulders tense. "I can be at the trials and help however I can, but I can't promise you won't get caught. And if you do, I can't stop them from killing you."

I lower my eyes. "I know."

"I'll risk my life for you, but if anyone finds out, I won't hesitate to say you threatened me and Marianne to help you. I'll stop at nothing to protect her."

Thea goes rigid, and her hands curl into fists.

I rest my palm over them. "I understand."

And I do. Without hesitation, I'd burn down the kingdom to protect Thea. And she'd do the same for me.

"I swear, no harm will come to Marianne," I promise.

Gemma worries her bottom lip. "Just don't get caught, please."

13

I slide my fingers along my collar and fail to loosen the fabric chafing my throat.

In front of me, Kressa shrugs her hair over her shoulder. Judging by her unbound strands cascading in waves down her back, she must have denied help from the staff to get ready for the ceremony.

Delicate white piping sweeps down her sleeves, matching mine and every other competitor's court-issued uniform. But unlike everyone else, she doesn't tug at her cuffs or strain against the neckline of her shirt.

Simon shuffles and glances over his shoulder at her. "How long is he going to keep us waiting?"

I scan the hallway. Nobles flooded the great hall nearly an hour ago, and since then, we've been waiting behind the closed doors, listening to the garbled conversations coming from the other side.

I wind my finger into the hair at my temple and pull a lock of hair from my updo, letting it rest in my periphery. If they begin to darken from blonde to brown, I'll have to make a run for it.

A guard strides around the corner and whispers to the one stationed at the door. He eyes us and nods, grabbing hold of the door handle.

I roll back my shoulders and tip my chin, calming my racing heart. As the doors swing open, the air takes on a charge. Our two lines filter into the room, and I lean to the side, peering around the bodies and scanning the head table perched at the dais.

Isolde takes up her seat, her head adorned with a crown of inverted icicles—her eyes just as cold. But the chair beside her is empty. Vacant.

Caelus isn't here.

My stomach sinks.

A hand shoves me in the back. "Are you going?"

I swallow and force myself forward, crossing the threshold into the great hall.

The announcer's voice booms in my ears. "King Caelus is pleased to introduce the participants of The Gales."

"All hail the king," the guests recite.

I seal my lips tight and palm the dagger hidden at my thigh. Tables cram the space—a sea of nobles and governors gawking as we pass. I squirm under their gazes and their scrutiny, wondering which of us will live and which will die.

Money exchanges hands under the table.

Kressa glances at Simon, her lip curled. "They're betting on us."

A sour taste fills my mouth. This is what we are to them—not lives, not people, but entertainment. They'd think different if they knew the power of their court hinged on their king holding this competition.

Our lines split at a long table parallel to the dais, and I keep my head low, noting the way Isolde's hand tightens on her cup. I can't imagine her with us—marching in a line, risking her life.

I wouldn't let her.

I sink into the seat across from Kressa, and she catches my gaze. She lifts a brow, reading something on my face, but shakes her head and turns her attention to Simon.

Servants bustle from the kitchens and lower glasses of red wine in front of us. I take a long sip and search the ballroom.

Clouds blot out the moon, and rain pelts the windowpanes. In the decade I've been here, Caelus has never not controlled the weather when guests are dining with us. There's an uneasiness in the air, as if everyone is just as curious where the king is.

I pull my gaze from the window and find Gemma and Marianne at the back of the room.

Gemma nods, and my skin tightens, the glamour reinforcing.

The competitor beside me leans his elbows on the table, and to no one in particular, says, "Why would he keep everyone waiting?"

I shrug. "He's not usually this late."

Kressa's glass pauses halfway to her mouth. "And precisely how many of the King's dinners have you attended, Harriet? I didn't think pirates were particularly welcome."

My chest tightens as she studies me, parsing out the background of the person I'm pretending to be yet know nothing about.

"From what I've heard, I mean." I drown my words with a long sip of wine.

She hums. "From who?"

"Thea."

"Ah." She sets down her glass with a clink and drags her thumb over her bottom lip, wiping away a drop of wine. "The courtesan who walked into your room, huh? Pretty, that one."

My fingers curl around the stem of my glass. She straightens and twists her head over her shoulder. I follow her gaze to the table of courtesans in the back corner, each dressed in shades of cobalt and sapphire.

Thea rubs the back of her neck, watching the door.

"Someone else is missing," Kressa says.

"Who?"

She takes a drag from her glass. "His favorite courtesan."

The wine sours in my stomach, and I let out a low hum. "Not familiar."

"What's her name again?" Simon whispers.

Kressa sets down her glass. "Briar."

My pulse quickens as my name rolls off her tongue, the way she tastes the letters, possessing it like a mark on her list.

"What do you want with her?" I say, too eager.

"Wouldn't you love to know?" She smiles, but there's no kindness behind the gesture—no camaraderie. It's an oily toxin as she eyes me. "Don't worry yourself with it. Come the first trial, you'll be gone anyway."

I clamp my mouth shut and bite back a retort. If she wanted a reward for turning me—Briar—in as the thief, she would have by now. Unless she's waiting for Caelus and I to arrive to the ceremony, where she can announce it publicly.

Valuable.

Simon watches me over the rim of his glass, but I don't dare look away. I've already calculated his weak left side and noted the way he leans too far back when he throws a punch. It's not him I have to watch out for.

It's Kressa, and the lightness on her feet—how her attacks can't be anticipated.

What she wants with me.

The competitor beside me bumps my shoulder. "What will you wish for if you—"

The doors burst open on a violent gust of wind. It whips down the aisle, clawing at tablecloths, yet Isolde only scans the open doorway, her fingertips clenched against the table.

She's wondering where I am, too.

Caelus strides in, every muscle taut, a vein protruding in his neck.

Shit.

"Maybe I was wrong about Briar holding him up." Kressa smiles against the rim of her glass. "Perhaps she's the reason he's so angry."

Caelus halts at the courtesans' table and wraps a hand around Thea's arm, jerking her upright. I jolt to my feet, but behind me, Isolde clears her throat. A warning.

I sink back down, nails digging at the wooden arms of my chair.

Teeth bared, Caelus squeezes Thea's arm and whispers in her ear. She flinches back and nods, her eyes wide. He throws her toward the doors, and she stumbles over her feet, getting tangled in her dress. She balances herself against a crowded table and glances over her shoulder. Our gazes meet for only a heartbeat, but long enough to send a message.

He's looking for me.

My heart trips over itself as lightning flashes outside the windows, silencing the whispers. A clap of thunder follows and rattles the room, but within the length of a breath, the storm clears.

Caelus adjusts his collar, and the wind calms to a warm, mild breeze.

Tucked along the wall behind the dais, the kitchen door beckons me. I hold my breath and ease out my chair, careful not to scrape it over the stone. Ever so slowly, I grip my hands on the armrests and push myself up.

"Where do you think you're going?"

I freeze. Caelus looms over me and tilts his head, planting his palms on the wooden table. I glance at them—each fleshy finger. All I can see is the way he gripped Thea's arm so hard her skin puckered.

If I was within arm's reach when he grabbed her, he'd be walking out of the room with one less hand.

My nostrils flare as I lean over the table, meeting him eye to eye. "Apologies, *Your Highness*, but I must use the restroom."

"You'll leave when I allow it," he snarls.

Every noble in the room watches, waiting to see how the king will react, or how I might disobey. Ladies cover their mouths with their fans, whispering.

But I don't waver—this act of disobedience a luxury. As Briar, I don't have a choice. But as Harriet, he needs me as a willing sacrifice. He won't, *can't*, hurt me.

His hands curl into fists, and he inches closer. "I could make you wish you were dead."

I swallow.

Behind me, a chair scrapes against the floor.

"Let her go," Isolde says.

I don't react, not as Caelus's gaze narrows on her and my heart climbs into my throat.

He can't hurt me, but he can hurt her.

Silence stretches out. A muscle works in Caelus's jaw, and seconds tick by—ones where Briar goes unaccounted for.

He grits his teeth, his voice as sharp as the tip of a blade. "Get out of my sight, pirate."

I sweep an arm behind my back and dip my head. "It'd be an honor."

A blast of wind knocks me back. I stumble, gripping the back of a chair for balance. Caelus sneers, and I circle the table in controlled, even strides down the carpeted aisle.

Gemma stands like wallpaper in the back of the room, and I give her a faint nod. She returns it and slips through a passageway.

My heart races as I walk under the curved archway and through the open doors.

Rounding a turn in the hall, I run.

14

———————

I burst into the room. "Did he hurt you?"

She doesn't look up. Bent over her bed, Thea readies my corset, her hands shaking as she loosens the ties. I close the door and cross to her. Finger marks dot the upper half of her arm—ones that will surely leave a bruise.

I inhale a slow, steady breath and blanket her hands with mine. "Thea."

A tear falls from her eyes and splashes on the silk dress thrown over the edge of the bed. Her fingers pause, and she turns, tears glistening in her eyes.

"He hurt me," she whispers, jaw trembling.

I wipe a tear from her cheek. "We'll make him pay for everything."

"When you win and wish for that ship, I'm going to leave with you."

A weak smile tugs at my lips. "I know you will."

Firelight flickers as I help her loosen the rest of the laces. I trace over the half-moon indents where Caelus's nails dug in. "What did he say to you?"

"He asked me where you were, but when I said you were feeling unwell and stayed behind in the room, he got angrier."

I tilt my head. "Why?"

"Because he came in here and checked."

I stiffen and scan the room. "He was in here? Alone?"

Without waiting for her answer, I lunge toward the vanity. My pulse thrashes in my ears, and my legs drag, like I'm trudging through knee deep water.

I drop to the floor and rip the bottom drawer open. Various creams and perfumes shift at the disturbance, and I shove my hand into the very back.

My fingers scramble along the base of the drawer until they brush a small box.

I yank it out and rip off the lid. A shuddering, relieved breath escapes my mouth. He didn't find my compass.

Running my finger over the worn, wooden face, I press until the ridges bite into my skin. Rather than cardinal directions, gold constellations act as guides. Aethra—effortlessly drawing back an arrow—points the way to Delterran.

Thea's hand falls on my shoulder. "Everything okay?"

"Yes." I replace the lid and slide it to the back of the drawer, concealing it with layers of washrags. "I'll tell him I was out, searching for a healer."

The servant's door cracks open, and Gemma slips in. She gathers her hair into a low bun and crosses her arms, eyes narrowed. "Are you trying to get yourself killed?"

Thea's gaze swings to me. "What is she talking about?"

I raise my hands. "We don't have time to argue—"

"Briar—or should I say *Harriet*—went toe to toe with Caelus when she was meant to lay low."

Marianne follows her through the door, eyes sparkling. "It was brilliant."

"He hurt you," I whisper, glancing at Thea. "I was angry."

She rubs her hands over the blossoming bruises and looks away.

Gemma sighs and crosses the room, cupping my face in her hands. "You're a damn fool, Briar, but I admire your courage."

I close my eyes as her power slips beneath my skin and removes the glamour. My hair snakes down my back, and in the mirror I catch it shifting from ashy blonde to a deep, chestnut brown.

"We're more alike than you think," I say. "You're just as brave."

"Maybe." She swallows, and her eyes go distant. "But I wish I didn't have to be."

Marianne slides her arms under my ballgown and lifts it from the bed, nodding at me. "Go on, then. It'll take a moment to lace you up."

I unbutton my dress shirt and slide out of the pants, passing them to Gemma. Without meeting my gaze, she slings them over her arm. "I'll take these to the east wing."

She disappears through the servant's door, and Marianne tightens the corset around my waist, fingers nimble on the laces. She glances at my thigh. "Do you usually have that on you?"

I trace my fingers over the dagger. "Always."

She maneuvers around the dress and fastens the buttons. Leaning over my shoulder, she whispers, "Can you teach me how to use it?"

Smiling, I meet her gaze in the mirror. "Of course."

Thea dusts a layer of powder over my face and pauses. "Can you teach me, too?"

I suck in a breath and bite down on my cheek, fighting the sting behind my eyes. When we were young, we learned together, and our spars frequently spiraled out of control. The pin-sized scar on the top of her shoulder is proof of that. But, of course, she doesn't remember.

I shove back the memory and say, "I thought you'd never ask."

Thea and I leave the safety of our room, our heeled shoes tapping against the marble floor. I hold my breath as we approach the great hall doors, and Thea reaches for my hand, giving it a squeeze.

"To the ends of the earth," she whispers, as the guards bow and swing the doors open.

Muted voices and the occasional clink of silverware echo off the vaulted ceilings. My stomach churns, and I lower my eyes to the carpeted runner as I cross into the ballroom.

Conversations halt. A bitter taste floods my mouth, and I swallow, focusing on the way my heels sink into the low carpet. My lungs strain against the corset, unable to inhale a full breath.

A warmth runs down the back of my neck, easing the tension in my shoulders. I blink and lift my gaze.

Kressa's stare pins me like a moth to a board, and my stomach hollows out. As Harriet, I've seen her plenty, protected from her blade only by the competition's rules. But as Briar, this is our first encounter since she found me with jewels weighing down my pockets.

When I held a blade to her throat.

Her eyes skim down the bodice of my gown and stop at my thigh, where my dagger rests. Her gaze lingers, as if she can see straight through the layers of fabric.

She lifts her glass and tilts it in my direction. Taking a sip, her eyes hold mine as she swallows it down, her throat bobbing. I search her face for what she might want from me or how she knows my name, but she gives nothing away.

My mouth goes dry. She's trying to get under my skin, like she did to Caelus this morning. But I've dealt with my fair share of overconfidence and arrogance. And unlike Caelus, I know the winning blow.

Ignore their existence.

I school my face and dismiss her, focusing on my steps on the runner. Whispers filter through the space, buzzing around me like bloodthirsty mosquitos.

My feet stop at the dais, my dress brushing the first step. I lift my gaze, first to Isolde. Her shoulders stiffen, chest unmoving, but her attention is pinned to the far wall.

Either terrified what is about to happen to me, or livid she didn't know where I was.

Maybe both.

My chest aches, and I silently beg her to look my way—to give me the barest acknowledgment. She doesn't.

I swallow the knot in my throat and turn to Caelus. "Your Highness," I say, dropping into a low curtsy, "I apologize for my tardiness. I felt unwell, and it took me ages to find the healer, but I'm much better now."

He sits relaxed, ankle propped on his opposite knee as he regards me. "You seem quite sparse lately, courtesan."

A servant sneaks behind him and sets down two plates of food—one before him, and the other in front of Isolde. They go unnoticed.

I soften my eyes and relax my jaw, camouflaging into the apologetic courtesan and trustworthy spy he favors. "I'm sorry, Your—"

"I don't want an apology." He leans forward and clasps his hands on the table, lowering his voice. "What I want, is for you to be where I tell you, when I tell you. You are *my* courtesan, and I will not be made a fool searching the castle for you, especially as a dinner guest."

I stiffen at the insinuation, but Isolde doesn't so much as flinch.

Blinking, I seamlessly smooth my expression with a practiced, easy smile. I'd take his yelling and thrashing windstorms over the smug glint in his eye. "Dinner guest?"

The servant reappears with a chair between his hands, matching the ones Caelus and Isolde occupy. He sets it down, the legs scraping against the floor.

"Is there something wrong with that?" Caelus says.

"I can't sit there," I whisper. Not where a guest of distinction would sit. Nobility. A queen.

One who would replace Isolde when her power runs out and she dies.

"It wasn't a request." Caelus says.

Isolde's gaze slides to me, but I can't decipher her blank stare. Her cheeks, hollowed under this lighting, give nothing away. My hands ache to cup her face and reassure her I'll let no harm come to her.

In my periphery, Kressa smirks. Her eyes dart to my thigh again, and she raises a brow. A reminder she knows me as the thief—the woman who threatened her, not as the compliant courtesan.

Little does she know, I'm more than that. I'm manipulative. Cunning. Ruthless.

Vengeful.

And if she plans to expose my thievery to Caelus, my word would be far more *valuable* than hers.

I tip my chin to Caelus. "I'd be honored."

He holds out a hand, and I accept it as I climb the short set of stairs. I reach the top, and he lifts the back of my palm to his lips, pressing a kiss against my knuckles.

The image of his hand around Thea's arm flits through my mind, but I force a weak smile. I may not be able to drown him with half a thought, but I can feed his ego—until it's so full he never expects my hand to be his downfall.

"You look stunning," he breathes.

I relax my hand and stop myself from digging my nails into his wrist. "As do you, Your Highness."

A breeze rustles my dress and caresses my face. I lower into the chair, and he pushes it in, taking the spot between Isolde and me.

I stare at my lap, unable to look at her or the crowd and their piercing, assessing eyes.

I'm the heir to the sea. I'm no prize—no ornamental trophy meant to collect dust on a shelf and be gawked at.

Gritting my teeth, I dig for my power and will it into existence, but I come up empty. My hands fist the fabric of my dress.

Caelus unfolds his napkin and spreads it across his lap. Gilded wings adorn the shoulders of his jacket and glitter under the light. Jewels line the feathers, each decoration representative of the lives he's taken from the sea.

Forks and knives scrape against plates as dinner begins, and I push my food around, my stomach tying into knots.

Something brushes my shoulder, so featherlight I almost missed it, and I sneak a glance out the corner of my eye. Isolde keeps her gaze trained on her plate, but her fingers hang low behind Caelus's seat. Reaching for me.

I drop my arm to the side of my chair, shifting until our fingertips lace together. My heart slows, growing heavy in my chest, and my throat thickens with the words I want to say but can't.

But as her thumb drags over the back of my fingers, my pulse calms. My head clears. Her silence says everything I wish I could.

"It's a bit excessive," Caelus says.

Isolde drops my hand.

I snatch my fork. "What do you mean?"

Caelus gestures to the table of competitors. "I'm expected to share my castle and feed people competing for a single wish." He scoffs. "If you think about it, it's pathetic, really, that they're all so desperate for something they don't have."

I bristle and scan the participants. My—Harriet's—chair

sits empty, but Caelus seems to have forgotten all about the pirate.

Kressa's whispers to Simon, and that familiar shiver creeps up my neck. As if she senses my stare, she straightens, and a swallow makes its way down her throat.

Caelus leans closer, stealing my attention. "There's something I need your *expertise* for."

"Of course." I dab my mouth with the napkin, pleased to have something to distract myself with. "What is it?"

"When I bound the competitors to The Gales, I sensed something—another power, perhaps. But it wasn't like Isolde's. It was wilder, stronger."

Bile rises in my throat, and I inhale a small, controlled breath. I hold it until my lungs scream. My chest stings at the memory of his gritty power clawing through me, inspecting me. "But why would someone with power enter the competition? That doesn't make sense."

He shrugs. "I can't pinpoint it, but I think she's the one hiding something."

I follow his line of sight, not to Harriet's chair, but to Kressa's. A slow smile pulls at my lips, and I rest my chin on my hand. Perhaps my problem found its own solution. "What do you need me to do?"

"I want you to get close to her."

I blink. "What? No." I glance at Kressa, and my stomach tumbles. "She's one of the competitors. What will people think?"

"I don't care what anyone thinks," he snarls. "You have my permission to do whatever it takes to gain her trust, and you'll relay any information to me. If she has any power, or any motive for entering, I want to know why she signed up. If she's a threat, or commits crimes against the court, I am free to execute her."

I consider his words. Kressa doesn't have power. If she did, she would have used it against me when I attacked her back in the alley. But perhaps I can get close enough to find out why my name was on that list.

"Do you think I can earn her trust that easily?" I ask.

Caelus scoffs. "You're a good courtesan, and an even better spy. You've done it before, to men and women alike. You can do it again."

I tilt my head and press my tongue into my cheek as I study her. She turns her head to the side, calling attention to the scar disappearing into her hairline.

Discover her secrets, make her a threat, and I'm free of her. One less person to compete with in The Gales. One less person hunting me down.

"What do you say?" Caelus asks, as if I have a choice.

I swirl the wine in my glass and take a sip. It goes down and pools with the revenge waiting to strike like an asp. "Consider it done."

15

———

Thea leans against the archway to the ballroom and worries her lip. "Are you sure about this?"

Dinner ended an hour ago, and couples twirl to music on the dance floor. Men and women lounge on low chairs and settees scattered throughout the room as a breeze flits through from the balcony.

"What other choice do I have?"

"But what if she hurts you? What if she does have power?"

"She doesn't." I press myself against the wall and scan the room for Caelus. "And she won't, hurt me that is. Not in front of everyone at least."

"Right." Thea drags her heel over the carpet. "But still, promise you'll be safe?"

I smirk. "As safe as pretending to be a pirate in a deadly competition?"

We share a smile, and the gleam of her teeth cuts through the tension. I study her face, searching for a hint of my first mate, but her eyes are flat, the blue ring around her pupils calm. There's no recollection beyond what courtesan Thea remembers.

A stone settles in my gut, and I add it to the collection—a growing mountain of guilt. Perhaps one day it'll be high enough to climb out of. Or crush me.

I straighten my bodice and run my fingers through my hair, coaxing the curls into place. "You don't need to worry about me. This is my job, is it not?"

My hands pause on the ends of my hair. Across the space, Kressa lounges on a low couch, sipping whiskey out of a short glass. And, like I called her name, our gazes lock.

It's as if a black pit opened in the center of the room and sucked out the air, leaving my lungs empty and aching. A tingle creeps up the base of my neck, and she takes a sip of her drink, piercing eyes staring at me over the rim.

I swallow hard and paint an uninterested smirk on my face. I am Briar, Princess of the Sea. I am feared. Kressa may know I have a dagger strapped to my thigh, but she's unaware I'm a weapon far deadlier than any blade.

"Do you really think this is a wise decision?" Thea whispers. She grabs two glasses of champagne from a passing server and hands one to me.

"No." I take a sip and let the bubbles clear my thoughts and calm my stomach. "But I've never been known for my wisdom."

With the confidence of the most feared captain in the world, I pin back my shoulders, lift my chin, and stalk across the room in slow, languid steps. Kressa watches every movement, every sway of my hips. Her free hand taps the arm of the couch in time to my footsteps.

I pause before her. "May I join you?"

"By all means."

I sink to the couch, and nothing but inches separate our legs. Since dinner ended, she's undone the top two buttons of her shirt, and her hair dips into the space between her breasts. Freckles dot the skin there like a constellation.

She regards me with a slow sweep of her eyes. "It's easier to admire how beautiful you are when I don't have a blade to my throat."

I let out a hum. "Don't speak too soon."

A low chuckle. "Ah, there she is. I was beginning to think I imagined being pinned against a wall, the tip of a dagger at my throat. Surely the same woman who did that wasn't the same one who fell to the king's feet and apologized for being late to dinner."

My jaw clenches, and I look away, sucking in my cheek. "I believe I gave you the wrong first impression."

She shakes her head, teeth skimming her bottom lip. Setting her drink on the low table, she slides closer until our legs touch. Her arm weaves behind me and rests on the back of the settee, her finger drawing small circles on the bare skin of my shoulder.

My breath turns ragged, serrated. Like her presence thins the air and makes my lungs work twice as hard.

She dips her mouth to the arch of my ear, her hair weaving into mine. "You mean to tell me"—her hand skims my knee and trails a slow line up my thigh—"there isn't a deadly blade strapped around your inner thigh?"

Blood rushes up my neck and spreads across my cheeks. Her gaze pins me to the couch like a weight, and I shake my head. "Of course not."

Her lips tilt into a knowing smile, and her fingers inch up, over the thin fabric of my dress, and brush the tip of the sheath.

"Of course not," she whispers.

She spreads her palm out over my thigh. The warmth of her touch seeps through the dress, under my skin, and into my bones. I wrap my hand around her wrist and dig my nails into flesh.

She tsks. "Quite violent, aren't you?"

"Does it intimidate you," I snarl between gritted teeth, "to know I could pull it out and sink it into your chest?"

"Not in the slightest, love." She drags her thumb over my jaw and stops at my chin, holding my head in place. "But I know not to underestimate you."

I reel myself in, steadying my thoughts. "I'm not here to threaten you, Kressa."

She leans closer, and the green outer ring of her eyes darkens. "I don't remember telling you my name, *Briar*."

My breath hitches. I jerk my face from her grip and cross my legs, feigning indifference. "I don't remember telling you mine either."

"Ah, but the guards have a lot to say about the king's favorite courtesan." She reaches up and tucks a strand of hair behind my ear. "But interestingly enough, no one mentioned her being an accomplished thief."

I bite down on the inside of my cheek. "I came to apologize, nothing else."

She unravels the champagne glass from my fingers and sets it beside hers. "You're a horrible liar."

"Liar?"

Without explanation, she rises to her feet and extends a hand. "Dance with me?"

I stare at her outstretched hand as music floats through the room, and the bow of a violin whines against its strings. In the opposite corner, I catch Isolde's gaze.

Her fingers tighten around the stem of her wineglass, tension bracketing her shoulders as she glances between Kressa's outstretched hand and me.

My chest tightens.

"Well?" Kressa says.

The last thing I want is to trap myself on the dance floor with her, but Isolde understands what I have to do. She knows what Caelus is asking of me. And I have to get *something* out of Kressa—anything that will get her pulled from the competition.

Stomach sinking, I tear my attention away from Isolde and accept Kressa's hand, rising to my feet. "I'd love to."

She cocks her head, a maddening tilt to her lips. "Can I trust you not to stab me while we waltz?"

I drag a hand down her arm, the cuff ending at her elbow. "You should never trust me."

"Likewise." She settles her hand on the small of my back. "Let's go talk about the agreement you made with the king about spying on me."

The blood drains from my face.

I open my mouth, ready to spin an intricate lie, but she drags me through the crowd to the dance floor. I settle a shaky hand on her shoulder, the other wrapped in her palm as she pulls me close.

My heart smashes against my ribs, and a longing note fills the air.

She sweeps me into a waltz and presses her lips against the shell of my ear. "I'm offended you find me so gullible."

"I have no idea what you're talking about."

She clicks her tongue. "I was suspicious at dinner, but do you know what gave it away?"

"I assume you're going to tell me anyway."

A chuckle. "The way you looked at me while we were eating. It wasn't a simple glance, or even a curious one. It was the way I look at my marks. You were studying me, attempting to pick me apart, find my weaknesses, see how you could get close." She scoffs. "But, you never will."

I try to rip myself out of her grip. She tightens her hold on me, keeping me too close to reach for my weapon.

I manage to pull back far enough to look her in the eye. "Did you ever consider that perhaps I simply enjoyed the view?"

"Now that, I'd believe." Her eyes hold mine, unwavering. "But I see through you, and I know that wasn't it."

"You know nothing about me." My words are clipped, biting as the tempo picks up and our feet quicken.

"I know enough to know you wouldn't want the king finding out about the jewels you hand over to pirates. The women you trade for them."

I stiffen, narrowing my eyes as the champagne turns to acid in my stomach. "Is that a threat?"

"I don't threaten, love." She breaks eye contact long enough to untuck my hair from my bodice and drape it over my shoulder. "I simply do."

"Blackmail, then. What do you want from me?"

Every hint of amusement wipes from her face, and her lips press into a thin line. "I'm looking for someone."

Her list.

Ice fills my veins, and I will my voice into submission as I whisper, "Who?"

"It doesn't matter. But I have reason to believe Caelus is holding him prisoner in the castle, and you're going to help me."

Him? I rack my brain for her list, but there weren't any other names—no marks left but me. But whoever he is...

"That's why you joined The Gales," I say. "Unrestricted access to the castle."

"And you won't tell anyone."

"What if I do?"

"I won't hesitate to tell Caelus exactly who took all those precious gems from the nobles." Her fingers tighten around my waist, my hand. "If you ruin this, I'll ensure you rot in a dungeon."

I dig my nails into her shoulder. "Or perhaps you will."

She clicks her tongue. "Such harsh words from someone who also benefits from this arrangement."

"How so?"

She spins me out, and in a blur, pulls me in, tucking me

close to her chest. "You help me find who I'm looking for, and you get to tell Caelus you're spending extra time with me, trying to get information. A perfect excuse to avoid him."

My lip curls. "What makes you think I want to avoid him? He's the king, after all."

"It's impressive how you've convinced an entire kingdom that you're interested in him." A laugh, laced with sarcasm and a hint of pity. "I see the way you look at him, the way your hands curl into fists when he touches you. You loathe him."

I shake my head. "You're imagining things."

"Am I? I'm quite observant, Briar." She hums, low and rumbling. "So, am I also imagining the way my touch makes you shudder?" She drags her hand from the small of my back to the tip of my spine, cradling my nape with her palm. "I can almost hear your heart racing." On an exhale, she lowers her mouth to my ear. "Perhaps you like the view after all."

Heat laps at my core, but I pull back and lower my voice to a snarl. "I wish I killed you when I had the chance."

She grins, wisps of hair hanging over her eyes. "Beautiful, awful liar."

The music fades and comes to a halt. Dancers around us stop and bow to each other, but we stay standing, locked in a glare.

Finally, she unravels herself from me and bows. I don't return it.

"It's been a pleasure," she says. "I'll see you in my room after tomorrow's trial."

"If you survive."

Her lip quirks. "Good night, Briar."

She turns on her heel and strides from the ballroom. I narrow my eyes on her back, burning a hole straight through her shoulder blades and into her heart.

She cannot walk out of tomorrow's trial alive.

16

———

At sea, bribes and threats trade hands like currency.

I am no stranger to extortion and intimidation, but over the years, I've lost my touch. This isn't something I can fight my way out of with brute force.

No, this is a battle of smarts. A game of lies and secrets. A war of words.

"Did you get what I asked for?" Caelus asks, lounging at the fireplace in his chambers. He sips from a glass of whiskey, his ankles crossed on the low coffee table.

I meander around the ample sitting room, scanning the top of his desk for any information about the war. Nothing jumps out.

I suck in a cheek and brush my fingertips over the door handle leading to his infamous room of collectables. I've only heard rumors of the priceless trinkets he keeps from various courts, but I've yet to explore it.

Pausing by the roaring fireplace, I lower myself to a wooden chest and fan out my dress, clasping my hands in my lap. I have the exact information Caelus wants, but haven't decided how to use it to my advantage.

There must be something Kressa isn't telling me—a sliver of the truth she's holding back. Caelus doesn't keep prisoners for the hell of it. He wouldn't waste resources on keeping them fed or living. So, who is this man, and why is he so important?

Caelus peers at me with a lifted brow.

I sigh and trace the intricate carvings etched into the lid of the chest. "No. Whenever I brought up the competition, she changed the conversation. I didn't want to come off too eager in case she became suspicious."

He abandons his drink on the coffee table and lowers his legs, resting his elbows on his knees. "Try harder. If I thought it would be easy, I would have asked one of the other courtesans."

My fingers close into a fist, my nails scraping at the wood. I glance over his shoulder, at the carpets and tapestries hung on the walls depicting images of birds caught mid-flight in raging storms. "I just need more time with her, that's all."

A tall mirror stands in the far corner with a quilt draped over it, the uncovered slice at the bottom clouded and warped with age. Why Caelus insists on keeping it in his room, I'll never know. A part of his collection, I guess.

"If she didn't tell you why she's here, what *did* you talk about while her hands were all over you?" He purses his lips and tightens his grip on the arms of the chair. "In fact, I'd say you were enjoying her company."

The ghost of Kressa's hand traces up my back, and I shiver despite the fire licking at my skin. I grimace. I don't want the brand of her fingers on me or the phantom of her whispers against my neck.

Or the memory of Isolde's expression when I took Kressa's hand.

I shrug. "Nothing noteworthy. Bragged about her work in bounty hunting, the people she's arrested. Mostly spoke about how good dinner was."

He gives me a long stare and nods, plucking up his drink.

Ice taps against the sides as he drains the glass. "For some of them, that will be their final meal. In fact, tomorrow, many of them will become a meal themselves. With any luck, Kressa will be among them and our problem will be solved."

My stomach sours, but his words snag my thoughts, and I straighten.

Of course.

"A meal?" I lean against the wall and admire my nails, feigning indifference. "What do you have planned for tomorrow's trial, anyway?"

He stands and crosses to the bar cart nestled between two sweeping windows, giving a view of the night sky. Amber glass bottles crowd the two tiers, and he removes the top from a decanter, filling his glass. He stares out at Sarenia below and knocks it back.

Just as I think he won't entertain my curiosity, he opens his mouth. "I borrowed something from the sea. It was hard to track down, even harder to sedate and airlift all the way here. But it's the perfect opening for the competition. The perfect way to kill as many as possible."

I sit up straight, my heart beating wildly against my ribs. There's only one thing in the ocean that deadly.

"It's currently being held in the lake, unfed and furious," he continues. "The pirates will likely be the first to recognize it from their legends, although none have met it at sea. A ship has never survived its attack."

Wrong. One ship has. Barely.

My fingers tremble in my lap, and I fold them together. "If it's from the sea, wouldn't it die in the fresh water?"

He nods, refilling his glass. "It can survive up to three days without salt water, and tomorrow night will mark the third day."

A string tugs at my heart. One that leads directly to the ocean. "And what will you do with him after?"

"We intend to return it, of course." Caelus turns and leans against the window frame, smiling into his glass. "Once it has its fill. Or when half the competitors are dead."

Blood drains from my face, my breaths quickening. "It's late, I should get going." Standing, I hurry to the door and pause with my hand around the knob. "I arranged to meet with Kressa tomorrow. I'll get more information from her after the trial."

"Should she survive," Caelus adds.

"Yes, should she."

Should I survive.

"Good night, Briar."

"Good night," I manage, slipping through the door.

I stagger down the hallway, blood pounding in my ears. My exhales come out in rasps—talons scraping down my throat. I press myself into a shadowed alcove and suck in a slow, controlled breath.

Fresh water from the lake won't kill me, but the puckered, serpentine tentacles will. The rows of razor-sharp teeth, capable of ripping apart flesh and bone. The revenge promised should he ever come across me again.

The kraken.

17

"I got your note," Isolde says, slipping through my bedroom door.

I shift on the couch, my eyes aching as I stare into the flames licking the ceiling of the hearth. Curling over myself, I rest my elbows on my knees, fighting the sting in the back of my throat.

She crosses the room and sinks to her knees in front of me, pushing my hair out of my face. "It's the middle of the night. What's the matter?"

Embers dance through the log, eating it from the inside out. I lean into Isolde's touch as she cups my face.

It's rare that we send word for each other. It's too risky, considering any correspondence could be intercepted by Caelus or one of his advisors. We usually take advantage of his absences—wait until he visits the warfront or neighboring territories.

But I need her now.

"I'm scared," I whisper, finally letting my gaze stray from the fireplace. I print her featherlight touch onto my cheek and breathe in the warmth of her scent, letting my fingers trail over her curls.

It could be the last time.

Her brow furrows. "Of what?"

The kraken. My glamour failing. Losing her.

I chew on my lip. If she knew what was in store for me tomorrow, she'd stop me. If she knew my life was on the line, she'd pull me from the competition. Anything to keep me safe.

"Of Kressa." A half-truth, given the target the bounty hunter has painted on my back. "I've always done what Caelus asked and built trust with whoever he wanted. But this feels different, more dangerous, more at stake."

"Briar." Isolde's eyes soften, and she swallows. She chews on her words, her fingers tracing irregular circles over my cheeks until she finally whispers, "Let's leave."

"And go where?"

"Far from here. Let's run away."

I pull back, far enough for her hands to fall to my lap. "What are you talking about?"

"I never wanted to give Caelus my power." Her hands curl into fists, nails catching on the fabric of my pants. "But my court was weak, on the brink of failure, and I had no family or heirs to support me. There were people starving on the streets, Briar. We were nearing an uprising. A civil war."

My chest tightens. If that were my court and my people, I would have done anything to save them, too.

"I was desperate," she continues. "And he promised if I surrendered my power he would share his resources. His wealth would help me feed the poorest of my people, restart the infrastructure, and boost the economy." Her eyes hold mine, a fury brewing in their icy depths as she snarls, "He lied."

"We can't just run," I whisper. "He'd find us. I'd be executed, and you'd be exactly where you are now, unless he decides to let you live from behind bars. Your people need you. *I* need you."

She lifts herself onto the cushion beside me and clasps my hands in hers, stroking a thumb over my palm. "It's not *just* running. While Caelus has been busy coming and going from the warfront, I've been taking advantage of his absence." She sucks in a cheek, as if she's testing her words—testing my loyalty. "I've been recruiting forces to fight him."

My eyes widen.

"I know." She nods, staring into the fireplace. "My forces are weak, and they wouldn't stand a chance at this moment. But they're close, and I've caught wind of Callum planning to overthrow him. Caelus will never see me coming." Her gaze meets mine, and she squeezes my hands. "We could leave tonight."

"Isolde," I breathe, my voice swallowed by the crackling flames. So the rumors are true about Caelus's brother. In light of everything else—Kressa, The Gales, Isolde building an army—that seems irrelevant.

"I'm ready to fight, Briar." She presses her forehead to mine and pulls in a breath. "Will you fight with me?"

A weight settles on my chest, my breathing ragged. Everything in me screams to say yes, to take her hand and not look back. With or without my power, we could stand a chance.

But.

"I can't." I look away, unable to bear the hurt on her face.

If I left, I'd forfeit The Gales. It doesn't matter how ready I am to fight, I'd die the moment I didn't show up for the first trial.

"Why?" She swallows. "I thought we both wanted freedom. A chance to be together, really together."

"I do." My voice wavers. "But I can't have it yet. Not until I get Caelus what he wants."

She throws her hands up. "Fuck what Caelus wants. I'm sick of catering to him. What about what we want?"

I blink back tears, and an ache spreads through my chest. This isn't how I wanted tonight to go. I don't want my last memories of her to be the hurt painted across her face, and I don't want her to remember me as a coward. But it seems I have no other choice.

"*You* are what I want." I lean closer and cup her jaw with my hands. "And I want to fight alongside you, but I can't right now."

"Because you're scared?"

I nod. "Terrified."

I go to lace our fingers together, but she pulls hers back, away from my reach. "If I've learned anything, Briar, it's that sometimes you have to do it scared."

Inside the fireplace, a log splits. My attention is trained on the side of her face and the gentle curve of her lips. For years, I've entirely misjudged her. I assumed she surrendered her power in attempt to destroy the other courts. Or in a moment of selfish weakness.

But she did it to save her own. She did it scared.

She stands, but I wrap my hand around her wrist and pull her back to the couch. "Give me three weeks. Three weeks to get everything sorted out, and I'll fight with you to the very end."

A moment passes, and I hold my breath, my heart pounding. She scans me, her gaze trailing over every mark, searching for a truth in my words.

"Three weeks," she says, nodding. "That'll give me enough time to get everything sorted, too. My forces will be ready, waiting for my signal."

"Thank you."

She weaves her fingers through my hair and tilts my head to the side, peppering a string of kisses up my throat.

I'm not promised three weeks. I'm not even sure I'll walk

out of the trial tomorrow afternoon. But I know one thing—I won't leave Isolde's side.

For her, I'll do it scared.

18

I could die today.

I swing my legs over the edge of the tower, my leggings snagging on the rough stone as I settle into a seat. An aurora of shadows spills over Sarenia sprawled out far, far below. My hair dances in the predawn breeze, and I lean against the parapet, its jagged formation cradling me like missing teeth.

The sea stretches ahead, and the sun waits below the horizon for the perfect moment to show its face. A thin, silver band separates the sky from the sea, but somewhere out there, the war rages. Perhaps on the other side of the world. And there, wherever my mother and her army are stationed, the sun could be setting.

This could be my last sunrise, and for them, their last sunset.

Gathering my hair to the side, I tame it into a long braid. It's been ages since I faced the kraken, and the day still haunts me. Growing up, I was warned not to sail into his waters. We agreed to avoid his swath of the ocean, and in return, he wouldn't hunt outside of it. An agreeable truce.

Until I broke it.

I should have known better, but the sea serpents swarmed us and I knew they wouldn't dare enter the kraken's water. And I—naively—thought we could outrace him.

When the kraken showed his face and bared the rows of hideous teeth, he slammed his tentacles onto my deck and nearly pulled us under. Even my power proved to be useless against him. My crew and I barely made it out alive. With a souvenir.

I'll never forget his wide, yellow eyes when I swung my sword into his thrashing tentacle, severing it in a single strike. His silent promise for revenge.

The question remains to be answered, though. Will he recognize me? Without my power, will he sense who I am?

I sigh, and the sky seems to exhale a long breath of its own.

Heavy footsteps sound from the staircase.

My heart lurches. I swing my legs over the parapet and onto the solid floor of the tower. Fueled by instinct, my palm flexes against my dagger. Accessible only from a hidden door, no one knows how to reach this part of the tower. Unless they followed me.

Holding my breath, I narrow my eyes as a head of dark brown hair appears, followed by a set of honey eyes.

I pull my blade from its sheath. "How did you find me?"

Her face is set like granite, but her eyes widen for a heartbeat. "Find you? I want to see what could very possibly be my final sunrise."

My hand falters on my dagger, but I tighten my grip. "There are plenty of other towers to choose from."

"Yes, but this one has the best view."

She takes a step closer, and I raise my blade, pointing it at her chest.

"Trust me, love, if I wanted to kill you, you'd never see it coming. And it certainly wouldn't be as messy as pushing you over the edge of a tower."

"Then why did you follow me?"

Another step. "Follow you?"

"The entrance to this tower is hidden. No one knows about it."

She sidesteps the tip of my blade and leans her elbows on a tall crenelation. "Not hidden well enough, apparently. If you'd rather not be in my presence, that's fine, but I'm not leaving this tower."

I level her with a stare, but it wanes, softens. We're here for the same reason, after all. She won't be the kraken's target like me, but that doesn't mean she'll survive.

"Fine." I tuck my dagger away and thoughtlessly brush my hand over her pocket, lifting out a gold chain. I fold it into my fist. Everyone else has to pay to be in my presence, so why not her? "You can stay."

She nods. Shadows dance over her soft cheekbones and over the slope of her jaw. Her lips are parted, relaxed, like in this one place in time, she's at ease.

I pull my attention from her and flick a small stone over the edge. The sunrises I see from land are tallying up, my body aching for the day I can watch it again from the deck of *The Twelfth Night*.

Moments pass by with a calm stillness to the air. A comfortable silence.

She tilts her head, and whatever troubles were haunting her have been hidden, tucked behind a second skin. Her mouth curves into a small smile. "When should I expect you to return the chain you stole from my pocket?"

Cold sweeps over my body. I furrow my brows and drop my hand to my side, the necklace tucked in my fist. "What chain?"

She scoffs. "Has no one caught you before?"

Sighing, I shake my head and open my palm. "Only you."

A gold pendant stares back, etched with a mountain range. Swirling symbols crown the peaks—some sort of foreign or lost language. I thread a finger through the chain and dangle it, the pendant swinging in a light breeze.

She blinks at the necklace, and behind her eyes lies something I can't quite discern. Amazement? Concern?

"How did you learn how to do that?" she whispers.

Shrugging, I lower my arm and the chain pools into my palm like sand. "People have a tendency to look at everything except what's right in front of them. I simply take advantage of that."

I grimace and offer her the necklace. I'm not accustomed to being caught, let alone returning my prizes.

One corner of her mouth tips. "Keep it."

I shove my hand toward her chest. "I couldn't."

She shakes her head. "Its absence will be a reminder to pay attention to what's in front of me. And it's a good luck charm." Pinching the chain between her fingers, she lifts it out of my hand and unclasps it. "Turn around."

"If you push me over the edge, I'm pulling you down with me."

A laugh escapes her mouth, and her smile rivals the rays of golden light shooting from the horizon. "Just do it, Briar. You're no good to me dead."

I level her with a glare. "Charming." And yet, despite my years of training warning otherwise, I turn my back to her. "If it's good luck, I would think you need it more than I do."

Her hands slide around my neck, knuckles brushing my collarbone as the gold pendant settles in the center of my chest. "I have to disagree. I'd face these trials a hundred times over rather than spending time with the king. To endure him—that's true courage. Bravery no one should have to bear."

She secures the clasp, fingertips skimming my nape. A shiver snakes down my spine despite the lukewarm morning.

Then her hands disappear. I pinch the pendant between my fingers and lean against the parapet as the sun makes a dramatic entrance. It paints the skies a hundred watercolor shades of pink and violet, the underbellies of the clouds absorbing the light, swirling with color.

My heart aches at how I used to admire them from my ship.

"What do you do with everything you steal?" she whispers, as if speaking too loud would interrupt the sun.

I drop the pendant to my chest. "Hoard it like a dragon."

A dimple appears in her cheek, and the sun disguises the blush licking up my neck. I dig the pads of my fingers into the rough stone. "Tell me more about this person you're looking for."

She focuses on the sun casting its flames over the glittering sea, and hums. "A truth for a truth?"

The pendant hangs heavy over my heart. I can't safely tell her any of my secrets. They're too large, too dangerous, too easy to use against me. And discovering one of my secrets is what tangled me with her in the first place.

I swallow. "You first."

She inhales a slow, steady breath. "When this war began, the Sky Court took someone very important to me. I've spent a decade searching for him, and it's brought me here." She glances down at her hands. "I can feel him in the castle walls."

I study her eyes. Sometimes, but not always, eye color tends to lean toward the court one belongs to. There are blue ones among the Sea Court, occasionally green—the shade of seaweed. And I've seen hazel eyes from the Earth Court, but they are always muddied with warm brown or copper. I tilt my head. "What court do you belong to?"

A weak smile. "I said a secret for a secret."

I tear my eyes off her, to where the world awakes in the city below. A flock of birds sweeps across the sky, and sails appear on the distant horizon. A pang spears my heart.

Kressa shifts. "Well?"

Maybe I can tell her a secret that doesn't belong to me—one to replace the luck I'm wearing around my neck. I don't want to help her win the competition, but if she dies, so does the freedom of the person she's searching for.

Over my shoulder, the stairwell is empty. I lower my voice. "Have you ever heard of the kraken?"

She stiffens, fingers pausing on the stone. "Yes."

"This afternoon you'll meet him."

Her gaze swings to me. "How do you know?"

"It doesn't matter." I worry my bottom lip. "The trial won't end until half of the competitors are dead. If his tentacles wrap around you, you're gone."

The sun shows its entirety, turning dawn into day as Kressa raises a brow. "It sounds like you're speaking from experience."

I dig my nails into my palms. "I'm only telling you what I was told."

A nod. "Thank you. It—it means a lot."

Her tone is thick, genuine. My chest swells with an unfamiliar warmth, and I cross my arms, unable to meet her eyes.

The bell in the clock tower chimes six times.

Thirty minutes until the first trial.

"I have to go." I push away from the parapet and take a step, but a hand wraps around my wrist and stops me.

Kressa stares at me, her eyes vast and depthless. "If I die today, his name is Elias."

My heart stutters. If she dies, I have no reason to risk my life looking for him. I can focus on winning the competition and forget Kressa ever existed. But how many people have I met, suffering at Caelus's hand?

"I'll find him," I promise.

19

"Welcome to the first trial."

Loose gravel crunches beneath my boots as I come to a stop among the crowd of competitors. Caelus stands before a set of wooden doors built into the stone arena circling the lake. A heavy metal plank rests across them, securing them shut.

But the hefty lock isn't meant to keep the kraken in. No, it's to keep us from getting out.

I swallow and shove my hands into my pockets. The clothes Caelus provided for the trial would be more suitable—tight pants and a fitted blue tunic—and most of the others chose to wear them. But not me.

My sleeves billow around my wrists, and the cords of my collar are pulled tight, hiding the chain around my neck. I considered not wearing it, thought it too high a risk, but I need all the luck I can get.

"You made yourself quite sparse last night, pirate."

Her voice sends a jolt up my spine. Kressa circles me, her eyes just as sharp as the blade at my thigh.

She's donned head to toe in black, also choosing to forgo the attire Caelus provided.

"Did I?" I say, watching out the corner of my eye as Simon enters my periphery.

"It doesn't matter." Kressa clicks her tongue. "You won't make it out of this trial anyway."

Two royal guards heave the metal plank from its perch and open the doors with a sickening groan.

"Follow me," Caelus says.

I hesitate, but Simon shoulders my back. He strides around me and disappears through the doorway into a dark, cramped chamber. We funnel in, and I join at the rear, sliding into the small room.

Torches line every wall but one, where rows of swords hang from hooks.

An unnatural, otherworldly screech comes from the second set of doors leading to the lake, rattling the stones beneath our feet. I back into the cold, damp wall, and my breaths come out in shudders.

Half of us won't walk out of this trial.

I might not walk out of this trial.

If the kraken senses me, I'll be among the first to go. And it won't be quick.

Shadows dance over Caelus's face as he regards us. "On the other side of this door waits a sea creature so ferocious, none have ever faced it and lived. He's known to sink ships and annihilate entire crews in a single strike."

The pirates in the room blanch.

"The kraken," one whispers.

Murmurs reverberate off the walls, and my stomach hollows out. I slide my hand to my thigh. My dagger would be useless against the kraken, yet its presence sends a wave of calm over me.

Kressa clears her throat. "Actually, there's one person who faced it and lived."

Caelus narrows his eyes. "And who would that be?"

"The Princess of the Sea."

The room goes silent, and I swallow as I study her. It isn't awe or reverence on her face, but a scowl.

"May I remind you," Caelus snarls, "we do not speak of her. It is illegal to honor her. To do so, would be treason."

Kressa scoffs. "Nothing worth honoring."

A bitter taste fills my mouth, and I try to swallow it down, but it only grows. I glance to the pirates, waiting for them to come to my defense. But they remain silent.

Another ear-piercing roar shakes the foundation, but I'm unfazed. Since the curse trapped me here, whispered rumors of my power float through the castle—stories of the princess who disappeared, whose features or name no one can remember.

But this is the first time my guilt has been spoken aloud. My blame. It pierces through my heart and skewers me to the wall. Tensions were already high among the courts, but my actions tipped the balance to war.

Tens of thousands of deaths are the result of my selfish decision.

"Indeed." Caelus pulls his gaze from Kressa and gestures to the wall of swords. "You'll each be given a sword. But the kraken isn't the only thing you're up against."

My knees weaken, and sweat gathers on my brow.

"You will each be assigned a target—another competitor. If you succeed in killing them, you'll be granted immunity from the next trial. An immediate entry into the final."

Those who previously forged loose alliances back away from each other, exchanging wary glances. But my lips tilt. I could kill any of them with my eyes closed and earn myself a spot in the final trial.

Caelus steps to the side. "Retrieve your weapons."

The royal guards stride to the wall and hand out the blades one by one. I step up last, and the guard shoves the sword in my direction, the polished metal glinting in the low light.

The hilt is heavy in my palm. A Sky Court emblem is stamped onto the pommel, and smooth leather twists around the hilt. I test its weight against my old sword.

It's been a decade since I last wielded one—when I fought my way out of the castle after refusing to marry Prince Barren, then killing him. But muscle memory takes over, and my hand relaxes, fingers settling into a familiar grip.

"When the cannon blasts, the trial will begin," Caelus says. "When half of you are dead, the canon will blast a second time, marking the end of the trial. Good luck."

He strides to the exit and disappears into the daylight. The doors heave shut, and a clank echoes through the chamber. The metal plank, locking us in.

The man beside me worries his lip, and the tip of his sword clatters against the floor. His shirt hangs off his shoulders, arms frail despite his youth. My mouth tips into a smile. A beggar chose to wear his threadbare clothes rather than the ones provided by the Sky Court.

His brown eyes meet mine.

"What's your name?" I ask.

He swallows. "Geoff."

"If you win, what's your wish?"

He inhales a deep breath. "My wife is pregnant. A girl. Or, at least we think so." He beams, and the tremors of his hand ease. "My wife was livid when I signed up for the competition, but if I win, I'll wish for enough money to get us out of the slums. We'll have a house, food, an education for my daughter. All I want is for her to have a better life."

My nails dig into the handle of my sword. This shouldn't be the answer, yet Caelus has made people desperate.

"What's her name?"

"My wife?"

I nod, glancing at the door to the lake. Any minute now, the canon will blast.

He blinks, and the rapid rise and fall of his chest slows. "Dolma."

Dolma. I commit the name to memory. "What made you fall in love with her?"

A light blooms in his eyes, and he chuckles. "The first time we met, she threw a glass of water in my face. I've been in love ever—"

The cannon blasts, and a gust of wind throws the door open. Blinding light floods the room, and a screech rattles the walls. A tentacle thrashes in and wraps around Geoff's waist, the razor-lined suckers burrowing into his skin. He screams, drops his blade, and I raise my sword overhead, but the weight slows me down, and the tentacle drags him through the doorway.

My blade slams into the stone at my feet.

A splash cuts off Geoff's scream.

My knees buckle, and I brace a hand on the wall, steadying my breaths.

The competitors gawk at the doorway, the whites of their eyes stark in the low light. I stagger closer. If we stand here and wait, we'll be picked off one by one. I'd rather take my chances on the shoreline.

I step over the threshold, and the blinding sunshine blurs my vision. The arena spans the entirety of the lake—a stone oval topped with packed grandstands, where spectators cheer and scream as we exit, stumbling onto the damp shore.

Only two dozen feet of muddy sand separates the cloudy water from the arena walls. Across the lake, a pile of boulders protrudes from the ground.

I take a step toward them, but hesitate. Climbing them

would give me an advantage against the kraken, but I wouldn't be able to hunt my target, whoever it might be.

Ripples fan out from the center of the lake, and bubbles emerge from its depths. I retreat a step, my stomach roiling.

The man beside me shouts and falls to his knees in the wet mud, clutching at his hand.

Then a woman.

Followed by another.

And another.

Blood pours from their palms and pools around their knees. Their backs heave, jaws clenched.

A searing pain shoots through my hand, and I fall to the ground, my sword clattering at my side. Biting back a scream, I open my palm, where an invisible blade slices through my skin.

It spells out a name.

Kressa.

I grit my teeth, lungs heaving from the pain, and force myself to my feet. Sword forgotten at her side, Kressa kneels in the dirt a few feet away, her eyes shut tight as blood drips from her hand.

I pluck my sword from the mud and hiss as my bloodied hand clamps around it. Pain shoots up my arm, and crimson trails down the handle, splashing to the ground. I breathe through my nose until the pain dulls to a steady throb.

Kressa grunts, the knee of her pants soaked through. I tune out the world—the cheering spectators, the kraken waiting to strike, and hone my attention on her.

Blade ready, I stumble a step closer.

I'll make it quick, painless. A clean sweep. I know how to maim and torture, but also how to deliver a lethal, instant blow.

My fingers tremble, but I tighten my grip.

She won't feel a thing.

Panting, she braces a hand against the ground. Her head

hangs between her shoulders, hair a muddied curtain around her face.

I raise my sword, poised to strike the base of her neck.

Inhaling a deep breath, I steady myself. On the exhale, I swing my blade down.

20

ressa rolls, and my blade sinks into the ground, slashing through mud and sand and blood. The impact reverberates through my arm and tears at the open wound on my hand.

She grips her sword and rises to her feet. Her lips press together, and she unravels her fist, exposing the name.

Harriet.

My stomach hollows out.

A familiar scream comes from the stands. "Behind you!"

I twist to Thea's voice, but a tentacle sweeps my feet out from under me, and I crash to the ground. My temple slams into the grainy mud, and my sword soars out of reach, sinking into a puddle. I fumble toward it as the tentacle thrashes over the shore, knocking over anyone in its path.

A second shoots from the water. And a third.

Competitors scream, stumbling over each other, and a cry pierces the air as Simon sinks his sword into the chest of a man. Chills sweep down my spine and I rise to my knees, scrambling for my sword.

I reach for it, but a foot meets my side and throws me onto

my back. My vision swims, and Kressa's figure blots out the sun. Her hands grip the hilt of her sword, tip poised to my chest.

Lifting her blade, she readies it over my heart. Not quick. Not painless. "No hard feelings."

She brings it down, but I roll, and her sword pins my shirt to the ground. I rip it free and lunge for my sword. My palm screams as sand bites into the wound, but I grip it tighter and push to my feet, sprinting around the edge of the lake.

My boots pound the shoreline, heart hammering in my chest. The kraken thrashes men and woman through the air, pulling them beneath the surface one by one. Sunlight bounces off the churning water, and I risk a glance over my shoulder. Bloodied, prone bodies coat the open space where we entered the arena.

And between me and the bodies—Kressa gains, blade swinging at her side.

Hand throbbing, I pump my arms harder. Wet sand shoots into the air with each footfall, and the loose fabric of my pants catches the wind, slowing me down.

The sun beats down on the back of my neck. I bank around the curve in the lake, the pile of boulders inching closer. If I make it to them, I—

A large tentacle twists through the air and slams into my chest, pinning me to the ground. The air rushes from my lungs, and its weight pauses over my middle before it slowly reels itself back into the lake.

Two yellow, slitted eyes peer at me from the surface.

Hello, Princess.

Fuck.

It sinks back into the depths, and footsteps sound behind me, close enough for mud to splash onto my calves. I jump to my feet as Kressa raises her sword, her eyes locked on me. I duck, roll to my blade, and lift it in time to meet hers, the vibration of metal on metal echoing through my bones.

Our blades slide together, screeching.

I grit my teeth and look for an out, but there's no weakness or fault in her technique.

She smirks, as if reading my mind, and shoves her weight into me, blade slipping free. I stumble back. She takes the advantage, lunging forward, and slashes her blade in a wide arc.

It slices through my upper arm, and I scream. Deep, ruby blood blooms through the fabric of my shirt and seeps down my forearm. I snarl and regain my balance, forcing my attention off the gash

I've fought battles far deadlier than this, with and without my power. Growing up, I was trained by masters of the craft. I don't lose.

I narrow my eyes. Raising my sword, I inhale a deep breath and center myself—calm like the seafloor. I breathe out and pin my stare on the soft skin of Kressa's throat.

I attack.

My sword thrashes through the air—a flash of metal.

Kressa deflects my blow, but I advance and force her back until she's flush against the stone barricade. Spectators lean over the rail, cheering and shouting. Her blade scrapes the wall, the metal squealing as she dodges my assault. I slam my pommel onto her wrist, and it jerks open, her sword tumbling to the ground.

I swing my blade and point it at her throat, directly over her artery. "I was going to make this quick, but then you cut my arm and pissed me off." I narrow my eyes, my lip quirking. "No hard feelings though."

She blinks—the first time I've witnessed fear etched into her eyes, and I tighten my grip, swallowing down the lump in my throat. It has to happen this way. I entered this competition knowing I'd have to kill.

Kressa shifts and hooks a foot around my ankle, kicking out with her other leg.

My legs flail, trying to gain purchase, but I trip over a jagged stone and fall, my back sliding into thick mud. A fist connects with my jaw, and Kressa drops onto my chest, pushing me into the earth.

She wraps a hand around my throat and squeezes until my vision blurs. I gasp for air, fists pounding her sides, but my blows do nothing. Her weight, the leverage, is too much.

Lungs screaming, I inch my fingers into my pocket and find the hilt of my dagger. I ease it out, rearranging it in my palm, and slam it into Kressa's thigh.

She howls, releasing her grip as I yank my dagger free and push her off. Air burns against my raw throat, and I clutch at my chest, heaving.

"That dagger," she rasps, eyeing the handle. "Did she give that to you?"

I smirk. "Jealous?"

Sheathing my blade, I rise to my feet and pluck my sword from the sludge. I hold it over Kressa's chest.

A coppery rust taints the air. Blood dyes the shore crimson and the lake scarlet. The surface is completely still—not a ripple or bubble or disturbance in sight, as if the kraken has already succumbed to the freshwater.

I count those still standing along the bank, and my stomach flips. One more death until the trial ends.

Kressa's.

In the stands, Caelus observes with a grin, watching us the way he would a performance or an opera. Beside him, Isolde sits, stoic.

Nobles laugh and tap their tankards together, beer sloshing over the rims.

All this death—all this pain for the benefit of a king, the amusement of a court.

My stomach sours, and the cuts along my body throb, my throat a searing ache.

"Get it over with," Kressa says, trying to lift herself in the mud. Her foot slides out from under her, and a fresh wave of blood gushes from her thigh.

I shake my head. "No."

My weapon slides through my fingers and hits the ground with a slick thud.

Her gaze meets mine. "No?"

I tilt my chin to the crowd. "I'll play to win, but I'm not going to kill for their entertainment. I won't kill innocent people."

Even if it sacrifices my freedom.

I thrust out a hand, and she hesitates, but accepts it and allows me to hoist her to her feet.

Her face is pale and bloodless as she rubs at a scrape on her arm. "You're a far better person than I am."

A splash comes from the lake, and Kressa's eyes widen over my shoulder. I twist, and a tentacle pauses midair.

I curse under my breath.

The tentacle freezes, suckers flexing, and the very tip tilts in my direction. It darts toward us and slams Kressa into the barricade. She slumps to the earth, her head drooping at an unnatural angle.

I snatch my sword. "Kressa!"

The tentacle turns on itself and faces me, testing the air. Tremors wrack my body, but I raise my blade over my shoulder and bring it down, severing through a layer of leathery scales and muscle. The kraken screeches, and a second tentacle wraps around my waist, jerking me into the air.

My sword falls from my grip, and I wedge my hand between my waist and the kraken's hold, but it's too tight. I can't reach my dagger.

A scream comes from the stands, but it cuts off the moment I plunge underwater.

I beat my fists against the tentacle as I sink. Light at the surface dims, and through the haze, two yellow eyes come into focus—pupils nothing but a thin slit. Tentacles float around his grey, elongated head like snakes.

A deep, otherworldly chuckle floats across the mental bridge.

You look different, princess.

Do I? You're as revolting as I remember.

A massive, welded chain wraps around his body in a figure eight. The end disappears through the cloudy water, where it's secured to the lake floor. A prisoner.

He tightens his hold, nearly forcing the oxygen from my lungs. *It seems your power is missing. An interesting turn of events.*

I ignore him.

He shifts and flinches as the iron bites into his skin. Blood seeps from his wounds, clouding the water with crimson. I trace the path of the chain, where angry, red sores weep beneath each link. My chest tightens.

My chains aren't as visible, but the pain cuts as deep.

Where his largest tentacle would be, only a jagged nub remains. A reminder of that fateful day all those years ago. I relax my muscles and slow my heart, rationing the dwindling oxygen in my lungs.

The kraken scans me, his pupils dilating. *You're a prisoner, too.*

I struggle against his grip and lift my leg, but one of his razor-tipped suckers cuts my thigh. I clamp my mouth shut as blood floats into the water. *Yes, but at least you'll be returned to the sea when the trial ends.*

His eyes track the red liquid, widening with what I can only assume is hunger. They swing back to me with a slow blink.

Caelus has no intention of returning me to the sea.

My heart stutters. *But he told me—*

The false king lies.

He pulls taut against the chains and cringes as they dig into his open sores. His gills strain, searching for salt water the way my lungs beg for air.

They've kept him here for days.

The kraken and I may be enemies, but we come from the same waters. We share the same home.

We don't belong to Caelus.

My lungs scream for oxygen, and my vision blurs. *Spare me and I'll help you escape.*

He pauses, considering. Then the skin around his eyes wrinkles.

He catapults me up through the water, my head whipping to the side with the force. I break the surface and gasp for air, my throat like sandpaper from Kressa's chokehold. I push my hair out of my face and every set of eyes—spectators and competitors alike—focuses on me.

They're waiting for the final death.

I career down and suck in a final breath before I'm pulled under.

Yellow eyes appear in front of me. *I'm listening.*

Let me live, and I'll get you out of these chains.

A tentacle yanks at the metal holding him down, but the chain doesn't budge. *I've tried everything to release myself, and you think* you *can do it?* He pulls me closer. *You're nothing without your power.*

Take me to where it's fixed to the bottom.

His eyes narrow. *I don't take orders from you.*

I level him with a glare equally as menacing, and I swear he rolls his eyes.

Fine, he says.

He lowers me to the lake bed. My vision strains against the lack of light and I search the muck, fanning my hands for the base of the chains. My palms brushes metal and I grab hold.

My head and ears throb from the pressure, and I blindly follow the path, searching for a weak spot. There has to be a break in it, or a latch of some sort where they locked him in. There *has* to be. Otherwise, we're both dead. I grapple each link, running my fingers over the weld holding them together. Nothing.

I need air.

He huffs. *You're lucky I'm known for playing with my meals.*

He lifts me, but my foot catches on a link. It pierces my boot, shredding through skin and muscle, and I swallow the scream.

Wait!

He pauses. I pull my foot free and trace over the metal. My head swims from lack of oxygen and blood loss and thousands of gallons of water above me. My finger finds a rough, serrated break in the chain.

Get me to my sword. Now!

Sunlight races closer and closer. I throw a hand over my mouth and another over my nose as they threaten to inhale water. The kraken whips me from the lake and lets go. I soar through the air and slam into the ground, feet away from my sword.

Groaning, I push onto my elbows and find Kressa, unconscious and slumped against the stone barricade. My breath stutters, and I stare at her chest. Time slows to a stop, the cheers and screams above nothing but a hushed whisper.

Her chest rises.

I shudder a breath. Alive. She's alive.

Standing, I grab my blade from the mud and sprint back toward the lake, wind whipping at my face. Screams fill the arena as countless tentacles burst from the water and taste the air, coiling back like an asp.

I smirk. *Show off.*

I didn't earn my reputation from humility.

A single tentacle whips toward me. I tuck my sword against my side, careful not to cut him as he wraps it around my middle, lifts me high in the air, and plunges me into the depths.

Take me to the same spot.

So bossy.

Sinking through the abyss, I clutch my sword. If it slips undetected, there's no hope for either of us. He delivers me at the chain and I fumble the links, finding the weak one.

When I count to three, pull as hard as you can, I say.

He grunts.

One.

Carefully, I slide my sword through the narrow, rusted gap. My hands quiver, oxygen quickly depleting.

Two.

I brace myself against his tentacle, and he presses back, steadying me. My throat closes up.

Three!

The chain goes taut and I throw my entire weight onto the sword. The kraken screeches, blood pouring into the water.

It doesn't budge.

Pull harder!

My muscles twitch, but I keep my grip firm on the sword. He sinks as far as the chain allows, and his exhausted, luminescent eyes peer through the muck.

I'm getting you out of here, I promise.

His tentacle falters, but he gathers his strength and presses each of his long arms against the lake bed. I grip the handle. My fingers shake, heart palpitating. I clench my jaw against the imminent implosion of my lungs.

Thank you, princess.

His tentacles push off the floor, and he shoots up. The chain goes rigid, and I put everything I have on the handle, the blade bending beneath my weight.

A pop echoes through the water, and the sword slips from my hands. The kraken roars, his tentacle falling from my waist. I sink, weightlessly, into the depths.

My lungs can't stand another moment.

I'll never feel the ocean spray against my face—never feel the ocean churn beneath my feet or the untethered bliss of sailing stormy waters with my crew.

I'll never step foot on *The Twelfth Night* again.

I bump against the sandy floor. My mouth opens and I inhale a lungful of water.

A tentacle sweeps through the water, across the sun rays, and snakes under my arms, gingerly wrapping around my middle.

My head breaks the surface, and I cough out water as the kraken lays me on the shore, letting my head loll to the side. He screeches and scrambles to the lakeshore, hooking his tentacles over the edge of the arena wall. Screams burst through the air as he clambers over the barricade, tossing people out of his way.

He drops to the other side and climbs the hill toward the ocean, his sheer size a sight to behold.

The greatest, fiercest creature of the sea. Pausing at the top, he turns and sinks into a low bow.

Thank you, Your Highness.

A canon blasts, piercing the air.

My lips tilt, and the world goes black.

21

———

Cotton fills my mouth, dry and grainy like the beaches of Delterran. Thin rays of light filter through a set of gauzy curtains, dancing in the breeze from an open window. My dagger rests on a nightstand I vaguely recognize.

I groan, gingerly running my fingers over the tender spot on my jaw where Kressa landed a blow.

My eyes shoot open.

Kressa.

I bolt upright and regret it immediately. Stitches strain at my thigh and upper arm, and my head goes light, the room spinning.

A hand rests on my shoulder.

"You're okay." Thea whispers, guiding me back to the mattress. "Lay down."

My vision focuses on her face, pinched with concern. Yet her eyes narrow—a silent promise I'll get a tongue lashing later. Behind her, the room is bare, save for an armoire beside the window.

I furrow my brows. "Where am I?" My voice comes out as a

croak, and I search the recesses of my mind, struggling to piece together my memories.

She shushes me and glances over her shoulder. "You're in the east wing, where all the other competitors are."

"Is she okay?"

A huff. "Isolde is fine, she's—"

"No, Kressa."

The name hangs in the air, somersaults, but it's too late to reel it back in.

"Oh," she breathes, followed by a nod. "She's in her room, resting like you."

I hold my palms up, where the faint outline of Kressa's name mars my left hand. I turn them over. These hands don't belong to Harriet. They're mine.

An ache pierces my sternum and I swallow, shifting my gaze to Thea. "How long have I been asleep?"

The thin nightgown on my body is clean and dry. Not coated with mud and sand, or soaked through with lake water and blood.

"Nearly an entire day. I brought up some clothes and hid them in the dresser." She narrows her eyes at the stitches on my upper thigh. "What were you thinking when you ran into the lake? I thought you were *dead* when the kraken pulled you underwater. And when he escaped..."

Her voice trails off, and my cracked lips tilt. Escaped, not freed. "He got away?"

"Yes, and killed a handful of nobles in the process."

I cough, clutching at my side. Thea helps me lift myself against the headboard and hands me a glass of water. I take a sip and swallow, my throat like sandpaper.

The doorknob rattles, and we freeze. The breath in my lungs halts, and my eyes dart around the room, but there's nowhere to hide. If I bolted to the servant's door, I'd faint. The stitches would tear.

The door swings open. Thea jumps from the bed and blocks the intruder's view, but it's too late.

She saw me.

"Briar?"

Kressa's voice is strangled, throat likely as dry as mine. She walks in and scans the room, searching for someone she won't find. My chest tightens at the slight limp on her right side, where I stabbed her.

"Where's Harriet?" Her gaze lingers on the quilt in my lap and the nightgown bunched high around my hips. She blinks and looks away. "And why are you in her bed?"

I tug down the hem and fold my hands in my lap. She'd have far too many questions about her name carved into my palm. "I, um—"

"I brought Harriet to our room last night," Thea interjects. "She wasn't sleeping well on this bed, and Briar was kind enough to trade, so she stayed up here."

Kressa furrows her brow. "And where is she now?"

"Still resting."

She rubs the back of her neck and winces. "When she wakes, will you have her come meet me?"

My hackles raise, but Thea rests a comforting hand on my shin.

"I'd love to," she says.

"And could I have a moment with Briar? Alone?"

Thea's stance between us stiffens, but I grab her hand and squeeze. "It's okay."

Kressa's gaze slides to me and settles on the pendant hanging around my neck. "I won't harm her."

My lips part. Something in the air shifts, growing taut. Thea sneaks a glance at me and gives a pointed look at my throat.

I grimace and rub at my neck until I realize it's the hand with Kressa's name on it. I shove it under the covers. "I'll be fine."

Thea exhales a long breath and fusses with the pillow behind my back, propping me up. "Fine." Facing Kressa, she tilts her chin. "But I'll be standing on the other side of that door. If you so much as raise your voice at her, I'll flay you alive."

I bite down on my grin. There she is. My fearsome first mate.

Kressa's lips quirk. "Something tells me she'd do it herself."

Thea nods, offering me a final look before she crosses the room. She gives Kressa a dramatic once over and slips through the door, pulling it shut behind her.

I slide the chain off my neck and hold it out. "Considering you survived, I believe you'll be wanting this back."

She strides toward me, stopping at the edge of my bed, and folds my palm closed. "It's yours now."

I suck in my bottom lip and set the necklace beside my dagger on the nightstand. Through the corner of my eye, I scan her. My stomach clenches as the image of her slumped, unmoving body flashes through my mind.

"Are you okay?" I whisper.

I hate the desperation in my voice, the need for her to validate she's alive and breathing and didn't die in arena. With my name on her list and being her target in The Gales, I shouldn't want her to live.

And yet.

She shrugs. "I've been better."

Between her proximity and the thin fabric separating her gaze from my skin, I feel naked. The pillowy mattress presses against my bare legs, and my breath snags. It's too comfortable. Too vulnerable.

Ensuring my slip covers as much as possible, I throw the sheets from my lap and swing my legs over the side. My vision swims. I brace my hands on either side of the mattress and bow my head, taking deep breaths.

A pair of callused hands grip my shoulders, immersing me in hints of cedar and rain. "Slow down. Are you okay?"

Her voice sounds distant, but when I raise my head, she's a breath away.

"I—I'm fine," I lie, wounds pounding, head spinning. I blow out a breath and straighten. "Just moved too quick, that's all."

She releases my shoulders and extends a hand, the outline of Harriet's name etched into it. Swallowing, I shake my head and push myself from the bed. I teeter for a moment, and Kressa grips my arm, steadying me.

"Pull it together," she says, any sympathy leeched from her voice.

But her breath catches, and she leans closer, trailing a finger down the side of my face where she landed a blow. "Briar, who did this?" Her eyes darken, searching my face. "If Caelus laid a finger on you, I—"

"No." I push her hand away. "You don't get to blackmail me one moment and care for my safety the next. In fact, this *agreement* will only work if you keep your hands off me."

The light in her eyes dims, and she shoves her hands into her pockets. "Understood."

"Now," I say. "What did you want to talk about?"

She sidesteps and lifts my dagger from the nightstand. I should reach for it, or snatch it from her hands, but the way she admires the hilt gives me pause.

"I've never seen anything like it," she says.

Swirling, intricate lines decorate the gold handle, smoothed by time at sea. At one point, my name was etched into the metal, but years of wielding it have worn away the letters— fitting, considering the curse has erased my name from mouths all over the world.

She turns it over in her hands, and sunlight bounces off the blade. "I'm surprised you let Harriet borrow it. You must trust her."

"I do."

She lowers her eyes and drags her bottom lip through her teeth, setting my dagger down like it's a piece of artwork. "If you see her, let her know I'd like a truce. An alliance. I'll fight beside her until I have to fight against her."

A knot loosens in my chest. "I'm sure she'll appreciate that."

Without looking at me, she asks, "Are you two friends?"

"Something like that."

Tapping her fingers on the nightstand, she straightens and turns to the servant's entrance. "Caelus is hosting a dinner at the end of this week, followed by dancing and drinking, of course. We will take advantage of the distraction and search the dungeons for Elias. Until then, try to get information out of the king."

I narrow my eyes. "I'm getting tired of being told to use my body to get information out of people."

Frowning, she shakes her head. "That's not at all what I meant. I would never ask you to do something like that, Briar. Your words are far more powerful."

A thick silence stretches between us, hanging over our heads.

Her hands flex—the same ones that swung a sword at me and nearly plunged it into my heart. I swallow and twist the fabric of my nightgown.

A creak comes from the door, and Thea's head pokes in, eyes wide. "Caelus has guards searching the grounds for you. He wants to meet in the garden."

I grimace at my nightgown. "I'll have to go back to the room and change."

She slips in and scurries to the servant's door, pausing halfway through the room. Glancing between Kressa and me, she lets out a low hum. "I'll be waiting in the dark, scary, spider-filled hallway."

Her hair swishes around her head as she gives Kressa one final, searing look, then disappears through the doorway.

Kressa lifts the chain from the nightstand. She slides it through her fingers, running a thumb over the pendant, and flicks her gaze to me. "May I?"

I swallow and nod.

She circles behind me, and her fingers dip beneath my hair. My breath hitches as her knuckles skim my nape, and with a soft tap of metal, she secures the pendant around my neck.

Dropping her hands, she nods and crosses to the bedroom door. She pauses, opening her mouth, but closes it and shakes her head.

"What?" I ask, my voice more breathless than I'd like.

That mask slides back on, and her eyes harden, lips pressing into a taut line. "Don't disappoint me."

22

———————

My shoes click against the stone path as I stride under arches of flowering wisteria shading me from the afternoon sun. Honeysuckle, jasmine, and tulips of every shade surround ivory sculptures and bubbling fountains.

The garden should smell beautiful—and it did, a decade ago. But no longer. The fake flowers are only a reminder that nothing natural grows in this soil ever since Caelus conquered.

I round a bend to the center of the courtyard, my courtesan dress tailing over the fake grass, and a large fountain of Terra comes into view. She stands, mid-stride, arms held out. In one palm rests an eagle, wings tucked comfortably into its sides. Water pools in her other hand. And around her forehead—a twisted crown of vines, roses blooming beside thorns.

Her creation. Sea, Sky, Earth. No mention of the Fire Court that came from Serinos. No, that would be sacrilegious. Illegal.

"Briar."

My brows pull together, and my attention drags from the fountain to the stone bench. Isolde sits with her gown spread over her legs, crossed at the ankle.

"I thought I was meeting Caelus here."

"Sometimes the only way to get servants to do my bidding is to lie and tell them they're his orders."

Her tone is thorny, lacking the typical softness when she breathes my name against my neck. I tilt my head away from her. The bruise along my jaw faded this morning, and the stitches in my arm dissolved an hour ago, but I can't be too careful.

"Come," she says, patting the spot beside her. "Sit."

I hesitate, searching her eyes. There's a chill there, but it thaws as her lips tilt and she warms me with a smile.

The tension in my shoulders unfurls, and I close the distance between us, settling onto the bench. Between the sun-drenched stone beneath me, and her thigh pressing against mine, warmth seeps into my bones. "You wanted to—"

"I looked everywhere for you."

I swallow. "What?"

Her gaze remains fixed on the fountain. "During the trial." She turns her head, slowly, until her eyes bore into me. "Where were you?"

My words tangle on my tongue, a mess of half-truths and complete lies. The confession begs to be let free, but I can't put her in harm's way. "Isolde, I..."

The sentence bottlenecks in my throat, and I weave my fingers through hers.

"Yes?" she says, expectantly.

I blow out a breath. "My uncle had a fall, and I had to help take care of him. They're both getting older, and I'm so worried that the jewels I'm giving them aren't enough to pay for their care."

"A shame." Her thumb brushes over the back of my hand, and she lets out a hum. "What are their names again?"

My mouth goes dry, and the sun bakes down on me. She's

never asked their names—never doubted my lies about where I am when I'm not at the castle.

"Lydia and Malcolm," I manage.

"Lydia and Malcolm, what?"

I search the recesses of my mind for a single surname, one of many I've seen bolted above the front doors in Sarenia. "Lockett."

She nods, slowly. "Lydia and Malcolm Lockett?"

"Yes."

"Send my wishes for a speedy recovery."

"They'll appreciate that," I say, controlling my voice even as my heart pounds against my ribs. She knows it's a lie. I can tell by the set of her shoulders and the way she won't make direct eye contact. But I've burrowed this lie so deep, I can't admit what I actually do with the jewels.

She brushes my hair off my shoulders and plucks a fake rose from the bush behind us, twisting the stem between her thumb and forefinger. She flicks it to the ground.

I force my lips into a smile, my mind racing with a way to change the topic. She pauses, and her brows furrow as her gaze finds the gold chain resting against my chest.

The blood drains from my face.

She leans closer, hovering her mouth over my ear. "I saw a competitor wearing this chain, did I not?" She pinches it between her fingers, so tight her skin puckers around the edges. "Kressa, right?"

"This?" A laugh bubbles from me. I cup her face and trace her chin with my thumb, dipping my fingers into her hairline. "Isolde, there is nothing for you to worry about. Caelus wants me to get closer to her and figure out what she has to hide. That's all. This necklace means nothing to me."

She clicks her tongue and drops the charm. "A shame the vermin didn't kill her."

I tilt my head. "Vermin?"

"The kraken. Vermin, like all the other creatures who dwell in the sea."

The words are a slap to the face, but I school my features while a bruise forms on my heart. Her distaste for any court that isn't her own isn't a secret, like the other rulers. My own mother loathed the land, after all.

But it's a shock to hear it said so plainly.

"I know what's happening to me," she whispers, her gaze somewhere in the distance. "That it's only a matter of time before my power depletes until all I am is a husk."

I let a moment pass by, then, "Will your forces be ready before that happens?"

She shrugs, weak, the space around her collarbones hollower than it was just days ago. "They're going to have to be. Either I die trying to save myself, or I die doing nothing." She picks at a thread on her dress. "That's why I wanted to enter The Gales. To wish for my power back."

The light in her eyes dulls, and I weave an arm around her waist. Using my other hand, I tilt her chin until our eyes meet. "We'll find a way out of this."

She doesn't know how deep the promise goes—how I can't imagine a life without her gentle touch or the press of her full lips against mine.

Leaning into my touch, her gaze clears. "When I surrendered my power ten years ago and bound myself to this castle, I never thought I'd find love within these walls." Tears rim her eyes, and she sniffs. "But here you are, Briar."

"Here I am," I whisper, tracing her bottom lip with my thumb. "And here I'll be."

She melts into me, molding our bodies together. In the openness of the gardens, with little more than a hedge at our backs and a fountain at our front, she presses her lips to mine. My breath hitches, and my eyes flutter shut.

Yes, she surrendered her power to Caelus, but I'm the one

who fanned the flames of war. We're two sides of the same coin, living the consequences of our actions.

She pulls back first, eyes drunk. Then they narrow, focusing on the balcony over my shoulder.

I turn, and ice spreads through my veins.

Dressed in black and no longer favoring her left leg, Kressa stands at the rail, deep in conversation with Simon. Her hair is loose around her shoulders, and although she doesn't look my way, there's an expectant buzz in the air—a stiffness to her spine.

A shiver crests over my arms.

I expect Isolde to jerk away from me, like she does whenever our time is unexpectedly interrupted. But she teases the ends of my hair with her fingers and settles her mouth against the curve of my throat.

"What are you doing?" I breathe, warmth blooming behind my navel.

She drags her nose up the slope of my throat and hovers her lips over my ear. "Touching what's mine."

My breath comes out ragged, and I bite into my cheek—anything to stop myself from pulling Isolde behind the hedges. She presses kisses behind my ear, then my nape, leaving a blazing trail in her wake.

At the balcony, Kressa's gaze slides to me. Goosebumps wind down my spine, and as Isolde's hand weaves into my hair, Kressa doesn't look away.

She lifts a brow, as if to say, *Your words are powerful.*

"I heard Caelus is holding a dinner this weekend," I say.

Isolde pauses, lifting her mouth from my neck. Kressa disappears into the castle, and whatever tether she had on me snaps.

"He is," Isolde says against my skin. "There's also a ball coming up, before the final trial of The Gales, that he's already preparing for."

"What's so important about it?"

She presses a final kiss to the top of my spine. "Apparently, there's been an advancement in the war, large enough for Caelus to wish to announce it at the ball."

My attention piques. "What is it?"

She leans against the back of the bench and shrugs. "I have no idea. He doesn't tell me anything. If anyone were to know, I would think it'd be you."

My palms sweat. I could send a letter into the water like I've done countless of times over the years. But without a single response to show for it, I shouldn't get my hopes up. Yet my thoughts turn to my mother's smiling face—her ruby eyes as vivid as the brightest coral in the sea.

I rise from the bench and wipe my hands down the front of my dress. "I'd better get going. Thea is expecting me for tea."

Isolde shifts forward. "Wait."

"Yes?"

She eyes the dark clouds rolling in over the mountains. "Caelus mentioned to one of his advisors that he's getting impatient waiting for answers about one of the competitors. I'm worried he's talking about you."

I swallow. "Impatient? It's only been a couple days."

Her hold loosens on me, one finger at a time, until her touch is gone completely. "If I had to guess, he'll wait until this ball he's planning. Before the final trial."

Stepping back, I nod. "I'll have his information by then. And once I'm freed of that duty, we'll leave."

But even as I say the words, I watch her wilt. Her shoulders curl in on themselves, and there's a lifelessness to her hair—the weight of draining her power for an entire decade and bowing to a false king.

I make a silent vow.

One day, he'll bow to us.

23

———

"Caelus ordered it custom for you. For dinner tonight," the tailor says, hanging a garment bag in front of the full-length mirror.

"Are you sure? He didn't discuss it with me."

She slides a small envelope out of her pocket. "Are you Briar Rielle?"

No. "Yes."

I've gone the last decade using my real first name, but not my last. Calisdana belongs only to the royal family of the Sea. And although no one recognizes me, that last name would make me a target.

She holds out the envelope. "There's no mistake."

I accept it and run my fingers over the sharp corners, pressing them into the pads of my fingers. The tailor unzips the bag, revealing a gown so dark blue, it's nearly black. A layer of lace floats down from the waist, adorned with thousands of tiny diamonds.

The night sky.

She pulls it from the garment bag, and my chest tightens. The neckline plunges to the sternum, and a thin band of fabric precariously holds the two halves together. This isn't the dress of a courtesan, but a seductress.

Thea hides a grimace and runs the sheer fabric between her fingers. "You did a remarkable job. Didn't she, Briar?"

I swallow. "It's beautiful."

The tailor beams. "Let's try it on, shall we? I'll check for final adjustments."

Sliding out of my tunic and leggings, Thea helps me into the dress. Thin straps rest on my shoulders, and loose diamonds cascade down my arm. I pull the bodice farther over my breasts, but it's been carefully constructed to cover as little as possible.

Thea clasps a hook at the small of my back and meets my gaze in the mirror. She worries her bottom lip and steps away as the tailor bustles around the hem.

A slit runs up the side, exposing my leg to the hip. Sunlight dances through the fabric, outlining my entire body.

It's not that I hate it. In fact, it's something I'd wear in Delterran. I've never shied away from revealing clothing, but when it's my choice to wear it. Caelus, however, has a prerogative.

He wants me to be an object—to be stared at. To ease the minds and loosen the lips of anyone I speak to.

The tailor stands and smiles, but her gaze won't meet mine as she packs up her wares.

"Enjoy the dinner," she says, walking to the door.

"Thank you."

The smile on her face disappears as the door swings shut. Turning my attention to the mirror, I run my palm over the thin, diamond encrusted fabric and gauge the value of the dress.

Chills race down my spine, and I slide my hand over the generous slit, too high to conceal a dagger. Sighing, I flip over the envelope and slide my finger under the seal.

Briar,

I trust you'll enjoy the dress for this evening. Get me the information, but be careful. She could be dangerous.

I crumple the paper into my fist and toss it in the fireplace. Flames devour the note and turn it to ash, but it fails to erase one word from my mind—dangerous. Despite it all, he's right. I know nothing about Kressa or what else she could be hiding.

The servant's door creaks. I freeze, and a hand slips through the narrow crack, easing it open.

Kressa.

My ribs tighten. She ducks through the doorway and straightens, tucking her dress shirt into the waistband of her slacks. Our gazes meet, and it's as if a chasm opens in the room, swallowing me whole.

"What are you doing here?" I bite.

She doesn't answer. I step away from the mirror and snatch my dagger, closing the distance between us.

I ready my blade. "How did you find my room?"

She raises her hands, and Thea disappears into the bathroom, clutching at her robe and muttering something about lack of respect.

Kressa's lips tilt into a smirk, and she shrugs. "I followed you one evening. Just in case."

"Just in case, what, exactly?"

Her gaze dips to the dress, and her pupils spread wide. "In case we needed to talk, like right now." She presses the servant's door shut. "Dinner begins in an hour and we haven't spoken since sunrise before the trial. I haven't even seen you since you were with Isolde in the garden, and the next trial is tomorrow."

"Right." I set my dagger on the side table, well within reach.

"She told me that the night before the final trial Caelus is holding a ball and has announcements regarding the war."

Kressa curses under her breath.

"And she believes I have until then to tell Caelus why you joined the competition."

She nods. "Anything else?"

I shake my head.

"Are you sure?" She takes a step closer. "It seemed like a lengthy conversation."

I lift a brow. "Are you jealous?"

A scoff. "Not in the slightest, but it sure seemed like she was."

Ignoring the way my pulse speeds, I backtrack a step away from her. "There's nothing to be jealous of."

"My thoughts exactly." She steps closer again, her breath warm on my neck as she whispers, "Let the queen know she has nothing to worry about."

"Already have."

She leans back, a smirk playing on her face as she lifts her hand to my shoulder, where a strap has fallen. "May I?"

I nod, and she slides a finger under the strap, knuckles tracing my upper arm as she pulls it to the shallow curve in my shoulder. I hold my breath as her hand retreats, nails dragging lightly over my skin.

"Thank you," I breathe, my words thicker than honey.

She lets out a small laugh that hangs in the space between us. "I never thought I'd hear those words from you."

"Don't get used to it."

"To what, love? Hearing you thank me, or watching your mouth form words?"

I flick my gaze to hers, and she tilts her head, the corner of her mouth quirking up. A dare.

Blinking, I clear my throat. She's a distraction, that's all. "Tonight it should be easy enough to slip out of the ball without being seen. And if guards notice our departure, they'll think we're two lovers sneaking off."

She hums, low and deep, vibrating through my entire body. "Indeed." Her gaze dips to my leg. "Nowhere to hide your dagger tonight, I see."

"Or jewels." I bite down on my lip. "I won't be hiding much of anything in this dress."

A muscle feathers in her jaw. "No, I suppose not."

Her fingers find the pendant hanging around my neck, and she adjusts it so the clasp rests behind my hair, her fingers a whisper against my nape. "If you're worried about going to dinner without your dagger, I could carry it for you, even if the only person you ever wield it against is me."

I shake my head. "No one touches my dagger."

"Interesting." She drops her hand from the chain. "You let Harriet borrow it, and I haven't seen you talk to her once. In fact, I've never seen the two of you in the same room."

My pulse thrashes in my ears, the roaring fire suddenly stifling. I inhale through my nose. If she knew about my secret identity, she'd not only question why I wanted to enter in the first place, but blackmail me with that rather than my thievery. Twice as deadly.

I square my shoulders. "My relationships with others are none of your business."

She smiles, all sharp edges. "Well, it appears we both have our secrets. Don't we, Briar?"

Caelus's note haunts me. *She could be dangerous.* "It seems we do."

Her fingers toy with the diamonds hanging from my shoulders. "Would it be inappropriate to say I don't want anyone else seeing you while looking like this?"

My heart climbs into my throat, and I swallow it down. "Entirely."

"Then I won't." She pulls open the servant's door and steps out. Over her shoulder, she says, "I'll see you in an hour."

24

Shades of blue flood the ballroom—cobalt and indigo, some so pale they rival the shell of a robin's egg. At first glance, it could be mistaken Delterran, if it weren't for the billowing cloud nestled into the ceiling.

Lightning dances in time with the music, illuminating the room enough to discern shadowy figures, but not enough to expose where their hands roam. A servant brushes past us with a bottle of wine, headed to a crowded table surrounded by low settees.

"It's going to be one of those nights," Thea whispers, eyeing the figures intertwined at the outskirts of the room.

The music crescendos, and lightning strobes through the room. It reflects off the diamonds coating my body and scatters rainbows onto the marble floor. Dinner finished not long ago, and within minutes, the guests gathered here, ready to celebrate the upcoming second trial.

A tingle creeps up my spine and ripples down the base of my neck, pulling my attention to the opposite side of the room.

Kressa.

Her gaze is locked on me, lips slightly parted.

My pulse kicks up, pounding like the footsteps on the dance floor. Her eyes sweep down my body, and my skin shivers as if it were her fingertips grazing my skin. A burning warmth spreads across my chest, and a tight knot unravels, urging me toward her.

Thea rests her hand on my shoulder. "Are you okay?"

I nod and pull my attention from Kressa. "Do you remember what you have to do?"

"Talk to nobles and mention seeing Harriet in the room." She pinches her lips. "You don't think Caelus will notice her missing?"

Rain pours from the cloud overhead and disappears before drenching guests, as if there's an invisible umbrella stretched over the crowd.

I shake my head. "There are too many people here for him to single out Harriet. But if he does ask around, people will assume she was here based on what you said."

A noblewoman comes up to Thea's side and extends a glass of wine. She accepts it, her lips tilting into a suggestive smile as she gives me a nod. "I'm nearby if you need me."

I swallow, my stomach hollowing as she's pulled away. It never gets easier watching her walk off with someone who isn't Celia, but it's the one thing I cannot interfere with, no matter how hard I try. I can't force her to love someone she doesn't remember.

The rain from the cloud ceases, and lightning crests as another song begins. Nobles smile across tables, tapping their glasses together, and my nostrils flare.

Men could die in tomorrow's trial, and these people are celebrating.

A breeze drifts across my shoulders and spider crawls down the front of my dress. A hand snakes around my waist. "I've been waiting all evening for you."

I clench my jaw. The absence of my blade is like missing a

limb. I've never wielded it at Caelus, but knowing I *could* wraps me in comfort. Without it, I'm bare. Vulnerable.

Admiring the room, I slide out of his grip. "You've outdone yourself tonight."

At Isolde's expense, no doubt—considering she was too tired to attend this portion of the evening. Or she's off, busy strengthening her army.

He scans my body, gaze slithering over my hips and my breasts. "Indeed, I have."

I suppress a shudder and square my shoulders, refusing to make a smaller version of myself.

"Come," he says, grabbing my hand and leading me to a settee.

I sink into the cushioned velvet as a servant emerges from a doorway, bottle of wine in hand. She pauses before us and drops into a low curtsy, her grey uniform snagging on the raw edges of the table. Eyes downcast, she sets the bottle on the table and mumbles, "Your Highness."

Caelus reaches for the bottle, and I watch the servant retreat to the kitchen doorway. She pauses and, as if she expected my attention, glances over her shoulder.

"Don't drink it," she mouths.

I blink and furrow my brows as Caelus pours a glass. I rise from the seat. "I'll be right back, I have to—"

He wraps a hand around my waist and yanks me to his lap, hands brazenly roaming my body. "You don't go anywhere without my permission."

I lean away from his touch and distract myself with the couples twirling on the dance floor. At least Isolde isn't here to witness the way I'm being used.

"Wine?" Caelus asks, handing me a glass.

I accept it and bring it to my mouth, but I don't let a drop pass my lips. Caelus swallows a mouthful, his chest shifting behind my back.

Leaning forward, he sets his glass on the table and rests a hand on my bare thigh. "What do you think of the dress?"

I turn my face away from him. "It's beautiful."

He toys with one of the small diamonds dangling from my shoulder, each touch chipping away at my patience. "I could have a hundred of these made for you, if you'd like. With the taxes we're collecting."

My brows furrow. "Taxes? On what?"

"The competition bets, of course."

A sour taste fills my mouth. My vision tunnels on the gauzy lace floating over my body and the diamonds that are nothing more than a token of bloodshed—this dress a symbol of death.

It belongs on the seafloor.

"It's not right to bet on their lives."

Caelus goes rigid.

His hands pause their aimless roaming. "Look at them." He tilts his chin at the crowd, the participants sticking out like stones in a bed of sapphires. "Their lives mean nothing. If my power is at Terra's mercy, I'll exploit the competition however I see fit. With any luck, this will be the final one I have to agree to. After that, my power will be limitless."

Lighting strikes in a flurry overhead, and I wring my hands in my lap. "Have you discovered how to do that yet?" I don't dare leak judgment into my words, even though every inch of my being revolts.

Not only is it against our entire nature, but it would make him invincible. Without having to siphon weakening power, Caelus could create an entire immortal army.

We wouldn't stand a chance.

He shakes his head. "Not yet. But I found an ancient text buried deep within the library. It's in another language, so I'm working through translating them. It seems to be some sort of elemental sorcery from the Fire Court."

I lower my voice. Even my mother doesn't speak of that time

—when the court established by Serinos ruled. The first court. "Before it disappeared?"

He gives me a slight nod and lifts his glass, washing his words down with a sip of wine. If this book predates the courts' existence, it's a miracle it exists at all.

"But I have no interest in bowing to either God," Caelus says. "If I escape the bonds of Terra's rule, I'll bow to no one."

At those words, his hands sneak under the slit in my dress and trace jagged lines on the soft flesh of my inner thigh. When my power returns, I'm going to smile as I break those fingers off one by one.

But for now, I'm desperate. Desperate for something that will get his power-hungry mind off my body.

"Do you really think Kressa is dangerous?"

He hums into the crook of my neck, and the hand gliding over my leg folds into a fist. "Since The Gales began, reports of missing people have spiked all over Sarenia. Most notably, young women who have no family in the area."

Phantom fingers close around my throat, and a weight drops onto my chest. "You think she's involved in the disappearances?"

"She's quite the accomplished bounty hunter, perfectly capable of making sure people aren't found. But beyond that, I think she may be a spy from the Earth Court."

My skin goes cold. Earth Court. "What makes you think that?"

"There's no record of a Kressa Beaumont in any court. If she's lying about her name, what else could she be lying about?"

My stomach churns. Briar Rielle doesn't exist either.

"If you can confirm she's a spy," he continues, "or involved with these missing women, I can have her arrested."

My gaze floats around the room. Other than this evening, I

haven't seen her since after the first trial. Nearly an entire week of movement I haven't kept tabs on.

A shiver climbs up the back of my neck. Kressa rises from her seat and heads our way, her gaze pinned on me. Unlike when I saw her in my room, the top buttons of her shirt are undone, sleeves pushed to her elbows. And, despite the warning in my head to stay away, my heart tugs in her direction.

Something forgotten—deep in my chest—flickers.

Caelus's hand twists into my hair, and he yanks my face to his.

I struggle against his grip. "You're hurt—"

He smashes his lips against mine. His tongue plunges between my pressed lips, and my entire body stiffens. I push against his chest, lean my head back, anything to break this unwelcome kiss. He only tugs me closer.

Ringing fills my ears, and my heart thrashes against my ribs. My hand finds the spot at my thigh where my dagger usually rests, but there's no hilt. No security.

He pulls away with a satisfied grin. I fight the urge to wipe my forearm across my mouth and erase his touch. But it's there. A brand on my lips.

"Kressa," Caelus drawls. "What can I help you with?"

A muscle tics in her jaw, and her gaze slides to me, eyes softening for a heartbeat before returning to Caelus. "Briar promised me a dance."

Caelus slides his hand from my knee to the curve of my hip, palming the skin. "I'll allow it."

I grit my teeth and rise from his lap, my feet unsteady beneath me. Kressa braces me with a firm hand at my elbow, and I stop myself from leaning into it.

Caelus leans over the table and refills his glass. "She's quite a sight, isn't she?"

Kressa's eyes linger on me. "Beautiful."

My breath catches in my throat, and she cups my hand in hers.

"But what I admire more than that"—she brings the back of my hand to her lips—"is her bravery."

Lightning flashes, blinding against the walls. Kressa wraps her arm around my waist and leads me to the dance floor. "Are you okay?"

Her voice soothes the edges of my nerves, but my resolve crumbles. The dress constricts over my skin until I can't breathe, and I shake my head. "No."

Kressa brushes a hand down my hair and lets it settle on the small of my back. A low tune plays, and she takes my hand, leading me into the steps. We revolve around the floor in silence, nothing but the music lulling me out of reality.

Kressa dips her head. "If he touches you like that again, I'll kill him."

My jaw sets into granite. "No."

"No?"

A noblewoman bumps into me, and her sleeve slips off her shoulder, wine sloshing over the rim of her glass. Her lips tip into a sorry smile.

I don't return it.

Has she bet on me? Did she cheer when the kraken pulled me into the lake?

She rakes her gaze over my dress, the plunging neckline.

"I could dance with you next, if you'd like a better look," I coo.

She grimaces, and as she turns, I slip the diamond bracelet from her wrist.

I press myself against Kressa and rest my hand on her waist, bracelet pinned between my thumb and palm. I slide it down her body, over her hip, and dip my hand into her pocket.

She inhales a sharp breath, fingertips digging into my waist.

A smirk creeps over my face. If they turn my body into a weapon, it'll be mine to wield.

I tilt my chin and, against the curve of her neck, whisper, "No, because he's mine to kill."

Depositing the bracelet, I slide my hand out of her pocket and trail my fingers up the front of her shirt. I toy with the buttons until I reach the top.

She swallows and folds her hand over mine. "We should go before Caelus orders you back to him."

"Why? Is he watching us?"

She sneaks a glance over my shoulder and nods.

My lip quirks. "He put me in this dress for a reason, right?"

I push Kressa back until she's flush against a marble column. Stars wink at me from the open balcony, and from the cloud overhead, thunder rumbles.

"What are you doing?" she says, heart thundering under my hand.

I snake my hand to the nape of her neck, weaving her hair between my fingers. "He wants me to seduce you for information? Fine. But don't worry. Like Isolde, he has nothing to worry about, right?"

"Right," she says through gritted teeth.

Her chest heaves against mine, hands light against the swell of my waist. Like she can't trust herself to touch me.

I float my lips over the curve of her neck. "Be a good girl and play along."

She shudders, and I press my mouth to her neck. Once. Twice. Each of my nerve endings fire in succession, and warmth pools low in my stomach.

I lift my head and lock eyes with her for a moment, or an eternity. Perhaps entire worlds are made in this short span of time. Or maybe they end.

I tighten my hold on her waist, and she wets her lips, dragging the lower one through her teeth. She doesn't inhale a single breath, hands nothing but a whisper against my skin.

I pull her mouth to mine.

The world freezes—coming to a screeching halt.

Something snaps in my chest, and churning waves break free.

My power.

I gasp and pull away, and that wonderful, delicious warmth disappears the moment my lips leave hers. As if dumped through a sieve.

She searches my face. "Did you feel that?"

"Stop talking."

I arch into her and crash our lips together. My power floods back into my body, seeping through my bones and trickling between the small, parched crevices.

A moan tumbles from my mouth, and I press myself closer, desperate for more. My power swells, singing a sweet tune I haven't heard in far too long. Her lips meld against mine, soft and assessing.

Her arm clamps around my waist, and she tugs me flush against her. Her other hand tilts my head back, deepening the kiss.

A fire lights inside me.

Her tongue teases my lips in request, and I open them enough for her tongue to brush over mine. Flames spread over my body—licking, smoldering. Her hand travels lower, against the bare skin at the curve of my hip.

A throat clears, but I'm too drunk on my power—on Kressa —to care. A deep rumble comes from her, and her grip on me tightens, her kisses frantic. Like she'd rather drown in me than ever break away.

"Briar," that voice says. Harsher this time.

A hand touches my shoulder, and I jerk back. My power silences and retreats from my veins as if it was never there.

"Thea?"

She points out the balcony, where far beyond Sarenia, the sea rages. Whitecaps crash against ships, waves cresting over the levees.

Aftershocks of my power.

Kressa grabs my elbow. Her face is stone, every hint of desire gone. "Congratulations. Your king didn't even see your stunt."

Caelus's drink tilts at a precarious angle between his fingers, and his head rests on the arm of the settee, his eyes shut.

Is that all this was to Kressa? A stunt?

My gaze trails back to her, and a thousand questions hang off the tip of my tongue. Ones I can't ask until I have her alone.

"We're going to the dungeons. Now," she says, guiding me toward the open doorway.

I brush my fingertips over my lips. The absence of my power is like a lost lover—a hand extending to me, just out of reach.

It's tethered deep down. Caged. But there.

I sneak a glance at Kressa.

She awoke it.

25

The open hallway greets us, and Kressa pulls me to a stop.

"What is it?" I ask, glancing to the ballroom. Our exit went unnoticed, and no guards wait at the opening ready to interrogate us.

"Wait here."

Turning on her heel, she disappears into the coat closet. She emerges with a cloak draped over her arm and circles to my back, wrapping it around me.

I furrow my brows and shrug it off. "This isn't mine."

"It's yours if I say it is." Her lips tease the arch of my ear as the pad of her thumb brushes my collarbones.

My power roils against its cage, begging to be released from the chains anchoring it down. I suck in a breath, but the air in the room is suddenly too thin.

She comes around to my front and threads the button through its hole. "This dress draws too much attention. It's distracting."

"Distracting?" I take in the dim, empty hallway. "To who?"

She looks over the top of my head and straightens the hood. "Me."

I inhale a sharp breath. A shadow crosses her face, and her eyes sharpen to unreadable points. A tune floats from the ballroom, and she drops her arms to her sides.

My entire being begs for our lips to meet again, to release the fleeting, blissful thrill of my power. To discover exactly why she rouses it.

I wet my lips, and she watches, her mouth parting slightly. My skin buzzes with an insatiable need, and I risk a step closer, toeing a very dangerous line.

She clears her throat and retreats a step. "We have somewhere to be."

I lower my gaze and pull the edges of my cloak over my dress, as if it could stop my heart from hammering against my ribs. "Right. We need to find Elias."

She nods, her lips pressed into a thin line. I straighten and lead her through the arched hallway, clearing my thoughts with each footfall. Whether she stirs my power or not, I can't get distracted.

Like me, she could be a spy, and I can't forget that she's hunting me for reasons I have yet to discover.

She's as much my enemy as Caelus.

We pass through the unused hall with the grand piano, and she trails a finger over the top, disturbing the thick layer of dust. "Did you ever attend any of the balls here before the Sky Court invaded?"

I don't slow. "Only one."

My first and last. When finery draped these walls in shades of gold and honey. The night I killed Prince Barren.

When I lost my power.

The hallway curves to a part of the castle only frequented by guards and the prisoners they escort to the dungeon. We pause at the end, and I press a finger to my mouth. I lean around the corner, where a pair of heavily armed guards flank a set of doors.

Righting myself, I whisper, "We won't be able to get past the guards."

Sconces cast firelight over her face. "Give it a minute."

"We don't have a minute."

But as the words leave my mouth, a thud comes from around the corner. I glance to Kressa, and she smirks. "The sleeping tonic is tasteless in water, too."

"That servant is working with you?"

She nods and steps around the corner. I follow, where the guards sit slumped against the wall, their chests rising and falling with slow, even breaths.

I toe the one closest to me. "If you planned to knock them out, why do you need me?"

She sinks to her knees in front of the other guard. "Perhaps I simply enjoy your company."

I cross my arms and glare at her.

She pulls a set of keys from the guard's belt and twirls them around her finger. Looking up at me from under her lashes, her lips tilt into a smug grin. "Fine. I need you—one—because the sight of Isolde's hands on you in the garden has haunted me all week."

"Don't speak of her," I snap.

A smirk. "Wouldn't dare."

I swallow. "And two?"

She flips through the keys and pulls out a skeleton one, bent and knotted like a crooked finger. Rising, she fits it into the lock and slides the bolt. The door pops open with a click.

"And two, if we get caught, you'll take the fall for it. I'll tell the guards the king's favorite courtesan wanted to borrow some chains to try out something more...adventurous in the bedroom."

I grind my teeth. "They wouldn't believe you."

Stagnant air rushes out of the dungeon. "Oh, love, they saw you pin me up against the wall."

"I was pretending."

"Then it was quite a convincing performance."

A blush crawls up my neck, and before she has a chance to notice, I shoulder past her into the maw of the dungeon.

My feet meet slick, black stones, and a chill sweeps over my skin. Damp, cloying air seeps into my lungs and somewhere nearby, water drips onto the floor.

Kressa pulls the door shut, blotting out any light from the hallway. Dim, flickering lanterns reflect off silver chains hanging from the walls.

She threads her arm through the scant gap between my cloak and lower back. "Stay close."

A shiver runs the length of my spine, and my body aches to lean into her, to test if her skin has the same effect as her lips. But I jerk away. "Don't touch me."

Her hand falls. In the shadows, a mouse skitters across the floor.

"Do you know where you're going?" she whispers.

"Yes."

"How?"

Searching for my crew. "Caelus gave me a tour when I was first hired."

"And he showed you the dungeon?"

I shrug. "I asked to see it."

And after I saw the harrowing conditions he keeps his prisoners in, I never wanted to return.

We come upon a spiral staircase, and I go first, trailing my fingers along the rail as I descend. I don't need to look to know Kressa's hand remains out, ready to catch me if I fall.

At the base of the stairs, we step into a narrow, windowless dungeon lined on either side with barred metal doors. Whispers float out from deep within the shadowed cells, chains rattling.

My skin crawls, like it did during my first visit. Prisoners spend every hour behind bars, without a single window or sliver of natural sunlight to warm their faces.

Some of these people may have forgotten what the outside world looks like.

An arm shoots between the bars and a brittle, twisted hand wraps around the collar of my cloak. It yanks me to the cell and presses my face against metal. I grapple for the button at my neck, but it's pulled too taut against my skin, constricting my airway.

"What's this?" A tendril of hot breath brushes against my cheek. "A pretty little plaything?"

The man's rough, corrugated voice sends a wave of nausea over me. I jerk myself away, but the hand holds tight. I press my eyes shut and try to inch my arm up, but it's wedged between my body and the cell.

The hand disappears. I stumble back, pressing a hand to my throat as I inhale mouthfuls of stale air.

"Don't you dare touch her."

Kressa's hand wraps around the prisoner's collar, pulling him flush against the bars. Wide, brown eyes blink, and a thick layer of stubble brackets the curl of his lip.

His hands speak of someone much older than he appears to be, yet I've never witnessed the torture that takes place here. I only hear the screams while I lie in bed, unable to sleep.

"Who are you?" the prisoner snarls at Kressa. "Her keeper?"

I swallow and loosen the cloak, my skin raw from where the fabric dragged against me.

Kressa tightens her grip. "Apologize to her."

The prisoner smiles, his teeth rotten. "No."

I come to Kressa's side and wrap my palm around her upper arm. "We don't have time for this. Let's go."

As if she doesn't hear me, she slips a switchblade from her pocket and flicks it out, holding it to the man's throat. "Don't make me tell you again. Apologize."

Her words come out as a threat, a command. A tone only someone comfortable with doling out orders could use.

The prisoner swallows, his throat trembling against the sharp blade. "I'm sorry."

Kressa turns her eyes to me, dark and unreadable. "Do you forgive him?"

Her jaw ticks, teeth gritted together with barely controlled restraint. I blink. She'd end this man if I so much as gave the word.

The prisoner shudders a breath.

I nod. "I forgive him."

Kressa drops the man and folds her blade, stashing it in her pocket. The prisoner rubs at his throat and retreats back to the shadows.

I take a step toward his cell. "Wait."

Kressa stiffens and slides a hand around the front of my waist, putting herself between me and the prisoner. I thread my fingers through hers and give a reassuring nod. "It's okay."

She lowers her hand, but I don't miss the way she slides her blade back out.

I turn to the prisoner, half cast in a shadow. "We're looking for a man."

Chains and shuffling feet echo through the hallway. Other prisoners press their faces against their cell bars. They range in age, yet all as unkept and mistreated as the man before me.

"You'll need to be a little more specific," he says.

I tilt my chin toward Kressa.

She pockets her blade, but her hands remain clenched at

her side. "He has blonde hair, dark brown eyes, and was captured when the Sky Court invaded Sarenia."

The prisoner leans his arms against the bars and shakes his head. "Sorry, don't think I've seen him. I've been here less than a year."

I swallow. Only a few months, and he already looks like this.

The prisoner glances at the other cells. "Anyone else?"

They shake their heads, but in the last cell, shrouded in shadows, a gravelly voice speaks up. "I may have seen him."

Kressa bolts down the hallway, and I follow at her heels. The lanterns' glow doesn't reach this far down the corridor, and my eyes struggle against the low light.

She wraps her hands around the bars and leans forward. "When?"

"They arrested me the same day, if I'm remembering right. When they brought me to this cell, I passed by a man being led out by a host of guards. There was a rhodium helmet over his head, masking the majority of his face. But I'll never forget those knowing brown eyes."

My stomach loops into a knot. A rhodium helmet? I've seen shackles and chains constructed of the metal, used to extinguish the power of the wearer. But a *helmet*?

"Elias is a mind reader?" I breathe.

Her silence is answer enough.

I stumble back a step, feet sliding over the slick stone. Mind readers are an unnatural anomaly. Their power isn't bestowed by Terra or Serinos—isn't gifted from a noble family. No, they're born with the ability and killed as soon as their power manifests.

He's not some harmless prisoner. No. This man is a weapon.

"Do you know where they took him?" Kressa asks.

The prisoner taps a finger on the metal bar. "No, sorry. But once he left, he never came back."

Kressa bows her head against the cell and pulls the keyring from her pocket. She slides a key into the lock.

I lunge forward and grip her hand. "What are you doing?"

"Freeing them."

"But they're prisoners. Criminals."

She nods to the cell. "This man stole food to feed his malnourished granddaughter. Another down there was arrested for sleeping behind a house, near a chimney, to stay warm during the winter. I saw their intake files, Briar. None of them have done anything to be behind bars, not even the man who put his hands on you." She blows out a long breath. "Imagine. A lifetime in this place for a petty crime."

I pause and drop my hand from hers. The bolt slides, and the door sways open with a squeal, like it hasn't been opened since the prisoner was locked in. An elderly man stumbles out.

He wraps his hands around Kressa's. "Thank you."

"You have nothing to thank me for."

I wait at the base of the stairs as Kressa unlocks the rest of the cells. The prisoners step into the corridor, each with a sore on their ankle where chains held them in place.

They gather in a small circle, and Kressa whispers to one of them, her voice too low to overhear. The man nods, eyes set with determination. He turns to the next man and passes on whatever was said.

Kressa turns to me. "We can go now. They know the safest way out of the castle, and with the ball going on, they shouldn't run into any trouble."

We step to the side as the group passes in a single line, a dozen pairs of brown eyes staring at me.

"They're all from the Earth Court," I breathe.

The freed prisoners climb the stairs, their knees wobbly and feet unsteady from the days, months, years spent in a small cell.

Kressa motions for me to follow her up. "They are. And like

so many others of the Earth Court, they've been wrongly accused and imprisoned of crimes. These ones are lucky though. They haven't been executed."

We emerge into the hallway, empty save for the guards slumped against the wall. The prisoners have already vanished, gone without a trace. Kressa locks the door and returns the key ring to the guard's belt.

"That was very kind of you," I say. "To free them."

She swallows and lowers her gaze. "Elias would've wanted me to do it."

Something slimy twists in my gut. If she expects me to help her find him, I need the truth of who he is. "Kressa—"

Footsteps sound from around the corner, and she clamps her hand over my mouth. Shadows dance on the hall, growing in size.

My eyes shoot wide, my heart a hammer in my chest.

Kressa lowers her hand from my mouth and drags me down the hallway. A curtained alcove comes into view, and she throws me behind it. My back presses against a cold wall, and Kressa settles herself over me, her arms caging me in.

Her lips brush my ear. "Don't make a sound."

The footsteps grow closer, drowned out only by the blood pounding in my head. My hands naturally fall to Kressa's sides and, as if they've traced this path a thousand times, my fingers drift up her waist.

Our gazes lock.

"Briar," she breathes.

Her hand weaves through my cloak and settles on my lower back. Warmth pools in my stomach, and my power swells in its cage, begging for release. Her grip tightens around my waist, her thumb rubbing slow, soothing circles over my spine.

An oily sensation flips through my stomach. I promised Isolde that Kressa meant nothing to me, yet here I am, shoved into an alcove with her while our hands roam each other's bodies. But I can't seem to pull away.

Footsteps pound closer, and a pair of shadows pass in front of the curtain, heading in the opposite direction of the dungeon doors.

I drop my palms from her sides and shove her away. "My room. Now."

26

I slip into my room and lunge to my bed, yanking out the dagger I keep stashed beneath the mattress. Kressa follows through the doorway, and as she presses the door shut, I slam her against it. I angle my arm across her chest, dagger poised at her throat.

"Who are you?"

She swallows, and a chuckle rumbles from her throat. "You know, we could have a normal conversation for once."

"But I don't trust you."

"And I don't trust you."

I press the blade higher, just below the white scar spanning her jawline. "Caelus said you're from the Earth Court. Is that true?"

"And you're from the Sea Court."

I falter.

"I thought so." She smirks, as if completely at ease with my weapon to her skin. "What're you doing so far from home?"

I even my breaths. It isn't possible for her to know who I am. If she did, she'd have me bound in chains, crossing my name off her list.

"Is Briar Rielle even your real name?" She lets out a low hum. "It really rolls off the tongue nicely, doesn't it? Perhaps a little too nice?"

I tighten my grip on the dagger. "I'm the one asking questions."

"And an hour ago, you were telling me to be a *good girl*. Does that ring a bell?"

"It was a lapse in judgement."

Her mouth tilts into a knowing smile. "I'm sure it was."

My mind swarms with a labyrinth of questions about the kiss and why it woke my power, but I shove them aside. Unless Kressa can somehow release me from the curse, that information isn't useful.

"Elias has power," I say, not so much a question as a statement. An accusation.

"A lot of it."

"I'm risking my life to help you find your lover, and you didn't have the decency to mention he's a mind reader?"

My voice comes out unsteady, and my knuckles blanch against the hilt.

"Would it be so upsetting to you, Briar,"—she leans into my blade—"if I did have a lover?"

My nostrils flare, and I lower my voice to a growl. "I pity anyone who willingly frequents your presence."

She scoffs and leans her head back against the door. Firelight dances in her eyes, catching on the golden flecks. "I believe Elias would say the same, considering he's my brother."

The blade falters. "Brother?"

"Yes."

I weld my lips together. Then, quietly, as if the flames would betray us, say, "How is he—a mind reader—still alive?"

She sighs, and the amusement fades from her eyes. "Lower the blade and I'll answer your questions."

I raise a brow. "Truthfully?"

"Not that you'd know otherwise, but yes."

I search her eyes and dig for any hint of deceit, but find none. Slowly lowering my blade, I step away and point my dagger at the armchair. "Sit. I'll be right back. If you get up, or try to leave this room, I'll kill you."

She rubs at her throat. "Where are you going?"

"To get out of this fucking dress."

She turns her back to me and strides to the chair without so much as keeping an eye on the dagger. So confident I wouldn't bury it in her back.

Fool.

I hang the stolen cloak and stalk to the dressing room, barely shutting the door before I rip off the dress and toss it to the floor in a heap. It'll be nothing but rags in a few moments anyway. I cross to the armoire and rip open a drawer, pulling out leggings and a long sleeve tunic.

My pirate clothes peek out from the back—a bleak reminder that I discovered nothing about tomorrow's trial. Perhaps I'll find an excuse to talk to Caelus in the morning. I pull on my clothes and sling the dress over my arm on the way out.

Kressa says nothing as I settle on the floor in front of the fireplace and gather the dress onto my lap. I angle my dagger in my hand and slide the blade beneath a diamond, cutting it free from the gauzy fabric. Placing it on the floor, I move to the next.

"What are you doing?"

I add another gem to the pile. "I'm sure you're aware people are betting on the competition?"

"I am."

"Caelus is taxing the bets and used that money to get this dress made. The sheer number of diamonds on this dress—I can't imagine how much it cost." I rip another diamond free. "It's one thing to bet on us, but I refuse to benefit from the innocent deaths."

A pause. "Us?"

My hand falters, disturbing the pile of diamonds. Flames lick at my back, scorching straight into my bones. I mask my racing heart with a shrug. "I meant you and Harriet." I brush my hand along the floor, gathering the scattered diamonds. "Anyway, you promised to answer my questions."

She lowers herself to the ground and pulls the switchblade from her pocket.

I flinch back. "What are you doing?"

Her ankle brushes mine as she gathers the train of the dress into her lap. "You'll be here all night if you do this alone."

My lips part. I watch her slip the short knife beneath the threads and pull a diamond free. She leans over the dress, fingers skimming my leg as she sets it onto the pile.

"These diamonds were funded with my life on the line," she says. "And Harriet's. She spared me in the first trial, so it's the least I can do. But what's in it for you? She was a pirate who was hunting people from the Earth Court. Why are you helping her in the competition?"

I grimace. That's why Harriet was on her list. And if Kressa thinks I let Harriet borrow my dagger, she likely assumes I shared the information about the kraken prior to the trials, too. I blow out a long breath and look at her from under my lashes. "A truth for a truth?"

She leans over me again and adds to the pile. Pausing, her face inches from mine, she nods. "By all means."

A knot in my chest loosens—one that has been comfortably tight for years. My eyes slide to the dressing room, where the pirate clothes lie wrinkled and shoved in a drawer. Chewing on the inside of my cheek, I turn over the truth and spin it into something that isn't quite a lie.

"If she wins," I whisper, rubbing the lace between my fingers, "she promised to give me a ship to captain. So I can go far, far away from here. So I can be free."

She keeps her head down, working along the dress. "Ah, right. Sea Court." Her hands pause. "Have you even captained a ship before?"

I'm toeing a dangerously thin line. If she is a spy, how much of this will be relayed to whoever is ruling the Earth Court now? I worry my lip. To lie would be a betrayal to my past, so I settle on the truth. "Yes, before I became a courtesan."

"What happened to your ship?"

I suck in a deep breath. "It was stolen."

"By who—"

"It's your turn now."

She leans over, and a chuckle teases the air against my face as she sets down another diamond. "Ask away."

My power lurches toward her, but I avert my gaze and swallow down the heat rising up my throat. "What did you feel when we kissed?"

"Other than your hands all over me?"

My lip curls, and I yank another gem free. "Yes. Other than that."

She pauses, teeth dragging over her lower lip. She twirls a diamond between her fingers and lifts a knee, resting her forearm on it. "It was like I was lit on fire from the inside."

I furrow my brows. I thought perhaps my power would surge into her, or she'd at least feel it somehow. A cresting of waves, salt air in her lungs.

"It only lasted for a second though," she continues. "Then all I felt was your tongue against mine."

A diamond slips from my fingers and bounces across the floor. She retrieves it and places it in my palm, touch sparking my skin.

She tilts her head. "Why? What did you feel when we kissed?"

I pull the final stone free and set my dagger to the side. I could tell the truth—that her kiss unraveled the tether on my power. I could reveal myself as the Princess of the Sea. Perhaps tell her I'm Harriet, and I entered the competition to break the curse.

But I can't trust her. She blames me for the war that tore her kingdom apart, rightly so. She'd arrest me immediately.

I hold her gaze and shrug. "I didn't feel much of anything."

She examines my face longer than necessary, and I swallow. *Hard.* Anything to keep from crawling into her lap and pressing my lips to hers—if only to bask in the sweet taste of my power for another moment.

Her gaze slides to the fireplace and she leans against the legs of the armchair. "I'm not like Caelus, you know. I'd never force you to do anything you didn't want to."

She sucks in a cheek and drags her attention back to me. A shadow passes over her eyes—something I can't quite discern, or a history I have no business wondering about.

"I know."

A long pause passes between us—the air taut, pressurized. What else is there to say? We know enough damning secrets about each other to earn a trip to the gallows. But if one mutters a word, we'd both go down.

I stand and tug at the hem of my tunic. Stepping to my dresser, I pull a small drawstring bag from the top drawer and scoop the diamonds in. The smallest ones are no bigger than a grain of sand, yet even those would be enough to buy someone out of the slums.

Kressa digs her hand into her pocket and pulls out the diamond bracelet, adding it to the top of the bag. I secure the drawstrings and strap my sheath around my thigh, threading the leather through the bag's cords.

"Where are you going?"

I sheathe my dagger. "Out."

Crossing the room, I grab the cloak and drape it over my

shoulders. I glance at the clock and press my lips together. Hopefully it's not too late for a visit.

"I'm coming with you."

"No." I braid my hair back and button the cloak around my neck before throwing the hood up. "If you get caught leaving the castle at night, you'll be killed."

I cross to the servant's door, my footsteps silent on the stone.

"I won't get caught. What if you run into trouble?"

"I'll take care of it. Myself."

She sidesteps in front of me.

"If you follow me," I hiss, "I'll scream until every guard comes running. I'll tell them you were trying to take me out of the castle."

She narrows her eyes. "You wouldn't."

I give her a wicked smile. "Would you like to find out? I'm a woman of my word, Kressa."

"I don't doubt it."

"Good. I trust you remember how to get back to your room?"

She gives me a curt nod.

"Splendid." I step around her and pull open the servant's door, looking over my shoulder. "Good luck at the trial tomorrow."

27

My feet pound the cobblestones, slick from the mist blowing off the ocean. A thick fog has rolled in, blotting out the glow of the lanterns lining the street and masking the brick homes with a haze. Not even the stars blink down to light the path.

I keep my steps even, dodging shallow puddles as I sneak through alleyways. It's not that late, but few people wander the streets when they're coated in fog. Even though my name has been erased from their minds, many still believe the Sea Princess lurks the shores on nights like these.

My lip quirks. It was only once. Thea wanted to see how many men I could make scream.

It was a lot.

I emerge onto the road that separates the well-built seaside homes from the slums. The hairs rise on the back of my neck and I freeze, hovering my palm over my dagger.

A foot splashes into a puddle. Then another. And another.

I scan the dense fog, but I can't see farther than a couple feet in front of me.

"Who's there?" I say, my voice firm despite my heart rattling in my chest.

Three tall, broad shadows manifest.

"What have we got here?" one says, his voice deep.

I wrap my hand around the hilt. "I don't want any trouble."

They step closer, and their outlines morph into solid figures. Three men, each donning the uniform of the Sky Court armada appear before me. Gold falcons substitute typical buttons on their white shirts.

At the collar, above the medals depicting their distinguishes and rank, their names are embroidered in light blue thread.

"Don't worry," the one closest to me says, his shirt untucked from his pants. His breath reeks of beer, and the end of his nose is a splotchy purple. "We won't hurt you. Just want to talk."

"Yeah," another cuts in. "After lugging those selkies to the castle, we could sure use some company."

I freeze, and my heart leaps into my throat. "Selkies?"

"Screamed the entire way there, even more so when we took their tails."

My blood turns to ice. They must be for the trial tomorrow, and if they're without their tails? A lump forms in my throat.

A sick grin spreads over the face of one of the men. "Nasty sea vermin."

Red clots my vision. "Shut your fucking mouth."

His back goes rigid, and his grin twists into a sneer. His blonde hair is neatly kept despite the stain running down the front of his shirt. "I like a woman who's got a bit of a mouth on her."

I slide the blade from my thigh as he stalks forward and runs a finger along my jaw. "What's a pretty little thing like you doing out here all alone?"

His tone speaks of intentions I've skinned men for. I catch the surname embroidered on his shirt. *Beswick.*

"None of your business."

His gaze dips to my chest. "You'd be a fun time, wouldn't you?"

"I hope those Sea Court vermin kill every single one of you." I spit in his face.

He flinches back and wipes a forearm over his eyes. "You bitch."

I go to flick out my dagger, but a large pair of hands appear from behind and pin my arms to my sides. I struggle against them, but they're clamped down too tight. Hot breath grates against my ear, down my neck.

The man in front of me sneers. "You were saying?" Winding a hand back, he slaps me across the face.

My head jerks to the side, cheek stinging from where his hand met skin. I pause, then turn back to him, an amused smile tugging at my lips. "Perhaps I want trouble after all."

I plant my feet against the ground and throw my head back, slamming it into the man's nose. A satisfying crack echoes through the silent street and I spin, sinking my dagger into the soft flesh beneath his ribs. A lethal blow, but slow and painful.

He falls in a heap, grasping at his side.

The third man sidesteps in front of me and swings a fist toward my jaw, but I duck and knock his feet out from under him. He clatters to the ground on his stomach, and before he can get his hands beneath him, I yank his hair and drag my blade across his throat.

Standing, I suck in a deep breath. I've missed this—the thrill of being feared. The surprise on a man's face when he realizes he's about to meet his demise at my hand.

I turn on my heel, where a hard gaze is pinned on me, hands readied into fists. The drunken haze has disappeared from his eyes. Yet his jaw trembles.

Canting my head, I give him a sinister smile. "Oh Beswick, you aren't afraid of me, are you?"

"I'm going to kill you."

I step closer, slowly. "What, you don't think I'd be a fun time anymore?" I frown. "Pity. I'm having a blast."

He snarls and throws a right hook. I dodge it, his knuckles nothing but a breeze against my skin.

I laugh. "Does Caelus truly do such a terrible job training his soldiers, or are you lot the runts?"

His teeth clench together, crimson rising up his neck. "Didn't stop me from slaughtering hundreds from the sea."

My power thrashes against its chains, begging to burst free, but it's held down tight. No matter.

He pivots and throws out a leg aimed for my middle. I leap back and slice my blade along his ankle—not enough to maim, but enough to keep him from running away. He lands on the foot and crumples, palms digging into the gravely stones.

I kick his side and he sprawls to his back—into the blood seeping from the bodies of his friends. I settle my knee on his chest and pin him to the ground. He beats against my thigh, but it doesn't register as I dip my face closer to his.

"You do know who hunts these streets when the fog rolls in, don't you?" I whisper, twisting my mouth into a grin.

His face blanches. "That's a myth. The Sea Princess is gone."

I let out a low laugh and tease the tip of my dagger down his cheek. "How could she have disappeared when you're staring at her?"

His eyes widen, and he opens his mouth—either to insult me or beg for mercy. I've heard both. I don't give his words a chance to form as I raise the dagger high over my head and plunge it into his chest. Blood gushes from the wound, retribution for every soul he's stripped from the sea.

I lean closer as the life leaves his body, and whisper, "I've come back for revenge."

When his chest no longer rises, I stand and wipe my dagger

on his shirt. I survey the other motionless bodies, their blood streaming through the divots between the cobblestones.

Footsteps sound from the alleyway behind me. My stomach hollows and I flick my hood up over my face, turning to the thick shadows. I grip my dagger so hard my knuckles burn.

Kressa emerges from the shadows and gives me a slow clap. "Impressive."

A vise wraps around my throat. "I told you not to follow me. You'll be killed if a guard catches you."

She leans against a stone wall, perfectly comfortable wandering the streets at night. I narrow my eyes. How often has she left this past week?

An amused smirk teases her lips. "I won't be caught."

I scan the street. "You didn't think to step in when they attacked me?"

"You told me you'd handle it." She shrugs. "And I knew they didn't stand a chance."

Something in my chest warms. Flickers. "Since I've proved I don't need a warden, you can go back to the castle now."

She steps closer. "I'm coming with you."

"No."

"Why not?"

"You'll slow me down."

She laughs and closes the space between us. Lifting a hand, she drags her thumb over my lower lip. Blood that is neither mine nor hers coats her finger, and she wipes it on my cloak. "But what if I told Caelus there's a woman out here impersonating the Princess of the Sea to scare men?"

My knees threaten to buckle, hand slipping on the hilt. But I search her eyes. There's not a trace of accusation, only amusement. "Your threats are beginning to bore me."

She smiles, eyes twinkling in the low light. "I'll take that as a yes."

"Fine, but do me a favor and keep your mouth shut."

I step over the soldiers and follow the curve in the road where brick houses turn into dilapidated shells. The road ends, then drops off to packed dirt. A carefully constructed tent borders the narrow pathway with its flap open, buttery light spilling out.

I hold my arm out, keeping Kressa back, and dip my head into the tent. An elderly couple sits at an overturned wooden crate, splitting a meager meal of dried meat and bread.

"Excuse me," I say. "I'm looking for a woman named Dolma."

They scan me, their gazes lingering on the thick, expensive cloak secured around my neck. I unfasten the button and sling it over my arm.

"May I come in?"

The husband glances to his wife, and she nods.

I duck under the opening and stride to the small table, holding out the cloak.

"We don't take handouts. Or bribes," the woman says, her voice fierce despite the tremor in her hands.

"Would it help if I told you I stole this from a noblewoman?"

The deep wrinkles around the woman's eyes soften. "I suppose the threaded initial would be easy enough to remove."

I nod. "It's ugly anyway."

She smiles, and the sight warms the tent more than the lantern. "Last I saw Dolma, she was huddled around a fire with a group a few rows down." She tilts her chin in the direction we were headed. "But be easy on her. She lost her husband in The Gales."

My chest swallows my heart. "I will."

I exit the tent, and cool air kisses my face. The slums are quiet without carts bumping over rough roads or soldiers barking orders.

"Where's your cloak?" Kressa says.

"What cloak?"

I stride past her, but not before I catch the quirk of her lips.

We weave through rows of tents and ramshackle buildings until we come to a fire, burning like sunshine through the fog. A group sits on driftwood logs set in a circle around the flames, warming their hands and passing around bits of food.

"Stay here," I whisper.

She nods, and I stride closer as men, women, and children watch me approach—like I'm a debt collector ready to snatch whatever they have left. Their clothes hang from their bodies, many of them barefoot.

"I'm looking for Dolma."

A woman on the far side, holding a round belly, raises her hand.

My stomach lurches at the red, swollen ring around her sandy eyes. She goes to push herself up from the log, but I hold out a hand. "Don't. I'll come to you."

I circle the group and kneel down beside her. In the distance, Kressa stands against a building, watching with a raised brow. I turn my attention to Dolma and unhook the drawstring bag from my sheath.

"I met Geoff," I say.

Her eyes widen at the name, and her chin shudders.

"He told me all about you, and how excited he was to be a father. All he wanted was for his daughter to have a better life." I press the satchel into her hand and lower my voice to a whisper. "There are enough diamonds in here to buy you anything you want. A better life. The kind of life Geoff died to get you."

Her eyes shine with tears threatening to spill over.

I swallow and close her fingers around the bag. "He was a brave man."

She stares at me, wide-eyed. "I don't"—her voice breaks—"I don't know how I could ever thank you."

"You don't need to. I only wish I could do more."

She squeezes my hand. "My daughter—we wanted to name her after the Princess of the Sea, but we can't find any reference of her name before she disappeared."

I flinch back. "What?"

"I may have married someone from the Earth Court, but I'll always be from the sea. I've never stopped honoring her." She looks out to those gathered. "None of us have."

"I'd be very careful who you share that information with," I say under my breath, glancing at the others. "It's treasonous to worship her. Punishable by death."

My voice has more venom than I intended, and she stiffens.

But the man beside Dolma smiles, his wrinkled hands wrapped around a stale piece of bread. "She'll return one day."

My mouth parts, and I swallow, studying the flames licking the metal barrel. Firelight dances over their faces, blue and brown eyes alike staring back at me. Pride swells in my chest. These people, without homes or warm clothes or steady meals are, unconditionally, the bravest people I've ever met.

I crouch and bring my mouth within an inch of Dolma's ear. "Her name is Briar. And she will return."

"Briar," she whispers.

I leave the warmth of the fire and join Kressa. She reaches a hand out, brushing her knuckles over the pendant hidden under my tunic. "Did you just give that woman those diamonds?"

"Yes."

She blinks. "You're not what I expected."

I lower my eyes at the way her words wash over me, how they fill me to the brim. Swallowing, I say, "Let's go."

We navigate through the fog, back to the city proper where chimneys puff out smoke and Sky Court families gather around plentiful dining tables. My jaw tics. They live a life of luxury with poverty in their backyards.

Most of the people in the slums aren't my own subjects, but the injustice sinks its poisonous claws into me.

The fog thickens the closer we get to the castle, cloaking the balcony in a cloud. Music floats through the night, mixed with voices of revelers soaking in the last few hours of the ball. Nobles stagger down the steps to their carriages, whispering into each other's ears.

I lead us around the side of the castle, and we slip in through the side door to a silent corridor.

"Those people in the slums worship your princess, don't they?" she says. "Sympathizers."

I note the cold tone in her voice—the same venom that coated her words in the chamber before the first trial. "What if they are?"

"I couldn't imagine celebrating someone so incredibly selfish."

My steps falter. "Selfish?"

"Yes," she says, her voice like a whip. "She could have joined our two courts together and held Caelus in place. She could have prevented all this bloodshed. But instead, she made a single selfish choice. Tens of thousands have died because of her decision."

I tug at my collar, my tunic suddenly stifling as we round a corner and climb the stairs.

"It's not like she knew that would happen," I whisper, my voice fragile. But my stomach roils. I *did* know, but I thought I'd be able to fight my way out, alongside my crew. I didn't know my mother had made a blood oath with Serinos.

I didn't expect to be cursed, learning about the war from whispers on the docks, spending my days desperately searching for my crew—the women who promised themselves to *The Twelfth Night*. Killing soldiers at night is my only contribution, but that's like bailing water from a sunken ship.

"Ignorance doesn't forgive what she did."

The knife in my chest twists, and my feet grow heavier with every step up the curved staircase. "Maybe she'll come back. Redeem herself."

"No. If she does, she'll meet the tip of my blade."

My breath catches in my throat, and we come to a stop in front of my door. I narrow my eyes. "Let me remind you, that's my princess you're talking about."

"You should be as eager to kill her as me, considering what she did to those you love."

The killing blow. I've hurt everyone I love. Everyone she loves. Her brother is in a rhodium helmet because of me. Thea can't remember anything from her past, and my crew is somewhere, scattered across the ocean. Or dead.

The space behind my eyes burns. "Perhaps you're right."

I twist the knob. If Thea is in our room, maybe I'll linger in my guilt and tell her who she is. Just to be reminded of what I've done.

"Selkies," I whisper.

"Selkies?"

I nod.

Kressa's eyes widen. "For tomorrow's trial?"

"They won't have their tails, so they'll be lethal. Good luck."

I slip into the room, but she slides a foot into the door opening before I shut it all the way.

"What you did tonight—I admire you for it."

My throat tightens. "Good night, Kressa."

28

"He's coming," Gemma says, peeking through the narrow slit in the door. She pushes Marianne back into the room and shoves an empty pail into her hands.

The healer on the low stool beside my bed stiffens.

Veronica swore her secrecy after the first trial when she stitched me up. Thea claims it was a mutual agreement, but Marianne insists it was more of a threat.

Thea leans over me and presses a hot rag to my forehead. "Are you sure this will work?"

"Yes," Veronica bites, tightening the white apron wrapped around her waist. She tucks her greying hair behind her ears. "He has no reason to think I'd lie."

I tug the sheets to my chin and cover the collar of my pirate shirt.

Thea bares her teeth. "You better make it convincing."

"Quit your bickering," I hiss.

Heavy footsteps sound from the doorway. The door swings open, and I turn my head away, closing my eyes.

"Where's Briar?" Caelus says, voice hard.

"She's ill, Your Highness," Gemma says. "We were delivering clean rags."

"And emptying the bucket," Marianne adds.

I keep my breaths even and stop my feet from squirming at the foot of the bed. I feel his glare rake over my body. Gemma and Marianne pad to the servant's door and slip out, Marianne sneaking a nod to me, as if to say, *We'll be waiting.*

"Your Highness," Thea says, removing the rag from my forehead. "I thought word was sent. Briar has been ill all morning. She's only been lucid for a few moments at a time."

"I've requested her presence at the second trial."

My skin goes cold, and his booted footsteps creep closer.

"She's unable to get out of bed," Thea says, pressing her hand to the mattress. Like she could keep him from pulling away the covers.

"Then I think it may be time to get her up."

His tall shadow looms over the bed, and I fight a tremble as his hand presses against my forehead. His fingers dip under the sheet. I clench my eyes shut and swallow a whimper as my heart thrashes in my chest.

"I wouldn't do that, Your Highness," Veronica says.

The hand disappears.

"She's extremely contagious. In fact, you shouldn't be in here until it's sterilized."

A long pause fills the room, and a bead of sweat rolls down my hairline.

Caelus's footsteps retreat to the doorway. "Thank you, Veronica. Send word when she's well."

"Will do."

The door shuts with a click, and Thea bolts from her seat, sliding the lock into place. I throw back the covers and leap from the bed, steadying my feet beneath me.

Thea shoves the boots into my hands. "Go. Don't put them on yet. You only have five minutes."

Swallowing, I nod to Veronica. "Thank you."

"Thank me when you win, girl."

I slip into the empty servant corridor. Everyone has already filtered to the streets, ready to watch the procession to the trial. I blow out a long breath and steady my pulse. On the inhale, I break into a dead sprint, my bare feet silent as the boots swing against my hip.

I count down the seconds until I'm meant to be in the east wing on the opposite side of the castle. If, for whatever reason, Gemma and Marianne didn't make it to Harriet's room, I'll be a forfeit. Instantly executed by the power Caelus used to bind us to the competition.

Three more minutes.

I skid around a corner, and my heart leaps into my throat. Ahead, a pair of servants exit a room, arms piled with linens. I slink into a shallow alcove and press myself to the wall, covering my mouth with a hand.

My pulse drums in my ears.

Two minutes.

The servants pass, and their whispers echo through the hallway.

"Another missing this morning."

My ears perk, and I hold my breath, quiet the pounding in my ears.

"Said they found a folded note in her bedroom, and—"

They disappear into the laundry room, and the swinging door cuts off their voices. I push from the wall and barrel down the corridor.

I shove a heavy oak door into the ancient east wing and sprint past unexplored hallways to the staircase at the end. My bare feet splash through stagnant water, and I slip on a worn step, the jagged edge of wood biting into my knees.

I grit my teeth and heave myself up, ignoring the searing pain shooting up my leg.

One minute.

A landing opens up and I throw myself into the musty, cobweb lined corridor. Light spills out of a doorway and my muscles ache, lungs scream, knees drip blood. I hurl myself into the room and trip over the threshold, slamming to the ground.

Gemma stretches out a hand. "Took you long enough."

I rise, the edges of my vision blurry.

"Hurry," Marianne whispers, eyeing the bedroom door.

Voices come from the hallway.

Gemma cups my face. "This fast, it's going to hurt."

Power stabs under my skin like a blade, morphing and cutting my features. My hair shortens to my shoulders and lightens to a sandy blonde. I swallow a scream as my shoulders shift and legs lengthen—muscle and bone stretching and twisting until I no longer resemble myself.

Her hands fall. "Done."

I heave in a breath, body aching from the sudden change, and slip the boots onto my feet. The voices in the hallway grow louder. I gather my hair and secure it at my nape. "Thank you."

Gemma nods. "My power is stretched thin, so the glamour might not last as long, but I'll be in the stands to reinforce it."

A knock comes from the door. Marianne wraps her hand around Gemma's wrist and drags her to the servant's entrance.

"Wait," I say. "If you hear talk about where selkie tails might be hidden, listen closely. Please."

A knock comes again. Louder this time. "Harriet? Are you in there?"

"We will," Marianne says, pulling them into the corridor.

She shuts the door, and I stride across the room, taking one last glance at myself in the mirror. Every bit of myself is undetectable, other than the pendant shoved beneath my shirt.

I turn the knob and open the door.

Kressa scans me, paying close attention to the spot beneath

my pants where the dagger rests. "Where have you been? I haven't seen you since the trial last week."

Behind her, the hallway swarms with competitors.

"I must have missed you at last night's dinner."

Her brows furrow, and she presses her tongue into her cheek. "Have you spoken to Briar? About our—"

"Alliance." I nod. "Yes, she told me."

She holds out a hand. "Well?"

I hesitate. I spent the small hours of the night staring at my ceiling after what she said. Selfish. Ignorant. Each of her words rang true. But with two trials standing between myself and victory, I could use an alliance. And when I win, I'll atone for every decision I've made.

"As long as you don't try to kill me again," I say.

"I'm a woman of my word. And, well, I owe you for not killing me when you had the chance."

"Fair enough."

I grip her hand, and the moment our skin touches, my lungs empty. The space beyond her blurs into a vast expanse of nothing. Nothing exists but Kressa and me and my power singing below my veins, tendrils slipping from its cage.

I rip my hand away, and the power blinks out like a snuffed flame.

She rubs at her palm, gaze pinned to the lines running across it. A crease forms between her brows, and her eyes meet mine.

She shakes her head and turns away.

I pull my door shut, and the air in the crowded hallway is taut, fizzling with anticipation. I furrow my brows. There should be about two dozen of us left, but I count less than twenty.

Caelus appears at the mouth of the hallway, flanked by royal guards standing at attention. He adjusts his collar and the space silences.

"Welcome to the second trial. As you've likely noticed, a handful of your peers are gone. They were caught escaping the castle last night, and were executed on sight."

Goosebumps break out over my flesh, and I sneak a glance at Kressa. Her jaw is sewn shut, hands fisted at her sides. That could have been her last night, and if she was caught, there's nothing I could have done. No begging or bribing on my part could stop Caelus from killing her.

My chained power balks at the thought of a sword through her chest. A noose around her throat.

At the front of the crowd, Simon stands with the five others who earned immunity. He crosses his arms over his chest and shoots me a smug grin. I return it with a snarl.

"Let this be a warning to all of you," Caelus continues. "You knew the rules when you entered this competition."

The guards order us in two lines for the procession, and I settle in beside Kressa.

She leans closer. "Briar told me there will be selkies."

I bite back a smile. Somewhere deep in that cold, bleak heart, Kressa genuinely wants to help Harriet. "Yes, I heard."

She glances down at my hidden dagger. "And she told me you'll give her a ship if you win. Thank you."

I blink as we start our descent down the stairs. "For what?"

She averts her eyes, focusing on the treads at her feet. "She's a good person, and she deserves freedom—to leave Sarenia behind and never look back. I wish I could give that to her, but I'm glad you can."

The air rushes out of my lungs, and I stumble, grasping the rail so I don't knock down the man in front of me. Questions swirl in my mind, but as Harriet, I can't ask any of them. So, I settle on, "You're welcome."

We exit the castle and stride down the polished stone steps where nobles gawk, their velvety blue carriages waiting on the outskirts of the courtyard. I tilt my chin high, refusing to give them the decency of an acknowledgment.

Onlookers line the cobblestone streets, pointing and whispering amongst each other. People lean out of second story windows, cheering and waving Sky Court flags. Others simply stare like we're exotic animals.

I clench my jaw and stare back. How much coin did they drop at our expense?

Sprinkled amongst the wealth are servants from the castle and people dressed in plain grey clothing, tight lipped as the procession passes. Ahead, a woman pushes herself from a wall, reaching out to one of the men—Damian. He pauses and mouths something, stepping out of line.

A blast of air throws him back.

"In line!" Caelus yells.

The woman flinches back and sinks into the shadowed alleyway, her eyes glistening.

Rays of sun beat down on us as the street ends, and we stop in a grassy field. In front of the tree line, a wooden, half-moon structure arcs around us. Hundreds of bodies cram the stands, wide eyed and eager for bloodshed.

Thea nods from the second row, and a weight lifts from my shoulders. Marianne and Gemma sit beside her, hands pressed into their laps. Power ripples over my body and my skin tightens. I tilt my chin at Gemma, thanking her.

The two lines of competitors fan out into a semicircle in front of the stands, and applause roars from the crowd.

I squint at the box seats that Caelus will soon fill, then the row behind it. My heart races, and I scan the rest of the audience, eyes darting from face to face as my mouth dries. No Isolde.

But Caelus raises a hand and the crowd silences, spectators leaning forward in their seats. "The second trial is simple. You have an hour to find your way back to this arena."

My gut roils. Back from where? I brush my fingertips over my dagger and glance to the west, where the ocean spreads into the horizon. My limbs go cold.

None of us stand a chance against a rabid selkie in the water, let alone on land.

Caelus's lips curl into a smile. "If you survive, you'll join the six others in the third and final trial." The wide set of doors behind him ease open, and his smile grows. "But for today's, we have a visitor."

A figure clad in long midnight robes emerges from the chamber, its face obscured by a hood. Long, flowing sleeves hide hands clasped at his front, and sunlight hits his body, illuminates the pallid, grey skin of the bottom half of his face.

He tracks the competitors and pauses on me. A bone chilling dread sweeps through my very core and dives into my soul. His head tilts the slightest, and his mouth twists into a smile, revealing fangs.

"A Sopor," Kressa breathes.

"What's that?" I whisper, but the Sopor snaps his fingers and the world goes black.

29

I slam onto a shore, and salty sand fills my mouth, burning my eyes. A roaring din fills the air. A crash of a wave.

The ocean.

Wiping my eyes, I force them open against the sting as a wave shoots up the beach, toward me.

I scramble onto all fours, but my hands sink into the sand and slow me down. My throat constricts, and my elbows buckle as sea foam teases the rubber sole of my boot.

Digging my hands down, I blindly throw myself forward and slam into a solid mass. It shifts, and my hands lose purchase, but my fingers loop around an opening, and I hold tight.

Whatever is beneath me steadies, and I rest my head.

The wave retreats with a promise to return. I blow out a long breath, and the heap beneath me does the same, with a steady thump against my ear. Cedar infiltrates my nose and calms my racing pulse.

My power sings, and I settle into this space.

Then it coughs.

I jolt up, and my burning eyes focus.

"Harriet?" she croaks.

I glance down at my fingers laced between the buttons of Kressa's shirt, rubbing against bare skin. Yanking them free, I throw myself off of her and rise to my feet. Sand cakes my pants, weighing them down.

"Sorry, I tripped," I stammer, holding out a hand.

I pull her up. Other competitors groan and push themselves from the sand, rubbing at their heads and shoulders. A full moon illuminates the dunes at our backs—too high to see what's on the other side.

I brush the sand from my pants. "Where are we?"

"Impossible to know." Kressa rolls her shoulders and rubs the base of her neck. "Sopors get their power from Serinos. They can contort reality and transport people. We could be on the other side of the continent, or still in the arena."

"I've never heard of them before."

"They were executed with the fall of the Fire Court, but it seems Caelus managed to get his hands on one."

Just like he got the kraken. I tilt my head to the sky and point toward the dunes. "We should go that way."

She lifts a brow. "How do you know?"

Only someone from the Earth Court wouldn't know how to navigate. "The stars."

I point to the brightest constellation in the sky, Aethra. The matching one to my compass, and one that—if I had a ship— would guide me home by the tip of her arrow. "The ocean is due west, which, if we're still on the same shoreline as Sarenia, means the arena is that way." I nod northeast toward a mountain range in the distance.

But I pause, and my confidence flounders. This is too easy. I twist, and in the opposite direction, a second mountain range. I worry my lip and study Aethra. Something is off.

"Let's not waste time then," Kressa says, taking off toward the dunes.

If I spend too long debating which direction to go, I risk the glamour wearing off. Blowing out a breath, I jog to catch up with Kressa, and we climb the dune. At the peak, we pause—a dense forest sprawling out before us.

I swallow. "Is this—"

Kressa nods. "The Elkbane Forest."

The green expanse stretches to the horizon, and the dense canopy shifts with a breeze. As vast and deadly as the deepest reaches of the sea.

Competitors crest the dunes on either side of us, eyeing the forest with equal hesitation. Throats bob on swallows, blood draining from their faces.

"No one is making it out alive," Kressa whispers.

My fingers tremble, and I press them against my sides. "If the selkies don't kill us, the forest creatures will."

I survey the length of the beach behind us. It curves into itself on either side, cradled by the forest. We have no choice but to go through.

An unholy screech comes from the woods, rustling the canopy and sending a flock of birds into the night sky. Kressa stiffens and retreats a step. My pulse skitters, but I square my shoulders, and unsheathe the dagger at my thigh. My fingers find the familiar grooves on the hilt.

I fear nothing. In a blink, I could flood the forest and send its creatures to the depths of the ocean, the pressure killing them before lack of oxygen does.

Another shriek shakes the ground and rattles through my bones.

My grip falters, yet my resolve holds strong. "We only have an hour. We can't waste time."

I bound down the embankment, and sand floods my boots. Kressa curses under her breath and follows, feet pounding behind me. The forest beckons, limbs reaching out like twisted, gnarled hands.

The tree line swallows us, and moonlight speckles across the forest floor, spearing through small, insect-eaten holes in the leaves. The canopy hides the stars, and my stomach hollows. My only navigation.

I point my boots in the direction of the northeast mountain range. "We have to keep in a straight line. If we get turned around, one of us will have to climb a tree. And that will slow us down."

"Noted."

She follows close behind, and I keep my hand steady on my dagger, scanning the twisted tree trunks for glowing eyes or bared teeth. Protruding roots slow us down, some higher than my chest.

A scream echoes through the forest and silences the birds in the trees. I halt, and my blood drains to my feet.

"That wasn't a selkie," Kressa whispers, the whites of her eyes visible in the dark.

No. It was a man. A competitor. "We need to run. Now."

I take off without bothering to check if she follows, but her footsteps pound in sync with mine, and her breath fogs in front of her. Tree limbs reach out, whipping me in the face as I leap over roots and weave around dense bushes.

The canopy thickens and blots out the light from the moon. I slow my steps.

"Can you see anything?" I whisper.

"No—"

The breeze dissipates, and the temperature plummets. The forest quiets—stills as if holding its breath. A clearing opens and I freeze, throwing my arm in front of Kressa.

"Get down, and don't make a sound."

Moonlight filters into the clearing like a spotlight and illuminates a competitor, frozen to the spot.

A woman steps out. Glittering scales protrude from her chest and cascade down her waist and across her hips. Shiny black hair falls past the tips of her ribs, and her lush lips tilt into a smile.

She stops before the man and runs a finger down his arm. "Are you Anson?" Her voice comes out as a purr, and her eyes settle on his face.

"I can be whoever you want me to be."

"Where is it?" she whispers, toying with the collar of his shirt.

"Where's what?"

My fingers dig into the earth as she blinks, and the whites of her eyes disappear, replaced with a shade of black darker than the surrounding forest. Darker than the water kissing the seafloor. Her face contorts, her luscious smile widening until the edges of her mouth meet the hinge of her jaw. White teeth morph into a row of fangs sharp enough to shred flesh.

The man lurches back, but her razor-tipped nails dig into the skin around his neck and pin him in place.

"My tail!" she screams.

The man grips her hands and tries to pry them from his neck, but it's no use. "I—I don't know. I don't have your tail."

"Liar!" She leaps onto him and clamps her teeth around his throat, tearing it out before another word leaves his lips. She spits it out and returns to his body in a frenzy, shredding his skin into ribbons. She bellows, her bloody face tipped to the sky.

I inch up from my knees, fingers trembling around the dagger. "Run. Now."

We burst from the forest floor and sprint along the edges of the clearing, the selkie too busy feasting to notice us.

"*That's* a selkie?" Kressa says between pants.

"One on the brink of losing her ability to live in the ocean." A pang spears my chest. Unable to roam the open ocean, selkies' hearts wither, and they die within days.

My lungs ache, and frigid air bites the lining of my throat.

But I can't stop. We have to get to the other side of the forest and reach the mountains, or break through the mental barrier the Sopor threw over us.

The trees thin out, and my breath hitches. We're almost there. Forcing my legs faster, I pump my arms and push against the fog clouding my vision.

I trip and careen forward, slamming my face into a gnarled root. Rolling to my back, I press a hand to my throbbing temple and groan. Something shines behind my closed eyelids and I blink them open to the bright moon overhead. My muscles relax. We made it.

"Harriet," Kressa whispers, voice shaky. She taps at me with her boot. "Harriet, get the fuck up."

The hair along my neck rises. I push my elbow against the ground—no, against sand. I raise my head, coming face to face with the back of a dune, and my breath hitches. It's the beach we left nearly an hour ago.

"You must be Kressa," a female voice croons.

"And Harriet," another intones, sweet and silky.

30

———————

The selkie runs her tongue over a fang, the point honed to a tip. "Kressa, the king tells me you have my tail." She stalks closer, hips swaying with each silent step. Her head tilts. "Don't you know it's not nice to take from others?"

Ignoring the throbbing at my temple, I push to my feet. Fresh cuts burn my hands, raw from sliding against the knotted tree root. Kressa retreats a step from the advancing selkie.

While I don't recognize her, I know the one in front of me. She helped raise me, taught me how to navigate with the stars. One of my mother's oldest friends.

Tertia.

I sheathe my dagger and raise my hands, risking a step forward.

Kressa's eyes widen. "What are you doing?"

"The king is lying." I focus my attention on Tertia and cross the mental threshold. If it worked with the kraken, it might work with the selkies too. But I slam into a wall and flinch back. She's too frantic to let me in.

"He said you would say that," the other selkie hisses, her hungry eyes trained on Kressa.

"We're telling the truth," Kressa says.

The creatures blink in unison and pad closer.

"They smell delicious," Tertia croons. She closes her eyes and inhales a deep breath, the gills along the sides of her neck straining as if searching for saltwater. Her delicate nostrils flare, and her eyes fly open.

"You smell different, Harriet." She tilts her head. "Familiar. Have we met before?"

My heart leaps, and I ease my way across the mental gap again. If she senses me, maybe she'll pause long enough to let me in.

"She's a pirate," the other snarls, satin voice tipped with poison. "Of course you've met her kind before. They're notorious for stealing our tails." Her lip curls at me. "Aren't you?"

Tertia shakes her head. "She smells like the sea. No"—she blinks—"the sea smells like *her*."

Kressa furrows her brow. "What is she talking about?"

The selkie before her releases a blood chilling screech. I flinch back, but hold my ground and keep my dagger safely secured at my thigh.

Her lips widen, eyes turning a soulless black. Unnaturally quick, she lunges at Kressa and sweeps her talons at her face. Kressa dodges, but the selkie's nails slice long lines down her forearms, drawing blood.

It streams to the sand, and Tertia watches it drip into a small puddle, her eyes lolling in their sockets. They glaze over with bloodlust and jerk to me. She growls, low and fierce as the whites of her eyes disappear.

"Please," I whisper, palming the hilt of my dagger. "I don't want to hurt you."

A hideous laugh escapes her throat, and she bares her teeth. "Where is it?"

"We don't have them. I swear."

"Filthy, lying pirate."

She releases a shriek that rings in my ears. In one fluid motion, she leaps, fangs aimed at my throat. I whip out my dagger and duck, but she tackles me to the ground. Her nails tear through my shirt, and I scream as they shred my skin. My blade flies out of my grip and lands behind my head as she pins my arms down, mixing blood into the sand.

I flail and try to buck her off, but she only chuckles, low and guttural. Hot, salty breath skates across my cheek, and out of the corner of my eye, Kressa lands a blow to the selkie's jaw.

Tertia hovers her face over mine. "Give me my tail, and I'll let you live."

A lie. Even if I returned it, she'd kill me out of vengeance. Her nails dig into me, puncturing skin and drawing blood.

"It's me, Tertia. Taste my blood," I say, nodding toward the crimson leaking from my arm. "You said I smell different. Taste it and you'll know."

A harrowing screech comes from beside us, but I don't dare look. Tertia narrows her eyes and drags a nail down my cheek, splitting skin. She dips her finger into my blood and brings it to her lips. Those black eyes clear, and the whites return. Her throat bobs, jaw slackens, and the claws digging into my arms retract.

"Briar?" She blinks. "Your Highness?"

I nod, and tears spring to my eyes. I haven't been called that in a decade. "We don't have your tails. None of us do. Tell them —tell your sisters they're hunting the wrong people. It's the king who has your tails."

Her eyes glaze over, the slitted pupils darting back and forth. They clear and her porcelain skin pales. "He lied. He said if we retrieved our tails from you, he'd set us free. But they must still be in his quarters."

I pause. "They're in his room?"

Her chin dips. "They took us to an open-air prison facing the sea and chained us to the walls, torturing us one by one until we shifted into our human form. They collected our tails and the guard who was in charge ordered them to be taken to the king's quarters."

To add to his collection. My nails dig into the soft sand, but it gives far too easily to quench my rage. "After the trial, I'll find the tails. Tell the others to meet me at the most northern dock at midnight."

Her eyes gloss over, then clear with a blink. A faint tap echoes against my mind, and I open it up for her.

Princess, why are you with her? She tilts her head in Kressa's direction, and her upper lip curls. *I thought you—*

Her body jerks, and blood sputters from her parted lips, cutting off her words. She rolls to the ground, and her eyes slide to me, hand reaching in my direction. Black blood gushes from a wound at her side. *Your mother, she—*

Kressa sinks my dagger into her chest, and I scream, the noise reverberating through the forest and across the ocean. It ripples through my very being.

"No, no, no."

I flip over and scramble to her, tears streaming from my eyes. Her chest shudders on an inhale, then freezes. Nearby, the other selkie lies in the sand, motionless, in a pool of inky blood.

"You killed her," I whisper. Fire coursing through my veins, I jerk my gaze to Kressa and scream, "You killed them!"

Her lip pulls back, and she drops my bloodied dagger into the sand. "Of course I did. She was about to kill you! Briar cares too much about you for me to let you die."

I jump to my feet and slam my fist into her cheekbone. I pluck my dagger from the sand and ready it to plunge into her chest, but freeze. The world spins around me, tilts on its axis. Kressa's shouts hollow out, muffled by the roaring in my ears.

It's not Harriet's hand I'm staring at.
It's mine.

31

The fight drains from my body, and I shove the dagger in its sheath. I turn my back to Kressa and bring my hand to my hair, pulling out the bun. The ends hit my shoulders, short and blonde. I'm still Harriet, mostly.

But how long do I have? Minutes? Seconds?

I stare at the horizon. Gemma can't reinforce the glamour from here.

My throat seizes up.

Kressa takes a step and stumbles, falling to her knees. That's when I spot it—the black shirt clinging to her side. The shredded fabric. The thick blood gushing from a deep puncture wound.

"Kressa," I breathe. My heart thrashes against my chest, my power yanking at its chain.

She follows my line of sight. "The selkie bit me."

Before I can stop myself, I scramble to her. "You're losing too much blood. You—we can't make it to the mountains."

I retreat a step. I shouldn't care. Alliance be damned, I should sink my blade into her for killing those selkies. One less competitor. But a knot in my chest loosens. She could have walked away after killing that selkie, but she didn't. She thought she was saving me, and did so for Briar's sake. For *me.*

Her blinks grow heavy. "I think the forest is an illusion. Or a distraction. From the Sopor." She pushes her foot into the sand and goes to stand, but her legs buckle beneath her.

She deserves freedom. I wish I could give that to her.

I swallow. I can't let her die. Not like this.

"Take off your shirt," I say, dropping to the sand.

Her fingers fumble with the buttons, and I brush away her hand. "I've got it. You just breathe."

I make quick work of the buttons, and her shirt falls open, revealing an expanse of light brown skin. Blood coats the white fabric wrapped around her chest and drips down her waist in rivulets. I bite down on my cheek, easing her arms out of the sleeves. My fingers brush against her bare skin, and my power roils at the touch. If she feels it too, she doesn't show it.

"Your eyes," she whispers, lids heavy, "they look like Briar's."

My stomach hollows. "The blood loss is getting to you."

I angle my head away from her and run my dagger through the center of her shirt, ripping it into two strips.

The corner of her mouth lifts. "Blue, like the depths of the ocean where the sunlight barely filters through. Before it plummets into darkness."

My hands pause, gaze drifting to her pale face as my chest flutters. I shove down my power singing from its cage.

Focus. I have to get us out of here.

I crumple one strip into a ball and press it flush against the wound. She winces, but doesn't resist as I wrap the other strip around her middle and tie it tight, staunching the flow of blood.

"I'm not going to let you die," I say, double knotting the fabric. I lay her down and jump to my feet. "Stay here."

I sprint to the top of the dune and stare out over the forest.

It's too far to the mountain. She'll bleed out before we make it there, or we'll run out of time. And even if we made it, the glamour will be long gone. I'd be arrested the moment I appear in the arena.

What am I missing?

I whip to the churning waves. They're a stormy black, yet there are no clouds, no wind. Just a bitter bite in the air. My attention lifts to Aethra, twinkling in the sky.

The breath catches in my lungs.

Her arrow, the one pointing toward Delterran, has flipped —the constellation a mirror of itself. As if it senses my gaze, the stars rotate until the arrow points straight down. To the water.

We haven't been transported somewhere else, or at least not somewhere real. This isn't the ocean.

I sprint down the dune, sand flying as I slide to a stop in front of Kressa. Her eyes are pressed shut, and I drop to my knees, shaking her shoulders. "Kressa?"

She doesn't budge.

I shake harder. "Kressa, wake up!"

Nothing.

My breaths grow ragged, and I check her side. A pool of blood soaks the sand, and her chest shudders with every inhale.

Muscle and bone shift under my face. I bring my hand to my jaw, where the harsh angle gives way to my rounded cheeks. My nose shifts, and the slight slope returns. I swallow and glance at the crest of the dune.

If I left Kressa, I could make it. I could run into the water and break through the veil before the glamour wears off completely. Gemma could snap it into place before anyone sees. Only one trial would separate me from freedom.

Kressa lays prone, unmoving. Not yet dead, but close.

My throat constricts. She came to my defense when that prisoner grabbed me. She wants to give me freedom, but little does she know—in the last decade—my power has only felt this free with her.

I can't leave her.

Stepping near her head, I thread my hands under her arms and heave her up the side of the dune. My power goes frantic, thrashing, as if it can sense her life depleting.

Blood trails behind her, and my shoulders scream at the strain, but I dig my feet into the sand and fall onto the crest of the dune, pulling her up with me.

The ocean beckons on the other side.

I suck in a breath and grab her feet, carefully guiding her body down the embankment. My head pounds, and a searing pain grips my chest. I fall to my knees and we roll down the slope, slamming into the bottom.

Blood pulses from the deep wounds in my arms, dying my shirt a deep ruby. I groan, lifting my head.

I take a deep breath and run my fingers through my hair. Still short. Only a few more feet and we'll be in the water. We'll either survive the trial or die together.

Kressa's eyes open to slits. "Briar?"

The cold air on my face freezes over.

She reaches out and brushes her fingertips over my cheek. Her head sinks back to the sand, and a wave shoots up, caressing her hair. "Am I dead?"

I run my fingers over her knuckles. "It's just a dream."

"Don't leave me," she whispers, eyes falling shut.

"I won't."

Head throbbing, I push to my feet and drag her toward the water, each tug a screaming pain in my muscles.

A wave crests as my feet sink into wet sand. I suck in a deep breath and brace myself. If I'm wrong, I'll die. My knees tremble, and saltwater shoots up the shore, but I don't dare close my eyes. If it kills me, I want it to be the last thing I see.

Please, I beg the ocean. *Please let me be right.*

The waves swallow my ankles and knees, but I'm not wet. My clothes remain dry.

The sweat soaked strands on my head lengthen and brush against my collarbones.

No no no.

I hoist Kressa up and throw us into the surf. The ends of my hair reach my chest, and with a final lunge, I throw myself under the water, dragging Kressa down with me.

My back slams into hard ground, and dirt billows around me in a cloud.

Blaring cheers replace the roaring of the ocean, and the muscles and bones in my body shift and stretch and twist. I scream, but it's swallowed by applause.

The dust clears.

In the stands, Gemma digs her nails into the seat in front of her and rises, as if she's going to jump in the arena.

My gaze falls to the body beside me, shrouded by long grass.

Kressa.

I scramble to her. Her chest rises on a labored breath, her lips purple, and I put pressure on her wound. The shirt is soaked through with blood. I raise my head, searching the stands for a healer.

A strangled cry comes from my throat. Even if there was a healer, they wouldn't save her. Not in The Gales.

Beneath my hand, Kressa's chest shudders.

The back of my throat stings, and my power jolts toward her. "Don't die," I whisper, my eyes welling with tears. "Don't you dare leave me."

I swallow, and my power stutters, as if it senses her life snuffing out.

Her chest stops.

No.

A scream builds in my chest I grapple for my power. If I can just sink a sliver of my power into her, it just might bring her back. As long as her heart hasn't stopped.

I grab her wrist and order whatever dregs of my power are left to sink under her skin. A single tendril slips out and weaves through my arm in a dim cobalt glow. It floats over my palm and into Kressa.

It dissolves into her body, and I hold my breath, staring at the spot where her chest should be moving. I glance to where a pulse should thrum on her neck. Nothing.

A dim, emerald glow appears over her heart, and the hair on my arm stands on edge. It travels down her shoulder, twines around her bleeding forearm, and crosses her wrist.

Before I have a chance to let go, it shoots into my hand.

Lurching back, I grab my wrist as the light disappears under my sleeve, weaving like a warm caress over my aching muscles. It climbs my chest and sinks directly into my heart, where my power would be if it wasn't locked up tight. A ripple goes through me, like a pebble dropped into a pond.

Earth. Fresh rain. Trees.

I inhale fresh grass and flowers and the first hint of a spring morning.

Kressa heaves a breath and leans on an elbow, coughing out mouthfuls of blood. She groans, and fall back into unconsciousness.

I sit, motionless, as her breathing regulates.

Caelus was right.

Kressa has power. And we exchanged it.

32

———————

"You shouldn't be here," Veronica snarls. "Do you know how hard it was to hide Kressa when you dragged her here this morning?"

A healer walks by, her low heels clicking over the stone as she crosses the infirmary. She catches the look on Veronica's face and lowers her head, pushing through the nearest exit. The door swings shut, and the clock above it reads five minutes to eleven.

I tug my cloak around the canvas sack I lifted from the laundry room. "I had no other choice. The hallways were swarming with guards after the trial ended. They would have never allowed a healer through."

She narrows her eyes. "As if you were in any state to be helping her."

At her words, the recently healed wounds spanning my body ache.

"Please, just let me see her."

My voice comes out more desperate than I'd like. I had no intention of stopping to check on Kressa on my way to retrieve the selkie tails, but her power tugged me here and wouldn't relent.

Veronica sucks in her cheek and scans the rows of hospital beds, each cot veiled by a thick curtain. "Fine. But keep your voice down. I have other patients too, you know."

The dagger is a weight against my thigh. "I know."

"She's in the last one on the left."

I nod. "Thank you."

She gives me one final glare. "I'll be in the supply room preparing bandages for the next thirty minutes."

My lip quirks. "Thirty minutes."

With that, she huffs and turns on her heel, disappearing through a doorway. My stomach clenches, and I stride down the center of the rows of beds, all of them full, yet only one occupied by a competitor—Kressa. One other survived the second trial, but the state he's in, I do not know.

Only nine—out of fifty—remain.

Dim lanterns line the wall and cast an incandescent glow over the long, narrow room. My cloak billows around my ankles, and with each step I take, the figment of her power pulls me closer.

A moth to a flame.

My hand reaches for the curtain, but pauses midair. Maybe I shouldn't be here. I should let her rest until morning, when I can berate her with questions. I drop my hand and step back.

"Briar?"

Her voice isn't more than a whisper, but it sparks something in my chest—something new and steadier than the ground beneath my feet.

I part the curtains. "How did you know it was me?"

A pillow lies under her head, her body covered with a thin white sheet. Fading purple bruises jog along her temple and down her cheekbone. I cringe at the one I inflicted.

But she's alive. Breathing.

"I don't know." She shrugs. "I sensed you."

The vulnerability in her voice takes me off guard, and I slip into the narrow space between the side of her bed and the curtain. "Are you okay?"

"What's that?" Her lips tilt into a weak grin, honey eyes sparkling in the dark. "It sounds like you're worried about me."

"Well, now that I know you're alive, I need you to start talking."

She lifts onto her forearms and props herself against the low headboard. The sheet pools at her waist and exposes every curve and dip of muscle along her arms. White gauze is taped to her side, covering the wound that nearly killed her. And in the center of her chest, over her heart, barely hidden by the fabric around her breasts—

A dimple appears in her cheek. "What do we need to talk about, love?"

Heat climbs up my neck, and I glance away from her chest. Her uninvited power purrs between my ribs, but I swallow it down. "You have power."

A scoff. "No, I don't."

"It wasn't a question," I snarl.

I settle onto the mattress and trace the spot over her heart where my power dipped into her. A deep, cerulean light blooms beneath her skin.

Unbuttoning my cloak, I let it fall to the bed beside the laundry sack. Beneath my tunic and under my skin, a deep emerald green light glows.

I remove my hand from her, and the glow flickers out. "Now stop lying, and tell me the truth."

Her face pales. "Then let's start with you."

I bite my lip. Selective truths it is. "I felt ill, so I missed the trial. Harriet passed by me when she carried you here, and I—I thought you were dead. I grabbed your hand, and this"—I tap my chest—"passed from you into me."

She rubs a hand over her heart. "And this one?"

Saved your life.

I clasp my hands in my lap and stare at the space over her shoulder. "From me."

"You have power?" Her head tilts. "From the Sea Court? Or Caelus?"

"Sea Court."

"I assume Caelus doesn't know about this?"

"Would I be alive if he did?"

Something in her face shifts, then softens. "No, I suppose you wouldn't be. The same way I wouldn't be."

She leans over and pulls a shirt from the nightstand, throwing it over her head. A warmth pools in my stomach at the way her fingers skim her waist as she pulls the hem down.

I swallow and look away. "And yours came from the Earth Court?"

She nods, and my stomach twists. I want to ask her who gifted it to her. A lesser noble? King Golan, or Prince Barren, before they were killed?

But if I asked, so would she. And I'd rather not add another strand to my carefully spun web of lies.

"Is it strong?" I say.

She shakes her head. "Nothing noteworthy. Nothing compared to Elias's."

I nod, slowly. Not directly from a royal, then.

Her gaze meets mine. "What about yours?"

"Almost nonexistent."

It's not a lie, but she stares, scanning every facet of my face.

Her fingertips tease the curve of my knee. "I think you saved my life."

"What?"

"I think I was dead, or close, at least. I remember seeing your face at one point during the trial. Like it was a dream."

I clamp my lips together.

"But maybe that was when your power came into me. I was dead, and I think it brought me back to life."

"That's not possible," I say, my voice stone. It shouldn't be, at least.

She gives me an unreadable look. "Maybe it's not." Leaning closer, she reaches her hand to my face and rubs her knuckles over my jaw. "You lied."

I furrow my brows, unable to lean away from her touch. "What are you talking about?"

"About the kiss. You said you felt nothing."

"I didn't."

She threads her fingers through my hair at the base of my neck. "A lie then, and a lie now. The truth this time. Please. What did you feel when our lips came together?"

The green light at my chest flares, and I shake my head. "I don't remember."

"Perhaps you need to be reminded."

She pulls me close, and my chest flares brighter, lighting her face in an emerald glow. I swallow and angle my body toward her, lifting a leg halfway onto the bed. Her other hand wraps around my waist, our mouths nothing but a breath apart.

My heart rattles in my chest, pulse skittering in my veins. Her power, and mine, urge me closer. Her gaze dips to my mouth, and her pupils widen, a soft smile crossing her lips.

"I'll ask one more time," she whispers. "What did you feel?"

I glance to her mouth, watching the way her lips work around each syllable. I bite down on my cheek.

No, I'm not some sort of experiment. And she's nothing but an excuse to stay away from Caelus—a means to stay alive in The Gales. If I knew our power would exchange, I never would have saved her.

And Isolde. After the trial, I tried to track her down, but with no luck. I can't do this to her.

I push against Kressa's chest and bolt from the mattress, her sudden absence like a slap. "I felt the ocean, okay? The salty air, the churning waves—that's what I felt when we kissed."

She tilts her head. "Interesting."

I sling the laundry sack over my shoulder and replace my cloak, buttoning it around my neck. "And what did you feel?"

"I never lied to you. I felt flames licking up my skin, burning from the inside out."

"Well, I'm glad that's settled. Have a good night."

I part the curtain and air from the infirmary rushes in, cooling my face.

She throws her legs over the side of his bed and winces, pressing a hand to her waist. "Where are you going?"

"Back to my room," I lie. "Alone."

Her eyes darken, and a smile spreads over her lips. "You're going back to your room with a massive laundry bag?"

I glance at the bag peeking out of my cloak. "Yes. Goodbye."

The clock ticks above the doorway, and I step through the curtain, but she grabs my hand. As if charged, her touch buzzes up my arm and into my chest, jolting my power. I rip from her grasp and run my palm down the front of my cloak.

She stands. "Harriet told you about the selkies, didn't she? That their tails are somewhere in the castle."

"She did. And if I want to return their tails, I need to go now."

She looks over my shoulder, and a line forms between her brows. "She isn't going to help you?"

I shake my head.

She yanks a sweater hanging off the headboard and slides her arms through it. "Then I'm coming with you."

"No, you're not. I don't need a chaperone."

"Trust me, Briar. I'm well aware of that."

"And they killed those competitors for leaving the castle. They won't hesitate if they catch you."

She lowers to the mattress and tugs on a pair of boots,

fingers making quick work of the laces. She sighs, and through lowered lashes, looks up at me. "I killed two of those selkies."

My breath shudders at the memory of blood dripping from Tertia's mouth. "I heard."

A shadow crosses her face. "I didn't want to hurt them. But one had Harriet pinned down, and I knew if she died, you wouldn't get that ship. I know they aren't usually like that—that they were prisoners just like my brother. This is the least I can do." She blows out a long breath. "Please, Briar, let me help."

That hard stare I've become so accustomed to softens, and warmth spreads over my chest, whirling with her power embedded in my heart.

"Fine."

33

———————

"Where are we going?" Kressa whispers as we climb the stairs.

I don't look at her. "To get the selkie tails, remember?"

We come to the landing, and she pulls me to a stop. "Tell me where we're going. Now."

"Why? Do you already regret coming?"

"I will if you lead me straight into a trap."

I yank my hand from her grasp. "First of all—if this was a trap, it'd be too late for you. And second, if you get us caught, I'll kill you."

Something passes behind her eyes. "I'm not so sure you could, love."

I grit my teeth and lean closer. "I wouldn't hesitate."

A smile crosses her face. "Good, now tell me where we're going."

Blowing out a breath, I peek around the corner of the hallway. "Caelus's quarters. He has a collection of sorts in his room, and I think that's where the tails will be."

"You *think*? We can't just go into his room and politely ask for the selkie tails back."

"Of course not, but I have a plan. And you're wasting my time." I push past her into the empty hallway. "Just do me a favor, and keep your mouth shut."

We keep to the edges of the hallways and come to the corner before Caelus's quarters. I throw my arm in front of Kressa and peer around the wall, where two armed guards stand watch.

I hold my breath and count the seconds. The timing has to be perfect. I shed my cloak and pull the laundry bag from my shoulder, shoving them into her chest. She grunts, and I pull the elastic from my braid and shake out my hair.

Her knuckles blanch against my cloak.

I paint a smile onto my face and wet my lips, curling them into a pout. "Wait for my signal."

Emerging into the hallway, I saunter toward the guards. Their arms remain crossed over their chests, swords sheathed at their backs, but their gazes follow the sway of my hips.

"Good evening, gentlemen," I purr, stopping in front of them. "Is the king in?"

The one on the right shakes his head. "He's out with Isolde, celebrating the success of the second trial."

I bite down on the inside of my cheek. Isolde. "Perhaps I could slip in and wait for his return?"

"No one is permitted entry," the one on the left says, his voice hard despite the languid way his eyes roam my body.

My foot taps. Any second now.

Slippered feet pound from around the corner.

"Guards!"

Thea appears from a nearby hall, running with her nightgown bunched in her fist. She skids to a stop, chest heaving. "There's a thief in the kitchen. I need you to come. Now!"

They stiffen and run their hands over the hilt of their swords. The one on the left shakes his head. "We can't leave our post."

Thea gives me a pained look. "Please, I need you to come now. What if he's dangerous?"

"I'm sorry, we cannot—"

"I've got it covered." Julian strides up in blue pants and a white buttoned shirt, a dagger tucked in the sheath at his waist. "I'm meant to take over in fifteen minutes anyway."

He glances at me, and I avert my gaze.

The guards hesitate, but the elder of the two leaves his spot at the wall and steps toward Thea. "What did this person look like?"

"I'll show you," she says, motioning for them to follow.

The other guard rakes his gaze over me, but not out of concern or suspicion. No, I know that look. Covetous. He joins Thea and she leads them down the hallway, disappearing from view.

I blow out a breath. "Fifteen minutes?"

Julian nods. "Marianne has eyes on Caelus and will send word if he returns sooner." His nose shrinks, chin softens, and his hair lengthens from a crop to his shoulders, turning a shimmering black.

Gemma pulls the sheath from her waist and hands it to me. "That's all the time you have."

"That's all I need." I thread the holster around my thigh and tighten it. My shaky fingers brush over the hilt. "Thank you, by the way."

She nods. "You're welcome."

I turn and whistle.

Kressa steps around the corner, and Gemma stiffens, pinning her arms to her sides. "Be safe," she whispers, hurrying past Kressa.

Kressa comes to my side, her eyes narrowed. "I'm not a dog."

I grin and take the cloak from her, throwing it over my shoulders. "You sure did come like one."

Buttoning it, I take the laundry bag and scan both ends of the hallway. I wrap my fingers over the brass handle and crack the door. "It's clear."

In the sitting room, lanterns cast a dim glow over the table and chairs in front of the empty fireplace. I release a breath. Caelus isn't coming back anytime soon if he hasn't sent a servant to start a fire.

I stride to the narrow door tucked beside the covered mirror. "Over here," I whisper, turning the knob and pushing the door open. "Don't touch anything."

She doesn't respond. Over my shoulder, she stands frozen in the center of the room, gaze roaming the tapestries hung along the walls.

"What's wrong?"

She shakes her head. "Nothing. Let's go."

We step through the door, and moonlight spills into the room—not quite bright enough to light the vast space. I tiptoe past rows of glass cases housing various valuable items. Shelves line the walls, filled with trinkets of all shapes and sizes.

Kressa stiffens, her eyes shooting wide. "Briar."

A breath catches in my throat. I swallow down a strangled cry as I take in the selkie tails nailed to the far wall like hunting trophies.

Pressing the back of my hand against my mouth, I stifle the sting behind my eyes as I inch closer to them. Their iridescent scales shimmer, but a handful are missing, like they were torn one by one. Tortured.

I draw my dagger and slide the blade under the first nail, careful to avoid the paper-thin skin where the scales were plucked. My fingers tremble, and I pull back. One falter and the blade will slice through the delicate tail. I grit my teeth and clench my jaw so hard it shakes.

"What gives him the right," I snarl, my voice thick.

Tears threaten my eyes, and I suck in a shuddering breath. Slowly, I ease the tip under the nail head again, but a sob wracks my body, and the dagger slips from my grip.

It clatters to the floor, echoing through the room. I curse under my breath and wipe at the hot tears gathering on my cheeks.

A hand settles on my shoulder. "Let me."

Kressa bends over and collects my dagger.

I reach for it. "No."

She closes her hand over mine, her eyes full of somber understanding. "Please."

I go to argue, but my throat constricts, cutting off any words. Nodding, I retreat a step and gather the laundry sack, holding it open.

Kressa makes quick work of the nails, expertly prying them from the walls. She guides the first tail over her arm and gently folds it into the bag.

"Thank you," I whisper.

Her gaze lifts to mine, her eyes dark and serious, but she doesn't say anything as she turns back to the wall and starts on the next tail. Minutes pass by, and the bag grows heavier.

I glance at the open doorway, and my pulse quickens. "Julian's watch will start any moment."

Silent, Kressa stares at the final two. They each bear a brand —a large eagle, warping the scales at the edges. My chest tightens, and I brush a finger over the one missing the most scales.

Tertia's tail.

Another sob climbs into my throat. "When I was young, the selkies taught me how to swim. They were my friends. How you saw them in the trial? That isn't their true nature. They're kind and peaceful, and they didn't deserve this."

Guilt flashes across her eyes. "I'm so sorry."

I nod and wipe a finger beneath my eyes. "We're running out of time. We need to go."

"I'm not leaving until we get all of them."

My heart squeezes as she slides the dagger beneath the nails and pries them out one by one. She lays Tertia's tail across my arms, and I allow a single tear to fall from my eyes, splashing on the scales in a silent apology.

Kressa removes the final tail, and we set them into the bag, pulling the drawstring tight. She heaves it over her shoulder and winces.

"Your side." I reach for the bag. "It's too heavy. Let me take it."

"No."

My hand falls, skimming her shirt as it returns to my side. I note the hard set of her lips and the determination in her eyes. She isn't carrying it to lessen the burden on me, but as penance for the selkies.

I square my shoulders. "Let's go."

The clock in Caelus's quarters reads a half hour to midnight. It'll be close, but if we hurry, we'll meet the selkies in time.

I inch open the door and peek into the hallway. Empty. Drawing my hood, I whisper, "Stay close."

We file into the hallway, and I turn left. "The guards won't be manning the side exit at this—"

Voices call out from around the corner, followed by multiple pairs of footsteps.

"When we checked the kitchen, the thief had already escaped. Porcelain plates and cups were thrown everywhere. Shattered."

"Send guards to every entrance."

My stomach bottoms out. Caelus.

If we tried to run, we'd never make it. The hallway is too long, and they're too close. I grab the bag from Kressa's shoulder and shove it behind a heavy velvet curtain.

My heart thrashes wildly in my chest.

Caelus's shadow dances on the wall, growing closer. "Keep a tight guard on my room in case the thief decides to come this way."

I bite my lip. We can't run, but there's only one excuse for Kressa and I to be out of our rooms this late at night. I grab her by the collar and back up to the wall, pulling her flush against me.

"Play along."

She threads a hand through my hair, and her chest heaves as she angles my face up. "Are you sure?" Her voice is a gentle whisper against my mouth.

"No. Are you?"

My power buzzes, thrumming against its tether. A faint green glow appears from under my cloak, and Kressa tugs me closer, covering it with her body.

Caelus rounds the corner.

"No," Kressa says, crashing her mouth to mine.

I inhale a sharp breath. The kiss is a caress against my lips, and I allow them to part. My power flares and stretches from its confines like an animal unfurling from rest.

Kressa groans into my mouth and presses me harder against the cold wall, sliding a thigh between my legs. She winds her arm around my waist and I arch against her, tasting every corner of her mouth. Devouring.

A cough echoes through the hallway.

But Kressa tastes like spring rain—feels like being sucked into a whirlpool, laid against the soft sand at the bottom of the ocean. My power melds with hers, and I can't pull away. I would trade a thousand lifetimes for this moment to last into eternity.

"Courtesans," Caelus mumbles. "Good for one thing only."

Kressa stiffens, shifting as if she's going to whirl on the king. I fist my hands into her shirt and hold her in place.

I'm going to fucking kill him.

My eyes fly open, and I stop breathing. I break the kiss and press my hand against her chest.

That was her voice in my head.

Forcing a swallow, I smile and turn to Caelus and Julian. My fingers curl around Kressa's shirt to keep them from trembling.

"Gentlemen," I drawl.

Heels tap against stone, and before I have a chance to pull away from Kressa, Isolde turns the corner.

Her steps falter.

I go cold as her eyes sweep over me, then Kressa. The collar fisted in my grip. The flush to my skin.

Kressa backs away, running a hand through her hair. She bends into a shallow bow. "Your Majesties."

I search Isolde's face. For something, anything. But her expression is blank.

Caelus raises a brow. "I see you're taking your job very seriously, Briar."

"As always, Your Highness."

"By all means, don't let us interrupt you," he says, eyes boring into me. A warning.

Julian holds open the door, and Caelus nods a goodbye, striding into his quarters.

Isolde stands, frozen, her hair hanging in ringlets over her bodice, brushing her waist.

"Isolde," I breathe, stepping forward.

"Isolde," Caelus barks from the open doorway.

She flinches, blinking her attention away from me, and shakes her head. Without a word, she follows his voice into the room. I swallow past the lump in my throat and watch her go, the hem of her gown disappearing from view.

The door clicks shut, and my mind snaps into the present. Soon, I'll speak to Isolde and reassure her that everything will be okay. But for now—I whirl and shove Kressa, my face twisting into a scowl. "Why can I hear your thoughts?"

"I don't know," she whispers, collecting the bag from behind the curtain. "Because I can hear yours, too."

34

———

I stumble back. "Impossible."

The only creatures I've ever communicated with mentally are from the sea. Inhuman.

"Apparently not." She glances at Caelus's door. "But we can discuss it when we're out of the castle. Any second now, they'll come searching for the tails."

I reach for the bag. "I'm not going anywhere with you."

A smirk crosses her lips, and she steps closer, pulling the bag out of reach. *You think I taste like spring rain? So good that even if you wanted to, you couldn't pull—*

"Get out of my head," I snap, despite my power roiling at the silky words skimming my mind.

She leans closer and lowers her voice to a snarl. "If we don't go soon, neither of us are getting out of the castle. Now walk."

I grit my teeth. "Fine."

We weave through the castle and down a flight of stairs. Arched columns sweep above our heads as we cross through the grand hall, the clock high on the wall creeping closer to midnight.

We come to an unmanned side door and I pause. "Wait." I

unclasp my cloak. "You need this more than I do. If they spot you, you're dead."

She tilts her head. "First you come to my bedside, concerned for my health. And now you're worried I might die? I fear you're getting soft on me."

I narrow my eyes. "It would be terribly inconvenient for you to die."

"Ah, of course. Terribly inconvenient."

I slide one shoulder from the cloak, but she tugs it back into place.

The amusement disappears from her eyes. "If they catch me, I'll be killed. But if they spot you"—she slides the button back through the clasp and pulls the hood over my head—"there are worse punishments than death."

Like being stuck with Caelus.

Her fingers graze my cheek. "Yes, like being stuck with Caelus."

My eyes widen. My mental barrier was locked tight, shut from any interference. "I—"

Shouts come from behind us, and footstep pound through the corridors. Guards.

Kressa throws open the door. "Looks like they realized the tails are missing."

Night air blasts us, and wind whips at the edges of my cloak. Heavy storm clouds blot out the full moon, crackling with lightning. A blast of thunder shakes the ground.

A look passes between us. She presses her lips into a thin line and nods.

We take off across the street, twisting and weaving through alleyways.

Masts pierce the sky as the harbor comes into view. Waves crash against the aging stone barricade and crest over the maze of wooden docks jutting far into the water. I close my eyes and breathe in the mist, savoring the salt on my skin.

"How long have you been able to hear my thoughts?" Kressa asks.

I open my eyes to the tethered ships, bobbing in the waves. "That was the first time. How long have you?"

Her gaze lingers on the mountains in the distance. "When you came to the infirmary. They cut in and out, but I knew you were worried about me. And now, I can only hear certain things. Like when your emotions are heightened."

My chest tightens, and the possibilities of her discovering my secrets swarm my head. I kick a rock off the boardwalk, and the waves swallow it whole. "How did this happen?"

"Maybe when our power exchanged?"

I consider. If it's from my power, maybe I can control it. "Try to do it."

She raises a brow. *I thought you didn't want me in your head.*

Closing my eyes, I focus on the space in my mind. The mental bridge I share with the sea creatures is off to the side, but a new doorway gapes beside it, where her words filter in. I slam it shut and open my eyes.

"Try again."

She stares at me for a long moment. "Did you hear it that time?"

"No." The door in my mind is thin, and cracks splinter the wooden planks. It may not hold if my emotions heighten, but it'll do for now. "What did you say?"

"It doesn't matter." Her mouth tilts into a cheeky grin. "Now you try."

I crack open the door. *Can you hear me?*

Eyes shut tight, her lips rest comfortably together. Peaceful. I run a tooth over my bottom lip, where it was pulled between hers moments ago.

She opens her eyes, and I flick my gaze away.

Heat rises to my cheeks, and a faint emerald glow comes

from my chest. I tug the edges of my cloak together. "Did you hear me?"

"No."

"That seemed easy for you." I'm accustomed to closing my mind off to creatures, but Kressa has no such practice.

"My brother loved to read my mind when we were children. I never got away with anything because he always told my parents. As soon as I learned how, I blocked him out."

My lip quirks. "I like him."

"I think he'd like you, too." She glances sideways at me, pain etched into the lines on her face.

An ache spreads behind my sternum. "We'll find him."

We come around a bend to the northernmost tip of the docks. I reach across the pathway in my mind, bypassing the door that leads to Kressa.

Are you here?

Your Highness? a sweet voice whispers in response.

I smile. *Where are you?*

Pallid hands appear on the stone barricade. A selkie lifts her head from the water, black hair plastered to her face. Her sunken eyes study Kressa and she releases a low, menacing hiss.

The selkie bares her fangs. "Why are *you* here? I know what you did. We all do."

Her blackening eyes swing to me, filled with betrayal.

I lower to my knees. *She thought she was saving me during that trial, and wants to apologize. She helped me get your tails back.*

She blinks and the pathway closes, shutting me out.

Kressa strides to the edge of the barricade, and the selkie watches her like a predator. Her nails lengthen into claws, and a low growl reverberates from her throat.

I stand and throw an arm out. "Kressa—"

"It's okay," she whispers, lowering my arm. "They need to hear it from me."

The power in my chest shifts, and my heart warms.

She kneels close to the edge, pants soaking up water. The selkie doesn't look away as Kressa unties the drawstrings on the sack and pulls it open. Scales shimmer in the moonlight like gemstones, and the selkie stiffens, the whites returning to her eyes.

Other heads appear along the barricade, their faces ashen—nearly lifeless.

Kressa pulls out the first tail, and a selkie gasps. She pulls herself along the barricade and whispers, "You found it."

Kressa holds it out like a piece of fine silk and lowers her head. "I'm sorry for what I did to your friends."

The selkie's gaze darts over her shoulder and lands on me. It returns to Kressa, and the selkie nods. "You did what you thought you had to do."

Kressa lowers the tail to the selkie, and she sinks into the water. She resurfaces with a smile, the color restored to her face, and flicks her tail, disappearing into the depths.

Pulling the tails out one by one, Kressa mutters an apology to each selkie before returning their tails. Tears threaten my eyes, but I smile. Watching her interact with them with such respect, such gentleness—loosens a knot in me.

To her, they aren't vermin.

She glances over her shoulder. "How do you honor your dead?"

The final two tails rest in the bag, and I swallow at the sight of the charred scales. "We spend a night on the water, sleeping beneath the stars."

She nods and turns back to the selkie. Carefully, Kressa spreads the tails on the surface of the water, the scales catching moonlight. She whispers something under her breath. The selkie's eyes widen, and she nods.

Another selkie rises to the barricade. *Princess?*

Yes?

I have a message from your mother. One that I've been trying to share for a few years, waiting until we found you.

My stomach flips. I've sent countless messages to my mother via the sea, but never received a response. I can only assume the curse stopped the message from being delivered. Or disappointment outweighed her love.

I step forward. *What is it?*

She said she's sorry, for everything, and she loves you more than you know. And that one day, you'll understand why she did what she did. You'll know why she had to promise your hand in marriage.

My knees weaken, legs threatening to collapse. I swallow, hard. And although her words ease my hurt, I'm not sure I'll ever understand how a mother forces her daughter to marry.

And the war? I say. *Did she say anything about that?*

A shadow crosses her eyes. *We were evacuated from the front. We—we're losing a lot of soldiers. But last I heard, reinforcements are being readied.*

Guilt pierces my heart, but I shove it aside. *Reinforcements? From where?*

She bites her lip. *The Earth Court.*

My gaze swings to Kressa, and I furrow my brows. The Earth Court was dismantled a decade ago, and as far as I'm aware, Terra hasn't granted a new ruler with power. Powerless reinforcements will be useless against Caelus's aerial armada and his wielders.

I turn back to the selkie. *If you see my mother, tell her I'll be at the warfront in a week.*

Her eyes burst wide. *How?*

The trial you were subject to? I'm going to win and break this curse. Then I'll join you with my crew.

She nods and tilts her head in Kressa's direction. *What do I say about her?*

Her? I pinch my lips and shake my head. *Nothing. She's irrelevant.*

The selkie narrows her eyes. *But you've exchanged power. And she—*

I close off the pathway. Kressa has nothing to do with my power or my court. "Don't mention her to my mother."

She slinks into the depths. The wind whipping through the city has subsided, casting a sense of calm through the air.

"Ready?" Kressa asks, folding the empty bag under her arm.

I nod and say a silent goodbye to the selkies.

We turn from the edge of the water, and a tail slaps the surface. "Thank you, Your Highness," a selkie whispers.

My blood turns to ice, and my breathing halts. I don't dare turn and acknowledge her—to respond to a title Kressa doesn't know I have. *Can't* know I have. But judging by the blank look on her face, she didn't hear.

I relax my shoulders and tuck my hair into my hood.

We're silent as we make our way back along the boardwalk. I open the door to her mind, and knock.

Hers opens for me.

You didn't have to do that, I say.

Her gazes slides to me, the golden flecks in her eyes brilliant despite the dark night. *I wanted to.*

I pull my lower lip between my teeth. *Thank you.*

I close the pathway before she can say anything else—before she senses the way my power urges me to her, begs me to close the distance between us.

And how tempted I am to give in.

35

———————

I shut my eyes against the afternoon sun streaming through the window as Thea's voice echoes in the hallway. The door opens and her feet click through the room, stopping beside my bed.

"I know you're not asleep."

"Go away."

"I've never understood why you hate your birthday so much." She pads to the vanity and sinks into the chair, pulling pins out of her hair.

I push myself against the headboard and rub the sheet between my fingers. "It's not that I hate my birthday—"

"You just wish you could spend it with your family," she sing songs, reciting the words I say every year. "Where are they anyway? Your family?"

My heart slams into my back, and a burning sensation sinks into my throat. Thea is the only family I have left, and the rest? My mother?

"I don't know," I whisper.

"Sorry I brought it up." Sucking in a cheek, she pulls the

earrings from her ears and tucks them into a jewelry box. "It's a shame we aren't allowed to go out tonight and celebrate."

I grimace. My birthday was once a holiday people celebrated under the brightest stars of the year. But Caelus put a stop to that. Taverns are ordered to close before the sun sets, and gatherings of more than three are strictly prohibited.

I'll never forget that first year—the day after my birthday when Caelus arrested dozens who went against his law. He gave them a public execution.

Thea smiles in the mirror. "I can ask the cook to bring us up a slice of cake after we leave the tavern."

I groan. The tavern. "Do I have to go?"

"Yes, Briar. I'm dying to get out of the castle, and it would be suspicious if Harriet didn't show up when the rest of the competitors are going."

I fold my arms over my chest. "No one saw *Harriet* between the first and second trials, so I don't think anyone would miss her now."

She stands, dress shifting with the movement, and strides to my bed. "Yes, but that was before Harriet solved the king's trial. When she outsmarted a Sopor." She leans closer, leveling me with a glare that rivals the one she used to give me aboard our ship. "Before she saved another competitor when it would have been far safer and wiser to leave her for dead."

"We made an alliance," I whisper.

She straightens and throws her braids over her shoulder, the opal beads on the ends catching the light. "The Briar I know wouldn't risk her life saving someone who was collateral damage." Her voice lowers to a whisper. "So, what are you hiding from me?"

I search her eyes—not those of my first mate, but a friend nonetheless. A sister. One I trust with my entire life, to the ends of the world.

"Kressa has power."

She flinches back. "What?"

I nod. "Caelus was right. But it's more than that." I pause and worry my lip. I can't tell her about my power sinking into Kressa. She'll only forget. A sigh slips through my lips. "When I saved her, her power sank into me. It's a small amount, but it's connected us somehow. I don't fully understand it, but now we can communicate with our minds."

She opens her mouth, but I raise a hand, and she obliges. I pull the collar of my tunic down and tap at my heart. "When I touch her, or get too close, a light appears where her power sank into me."

And since the night in the infirmary, hers hasn't lit. Not once has a cerulean glow flared over her heart, while mine is uncontrollable.

Thea lowers to the mattress. "Why haven't you told me any of this until now?"

I reach for her hand. The words are sticky in my throat, but I force them out. "I wanted to protect you. It's dangerous, knowing Kressa has Earth power."

Her gaze jerks to mine, and she lowers her voice to a whisper. "Earth power?"

I nod. "If anyone finds out, it can risk everything. But it'll all end when I win this competition and we leave Sarenia forever."

A strangled laugh comes from her. "Now it makes sense why you saved her."

"What had you previously assumed?"

She huffs. "That you were in love with her."

A faint glow filters through my thin shirt. I pull the blanket up before Thea sees. "I'm not in love with her."

The servant's door opens, and a flash of red hair peeks through.

"Are you ready to go?" Marianne asks, pushing into the room. She hands Thea a pile of clothes, ones from the lower streets of Sarenia. Unless someone knows her personally, no one will think she's a royal courtesan.

Gemma follows close behind, eyes scanning me warily. "Are you feeling okay? After the trial?"

I nod and throw my legs over the bed. Rising, I stretch my arms. "Let's get this over with. I don't want to pretend to be a pirate any more than I have to."

Marianne circles to the dressing room and emerges with my pirate clothes, the hat perched on top. I make quick work of sliding into the shirt and pants, patting the dagger hidden beneath my pocket. I tuck Kressa's necklace beneath my collar, the metal cool against my skin.

Gemma cups my face, but flinches back. Her eyes widen. "You feel different."

"Different?"

She glances at my chest, directly where Kressa's power burrowed in. She shakes her head. "Never mind."

Replacing her palms to my face, she closes her eyes and glamours me inch by inch, bone by bone.

She lowers her hands, refusing to make eye contact. "I won't be at the tavern, so don't risk staying more than an hour."

I lean closer. "You can feel it in me, can't you?"

She searches my face and nods, lowering her gaze. "Please, be careful."

"I will."

Dressed in her disguise, Thea lowers the hat on my head, tilting it at an angle. She links her arm through mine and smiles. "Let's go have some fun, pirate."

36

Thick, sweaty air fills the tavern and clings to my clothes. Shouts ring out, and beer sloshes over the rims of tankards, splashing to the aged planks.

Thea winds her arm through mine. "I guess everyone is trying to enjoy the holiday before the taverns close."

My breath catches. "You can't say that too loud."

I scan the crowded tavern. The other competitors fill a long booth at the back, and I tug Thea in their direction.

"I don't see what is so wrong about celebrating her birthday," she says. "There must be a reason why so many people loved her, right?"

My chest aches, and I press my eyes shut. "Thea."

"What? It's a valid question. Think of how many people chose to be executed rather than bow to Caelus."

The ache spreads and wrings out my heart, threatening to shatter the wall I've built around my guilt. I halt and press my hands to her shoulders. "Thea, stop talking about her. For your own safety. Please."

"Easy tiger. I didn't know you cared so much." Her lip

quirks and she pokes a finger at my chest. "Harriet is kind of cute when she's angry."

I narrow my eyes, but her smile only widens, sparkling—so similar to the way she watched the ocean from our deck. A pang slides into my sternum. The hollow space behind my eyes stings, and I whisper, "I miss you."

A line forms between her brows, and she scoffs. "Your age is getting to you."

The roaring hearth taking up the majority of the side wall adds to the already stifling air. Sweat drips down the curve of my spine.

"Harriet!"

One of the competitors—Eric—waves his hand. He slides down the bench, leaving enough room for Thea and me. We sidestep through the bench and settle facing the crowd.

Eric's hazel eyes settle on me. "You saved my life in the last trial. If it weren't for seeing you run into the ocean, that selkie would've caught me."

Thea shifts beside me, and I swallow. "You saw me go into the water?"

If he did, he saw Briar. The glamour was all but gone.

"You disappeared a second after I crested the sand dune, so you were just a flash. I admire you for saving Kressa." He smirks. "Can't say I'd do the same."

"Me either," Thea grumbles.

A tankard of beer appears in front of me. The waitress bends over, her neckline low, and presses a kiss to my cheek. "On the house for the King's competitors."

I take a sip and scan the table. At the far end, Simon eyes me over the rim of his glass. I avert my gaze. I have no doubt he'll attempt to murder me in the final trial, regardless of the alliance I've built with Kressa.

He gives the other pirate, Mahone, an equally scathing look.

Cy—an Earth Court farmer—trails his fingers up the bare arm of a woman on his lap.

The chair across from me sits empty, and I gnaw the inside of my cheek.

Thea leans closer. "I think the person you're looking for just walked in the door."

The hair on the back of my neck rises, and a tug in my chest lifts my attention to the front of the tavern.

Kressa.

She looks up, and our gazes lock. The power in my chest sings, and I avert my eyes, my heart thrumming in my chest as she weaves through the crowd.

Thea slaps her hand over my heart. "You're fucking *glowing*."

Kressa approaches the table and settles into the seat across from me. She gives a pointed look at Thea's hand and raises an amused brow. I swallow.

The ruckus of the tavern bleeds into a din, and black clouds my vision. If she spots the light, she'll know who I really am.

Thea hoists herself up and slides onto my lap, pressing her back into my chest.

"Is Briar here?" Kressa says, as the waitress slides a tankard to her.

I clench my jaw together and glance at Thea.

She shakes her head, but her lips tilt. "No, she's not. Today is her birthday."

Kressa furrows her brow and stiffens, looking over her shoulder at the mass of bodies. *Briar? I can feel you.*

My skin buzzes, and I school my expression, slamming the mental door shut. It takes more effort to constantly keep it shut against her, when closing off the bridge to sea creatures is effortless.

She blinks and drags her attention back to us. "Interesting. She shares a birthday with the Princess of the Sea?"

"Yes, but she prefers to spend the entire day in bed. In fact, if you're looking for her, that's probably where she is now."

Thea wiggles in my lap, and I pinch her side. *Hard.*

She slaps my hand away and smirks. "Not now, Harriet. Save that for later."

I'm going to kill her. Flay her within an inch of her life and feed her to a sea serpent.

The corner of Kressa's lip tilts. "If Briar wants to spend the day in bed, I'll let her."

Eric grabs a handful of peanuts scattered over the table. "It's a shame we won't be able to go to any of the celebrations tonight."

"Celebrations?" I say under my breath.

Kressa narrows her eyes. "You shouldn't be going to them even if you could leave the castle. You'd be executed."

Mahone prods the table with the tip of his dagger. "You'll only be executed if you get caught."

I stiffen. There are no guards in the tavern to overhear, but Caelus pays a handsome reward to informants.

Mahone catches my hesitation. "Aye, you should know better than anyone that we still honor her." His lip curls, golden teeth glinting against his tawny skin. "Or are you one of the ones who gave up on the Princess of the Sea?"

Cy lifts his head from the woman's shoulder. "King Caelus can say whatever he wants about her—that she's dead or in hiding, but you'd be a fool to think she isn't waiting for the right time to come back."

My lips *almost* curl into a smile.

Simon eyes the men, but crosses his arms and presses his lips together. If anyone were to say something to Caelus, it's him.

Kressa sets her beer on the table and shakes her head. "If she was going to return, why would she wait an entire decade?"

I clench my hands into fists. "Maybe she's being held against her will, trying to get back."

"Tell that to the hundreds dying every day on the front."

I deflate, and guilt sweeps over me like a cresting wave. I lower my gaze and take a swig of lukewarm beer.

"She's a coward," she adds.

A twist to the knife already buried in my chest.

"I think we should go," I whisper into Thea's ear.

She turns and pushes out her bottom lip, pouting. Before she can object, the woman perched on Cy's lap leans over the table.

"Kressa, is it?" she says, brimstone in her eyes.

Kressa nods and takes another sip of beer, watching her over the rim.

The woman smiles, but it doesn't quite reach her eyes. "You call her a coward? Before she disappeared, her ship was attacked by a faction of the Sky Court's armada, and she single-handedly slayed them without a touch of her power." Her smile widens. "Rumor is she looked them in the eyes and laughed as she killed them one by one."

Thea stiffens, almost as if she remembers. If anything would spark her memory, it'd be that argument. She was livid when I ordered them to stay on shore while I took care of Caelus's soldiers that discovered Delterran's location.

None of them survived to share the secret.

Kressa lowers her gaze to her cup.

Cy nods, turning his deep brown eyes to Kressa. "When the war started, she calmed the waters long enough to give safe passage for those fleeing the Sky Court on the southern reaches of the world."

I sneak a glance at Kressa. She must know that story, considering I ferried thousands of Earth Court subjects across the sea. It's the reason why so many of the Earth Court honor me alongside King Golan. Or used to, at least.

Mahone points his dagger at Kressa. "She may be missing or hiding or imprisoned. Perhaps even dead. There's a lot of things she might be, but a coward isn't one of them."

My gaze travels around the crowded table. Over the past ten years, I thought my accomplishments—what makes me worthy—had died from word of mouth. But these people, from different courts, share stories about me with a gleam in their eye—one I recognize.

Hope.

My heart expands, filling my chest cavity.

Kressa finishes her beer and wipes her mouth, fingers dragging over foam. "I stand corrected." She presses herself from the table. "I have some things to take care of."

Thea tips her chin. "I'll let Briar know you were asking for her."

Kressa lowers her eyes and smiles—pure and genuine. I bite down on my cheek until a copper tang sweeps over my tongue.

She presses a palm to her chest, where my power settled in her, and scans the cramped tavern again. Shaking her head, she disappears into the crowd.

My tether to her stretches thinner the farther away she strides, and as she walks out the door, it snaps. My body stills, blood cools, and my power retreats to its corner.

I blow out a long breath. There must be a record somewhere of exchanged power, but as I search the recesses of my mind, I can't think of a single instance. My mother never mentioned the possibility, and I've never spotted this glow emanating from anyone else.

Thea stiffens and slides from my lap. "Why is Rita here?"

My head snaps up to where Rita frantically scans the room, her glasses askew on the bridge of her nose. The pads of my fingers press into the seat, but I hold steady.

I can't approach her looking like this.

Her gaze lands on Thea, and she scurries over. "Thea, thank

goodness you're here. I sent word for Briar, but the messenger couldn't find her anywhere. Have you seen her?"

Thea sneaks a glance at me and nods. "Not long ago. Why? Is everything okay?"

Rita eyes me and the pirate clothing, and grimaces. Leaning closer, she whispers into Thea's ear too quietly for me to hear.

Thea's eyes widen. "Are you sure?"

Rita pulls back and nods, her throat bobbing.

"You have no idea where they are?" Thea's voice cracks.

My mouth goes dry, and my hands clench the outline of my dagger.

Rita wrings her hands and shakes her head, grey curls swishing. "They disappeared in the middle of the night. But I'm looking for them. If you see Briar, please let her know I'll be at the safe house."

Thea reaches for Rita's hand and untangles her worried fingers. "She'll be there as soon as she can."

Rita presses her lips into a thin line. "Thank you."

She sends one more wary glance my way and turns, heading out to the bright afternoon.

I twist to Thea, who stares at the front door. "What did she say?"

Her face pales, fingers fumbling over the ironed pleats of her dress. "Four women in the safe house disappeared in the middle of the night, and haven't been seen or heard from." She gnaws at her fingernails. "They didn't take anything with them."

Missing.

Ever since she joined the competition, missing people reports have spiked.

I bolt from my seat, and the rough edges of the bench catch on my pants. My pulse pounds in my ears, louder than the voices in the tavern. "Will you be okay getting back to the castle?"

Thea stiffens. "Gemma said you only have—"

"I'll be fine. Will you?"

She nods. "Be aware of my surroundings. If I'm attacked, palm to the nose and knee to the groin. Then run as fast as I can."

Removing my hat, I drop it into her lap. "And don't—"

"Hesitate," she says with a sad smile, running her fingers along the brim. "I know. Now go help Rita."

I plant a kiss to her head and shoot a glare at the men—one that promises death if they so much as look at her the wrong way.

Shoving my way through the tavern, I burst into the late afternoon and take off toward the safe house. As my feet strike the ground, every warm thought of Kressa turns to stone and plummets to the bottom of the ocean.

37

———

The town passes in a blur. Shopkeepers slide metal chains over their storefronts, and merchants pack their wares into their carts, closing for the rest of the day.

My hair comes undone and clings to the sweat coating the back of my neck. Water splashes into my boots as I round into the alley. The back door of the safe house comes into view, and I slow to a stop.

I scan the other end, but everyone has already tucked themselves inside, avoiding the royal guards' patrol. Creeping through the shadows, a sour taste fills my mouth, and a ripple slithers under my skin. My muscles shift, hair lengthens, and in a light tug, the glamour disappears from my face.

My breath hitches. The sensation travels over my shoulders and shifts my frame, shortening my legs.

Bodies dressed in blue fill the mouth of the alley—wing-capped shoulders, blades glinting in the late afternoon sun.

My heart stops. Guards.

I throw myself behind a pile of rotting crates and hold my breath, peeking through the narrow slats.

One takes a step forward. "Did you hear that?"

My pulse pounds in my ears, and I clamp a hand over my mouth, stifling the whimper crawling up my throat.

He takes another step, tilts his head, and narrows his eyes at the barrier I'm crouched behind. Another step. "I'll go check it out."

My shaky fingers curl around my dagger, and my foot slips, splashing into a puddle. The guard takes a step closer. I slide the blade free as the toe of his boots come into view.

A shout comes from the street. The guard halts and turns on his heel, but hesitates.

"Now, Bradley!"

He flinches at his name, and takes off down the alley the way he came.

I slump against the wall and suck a deep breath. Even though the sun still hangs in the sky, no one is permitted on the streets at this hour. And if I were caught, in pirate clothing, there would be higher consequences. Pirates aren't rewarded with a swift execution.

I grit my teeth and peel myself from my spot, my pants soaked through with putrid water. They sag under the weight, but I hoist them up, tightening the belt as I jog to the back door.

Before I wrap my hand around the tarnished doorknob, the door flies open.

"Briar, get yourself in here before I have a heart attack!"

Rita shoots her arm through the doorway and yanks me in by the collar. Her clothes are rumpled, errant hairs hanging loose from her usually prim curls.

"I thought that guard was going to catch you," she breathes, a pale hand pressed to her chest. She scans my clothes and retreats a step, brow furrowed. "Why did I see those clothes on a pirate in a tavern?"

I kick the door shut and slide the lock, tugging the curtain over the small window. My gaze darts up the quiet staircase, and I lower my voice. "I want to tell you, but I can't."

"That was you. A competitor in The Gales." Her breath catches. "Oh, Briar, what have you done?"

"That's not important right now. What is, are those missing women."

The wrinkles on her forehead deepen, and she shakes her head, leading me toward the stairs. "Right. I'll show you their room."

We climb the carpeted steps to the narrow hallway lined with bedrooms on either side. A large shared bathroom caps off the end.

Rita stops at a door and eases it open into a room lit by a window on the far side. Four small beds line the walls, each with the sheets pulled back, pooling to the floor. A pile of clothes lay neatly folded on top of a chest of drawers, like one of them did laundry but hadn't yet put it away.

"Their bags are still here," Rita whispers. "As well as any money they have saved over the last few months."

"Have you asked everyone if they know anything?"

She nods. "They know nothing. But they're all on edge, hardly leaving the house in fear they'll be taken."

I lift the mattresses one by one, but nothing has been hidden between the bed and the wooden frame. Circling the room, I pause in front of the tall dresser and pull a drawer open. I shove my hand beneath the clothes and slide it along the seam at the back. Nothing.

I open the next drawer. Nothing.

Dropping to my knees, I open the bottom one and dip my hand in. My fingers brush a slip of paper.

My breath hitches, and I ease it out.

Its edges are frayed, as if it was frantically ripped from a larger piece of parchment. Swallowing, I unfold the paper.

The room spins.

I bolt to my feet and yank the pendant from beneath my shirt. Holding it out, I compare it to the scribbled drawing on the paper—the mountains are drawn in shaky ink, and the swirling symbols are messy, but it's an undeniable match to the necklace.

Rage burns a trail under my skin, but not like the searing lick of flames. It's the cool calm of the sea before a tempest swells, the harmless eddy before it morphs into a deadly vortex. I crumple the paper in my fist.

"I need a change of clothes."

Rita looks over my shoulder, and her face pales. "Do you know where they are?"

"No, but I know who took them."

Her eyes widen. "Jenna's clothes should fit you."

She disappears into the hallway. I peel off the wet clothes and shove them into a canvas sack hanging on the back of the door. Making quick work of the sheathe, I undo the belt and set it on a mattress.

Rita returns with a stack of clothes, and I shrug them on, replacing my dagger at my thigh, well hidden beneath the hem of my tunic.

"Are they going to be okay?" she whispers, staring out the window at the ocean stretching into the distance. She turns to me. "Be honest."

I shoulder the canvas sack, its bottom soaked with water. I study Rita's eyes—the only part of her face untouched by time. "I don't know. But I'm going to find out. And if they're hurt, I'll kill who's responsible."

Rita nods, her brown irises darkening. "Make them suffer."

She leads me to the back door, and I braid my hair back. "Don't let anyone leave tonight, and going forward, they are not to leave alone, only in pairs or groups. If you find more of these"—I hold up the slip of paper—"send someone for me immediately."

She nods. "Be safe, Briar. Please."

I fold my hands around hers and run my thumb over the fragile skin. How many more goodbyes do we have? Tears prick my eyes, but I swallow them down. "You too, Rita."

Her eyes glisten, but she looks away and opens the door. She stiffens. "Who are you?"

My hand palms my blade, and I dart around her into the doorway. At the base of the steps, with a single foot on the stairs, stands Kressa.

Her brow furrows. "Briar?"

I guide Rita behind me and back into the house. "Lock the door. Don't open it for anyone."

Her jaw quivers, but she closes it and slides the bolt into place.

The top step groans under my weight, and I lower my sack to the stairs as I pin Kressa with a glare. "What are you doing here?"

"I thought I saw Harriet come this way."

"You were mistaken." With cool calm, I step down and yank my dagger out. "Where are the missing women?"

She retreats and draws a blade from her ankle. "I don't know what you're talking about."

My lips tilt into an icy, sinister grin. I pull the crumpled paper from my pocket and throw it to the ground at her feet. "You don't? Are you going to tell me this is for luck as well?"

She stares at the paper as it sinks into a shallow puddle, blurring the ink.

"Where are they?" I hiss.

My power swells, almost close enough to grasp. I reach for it, but it slips through my fingers.

"Briar," she says, no more than a whisper against the blood pounding in my ears. "You won't find them. Let me explain."

My vision glows red, and I bare my teeth. "No need to explain."

In a flash of metal, I slice my blade through the air. Kressa blocks and wraps a hand around my collar, but I plant a kick into her stomach. She flies back and slams into the wall.

She rubs at her shoulder and grimaces. "Must you always resort to violence?"

"I know enough about you to know your words can't be trusted."

She grits her teeth and rolls out her neck. "If that's how it's going to be, so be it."

Pushing off the wall, she lowers her shoulder and barrels into me. My foot slips on the slick stones, and I slam into a deep puddle.

Water splashes, soaking my clothes, and my dagger sinks into the muck, hilt glinting above the surface. Kressa pins my wrists to the cobblestones and throws a leg over my middle, straddling me.

Not so deadly without your dagger, are you? She lowers her face and smirks. *Your door is wide open, love.*

I narrow my eyes and throw my forehead into her nose. It hits with a crack, and she brings her hands to her face, cupping the blood. I buck my hips, throw her off, and snatch my dagger from the water.

My palm meets her shoulder blades, slamming her onto her stomach, and she grunts as her face meets stone. I settle my knee on her spine and bring the tip of my dagger to her throat.

You were saying? I put enough pressure on my blade to pierce skin. *Tell me where they are.*

She grabs my wrist and bucks, somersaulting me over her. Twisting, she captures my waist between her legs and throws me onto my back. She pins my wrists over my head with one hand, the other angling her blade at my throat.

I thrash, but it's no use.

She leans over, chest heaving. Water beads at her lips and

nose and drips onto me. Her dark hair is soaked through, hanging around her face. *I need you to trust me.*

I slam my mental door shut. "I'll never trust you. *Never.* You're no better than Caelus."

She goes rigid. The sharp edge against my throat disappears, and her weight lifts, legs untangling.

I push myself up, wet clothes clinging to my skin. Kressa stands frozen, water soaking through the thin fabric of her shirt, plastered to her body like a second skin.

Our gazes meet, and her hand loosens around the hilt of her blade. It clatters to the ground, the echo reverberating through the alley.

She taps against the door in my mind. I ignore it.

"I'm nothing like him," she whispers. "I'd never hurt you."

I exhale, and the inhale burns my lungs. Singes my nerves. "Bullshit."

I shove her into the brick alley wall. Her back hits with a thud, but she doesn't flinch, doesn't blink, doesn't fight back. Gritting my teeth, I fist her collar and slam her into the wall again.

Nothing.

My blood boils against my veins, and I bask in it—let it consume me until all that's left is pure, unadulterated rage.

Her face remains blank. Unfazed. *I'm not going to fight you.*

A scream climbs up my throat, and I flick my dagger, angling it directly over the thick scar spanning her throat. Her pulse thrums against the blade, as if in invitation. I lower my face within inches of hers. "Get out of my head."

Then learn how to keep me out when your emotions go haywire. Control it.

I press my lips into a thin line and slam the mental door so hard it rattles on its hinges.

She smirks. "That's better, love."

"Caelus said you're a spy from the Earth Court," I seethe. "I'll ask one more time, what did you do with them?"

A strangled laugh comes from her throat. "I'm not a spy. You are."

I press harder, until the scar puckers around the sharp edge, and ignore my power screaming to pull away. "Answer my question."

The amusement wipes from her face. "If you think I'd harm them, you know nothing about me."

"You're right. I don't. So start talking."

She presses her lips together, and her fingers brush over my waist. The water pooled in our shirts seeps into my skin, calling attention to every spot our bodies touch, the fabric hardly a barrier. My breath catches, blade falters.

"I'll take you to them. Tonight."

Her soft tone caresses my skin, and the power thrumming in my chest grows. I meet her gaze, and she holds it.

Something behind her eyes softens, and I lower my blade. "Okay."

"Meet me in my room tonight."

Nodding, I retreat to the steps and thread the canvas bag over my shoulder. I shoot one last warning glare at her. "If you ever return here again, I'll kill you."

"No, you won't."

I sheathe my dagger and stride past her. "I would. With a smile on my face."

38

———

I peer through the bedroom door into the east wing hallway. At the entrance, two guards stand watch, ensuring none of the competitors partake in tonight's forbidden celebrations.

My heart thrums in my ears. If I'm caught, I'll find myself on the guillotine by morning.

One guard lowers to his knee, fussing with the laces on his boots. I dart across the hallway—my feet no louder than the warm breeze floating through the open windows. Holding my breath, I reach for Kressa's doorknob, but it swings open and an arm catches me around my waist.

I gasp, and Kressa swings me into the room, silently pressing the door shut. Her arm tightens, and my cheek settles against her chest as I catch my breath. A steady beat thrums in my ear, and I lean into it, pressing my eyes shut.

Her other hand settles on the back of my head—a warm, comforting weight. My power sighs, as if it's been holding its breath.

"You're glowing."

The light emanating from my chest coats the room in an emerald glow. But my power rests dormant in her chest, unlit.

I pull away and back up a safe distance, snuffing out the light. "How did you know I was coming?"

She rolls the cuffs of her sleeves to her elbows and shrugs. "I felt you. I could almost taste your fear when you were crossing the hall. And just now, when your head was on my chest"—she swallows—"I felt your relief."

"I told you to stay out of my head."

"Trust me, Briar, I'm trying to," she says, voice hardening. "But everything you send through that passage slams into me. You need to learn how to control it."

Her final words aren't a demand, but a plea. She blows out a ragged breath and runs a hand through her hair.

"Why?" I tilt my head. "Why is it so important I control it?"

The soft edges in her features disappear, replaced with a hard, unforgiving glare. "Because I can't breathe when you feel sad. I can't think straight when you feel rage. I can't focus on *anything*. That's why."

I flinch at the accusation in her voice. "As soon as we find your brother, I'll be gone and you don't have to worry about it anymore."

Her hands fist at her sides, and a muscle tics in her jaw. "Good."

I check my mental door. Sealed tight. My emotions shouldn't spill into her, unless this connection we have is strengthening.

No. If that was the case, my power would flare in her chest.

"Were you in the tavern earlier today?" she whispers. "With Thea and Harriet?"

The breath entering my lungs freezes. "No."

She gives me a slow, assessing stare. "Interesting." Moonlight pours over her cheekbones and drips down the slope of her neck as she straightens her collar. "We're going through Harriet's room."

"Harriet's room?"

She nods. "We'll use the servant's door. She's never there, so I assume she won't care if we use it."

My eyes narrow. "You sound like you've used it before."

She strides to the bedroom door. "I have."

"How often?"

A pause. "Often enough."

I search her face, but it gives nothing away. "And where do you go?"

"I'll show you." She wraps a callused hand around mine. "Ready?"

I rip my hand from her grip. "I'm perfectly capable of walking on my own."

Her lips quirk, a sparkle in her eye. "Suit yourself."

The guards' voices seep under the door, too low to overhear, and Kressa eases it open, her chest unmoving as she peers into the hallway.

"Now," she whispers.

She slips out, and I follow close behind, keeping an eye trained on the guards. We pass, unnoticed, into Harriet's room, and Kressa darts to the corner. Her fingers trace over the wall and, as if she's done it a hundred times, she finds the seam within seconds.

My brows stitch together, and I shift on my feet as fetid air floats from the dark corridor. But I steel my spine. I don't know where she's taking me, but I'll follow her anywhere if it means getting those women back.

"I know you've used this passageway before," she says, "but it becomes treacherous. Impossible to see. If you don't know where you're going, you could fall and break your neck. So, I suggest you take my hand."

Her fingertips graze the back of my hand, sending a wave of shivers up my cloaked arm. I hesitate and take a step back.

A low chuckle rumbles through my bones, her face blanketed in shadows. "You've pinned me to a wall with a kiss and held a dagger to my throat, but you're too scared to hold my hand?"

I scowl and accept her hand, squeezing hard enough to make her flinch. "I'm not scared of anything."

"I know." Her eyes glint in the dark. "But I am."

A warmth seeps into my heart and spreads across my chest, wrapping around my muscles and bones. The tension in my shoulders releases—a reprieve I haven't had in weeks.

Kressa squeezes my hand. "Did you feel that?"

I nod, slowly. "Did that come from you?"

"I hope it helped."

She pulls me through the doorway.

Our footfalls echo as we descend the stairwell through the floors I'm accustomed to. I trail my free hand along the inner wall, mapping the number of floors we pass. Kressa runs her thumb over the back of my hand, soothing my nerves.

A puddle splashes at our feet, and we come to a stop. Thick, putrid air infiltrates my nose, and bumps coat my skin from the sudden drop in temperature. I inch closer to Kressa, my eyes useless in the pitch dark.

"We must be below the dungeons," I whisper. "We can't exit the castle from here."

"Who said we're leaving?"

A chill seeps into my marrow. My hand loosens, and I struggle from her grip, but she holds tight.

"Where are you taking me?" I snarl.

"A bit further. We're under the mountain right now, and if we don't hurry, we'll miss them."

She takes a step, but I plant my feet. "Under the mountain? But there's nothing on the other side. The maps—"

"Are wrong. How else would royalty get out during a siege?"

I blink. Only someone with prior knowledge of the castle and these passageways would know their way through the dark. That's how she found me on the tower before the sunrise. She didn't simply find the door, she knew where to look.

"You worked in the castle," I breathe.

Without answering, she urges me forward, and we bank around a sharp corner. At the far end of a corridor, light crawls through the cracks of a short, decaying door. A thick layer of moss coats the crumbling walls.

Kressa releases my hand, and I follow, copying her steps should the floor give way. She grabs the doorknob and throws her shoulder into the wood. It scrapes over gravel, and when it gives way, a roaring fills my ears.

Brine sneaks into my nose, and I breathe it in. "The ocean."

She smiles over her shoulder and ducks through the doorway. My leggings snag on the raw edges of the threshold, but I tug them free as my feet sink into rocky, black sand.

A cove stretches overhead, and at its mouth, the night sky twinkles. Waves sweep up the shore, parting for a small rowboat nestled into the sand. At the bow, a man dressed in all black nods to Kressa.

His face turns to me, and the air leaves my lungs.

"Simon?"

Kressa nods.

"He attacked Harriet," I snarl.

"Well, so did I." She shoves her hands into her pockets and shrugs. "Pirates killed his mother and sister, so you can't blame him. I've told him to leave Harriet alone, though."

"And you trust him?"

"More than anyone."

I suck in my cheek and scan the base of the mountain. A small dwelling sits tucked into a pile of jagged boulders, blending into the terrain. I'd miss it if it weren't for the small, golden lantern glowing in the window.

Four cloaked figures sit around a table.

"Go," Kressa whispers. "Check on them."

I bolt to the small shack, sand flying up around my feet. I whip open the door, and it slams into the wall, startling the women.

One stands, her short blonde hair masked by a hood. Her blue eyes widen. "Irene?"

Their faces are unmarred, hands and ankles free of ropes or shackles. Four rucksacks line the wall beside the hearth.

My lips part, and a cry almost escapes my mouth. "You're okay."

Heavy footsteps enter the room behind me, and the door squeals as it shuts.

"*You're* Irene?"

Kressa leans against the door, searching my face as if this is the first time she's seen me. Her head tilts, eyes softening.

I nod. "Of course, I am."

She leans forward and dips her mouth to my ear. "Not at all a dragon hoarding her jewels."

"I still breathe fire like one."

"I don't doubt that for a moment, love."

Her power stirs in my chest, and I pull myself away before I light the room green. I sink to a knee in front of the table and look up at one of the women. "Has anyone hurt you? Or forced you to come here?"

She shakes her head. "Even after everything you've done for us, we aren't safe here in Sarenia. But Kressa promised to take us somewhere where the Sky Court can't find us."

"And you trust her?"

"We didn't at first," another woman says, "but she's shown us nothing but kindness."

I recognize her from the trade I did a few months ago. Her hair is longer, face filled out. Healthy.

Kressa lays a hand on my shoulder. "I can answer all your questions after we get them in the boat. The ship can't wait in the harbor much longer without being seen."

I rise, and the women follow suit, collecting their bags from the wall.

Leaning to Kressa, I whisper, "If you or your men so much as lay a finger on these women, I'll slit your throats."

"If anything happens to them, I give you permission."

She doesn't blink, the intensity in her eyes is all the confirmation I need. I draw a deep breath through my nose. "Thank you."

Her thumb cradles my chin, and she tilts my head to meet her gaze. "Did you just thank me?"

"Unfortunately, yes."

So, she does have a heart.

I pull away and slam the mental door shut. "Don't get used to it."

But as I watch the women file out of the shack, each sending Kressa a teary smile, something in my chest thaws. The impenetrable fortress I've built lowers its guard, ever so slightly —for her.

She swallows, and her knowing eyes meet mine. For once, I don't look away. I offer the sliver of what I have—this feeling of gratitude and vulnerability. A long, silent moment passes by, nothing but the beating of our hearts and the women's footsteps trudging through sand outside.

"Thank you," she says, holding the door open.

Simon guides each woman into the hull, and they lower their heads between their knees. He throws a large tarp over them, and Kressa helps him secure it to the sides with ropes.

I stand on dry sand and worry my lip.

Kressa nods to Simon and whispers something I can't hear over the crashing waves. They push the boat into the surf, and Simon jumps in at the bow, collecting a pair of oars. Kressa returns to my side, the bottom half of her pants dripping with water.

Her shoulder brushes against mine. "The tarp is to hide them. If someone spots the rowboat in the harbor, they'll assume it's just a fisherman."

I swallow. "But on a night like tonight? The Princess's birthday? If anyone sees him—"

She tucks a strand of hair behind my ear, the pads of her fingers skimming my lobe. "This is his third trip of the night. I asked him to take them last so I could prove to you they're okay."

The small boat disappears around the mouth of the cove. My heart tumbles against my ribs and I hold my breath, praying we don't hear an alarm.

"So you *are* the reason why women have been going missing."

She nods. "I suppose I am."

I dig my heel into the obsidian sand, so dark I don't know where my shoe ends and the sand begins. "How do you get them here? Through the castle?"

"I can't tell you that."

I glare at her out the corner of my eye, but she shakes her head. "You can threaten me if you want, but people are risking their lives to help. I won't jeopardize their safety."

"You'd rather die than share their names?"

"Yes."

I study her face. "But you told me about Simon."

She weaves her fingers through mine. "It's not only them I worry about. The more you know, the more dangerous it becomes for you."

"You didn't seem to care about my safety when you threatened to tell the king about my theft." I stare at our clasped hands—the way our fingers fit so well together.

She lets out a soft laugh. "Things have changed."

The dark water reflects off her eyes, and she inhales a long breath through her nose, breathing me in. My heart rattles in my chest, and she leans in, ever so slightly.

A bird call floats into the cove and echoes off the walls.

Kressa releases a breath and drops my hand. "They made it."

I blink and take a small step away from her, but her touch on my hand lingers like a ghost. "Where are they going?"

"Ignata."

I tilt my head. "What's in Ignata?"

She opens her mouth. Closes it. Wind whips around the cove, tossing my cloak around my ankles and kicking up bits of dry sand. The door leading into the castle sways on its hinges.

Finally, she says, "The King is there."

I shake my head. "He's dead."

She huffs and drags a foot over the small strip of sand between us. "That's what everyone believes, even Caelus. It made it easy to rebuild the kingdom and strengthen our army. The night the Sky Court invaded, they escaped through this cove."

This is what the selkies meant when they said Earth Court reinforcements would arrive. Hope blooms in my chest, yet doubt claws its way in.

When I gain my freedom, will they fight alongside me after everything I've done? Will Kressa?

My mind snags on Kressa's words, and I freeze. "They? Others escaped with King Golan?"

She nods. "Prince Barren did as well."

The earth tilts on its axis, and my knees threaten to buckle.

I stumble back a step.

Barren's face slams into my mind—his deep brown eyes and

the way they widened when I told him I'd rather watch the world end than marry him. How I said I'd rather lose my crew and my power than rule by his side.

My blood thrashes in my ears.

"But I—that's impossible," I whisper. I watched blood flow from the wound at his neck and soak into his hair. I *smiled* as the life left his eyes.

"The Princess of the Sea tried to assassinate him that night, but she failed."

Failed. I bring a hand to my mouth. "Do you know him? The prince?"

A nod. "We're friends."

Friends. She probably worked for him. A spy, like me. "And he knows you've joined the competition? That you're searching for your brother?"

"No, neither him nor King Golan."

I swallow. "Were you here, in the castle? That night?"

She pauses for a long stretch of time, and I worry I've crossed a line. My curiosity could be dangerous, yet so could getting myself tangled in Barren's plans.

"I was," she says.

A tremor sweeps over my body, and I dive into my mind, checking the mental door. It's shut tight, protecting against an accidental confession. Questions flow through my thoughts, but I keep them to myself. The more I ask, the more suspicious I'll become.

"I have something for you," she whispers, cutting through my panic. She pulls a small drawstring bag out of her pocket and holds it out. "Happy birthday, Briar."

I step back, shaking my head. "I don't want it." I don't want anything from her—*shouldn't* want anything from someone so closely tied to Barren.

Her gaze lands on my collarbone, and she slides a finger under the chain around my neck, lifting the pendant free. She holds it against the moonlight and admires the etching. "You don't always have to have your guard up. Harriet told me if she wins, she's giving you a ship. Freedom. I see the longing stares you give the ocean. You miss it."

I shake my head. "You don't know me."

"I know enough to know you're brave." She steps closer. "That you'd risk your life for someone you care about. Hell, even for strangers. I've watched you go toe to toe with Caelus without batting an eye." Her eyes burn bright, and she cups my face. "I know you well enough to know you amaze me."

An emerald glow shoots from my chest, coating the cove. The hair on the back of my neck stands, and a shiver runs down my spine. My power urges—begs—me to close the distance between us.

Her gaze locks onto me as she holds the small gift steady in the palm of her hand. "You're brave, Briar. You always have been. But you don't need to be brave with me."

A wave crashes and sprays mist against the back of her head. It slams into my cheeks, burning my skin like a branding iron. Water arcs toward us and reaches the upper bank of the beach, covering her shoes to the ankle.

My heart stops.

I shove her away and scramble back. Foam tips the wave, reaching for me. I throw myself into the sand, and it halts inches away from my feet before retreating back to its home. I press my hand to my thundering heart and swallow down mouthfuls of air.

Kressa reaches out. "Are you okay?"

My fingers dig into the sand, and I glare up at her. She's blackmailed and lied to me. Friends with the man I tried to kill. And what the hell am I doing? I'm in love with Isolde—promised myself to her.

"Don't touch me," I say.

Her face falls, and her hand drops to her side. I swing my legs under me and rise, wiping the sand off my leggings.

"Briar, did I do something? You feel—"

"Don't tell me what I feel."

She flinches back, and whatever comfort she was channeling into my body disappears.

"I can find my way back," I add.

A cold, hard mask slips over her face. "Understood. Tomorrow night we'll look for Elias before the final ball."

I nod.

She turns on her heel, but hesitates and drops the gift at my feet. I watch her leave, and when the door swings shut, I pull the bag from the sand.

I loosen the ties and flip it into my palm. A small, carved, wooden figurine slips out.

A ship.

39

A drum jolts me from sleep.

Grey dawn seeps through the curtains, and a lead weight settles in my stomach.

"Briar," Thea whispers.

A lump rises in my throat. "I know."

Execution drums.

Jumping from bed, I dart to the dressing room. I throw a gown over my head and lace the corset, but my fingers tremble on the cords.

"Let me," Thea says, coming up behind me.

She pulls the laces from my hands and I twist my hair into a braid, letting it drape over my heaving chest. "I have to stop them."

Thea's fingers pause. "They know the law, Briar. They know they shouldn't have been out last night. There's nothing you can do."

The drums continue their chant, each beat a nail into my chest. "But I have to try."

She finishes the back of my dress and steps away, her eyes red and swollen.

My brows pinch. "What's wrong?"

A tear trails down her face, and she knuckles it away. "Every night I go to bed terrified I'll wake up to these drums—that it'll be you on the platform. If you get caught, they'll kill you."

I fold her into a hug. "I'm not going to get caught."

A shudder wracks her body. "I can't lose you."

Leaning back, I bracket her face with my hands and commit to memory every line of her face, the slope of her jaw, the fierce blue of her eyes. "You won't. To the ends of the earth, remember?"

She lets out a strangled laugh, but a smile doesn't follow. "To the ends of the earth."

A fist pounds on the door and tears us apart.

Thea swipes at her eyes and sucks in a deep breath, straightening her shoulders. She pads to the dresser and hands me my dagger. "I'll feel better if you have this."

"Thank you." I make quick work strapping it around my upper thigh.

A knock comes again, louder. I stride to the door and pull it open.

My blood runs cold.

"Briar," Caelus drawls.

His tailored navy suit is pressed free of wrinkles, and his lips curve into an easy grin. Like he's not about to order the deaths of innocent people.

I breathe through my nose and stop my hands from grabbing my dagger. "My king."

"You'll be joining me for the executions."

His words aren't a question or an invitation, but a demand. I glance into the room. Thea's throat bobs on a swallow, and her hand clenches around a bed post, as if that's the only thing holding her back.

"Of course," I say, lifting my cloak from the hook. I wrap it over my shoulders and follow him into the hallway.

A pair of royal guards trail at a distance, and even in the heart of the castle, the drums reverberate through the walls. I grit my teeth and keep my feet steady down the grand staircase.

Caelus holds my fingertips, guiding me as if I'm incapable.

His grip tightens until my knuckles crack. "The ball is tomorrow. You have until then to find out Kressa's secrets. You wouldn't want anyone to get hurt now, would you?" He squeezes harder. "I believe you're quite close to Thea."

My stomach tumbles. "You wouldn't."

He leans closer, his breath a brand on my skin. "You know, I could kill her now if I wanted to. My guards have seen her with that pirate. Harriet, if I remember right. And that belt I found in your room nearly three weeks ago? It wasn't really your uncle's, was it?"

The blood drains from my face, and he releases my hand.

He smirks. "I didn't think so. But, I'm willing to turn a blind eye if you find the information I want."

The words sit on the edge of my tongue. I could tell him who Kressa really is and guarantee Thea's safety. But she'd expose my theft. And even if she didn't, the people she's been sending to Ignata would have nowhere to go.

That gives me one option—get Thea far, far away.

I swallow past the rising lump in my throat and nod. "Yes, Your Highness."

Bodies pack the courtyard, cramming into the space for the execution they're required to attend. Lined against the back wall, surrounded by armed guards, stand a group of people dressed in rags, their eyes red and swollen. Family.

Royal guards part the crowd for us, and Caelus grips my upper arm in a vice. We come to the raised platform, and my chest grows heavy, bile gathering in my throat. I drop my gaze as we climb the set of stairs, unable to bear looking at those who will die for honoring me.

Another drum tolls, rattling the platform.

It should be me kneeling on the wood, waiting for a blade to strike the base of my neck. It should be me dying.

I swallow mouthfuls of air, but it doesn't reach my lungs, and my breaths quicken. Black blurs the edges of my vision, and I fist my hands into my dress, fighting the sting behind my eyes.

Briar, love. Breathe.

A single tear falls to the wooden board, stained with blood from prior executions. Head bowed, I scan the crowd and find Kressa staring at me.

You're okay. I'm here. Focus on me.

Another tear falls. Her words wouldn't be so calming if she knew I was the princess she hates so fiercely.

Caelus brings his mouth to my ear and snarls, "What's wrong with you?"

"I'm fine."

Isolde appears from behind a group of armed guards, and she stops on Caelus's other side. Diamonds drip from her gown like frozen raindrops, and I study her from under my lashes, begging her to look my way—to offer the comfort we so often give each other.

She doesn't.

Caelus regards her. "You'd think they would learn, after all these years."

"Serves them right," Isolde says, her lip curled.

Pressure builds in my chest. In an entire decade, I've never known her to be so cruel.

In the crowd, Kressa watches me, and a calm resolve sweeps though the bond, coating me like a quilt. I steel my spine and raise my head, giving my followers the dignity and respect they deserve.

Ropes bind the wrists of a dozen people kneeling on the platform, sacks thrown over their heads. The one closest to me shifts, his bare knees bloody against the rough wood. His skin is aged, hands wrinkled. Grey hair peeks from under the sack.

The elderly man from the slums.

My breath catches.

Dolma.

She must have been with him last night. My heart ricochets against my ribs as I search for a protruding belly. I stagger forward and trace a hand over my dagger.

Don't.

I freeze at Kressa's voice. Each of my muscles strain, ready to spring across the platform and take the blade meant for Dolma. *I can't let them kill her.*

She isn't up there.

I blink. *How do you know?*

Caelus waves a gust of wind over the courtyard, silencing the crowd. "Those before you have been accused and charged of worshipping the Princess of the Sea. An act punishable by death."

Cheers ring from the crowd, as if death should ever be reason to celebrate.

Kressa doesn't take her eyes off me. *She left on one of the ships, with a newborn daughter safely swaddled in her arms.*

My eyes widen. *You saved her?*

Another breeze silences the applause.

Kressa nods, her lips pressed into a thin line. *If she's important to you, she's important to me. But I couldn't save them all.*

"Remove the sacks," Caelus bellows.

The guards obey and tear the sacks off, revealing an entire group from the slums. People who sleep without a roof over their heads, not knowing where their next meal will come from.

My chest hollows out, and the platform spins beneath my feet.

That day I found you in the castle was my first time returning to Sarenia after it fell. I had just come off a ship.

My fists unfurl.

I understand why you love the ocean so much, Kressa says, her voice a salve to my nerves. *There's nothing more peaceful than the sway of a ship, the endless possibilities of the sea stretching ahead of you.*

"Guards," Caelus yells, "ready your blades."

I bite down on my cheek hard enough to draw blood, and my pulse thrashes in my ears, drowning out the drums gaining speed.

Briar. Focus on my voice. I'm here.

The booming crowd blurs, and my ears fill with a high-pitched ring, dulling each of my senses.

That morning, before the first trial, when I found you on the turret? I've never experienced anything like that sunrise, watching the way it painted your face in violets and golds. The way your eyes came to life at the sight of the sun kissing the horizon. It was the most beautiful thing I've ever seen.

Metal glistens, blades reflecting the sun as the guards lift them far over their heads. Tears stream down my face, and I hold on to my connection with Kressa like a lifeline.

A warmth sweeps over me, calm and steady, like my sun-beaten deck on a summer afternoon.

I'm here, my love.

"All hail the King," a guard calls, voice projected on a wisp of wind.

Blades arc through the air and meet the soft flesh of the men and women lining the platform. A scream escapes my throat, drowned out by the pounding drums, and a spray of blood coats the front of my dress.

As one, the bodies fall. Lifeless. Blood pools across the boards, seeping through the cracks.

I pin Caelus with a glare. "You're a monster."

Like a whip, he slaps me. My head jerks to the side, and somewhere in the crowd, a commotion stirs. My vision reddens, blocking out everything but seething rage.

I bring my fingers to the stinging skin where a welt is already forming.

He lowers his face within an inch of mine. "Do not forget who you're speaking to. One toe out of line, Briar, and I'll make you watch me torture her. That slap will seem like child's play." He grips my arm, fingernails digging into skin. "Do you understand?"

I pin him with a glare that promises death, and my power swells beneath the surface, just out of reach. Over his shoulder, Isolde watches me. Blood has splattered onto her face, and a single tear falls from her eyes, trailing down her cheek.

Caelus shakes me. "I said, do you understand?"

My exhale is like fire, and I blink my eyes, pulling away as if his words don't singe my very core. "I understand."

He releases me with a shove. Guards drag the bodies off the platform by their ankles, their arms dragging through their own blood.

"Good. Don't forget your place, courtesan." Caelus straightens the collar of his jacket. "Isolde, come."

He stalks down the platform.

"Are you okay?" I whisper—the first words I've said to her since the night in the hallway.

Isolde releases a shaky breath and opens her mouth, but she clamps it shut and swallows, following Caelus through the crowd. I should chase her, but my feet stay rooted to the spot as I watch the executed bodies disappear from the courtyard.

Those people so fearlessly honored me, knowing death was a certainty if caught. Yet none of them shed a tear when they met their end. No, they held their heads high while I stood back and watched.

A coward.

My vision tunnels to the fresh blood on the platform. Blood that was spilled because of me.

Bile rises in my throat. I've failed them.

Grabbing the rail, I stumble down the steps. I have to get Thea to safety and focus on winning the competition and—

Arms envelope me. I go for my dagger, but a familiar scent blankets me and soothes my racing thoughts.

"I've got you," Kressa whispers, pulling me into her chest.

Tears stream down my face, and I slump into her. Her hand runs down the length of my hair, and her heart beats a steady, calming rhythm. My fists unravel, fingers finding the fabric of her shirt.

"I didn't save them," I whisper against her chest.

"Even if you tried to, I would've stopped you. I would've cleared that platform myself to stop you from doing whatever you were planning."

"Why? Because I'm your ticket to getting information on Caelus?" I will my words to bite, but they fall short—breathy and weak. "Because, without me, you won't be able to find Elias?"

She leans back and cups my face, eyes fierce. "Because I can't bear the thought of losing you."

My lips part, and I search her face—the concern etched between her brows, the bob of her throat.

Her thumb trails lightly over the welt. "I'm going to kill him for this."

The courtyard clears of everyone but the two of us and the long wooden platform at my back. Sunlight crests over the castle walls, bathing us in gold. But its warmth doesn't seep into my skin. Only Kressa's does.

She lowers her forehead to mine, and my power crawls to her, pulling against its short chain. It's there, swirling and alive, but shackled down. Everything I am, bound to a curse.

I lift my gaze to hers. "Why does my power want you so badly?"

The words slip out unprovoked and saturate the sliver of air between us.

Her teeth skim her lower lip. "I've been wondering the same thing."

"It's never reacted this way to anyone before."

"Mine either." She breaks our embrace and holds me at arm's length. "I don't need your help anymore. I refuse to force you into something you don't want to do, so I'm breaking our agreement."

My breath hitches. I should be relieved, yet her words twist my stomach, stifling my power. This connection must mean something, or it wouldn't react to her the way it does. And my heart—well, my heart doesn't know what it wants.

I lower my eyes and nod.

When I look up, she's gone.

40

———

The sun sinks below the horizon, sending a chill over the dining hall. Goosebumps prickle my skin, and I push the meat and roast vegetables around my plate.

Caelus leans away from me, deep in conversation with a noble. Across the room, Kressa's head is bowed over her plate, yet she hasn't touched a thing.

"Any hint on what you're going to announce in the coming days?" the noble asks, voice lowered.

My ears prick up, and I angle my body closer. I force a small carrot into my mouth, but it turns to ash on my tongue.

"It's still in the works. But, this new advancement could mean victory."

I tighten my grip on the fork, and the metal bites into my palm. Victory over the Sea Court? My mouth turns to cotton.

Did they find Delterran?

A royal guard enters and strides down the center aisle. He pauses at the bottom of the dais and bows. "Your Majesty."

Caelus dismisses the noble and motions for the guard to climb the dais. The hair on my body stands on edge as he leans over Caelus's shoulder and lowers his voice to a whisper. I crane my neck, but I can't discern any of his words.

"Good. And you replaced the quilt?"

My brows furrow, and air rushes into my lungs. Of course. The mirror. The one I've never seen uncovered, hidden in plain sight.

I press my hand to Caelus's shoulder. "If you'll please excuse me, I have someone I need to talk to."

Isolde's fork stops halfway to her mouth, forgotten, as her eyes meet mine.

But what she said about the people executed this morning haunts me, replaying in my head over and over. The lack of sympathy in her voice, for those who suffered a needless death.

Ice forms behind her irises, and she returns her attention to her plate.

Caelus scowls, glancing at Kressa. "You're excused, courtesan."

My nostrils flare, but I blow out a breath and stand. Gazes follow me—Isolde's like a brand on my spine—as I step from the dais and stride past the tables. The runner sinks under my feet, and I shake out my hands, willing my heart to slow.

I knock on Kressa's mental door.

Yes?

Her voice floats straight through my head and down my body, soothing every muscle and nerve. My exhale nearly comes out as a sigh, but I keep my eyes trained on the door looming closer.

I know where he is.

Shock filters through the bond. *Are you sure?*

No.

A pause, then, *Tell me what you need.*

Meet me in front of Caelus's room in five minutes. We have to act while everyone is occupied.

I clear the archway, and the door swings shut behind me.

The castle is a blur as I take the marble steps two at a time, bolting down the hall to Caelus's chambers.

Hushed conversation comes from two guards stationed outside his doors. Pressing a hand over my heart, I sidle up against the cold wall. I comb through my hair and throw it over my shoulder, painting on a sleepy smile.

I turn the corner, and the guards stiffen, but their shoulders relax as their gazes rake along my swaying hips. I wet my lips, tugging the lower one between my teeth.

"Good evening," I purr, wrapping a hand around my dagger.

My nails dig into the hilt. These guards partook in the execution—severed the heads of innocent people without a second thought. Fresh hatred swells deep in my gut.

"To what do we owe this pleasure?" one says, eyes glued to my chest.

The other smirks. "Did the king agree to share his favorite toy?"

I wipe off my facade and replace it with a leveled, predatory stare. "I am no one's to be shared."

Unlike last time, I don't have the luxury of enlisting Thea and Gemma's help. But perhaps that's for the best. I have no intention of letting these guards leave the hallway.

I slide my dagger free.

A guard huffs. "Sweetheart, do you even know how to use that?"

"Me?" I bat my lashes. "Of course not. I found it on the ground and thought it was pretty."

The other guard takes a step forward and holds out his hand. "I'll take it from you before you hurt yourself."

I hold the dagger eye level and drag a finger down the side of the blade, marveling at the way it catches the light. Flicking my gaze to him, I wink. "I think I'll keep it."

His hand settles on the hilt of his sword, and the guards exchange a wary glance.

I swing the dagger at my side. "What? Not as confident unless I'm kneeling and bound by rope like the people you executed this morning?"

They draw their blades, metal screeching against the sheaths.

"If you'd prefer to be bound by rope," the guard on my left snarls, "we can arrange that."

I tap the point of my dagger to my chin, considering. Smiling, I run my tongue over the sharp edge of my top teeth. "As fun as that sounds, I think you'd both still end up bleeding out."

The guard to my right advances a step. His arm reels back, swinging his blade, but before it crests, I flip my dagger into my palm and plunge it deep into his chest. I yank it out, and he drops to the floor, gushing blood.

Through a curtain of hair, I smile at the remaining guard. "Did I do it right?"

Blood beads at the tip of the blade and splashes to the floor as the man at my feet goes still.

He grits his teeth. "I'll cut you to pieces while the other courtesans watch."

I chuckle. "Such a little man with little words."

He jumps and slashes his blade down in a wide arc. I sidestep and it hits the stone floor, the sound clattering through the empty hallway. He lifts it, but the sword slows him down, and I reel back my fist, punching him square in the jaw. His head twists, blood spurting from his mouth.

"That's for the innocent people you killed today."

He rights himself and drags a sleeve across his mouth, gaze pinned on me. Raw rage swims behind his eyes, and he lunges, the tip of his blade aimed for my chest. I feign left and raise my foot, kicking him in the side.

"That's for any people you've killed from the Sea Court."

He slams into the wall and slumps to the ground, his sword

clattering out of reach. I lower a knee to his wheezing chest and pin him beneath me.

"And this—this is for me. For the Princess of the Sea."

His eyes widen, and I slam the dagger into his chest.

Footsteps sound from the end of the corridor, and I yank out my dagger, wiping the blood off on his shirt. I stand and step away from the body as Kressa rounds the corner.

She stops short. "I heard fighting."

I glance at the fallen guards. "What fighting?"

She shakes her head and closes the distance, lips pressed into a fine line. Her gaze rakes over me. "Are you okay?"

Her words are so genuine, so gentle, that I pull her hand to my face and lean into it. "I'm fine. I promise."

She grimaces. "And the guards?"

"Need to go in the linen closet. Right now."

I step to the guard against the wall and grab him under the arms, dragging him into the narrow closet across from Caelus's room. Kressa makes quick work of the other, and I mutter a silent apology to the poor servant who will discover them.

Kressa grabs a rag from a wooden shelf and returns to the hallway, wiping up the streak of blood.

"I said you didn't have to help me." She tosses it into the closet and shuts the door. "So why the change of heart?"

I sort through the answers that don't have a reasonable explanation, and settle on, "Apparently, Caelus's announcement means victory for the Sky Court."

"Victory?" Kressa breathes.

Nodding, I pull open the heavy oak doors into Caelus's sitting area. The mirror stands in the corner with a heavy quilt thrown over the glass.

"We need to send your brother on the next ship with a message for King Golan that the Earth Court needs to join the war. Not when reinforcements are ready, but now."

Her face falters, but she nods.

My hands pause around the quilt. "And we're sending Thea with him. Caelus threatened to kill her if I don't tell him why you joined the competition."

She tilts her head. "So why don't you tell him?"

"Because you'd turn me in."

Her fingers trace my jaw and sweep my hair off my shoulder. "I think we both know that's not true."

I cast my gaze down. I have known—for a while now, that she wouldn't hand me over. But I belong to the sea, and whatever my heart wants can't come between that.

"Then it's because we make good allies."

"Indeed."

In one fell swoop, I tug the quilt down. The cloudy mirror ripples and distorts our reflections, but the glass fades away and reveals an entrance to a dark corridor.

Kressa waves a hand through the opening. "What is this?"

"Some sort of charmed mirror that hopefully leads to your brother." A shiver snakes down my spine. "But we don't have much time."

I spare a glance at Caelus's door and slip over the threshold into the mirror. Kressa follows, and the glass clouds over again, giving no hint of the room on the other side. The air squeezes in on us, denser.

The low ceiling curves into the narrow walls on either side of us, and I run a finger down the black stone. It stings, and I flinch back, taking in the metal door at the very end. But it's no normal metal—not iron or steel.

"Rhodium," I whisper. "It's made entirely of rhodium."

Her hands clench into fists. "We need to hurry."

We stride down the short hallway, past a single oil lamp casting a shadow on the walls. She knocks against the door. "Elias?"

No answer.

I try the heavy handle, but it doesn't budge. Lowering, I

drag my finger over the locking mechanism, but there is no combination, no keyhole.

"It must have to be unlocked with some sort of power," I say, biting my lip. Or whoever gets locked in is never meant to come out.

She curses under her breath and reaches for the latch on a small window, swinging it open. A dim light floats in the cell, illuminating a room only big enough to accommodate a cot on one wall. Across from the bed, not even a foot away, is a toilet.

"Briar," Kressa whispers, pointing at the wall above the cot.

My stomach bottoms out. Etched into the stone is the same design as the pendant around my neck. But that isn't what makes my blood run cold. It's the rows of tick marks—thousands of tiny, uniform scratches in the rhodium. Thousands of days—a decade, locked in this cell with no interaction, no sunlight.

But no Elias.

Kressa grips the bars. "Where is he?"

I step back. "Kressa, if he's been in here for this long, with only his mind—"

She closes the window and presses her forehead to it. "Don't. Don't tell me he won't be the same."

The air thickens, souring in my lungs. She must know that his mind is enough to drive him crazy. I swallow. "We're going to find him. I promise."

"If I don't find him before the end of the competition, I have to return to Ignata without him."

I cup her jaw. "I don't make promises I can't keep. But we need to go. If we're caught, we may find ourselves on the other side of that door."

She spares a wary glance to the metal that doesn't reflect any light, only siphons it, and nods. "Let's go."

We step into Caelus's empty sitting room, and the mirror clouds over again as the weight on my chest dissolves. I gnaw on my lip. How many times have I been in here, ignorant to the prisoner only feet away? But if I had known, would I have done anything about it?

I quickly replace the quilt over the mirror, and we slip out of the room.

"Dinner should be over by now," I say as we come to a junction in the hallway.

Two voices echo from around the corner—Caelus and another I can't discern. Kressa freezes and grabs my hand.

Her face turns ashen and she glances around the hall, yanking me toward a closet. She shoves me inside and throws herself over me as she pulls the door shut. A sliver of light sneaks through the crack underneath, yet not nearly enough to illuminate the closet.

I tap at her mental door. *What is going on?*

Her chest heaves against mine, so close her heart races against my ear. Her hands brace against the wall on either side of my head, enveloping me in her scent.

When she doesn't answer, I squirm. *There's a wooden shelf digging into my spine.*

She weaves her hand around my back and tugs me closer, her arm flush against the shelf. *Better?*

I swallow. *Much.*

Her thumb rubs a soothing line along the curve of my waist, and I breathe her in. She lowers her mouth to my ear, as if to say something out loud, but doesn't.

Don't make a sound, love.

My hips press into hers, my leg parting her thighs, but in the cramped space, I can't shift without risking something falling from the shelf. My fingertips meet skin below the hem of her shirt.

A glow lights the room.

Kressa curses under her breath and throws a hand over my chest. The light peeks through the cracks between her fingers.

As much as I'm enjoying your thoughts, now isn't exactly the right time.

I press my eyes shut and suck in a deep breath. But all that does is push us closer. Uncontrollable heat fills the space behind my navel, and power swells in my chest, begging me to get closer. My fingertips trace the edge of her waistband.

She shifts. *Briar.*

Her thoughts come through as a strangled rasp—a warning —as her fingers curl against my chest.

Caelus's voice sounds from the hall, and I stiffen. Kressa's arm tightens around my waist, and I press my hand over hers, blocking as much of the emerald glow as possible.

The temperature plummets, and our breath fogs. Ice snakes under the door in a frozen wave, stopping at Kressa's heel. I stifle a gasp and hold my breath.

Caelus's power, stronger than I've seen it in years.

"Has everything been collected for the final trial?" he says, voice like icicles down my spine.

In the dark, Kressa's gaze meets mine. *Collected?*

"Almost. It's taken more resources than we anticipated." A guard, or another staff member. "Some of them fight back more than others."

My stomach flips, and the icy air infiltrates my lungs, freezing them. Their footsteps fade around the corner, and the ice at our feet retreats. I swallow and press my forehead against the curve of Kressa's neck.

What if neither of us survive?

41

Early evening light streams through the gauzy curtains and illuminates the seamstress in the doorway, a garment bag draped over her shivering arms.

I furrow my brows. "But I already have a gown for the ball tonight."

She extends her arms. "King Caelus insists."

I have no choice but to accept it. A chill bites my forearms from the thin layer of ice coating the garment bag. The seamstress gives me a curt nod, her forearms blanched, and disappears down the hallway. Closing the door, I cross to the mirror and hang it on a small golden hook.

I pull down the zipper, and billowing white tulle bursts free. The dress is so light blue it's nearly white, and diamonds of all shapes cluster along the bottom like clouds.

"Oh, that's pretty," Thea says, sliding into the room.

Sunlight catches the marquis crystals spanning the bodice, and delicate gold wings cap the thin sleeves. My stomach churns at the thought of what funded this dress.

And that it looks like something Isolde would wear.

I shake my head. "I'm not wearing it."

Last week, I entertained him and wore the gown he sent me for the dinner. Not again. I abandon the bag, and Thea lets out a long sigh, settling into a chair in front of the fireplace.

I sweep to her side and kneel. "I need you to listen to me very closely."

Her eyes widen. "Is everything okay?"

Over my shoulder, I check the bolt is locked and that no shadows are peeking from under the door. No curious ears listening.

I return my attention to her. "Kressa has a ship ferrying people to Ignata, and you'll be boarding it tonight while everyone is distracted at the ball."

A vertical line appears between her brows. "Why?"

"Caelus is threatening to kill you."

She flinches back, eyes wide, but chews on the inside of her cheek and shakes her head. The determination of my first mate flashes through. "I'm not leaving you."

I fold my hands over hers. "I need to know you'll be okay, and it's only temporary. I'll get to you as soon as The Gales are over."

"If you don't die first."

Her words permeate the air—the ever-present concern looming over our heads for the last three weeks.

"I'm not going to die."

She gives me a piercing look, knowing as well as I do I can't guarantee my safety. But if I can guarantee hers, I'll lie a million times over.

A long breath billows from her. "I don't have a say in this, do I?"

"No. Because I cannot watch you die."

She swallows and wrings her hands in her lap. "Okay."

Tension drips from my shoulders. "Thank you. Meet me in Harriet's room at midnight, and I'll take you to the ship."

With a solemn nod, she runs her hands over her dress. A

creak echoes through the room, and the servant's door swings open.

Marianne slips in, holding my competitor suit, and grimaces at the dress hanging on the mirror. "Is that an oversized cotton ball?"

A strained huff comes from Thea as I stand. "You wouldn't happen to have a secret dress collection, would you?"

Marianne's lip quirks, then slowly widens into a mischievous grin. "What color do you have in mind?"

In Delterran, I traditionally favor deep shades of blue, but the dresses in my closet here mock me. I've been forced to wear nothing but blue for the last decade. But what could represent the sea without being blue?

Warmth fills my chest. The sunrise.

I smile. "What about gold?"

She beams and tosses Harriet's suit to the bed. "I have just the one."

Moments later, she returns with a long sheath of fabric draped over her arms and replaces the dress from Caelus with hers. It cascades in a sweep of gold, as if the sun itself painted it. The train pools on the floor in a metallic puddle, light reflecting off the strands.

I approach it and run my fingers along the silky fabric. The individual threads are so thin they're nearly indistinguishable from each other. My breath catches in my throat. "Is it—"

"Pure gold." She smiles and runs a finger down the fabric. "Shall we try it on before you get in the suit?"

I step into the gown and ease it up my body, the fabric hugging me like a second skin. Two thin straps lay against my shoulders, and the neckline dips to the center of my chest. Kressa's necklace hangs in the middle, the gold an exact match.

Marianne clasps the back, and I toy my fingers through the fabric, where a slit runs up the length of my thigh.

I bite my lip. "But my dagger."

She's nothing but a flash of red as she kneels down and alters the hem to a perfect length. "Check the other side."

My fingers trace down my covered leg and find a hairline slit—big enough to conceal a small weapon. I tug at the pocket as if I'm drawing my blade, but in my reflection, my hand rests, unmoving against my thigh.

"How is this possible?" I breathe.

"I can glamour clothing like Gemma glamours people, I just don't do it as often. There's a second pocket hidden at your hip, should you need to carry anything else."

Thea pulls her dress from the hook and gives me a slow, considering smile. "That's what you're wearing instead?"

I nod.

"Is that wise?"

"Probably not."

She stares, and a smirk tugs at her lips. "You look like royalty."

I tilt my chin and smile in the mirror. I *am* royalty.

Marianne steps away and admires the gown. "Perfect fit." She returns and eases the straps off my shoulders. "Gemma will be here any moment. We should get you in the suit."

I swallow and nod. The gown falls from my body and catches light from the descending sun, splattering gold around the room.

Thea passes me the suit, and I shove my legs into the pants, buttoning the fly.

She helps my arms into the sleeves, and I stare at her hands. Just over a decade ago, they wielded a sword with ability that rivaled my own. But since then, the calluses have smoothed over, her skin soft.

My first mate is still there, buried under layers of tulle and jewels, and I'm going to get her back.

I slide the suit jacket over my shoulders, stretching my fingertips through the cuffs.

"Midnight," I whisper.

She makes a low humming noise. "I'll be there."

Gemma enters through the servant's door and brushes her hair off her forehead. "I'm sorry I'm late." She cups my face. "Are you ready?"

No.

"Yes."

42

My fingers skim the delicate gold piping on my pants as I join the other competitors at the ball-room doors. Three weeks ago, fifty eager competitors crowded this space. And now, with the final trial in two days, only nine remain.

I scowl at the bird wings perched on each of my shoulders and clench my hands into fists. On the other side of the double doors, Caelus sits on a stolen throne, the blood of my fallen subjects on his hands.

Ahead of me, Kressa stiffens and scans the hallway.

Briar?

I freeze and reel in my emotions as I ease my mental door shut. She cranes her neck and furrows her brow, but the doors swing open, stealing her attention.

A permafrost settles in the air and claws at the skin beneath my clothes.

"King Caelus is pleased to present the final competitors in The Gales."

Applause sweeps the room, and I lift my head to the dais. Ice travels in a thick wave down the throne, and frost covers the raised platform. Caelus's icy eyes scan us, his golden hair sweeping away from his face.

And beside him, Isolde.

Her skin is pallid, her hair coiled and twisted like snakes hanging down her front. She sits, almost not because she wants to, but because her legs cannot support her should she try to stand.

I take in the ice—the sheer power being drained from her for this display. Caelus must know she's on the brink of death. And I've kept her here, asking for three weeks before she escapes.

My heart aches, twisting behind my ribcage. Seeing her like this tears a hole through my chest.

Icicles drip down the chandeliers like stalactites, and we fan out in front of the dais. I dip into a bow and my attention snags on Isolde once again.

She doesn't know me as Harriet, but our eyes lock nonetheless. I allow my gaze to soften—to send whatever comfort I can her way. She brushes her attention over me and scans the rest of the room, landing on the courtesan table.

Where she won't find me.

Her shoulders sag.

It takes all my strength not to rub away the furrow between her brows and pull her into my arms. Say a promise against her temple that I'll never leave her. One I'm not entirely sure I can keep—not anymore.

"Welcome." Caelus rises from his throne in a white suit. A velvet cloak drapes over his shoulders, falling to the marble floor in a sheet of midnight blue. "Before we begin, we have something to attend to. It has occurred to me that one of our competitors isn't who they say they are."

Every muscle in my body goes taut, and ice shoots down the stairs, cresting down each step like a wave. It wraps around our ankles, shackling us into place. It creeps up my ankle and dips beneath the hem of my pants.

My pulse pounds in my ears, and I shift my feet, testing the strength of the ice, but it doesn't budge.

Caelus strides to the edge of the dais and halts in front of me, his hands clasped behind his back. A bead of sweat gathers at my brow, freezing over as a chill sweeps the air.

I've been exposed.

He smiles. "Would anyone like to come forward?"

The hair on the back of my neck stands on edge, and I run my finger over the curve of my dagger.

Kressa clenches her hands into fists, and her voice breaks through my mind. *Did you tell him who I really am?*

My heart lurches, and I hold my breath. I shouldn't answer, but I can't let her think I told Caelus her secret—not if I'm minutes away from my execution. *I would never.*

Her hands relax, and she glances over her shoulder, as if searching the crowd for me. *But I can feel you. You're terrified.*

I swallow. *I am. Whatever happens next, please—*

"Last night," Caelus says, "we caught a ship maneuvering around unguarded water north of the castle."

My fingers go numb, and the blood drains from my face.

Kressa, I whisper in my mind.

She doesn't respond. Her throat bobs, and she lowers her gaze to the floor.

"Our fleet captured it, and we thoroughly questioned the crew. Most of them wouldn't talk, even with our methods, but the final one did. And he gave us a name."

My breaths grow rapid, and my chest tightens. I can't breathe. Evening sunlight reflects off the ice in the room, blinding me. I slam into Kressa's mind over and over again, but I'm locked out.

He's going to kill her.

He regards us down the bridge of his nose with a sneer

painted on his face. Isolde hasn't so much as shifted in her seat, as frozen as the ice encasing my ankles.

The king pivots on his heel. "Very well then. I was going to offer a swift death should he speak up, but now I'm not feeling as generous."

His booted footsteps echo through the room, and he stops in front of Kressa. A wicked smile twists his lips, and my heart thunders, fingers gripping my dagger.

"Simon, you are under arrest."

My hands go slack. The ice around Simon's feet thaws, yet his eyes are calm and clear. Like he was expecting this. Ice crackles at the edges of Caelus's fingers and forms icicles sharper than a blade.

Simon turns on his heel and bolts down the aisle. A guard blocks his path, but a sheet of ice throws the man out of the way.

"He's mine," Caelus growls.

Ice shoots through the air and plunges between Simon's shoulders, piercing skin. He stumbles to his knees, but rights himself as blood pours from his back. He clears the archway, but ice materializes beneath his feet and he slips, slamming to the ground.

He manages to stand, but ice captures his feet and roots him to the spot. My stomach hollows out, tears burning at the back of my throat. Simon straightens his shoulders and steels his back, stoic.

He nods at Kressa.

The temperature plummets, and a shard of ice shoots down the aisle, plunging into Simon's chest. It rips him from the ice and spears him to the wall.

A solitary scream echoes from the crowd. Simon's head lolls to the side, and blood streams down the stone, staining the floor as his breathing stops. My tongue turns to cotton. A guard strides to the doors and grabs the handles, but they freeze over.

"Leave them open, as a warning to the rest of the competitors," Caelus snarls. His black pupils are stark against his pale blue eyes. "You may take your seats."

The ice around my ankles thaws, puddling at my feet. I hesitate. If Caelus has an announcement, now would be the time to share it. But he takes his seat at the throne.

We bow as a group, but I don't sink nearly as low as the others. I twist my head and catch Kressa's gaze, her bow as shallow as mine.

Caelus dismisses us and turns to an advisor over his shoulder. "Where is my courtesan?"

I stiffen and pause at the back of the line. Beside me, a muscle feathers in Kressa's jaw, but her gaze is fixed on the floor.

"I'll find her," the advisor says.

"Good. I'll be needing the entertainment tonight."

Competitors filter around me. Everyone but Kressa, hands in fists at her sides.

Caelus tilts his chin at her. "You look disappointed. Don't tell me you actually thought Briar was interested in you? It's her job, after all, to make people feel important."

Kressa opens her mouth. Closes it. Her eyes dim. Anger coils in my stomach like an iron, hot enough to melt the frost encrusting his throne.

Isolde stiffens and leans forward, her gaze raking over me, then Kressa. "Ah, Kressa, right? I've heard a lot about you from Briar. She's particularly good at getting close to her marks, gaining their trust. Isn't she?"

I freeze. A ringing fills my ears and drowns my pounding heart. She wouldn't.

Caelus stiffens, lip curled as he regards Isolde. "You are only to speak when permitted. Remember your place."

Ignoring him, she smiles, stands, and climbs down the dais until she's an inch away from Kressa. On a whisper too quiet for

Caelus to hear, she says, "Tell me, Kressa, does Briar taste sweet to you, too?"

Kressa jerks forward.

I throw out an arm. "Don't."

Kressa swallows and presses her lips together. Her hand rubs at her chest, right where my power sank into her.

Isolde smiles, eyes twinkling. "Ah, you don't know, do you? The softness of her skin, her touch?" She clicks her tongue. "What a shame."

A muscle tics in Kressa's jaw, and despite her mind being shut off, her emotions slam into me.

Fire hot rage. A cool wave of doubt. A stab of betrayal.

The mixed feelings churn in my stomach and turn sour.

Leaning forward, Isolde whispers, "The sounds she makes for me are divine."

Before Kressa has a chance to react, Isolde turns on her heel and lifts her gown, climbing the dais. Caelus sends her a scathing look, his knuckles blanched against the armrests. An aching hurt spreads through my body, directly from Kressa.

My lip curls. "Don't you dare speak about her like that."

Isolde whips around, eyes piercing me. "Which one? Your whore, or mine?"

I bare my teeth and wrap my fingers around the hilt of my dagger, but a hand snakes around the crook of my elbow and jerks my hand from my pocket. Nails dig into my arm.

"Harriet," Thea breathes, her eyes wild. "I've been looking all over for you."

Her fingers tremble as she drops into a low curtsy. "Your majesties. It's a pleasure."

Caelus glares at her. "With a pirate, Thea? You know better."

Thea gives a shaky nod and drags me behind her, the runner muffling our footsteps. Nobles gawk as we pass, but a violin fills the air with a wistful tune, and servers pour from every doorway with plates held over their heads.

I tug at Thea, but she snarls and tightens her grip on my arm. She doesn't relent until we're in a secluded archway at the back of the ballroom.

She slams me into the stone wall. "What the fuck were you thinking?"

Music and the clang of silverware drowns out her voice.

I cross my arms. "Didn't you hear what was being said about you?"

"You don't think I've heard that hundreds of times? I'm a courtesan, Briar."

I slap my hand over her mouth and peer over her shoulder. "Harriet."

She glares and rips my hand away. "People think they own me, but I *know* they don't. I've made my peace with how I'm treated,"—she shoves me again—"so don't you dare get yourself killed trying to protect my name."

Her final words come out in a waver, and her eyes well with tears. A single one spills over.

My face softens, and I wipe the tear away with my thumb. "Do you remember how to get to the safe house?"

She glances out the windows overlooking Sarenia, the sun sinking low against the horizon. "Yes."

"The ship they seized was your escape, so when the dancing starts, you'll leave." I cradle her face with my hands. "Do you understand? Now that everyone has seen you with me, it's only a matter of time until Caelus orders someone to execute you. Go straight to Rita's, and I'll meet you there in the morning."

Her lower lip quivers, but she nods.

I wipe another tear away. "We'll figure something out after I win the competition. When I have that ship—"

Kressa rounds the corner, cutting off my words.

"Where is she?" she says, voice harsh. Yet her eyes are soft. Sad.

Thea tilts her head. "Who?"

"Briar." Kressa swallows, as if it pains her to say my name. "I need to talk to her."

"She's running late," Thea says. "Had a bit of a wardrobe malfunction with the dress Caelus delivered."

Over Kressa's shoulder, Caelus strides between tables and holds conversation with nobles. But his attention isn't on them. No, he's scanning the room.

My stomach hollows. He's looking for me.

I lower my mouth to Thea's ear. "We need to go. Now."

Her gaze settles on the king, and her eyes widen.

I grab her arm. "Let's go."

We sidestep around Kressa, and I find Marianne across the room. I pull Thea closer. "Go tell them it's time. I'll meet you in our room."

She nods and we break apart, heading in opposite directions.

The guards don't so much as blink as I leave the ballroom. Simon's lifeless body comes into view, and my chest constricts. Blood seeps to the floor and swirls in the trees etched on the tile.

Bile climbs up my throat, but my heart beats for only one thing.

Revenge.

43

———

I kick the door shut behind me, and my suit jacket falls to a heap on the ground. I leave a trail of clothing through the room and yank the gold dress off the hanger.

Thea dips in through the servant door with Marianne on her heels. Gemma follows close behind, her eyes red and swollen. She slides her fingers over her cheekbones, wiping away mascara.

My stomach lurches. "What's wrong?"

"They killed him," Gemma whispers.

I let out a long breath. "You knew Simon."

She nods on a shaky inhale. "We grew up together. He was like a brother to me. I"—she sucks in a breath—"I hadn't seen him in years. I didn't know he was going to sign up for The Gales."

An ache spreads beneath my chest bone. Another casualty of my decision. "Kressa showed me what he did for all those people. He was brave."

Swallowing, she closes the distance and cups my face with her hands. "He did what he could."

Warmth brews beneath her hands, and ribbons sink

through muscle and into bone. Her teary eyes blink, and the glamour disappears.

Marianne helps me into the dress and slides it over my shoulders. She comes around to the back and clasps the zipper, but before she can tug it up, the door flies open and slams into the wall.

"Everyone out."

Kressa fills the doorway, and our gazes lock. Her nails dig into the doorframe, barely holding herself back.

"Now."

Her voice is thick and demanding, and something deep in my core stirs as her eyes lower to the pendant hanging in the center of my chest.

Harriet's pants are sprawled at my feet, the shirt at the foot of the armchair. Thea notices the same moment I do, and she maneuvers herself over the clothing, her dress a cover as she kicks it beneath the bed.

Gemma offers Marianne a solemn nod, and they give Kressa a wide berth as they exit the room.

Thea hesitates.

"I'll be okay," I say. "Do you remember the plan?"

She wrings her hands. "Leave when the dancing begins, and go directly to Rita."

I nod, and my stomach tumbles. If a guard catches her, they'll take her to Caelus. But if she runs into a group of men like I did—I can't bear the thought. I can only hope she'll run fast enough, or land a lucky blow.

Reaching for my hand, she whispers, "To the ends of the earth."

A sharp pain shoots behind my eyes, and tears fill my vision. I thread my fingers through hers and squeeze. "To the ends of the earth."

Kressa taps at my mind, and I let her in.

I have people on the outside who will watch out for her.

I don't hold back the tears slipping free. *I don't know what I'd do without her.*

Kressa's eyes soften, but she doesn't look away, even when tears trail down my cheeks. *If she's important to you, she's important to me.*

Thea releases my hand and pauses at the door. She turns to Kressa and says something too quiet for me to hear, but I catch the words on her lips.

"Take care of her."

Kressa nods, and Thea disappears, the door shutting with a click.

I comb through my hair. "You know, it's considered rude to barge into someone's room unannounced."

In three long strides, she crosses the room and wraps her hands around the back of my neck. Her gaze skates over my face. "I had to make sure you were safe."

I furrow my brows. "Safe?"

"I felt you in the ballroom. But I couldn't find you, and the thought of you in danger, Briar—it nearly drove me mad. Because—"

I wet my lips. "Because, why?"

Her thumb rubs a line down the back of my neck. "Because you were afraid. And I've never felt your fear on my tongue until you thought you were going to lose me."

She tucks a strand of hair behind my ear, and her nose brushes mine. Fingertips skim over the length of my bare arm, and I shiver beneath her touch.

She tips my chin, and a breath away from my mouth, whispers, "Where were you?"

"I wasn't there." I retreat a step. "Perhaps our connection isn't as reliable as you thought."

I turn to the mirror and reach my fingers to the zipper at my back. She comes up behind me and traces the curve of my spine in an unhurried sweep. Warmth pools behind my navel, and I tip my head back ever so slightly, soaking in the way my skin buzzes at her touch.

She lowers her mouth to the shell of my ear. "I've never been more certain of anything in my life."

Nudging my hand away, she inches the zipper up. I catch her reflection in the mirror, her honey eyes so dark they're nearly unrecognizable.

"Kressa," I say, my voice weak.

She doesn't respond, only lowers her head and trails her nose over the dip in my neck. My vision clouds, and she sucks in a deep inhale, breathing me in.

"You smell like the ocean," she whispers against the space below my ear. *But all I want is for you to smell like me.*

A shiver crawls up my back, and the light in my chest flares to life. Smiling, she sinks a finger beneath a strap and slides it along my shoulder. I shudder.

She lets out a low laugh. "Our connection is so sure, I can feel the way you react to every touch. The way that—even when you have a dagger to my throat—you ache for me."

I press my back into her and let my head fall against her chest. She reaches around and lifts the pendant between two fingers.

"So, tell me Briar, where were you?"

The light in my chest snuffs out, and I pull away. "Maybe if you looked at what's directly in front of you, you'd know."

I suck in a sharp breath and lower my gaze from the mirror. Too close. Too dangerously close to revealing my secret.

"Trust me, there isn't a room dark or crowded enough where I wouldn't find you."

My heart skitters, but I reign it in before it floats to her. I hold my breath until I have enough control to change the subject. "I heard what Isolde said about me."

"I've known that you two are together." A muscle tics in her jaw. "There's nothing you need to explain to me."

Her hands flex at her sides, and the air between us goes taut as a bowstring. I pull my gaze to her reflection—eyes dark and stormy. A hot wave crashes over me and wraps a rope around my heart, squeezing it.

I blink and whisper, "I can feel that. You're jealous."

Her face hardens. "It's eating me alive."

Turning on my heel, I face her. "Why? Why does it concern you what I do with my time, or who I spend it with?"

The pressure in the room thickens, and my heart thunders in my chest, the vise tightening.

She reaches a hand to my chin and drags a thumb over my bottom lip, gaze pinned on it. "Because the thought of you with anyone else drives me mad. The thought of someone else's hands on you makes me so jealous I hardly remember my name. I can't stop it."

I tuck my fingers around the buttons of her suit jacket. "I can't bear the thought of you with anyone else, either."

"There is no one else for me."

A lump rises in my throat, tears stinging as my heart pulls in opposite directions. "I—"

"Don't," she interrupts. "It's okay."

The noose around my heart retreats, and something slips in, taking its place. Something warm and sweet, yet unsure. Curious, yet hesitant.

She inches closer and threads her hand around the back of my head. I fight the urge to fall into her—to fall into something that promises heartbreak at best, execution at worst.

The emerald glow in my chest illuminates the sharp edges of her face.

A small smile creeps over her lips, and she shakes her head. "This dress is torture."

An undiluted need pulls me closer, and my power swirls deep in my chest, begging to be freed. Her presence offers the smallest reprieve from the curse shackling me to the earth.

Just a sip. A taste of my power, and I'll pull away. For a blissful moment, I can pretend the curse isn't real—that the war raging across the sea doesn't exist. I can pretend the prince I assassinated didn't survive. That Isolde didn't just use me as a weapon.

It's just me and Kressa.

For now, in this moment, it can just be us.

My heart skitters around my ribcage. She inches closer, and I press my eyes shut, holding my breath. Power laps beneath my skin, anticipating the taste of her mouth on mine.

Then she's gone. My eyes open, and she retreats another step, gaze lowered. I run a finger over my bottom lip, where it still tingles from her touch. A stone settles in my stomach. Perhaps I've misinterpreted everything, and nothing exists between us but our shared power.

She shoves her hands into her pockets. "We should get going."

The light in my chest flickers, dims, and the warmth around my heart cools as if swallowed by ice. "You're right. I've spent enough time avoiding Caelus." I tilt my head. "Because that's all this was about, right?"

The words hang in the air and turn sour, but the barb lands all the same.

She works her jaw. "Right."

My reflection mocks me. A decade landlocked and forgotten—frozen in time. I step away and turn to the door. "Let's go."

She opens her mouth as if to say something, but presses it shut and takes the door from me. "We shouldn't be seen entering together. I'll go first. I'll be there, if you need anything."

"I won't."

With a curt nod, she slips through the door and out of sight.

44

───────

Sunlight spills into the hallway from the ballroom, and two guards border the archway, hands clasped behind their backs.

One nods to me. "Would you like an escort?"

My eyes catch Simon's slumped body, and fire fills my veins. I square my shoulders and tilt my chin. If someone from the Earth Court can face Caelus without fear, so can I.

I shake my head. "No need."

On an exhale, I round the doors and step into the ballroom. The room silences, and every gaze swings to me. An inexplicable force draws my attention to Kressa, and when our eyes lock, my power stirs.

The sunset bathes her in gold, and the corner of her mouth lifts ever so slightly. *You put the sun to shame, my love.*

Heat rises in my cheeks, and whatever reluctance I had wearing this dress and making a scene dissolves. As if Kressa pulled it right from me.

Caelus stands, and with a sneer, he adjusts the robe hanging off his shoulders. Frost swirls at his fingertips—a show of power. A warning.

Sunlight envelopes me, and my dress scatters a million hues of gold, gilding the ballroom.

Like the sunrise over the ocean. Kressa's voice is breathless, awestruck.

My lip quirks. *Like home.*

Nobles stare as I pass, leaning over and whispering amongst each other. I stride down the center of the room with my chin held high.

Isolde's lips press into a thin line as she rises and joins Caelus at the edge of the dais. My heart pounds against my ribcage—tipped with rage and betrayal at the way she used my love as a weapon. The way she spoke of me, like I'm nothing but a bartering chip.

A calming caress floats down my spine.

Breathe, Kressa says.

I stop, forgoing a curtsy. "Apologies for my tardiness, Your Majesty."

"Where is the dress I had delivered?" Caelus says, his voice as frigid as the ice coating the room.

"I'm afraid there was a bit of a wardrobe malfunction."

Ice snakes up his wrists and disappears beneath the cuff of his sleeve. He presses his lips together and takes a step down, extending an arm. I accept it, and he jerks me up the steps, squeezing my arm until it goes numb.

His mouth lowers to my ear. "Behave. If you don't, I'll kill Thea right now."

A lump forms in my throat. "You said I have until the end of tonight."

The crowd resumes its conversation, and Caelus guides me to a chair beside his. "Did I? I believe I was far too lenient."

I find her in the crowd. Her hands wring in her lap, and her back is rigid against the back of her chair. Roast meat and vegetables sit untouched on her plate, her wineglass full.

"But if you do as you're told," he snarls. "I'll keep my word, despite her display with that pirate."

I swallow and nod.

On the other side of the throne, Isolde spares me a glance. I pretend not to notice.

Caelus settles himself in his seat and leans closer, lowering his voice. "I believe you remember our conversation about my experiment."

"I do."

He spears his steak with his fork and saws a knife through it. His experiment. The one that would bypass Terra and Serinos and grant him unlimited power. Make him a god in his own right.

Give him ultimate rule.

"Have you considered my proposition?"

"I have."

"And?"

"I accept," I lie. Anything to keep his temper at bay long enough for Thea to escape unharmed.

Caelus regards me out of the corner of his eye and smirks. "I do suppose the allure of godliness would be enticing enough to bind your life to me."

The air unspools from my lungs, from the room, and leaves nothing but jagged shards of ice. My chest heaves, the pendant lying heavy against my heart. On instinct, I clutch it, the rough edges biting into my skin. "Bind my life?"

A forbidden practice. He would bring me to the brink of death, and before I take my final breath, he would flood me with his stolen power—overpowering and extinguishing mine. My life would be bound to his. Forever.

Caelus's nails dig into my skin. "See that guard?" He tilts his head at a man stationed beside Thea's table. "If I give him the signal, he will slit her throat. So, what do you say?"

At the table before the dais, Kressa grips her fork, knuckles white against the metal. My door is shut, but that doesn't mean she can't taste my fear.

"Of course." I turn to Caelus and swallow. "It would be an honor."

He lifts a brow. "Then we shall hold the ceremony after dinner."

My throat twists into a knot, and I scan the ballroom. Guards are positioned at every doorway, blocking every exit. If I tried to escape, they'd catch me.

A royal soldier approaches the dais, stealing Caelus's attention. My pulse ricochets, and I fold my trembling hands in my lap as I slide my gaze to Isolde.

There's only one reason why Caelus would want to hold the ceremony after dinner.

She won't survive the night.

Her eyes find mine—not a hint of warmth behind them, just chips of ice. She must know, too. She has nothing to lose.

Caelus dismisses the soldier and rises, clearing his throat. "If I may have your attention, I have an announcement regarding the war."

The roaring in my ears quiets with the room, and I lean forward.

Servants pour from doorways with trays of champagne balanced on their palms. I accept one of the glasses, pinching the stem precariously between my fingers as my heart hammers in my chest. Only the best announcements would call for champagne.

As if I'd fall through the floor without her as a tether, my gaze lands on Kressa.

Warmth seeps through me, filling every cold and decrepit crevice. But then it intensifies, and morphs into flaming rage. But it tastes familiar, and her mouth quirks.

This is your anger, not mine. Don't be afraid of it. Let it consume you until you fear nothing Caelus could say. If he sees you balk, he wins.

I hold her gaze and welcome the flames as they lick at the underside of my skin, scorching my bones.

She smiles. *Never lose that fire.*

Caelus holds out his glass, bubbles climbing the sides. "I am honored to announce we have executed the Ruler of the Sea, Queen Marina."

The glass slips from my fingers, falls to the floor, and shatters into a million pieces. Champagne bubbles through the grooves in the marble like sea foam.

I slam my connection to Kressa shut.

The Queen of the Sea. My mother.

Dead.

My pulse roars in my ears, drowning out the cheering nobles. I search for the slit in the dress, but my fingers shake too violently to find the secret pocket.

Caelus grips my hand, holding it in place, his eyes as sharp as the dagger at my thigh. He nods at the broken glass. "That glass of champagne was worth more than your life."

"My apologies." I rise on wobbly legs and step to the edge of the dais, my dress dragging through the liquid. "You'll have to excuse me for a moment. I need fresh air."

"Go calm down then," he says through gritted teeth. "Hysterics are unbecoming for a woman."

I pull out of his grip, and tears blur my vision as I stumble down the steps and throw myself through a servant's door. I sink to the ground and bury my face in my hands, my back heaving with every sob.

She's gone, and my last words were full of anger and hatred.

"I'm no daughter of yours," I had said.

The hurt in her eyes is the last thing I remember. And now she's gone. Forever.

I've failed her.

Caelus won.

I rest my chin on my kneecaps and stare at the alabaster wall across the corridor. It's almost the same sandy color as the grainy beaches of Delterran, yet lacking the warmth. My chest constricts and threatens to fold in on itself.

I'll never walk through those opal halls with her ever again. I'll never listen to her drone on about royal duties while staring at the ocean canopy above the greenhouse. We'll never again count the stars together.

Applause thunders from the other side of the wall. I grit my teeth against the cheers as hot, angry tears fall down my face and splash to the floor.

But I straighten and drag my hands beneath my eyes.

Caelus hasn't won, not yet.

In killing my mother, all he did was replace her spot on the throne. I'm no forgotten princess. Not anymore.

I'm the Queen of the Sea.

The fabric of my existence ripples. My power grows and swells against its confines, but not strong enough to break through. The ocean calls, louder than ever before, and beckons me home. To fight.

Grief gnaws at my chest, but something else burns through and lights the embers into a wildfire.

Vengeance.

Music filters under the door, louder than it was at dinner. A celebration for them—a funeral for me. And in some ways, a coronation. Standing, I smooth my dress and dip a hand in the secret pocket, checking my dagger.

Blowing out a breath, I let rage consume me.

45

Isit on the edge of my chair, dinner and the shattered glass long gone, swept up by a servant. Nobles twirl around the dance floor, while others lounge on low settees, veiled by shadows.

On the outskirts of the balcony, Kressa leans against the rail with a glass of wine. She brings her mouth to the rim and glances at me over the edge. I breathe in and stoke the flames climbing beneath my skin—welcome my rage. My hunger for revenge.

A temporary escape from the grief trying to gnaw its way through.

Kressa's throat bobs on a swallow, and her fingers trace a line down the front of her shirt, dipping over and under the buttons my fingers have begged to undo. The muscles along her forearms shift in the moonlight, and shadows dance over her body, emphasizing every curve.

My dress grows tight, stifling.

A chuff rolls through my mind. *Careful, or you'll start glowing.*

She studies the curve of my waist and the high slit of my

dress. I hold her gaze as I lift my leg and cross it over the other —the silky fabric draping to the side and exposing my skin to the hip. I drag a finger over my knee and up my thigh, watching as she follows every movement.

Her fingers tighten around her glass.

I drag my teeth over my bottom lip and smile. *Would you care to dance?*

She tilts her chin at Caelus. *You don't think that would anger him? Or Isolde?*

That's exactly the point.

Her head tilts.

Caelus wants to bind me to him, I say. *Tonight.*

Kressa sucks in a deep breath and downs her wine, her grip so tight the stem might snap. *Consider me at your disposal.*

I furrow my brow. *You don't want to know why?*

She strides into the room and sets her empty glass on a table. *I'm five seconds away from clearing the dais and slitting his throat. So no, I don't need to know why.* Her steps widen. *I need you to come to me. Now.*

Women dip on the dance floor, and I catch Thea watching me with an expectant look in her eyes.

"Ready?" I mouth.

She presses her lips into a thin line and nods.

I exhale a long breath and rise from my seat. If I don't survive the night, or if my power is stripped from me, at least she'll be okay.

Caelus stiffens in his seat beside me. "Where are you going?"

The music slows, the ensemble nearing the end of a song.

I train my eyes into those of a submissive courtesan—wide eyed and innocent—before leveling him with a glare that he could drown in. "I have a surprise for you, my king. Consider it a gift for our binding."

Beside him, Isolde shifts. "You weren't given permission to leave your seat."

I don't look her way. "I don't need permission." I tilt my chin, staring at Caelus down the bridge of my nose. "If you'll excuse me, Caelus."

His hands clench, and ice crawls down his arm in a layer of permafrost.

I lift a brow and smirk. "Careful, Your Majesty. Hysterics are unbecoming for a man."

A stone wedges in my throat—my mind warning me to stop baiting him, but I give him a saccharine smile and curtsy. For far too long, I've bent to his whims. No longer.

Ice snakes down the throne, frosting a path toward me, but stops inches from the toe of my shoes.

I back away a step and swallow. As a competitor, his power can't hurt me. A line appears between his brows, and he tilts his head as Isolde's eyes narrow.

You have three seconds until I turn this room into a bloodbath, Kressa says. Barely held restraint hangs off the edge of her thoughts.

Breaking Caelus's assessing stare, I escape down the dais and cross the room to Kressa. Her chest doesn't move as I approach, as if she can't breathe until I'm by her side.

She wraps a hand around my arm, and only then does she blink and inhale a breath. *If he gets anywhere near you, I'll kill him.*

Her teeth grind together, and I cover her hand with mine, reveling in the way it eases her nerves. The tension in her shoulders melts, along with the tight clench of her jaw.

I drop into a low curtsy. "Spare me a dance, Kressa?"

She presses a kiss to the back of my hand. "It would be my pleasure."

We weave to the dance floor, and I glance toward the exit. Cloaked in shadows, Thea nods and disappears down the hallway. My heart tugs, urging me to follow, but I need to be here, making time for her to escape.

A distraction.

Bodies crowd the dance floor, and I slip a bracelet from a woman, stashing it in the secret pocket at my hip. I slide a ring off the finger of another—more brazen than typical. But tomorrow's trip to the safe house could very well be my last.

A string of notes fills the air. Kressa guides me in a wide circle and brings me close enough for our chests to touch. Her hand anchors to my lower back, branding me with her touch. We move around the floor, our footsteps perfect mirrors of each other. As effortless as breathing and as thrilling as sailing my ship.

I catch her staring, and a blush creeps into my cheeks. *What?*

My life was so different before I met you.

She spins me out—a flash of gold in a sea of blue, and reels me back in.

I slide a finger beneath the edge of her collar and smooth it out. *It must have been quite dull, I suppose.*

Her gaze darts to my lips. *You have no idea.*

The music crests, and the strings work faster and faster, yet Kressa moves me around the floor as if we've spent a lifetime dancing together. As if our movements dictate the universe. In her arms, I'm at peace.

Warmth spreads under my skin, over my bones, and into my chest. But it's not the same feeling as when my power yearns for her. It's different. Unfamiliar.

I trace her features—the cut of her jaw, the way tendrils of hair brush the curve of her ear, the hints of green nestled into her eyes I hadn't noticed before.

The full moon shines through the balcony, as if it rose for us.

She dips her mouth to my ear. "Not for us, my love. For you."

I stiffen. "My mind was closed off."

She smiles against my neck, sending a wave of bumps over my back. "Maybe there's a reason you can't lock me out completely."

"And what would that be?"

"I'm trying to figure that out myself."

Uncertainty laces her words, but the music quickens and crescendos. I smile. "Should we give them a grand finale?"

She turns her face, brushing her nose over mine. "What do you have in mind?"

"Follow my lead."

Her hand tightens around me. "Anywhere."

Lush notes tumble over each other, and the room blurs until the final beat drags out in a mournful tune.

"Dip me."

In a slow, careful sweep, Kressa guides one hand to the base of my neck and lowers me. The ends of my hair skim the marble, and my dress catches the chandelier light, casting the dance floor in gold.

The music halts, but Kressa makes no move to raise me. She holds her breath, chest unmoving, as her mouth hovers above mine. Her thumb drags across the base of my neck, her eyes caught on my lips. She flicks her gaze to mine, and although shadows cast her face in darkness, her eyes shimmer. And like salt to the sea, my power calls to her.

Nothing exists beyond the two of us. Nothing but time and space and our intertwined power.

In a single, unhurried movement, she closes the space and melds her lips to mine. They soften and part, letting her in, and my power bursts from its confines. I swipe my tongue against her teeth, and a low groan rumbles from deep within her chest.

My power swirls, dipping with every stroke of her tongue—

every draw of her lips, clinging to her touch. It sinks into the empty cracks and breathes life back into me. My fingers tighten in her hair, and she angles my head back, deepening the kiss. Heat spears through me, and flames lap my core, scalding the water coursing through my veins.

I need more. I drag my teeth over her bottom lip and press myself closer. But it isn't enough—not nearly enough to sate this need.

Kressa pulls away and blinks, eyes full of awe. A small smile creeps over my face, and I run my teeth over my bottom lip, savoring every last drop of her. My power retreats to its confines, but the simmering heat doesn't withdraw.

She tucks my hair behind my ear and eases me upright. My chest heaves, lungs drawing air after being consumed by her.

From the dais, guards advance on us.

No, not us—me.

"Briar Rielle, you're under arrest for theft."

My heart stutters, and my gaze swings to the dais, where Isolde catches my attention. She tilts her chin, and if anyone recognizes the look on her face, it's me. The scheming tilt of the corner of her lip, the resolve nestled into her eyes.

She turned me in.

I turn my attention toward the guards, draw my blade, and hold it close to my thigh. *You stay here. They can't hurt you, only me.*

Guards shove through the crowd, some drawing blades, others pulling arrows from their quivers.

I'm not leaving your side.

Kressa grips my wrist and sprints toward the balcony as a vortex of icy wind blasts through the ballroom. Ladies shriek, nobles cowering to the corners of the room, behind guards. We break out into the night, our hair whipping behind us, and race down the curving marble stairs to the garden below.

Clouds materialize across the clear sky, lightning dancing in their full bellies. Another boom shakes the ground, and rain pours in a sheet, flooding the fake lawn. I slip and kick off my heels, flinging them into the darkness.

My heart races in my throat, but it's not fear on the tip of my tongue.

It's freedom.

A wild grin crosses my face, and as my bare feet pound against the ground, I welcome the downpour, the rain blurring my vision.

After a decade, I'm me again.

Guards shout from the balcony, muffled by the wind and rain soaking my hair. Kressa's is plastered to her face, yet the look in her eyes—a mix of fear and awe.

Something whizzes through the air and lands at our feet.

An arrow.

I swallow a shriek, and she yanks me by my hand. We clear a row of hedges, banking toward a cropping of thick trees as a second arrow pierces the air. It nicks my cheek, drawing blood, and Kressa pulls me down as another shoots over the top of my head.

She guides me behind a tall bush, its synthetic twigs scratching my skin and snagging the dress. A group of guards enters the tree line, swords at the ready.

Kressa wraps an arm around me. *As soon as they pass, we'll head to a hidden door on the other side of these trees.*

I nod and sink into the warmth of her side.

And that's when I smell it.

Fresh, bitter grass. The sweet aroma of a freshly opened flower. Earthy, wet dirt.

Beneath our knees, blades of grass press through. Real grass. Buds gather on the bush and bloom, opening to a brilliant pink. I brush my fingers along the silky petals. Real.

I whip my head to Kressa, but her gaze is pinned on the guards.

They step closer, and twigs crack beneath their feet. One trips over a raised root and slams into the ground with a grunt. Kressa pulls me to her chest and blankets my head with her arms as they pass by.

As soon as they're out of sight, she grabs my hand.

Let's go.

I follow, searching for the root the guard tripped over.

It's nowhere to be found.

46

Silence greets us as we push through the servant's door into Harriet's room. I stride to the window and part the curtains, looking into the courtyard below. Guards pour from the castle gates and swarm the perimeter, blocking each possible exit.

I rest my head against the wall. Rainwater drips from my dress and pools into a puddle on the floor. "Do you think we gave her enough time?"

"More than enough." She scans the room. "Where's Harriet?"

I stare through the sliver of space between the curtains. Raindrops race down the windowpane, blurring the outside world. "She went with Thea to make sure she got there safe."

She freezes. "And risk being caught outside the castle at night? This close to the final trial?"

I turn from the window. "You'd be surprised what some people do for love."

A pause. "No. I wouldn't be surprised at all."

Her words hang heavy, floating midair like a wave waiting to crest. A spark slides under my skin and urges me to her. The front of her shirt is soaked through, hinting at the expanse of toned muscle hiding underneath. She takes a step closer, but stops, closing her hands into fists.

I lower my gaze. "You should probably go to your room."

"And what about you?"

"My room is the first place they'll search."

"But what if Harriet comes back?"

I bite back a laugh and grab a towel from the unused bathroom, wringing out my hair. "I'm not worried about that."

"Come with me," she whispers.

My stomach flips, and I drape the damp towel over a chair, masking the heat crawling into my face. "You'd rather I share your—"

"To Ignata."

The towel slides to the floor, and wind howls against the window, rattling the panes.

I look past Kressa and swallow past the knot in my throat. "I can't."

"Can't, or won't?"

I don't answer, and she stalks closer, closing her fingers around my chin. She tips my head up. Honeyed, stormy eyes pierce through the darkness and bore into me—stare into the very fabric of my being.

"Briar, why can't you touch the water?"

My body stiffens, and I flinch out of her grip. "What are you talking about?"

"I've seen the way you look at the ocean. Your eyes glaze over and go to some faraway place where you're calm and carefree. Yet, each time you're near the water, you recoil."

I bite my lip. So, she did notice the way I avoided the shallow puddles when we returned the selkie tails. How I threw myself back from the wave in the cove.

I cross my arms, as if it could stifle my pounding heart. "Why did the garden come to life in your presence?"

She closes the distance and backs me up to the wall. Frigid stone meets my skin and seeps through my dress, sinking a chill into my bones. She settles her hands on either side of my head, caging me in.

On instinct, I unsheathe my dagger.

I flick it to the base of her throat, but she only smiles.

"You still don't trust me? Even as my power calls to yours, you think I'd harm you?"

"You know nothing about me if you think I'd trust you."

Her hand wraps around my wrist and lowers the dagger. One by one, she untangles my fingers from the hilt, and my blade clatters to the ground.

"I know nothing about you?" A smile tugs at one corner of her mouth. "I know you ache for me, and I know how delicious that feeling tastes. But you never act on it." She parts my legs with her thigh. "Why? Would it make it too real?"

"Nothing about this is real."

Dipping her mouth to the crook of my neck, she presses a velvety kiss to the skin, and the light in my chest flares to life. She chuffs, breath skimming over me. "Your mouth says one thing, yet your body says something entirely different. If I were to guess, this is the realest thing you've ever felt."

Her fingers dip below the chain around my neck and slide along my collarbone in a long, languid path. Where her chest presses into me, my skin burns.

And yet, the glow of my power within her chest remains dormant, even as she leans in and presses another kiss below my jawline. A shudder washes over me, and her mouth spreads into a smug grin. A low laugh escapes her lips.

I scoff and push her off of me. "This is a game to you."

Her eyes darken, hands flexing at her sides, but she retreats. "What do you mean?"

"The light in my chest flares at your touch. Without it, even. Yet the light in yours hasn't so much as flickered since the night in the infirmary." I grit my teeth. "It's a game—seeing how little you need to do to unravel me."

She looks to the window and swallows. "It's not a game."

"It is. And you feel *nothing*."

"Have you ever considered, Briar, that not everyone has the luxury of feeling whatever they want to feel? That sometimes things need to remain hidden because the truth could hurt others?"

My voice lowers. "I'm more familiar with that than you think."

"Whenever I dip into your thoughts, they say otherwise."

I flinch back as if I've been slapped. "What do you mean *dip into my thoughts*? I keep my mind closed."

"Apparently not closed enough." She shakes her head. "I never get far, like there's an invisible force holding me back."

My throat constricts, the air in my lungs souring. I should scream at her for invading my thoughts, but a question burns to the front of my mind. "What did you learn?"

I calculate how long it would take to retrieve my dagger if she knows my secret. The resolve I'd need to plunge it into her chest.

"I know guilt follows you around like a raincloud. But guilt for what, I could never piece together. I learned how fiercely you care for Thea, and I saw you captaining a ship. But the name etched into the side is always blurry." She steps closer and tilts her head. "What was the name of your ship?"

I calm my face and dive into her mind, digging and clawing for her thoughts, but I hit a wall. I slam against it and try to break through, but it doesn't budge.

Anger rakes down my spine, and I bare my teeth. "I should have killed you when I had the chance."

"Or perhaps I should have killed you."

I blink and clench my jaw. "Then you wouldn't have someone helping you find Elias."

"Yes, but then I'd be able to sleep at night. I wouldn't have you haunting my dreams."

Heat climbs into my throat and singes my tongue. My thoughts spin, and the light in my chest vibrates, rattling. I swallow it all down and stride to the door. "Get out."

Threading my fingers behind my neck, I unfasten the chain and hold it out to her. It sits like a lead weight in my palm, the pendant seeping warmth into my skin. She hesitates, but I shove it into her chest and let go, giving her no choice but to catch it.

She opens her mouth.

I shake my head. "Out."

She presses her tongue into her cheek and nods, stepping into the dark hall. Without another word, I shut the door.

47

———————

I wake with a start. Sweat coats my brow and drips in a rivulet down the curve of my spine. Throwing off the sheets, I sit on the edge of the bed, but the heat only expands down my legs and envelops my arms. My toes tangle in the gold dress I abandoned in favor of the nightgown Marianne hid in the dresser.

I slide to the floor and root beneath the mattress until my fingers close around the small drawstring bag storing the jewels. I exhale a breath. This will be the last delivery, so it has to count.

Rising, I pad to the window. Outside, guards patrol every gate, still scouring the roads. Music doesn't float from downstairs, and the courtyard is empty of carriages.

I press my back against the cold pane of glass and sigh at the reprieve. But the heat only burrows its claws into my core and spreads like molten lava to the space behind my navel. A dim light illuminates the room, and I catch my reflection in the small mirror. My chest lights like a beacon, tugging me to the hallway.

My vision blurs, and heat swarms my mind until only one thought surfaces.

Kressa.

I slide my dagger from beneath the mattress and stumble to the door. Through the fog in my mind, I scan the hallway. Clear. I cross the space, and the heat intensifies the closer I get to her room.

My heart races, pumping boiling blood through my body. Even my lungs burn—every inhale a scorching ache, like it's going to burst free from my skin.

I push myself through her door and freeze.

Kressa stands at the foot of her bed. A blinding cobalt light emanates through her thin shirt, illuminating the pain painted across her face. Her brows are drawn, lips twisted into a grimace.

"This, my love, is what it would feel like if I lowered the barrier." Her words come out rough, serrated. Like even uttering them is agony. "This is the torture I endure each time I'm around you—when you even cross my mind. I hold this back because I couldn't give you this pain." She takes a step closer, and a fresh wave of heat crashes over me. "You might ache for me, Briar—but I burn for you. I endure this pain, for you. When you asked me about the kiss, I never lied. You light me on fire."

The flames that lick my skin when I'm in her presence, the heat that braids through my waves when our lips touch—that's from her. I inhale a deep, shuddering breath.

The room might as well be full of smoke and uncontrolled flames, but nothing exists except Kressa and me and the strands of power between us. And this pure, unavoidable need.

I scan every valley along her body, the rise and fall of her chest beneath the thin sleep shirt. The way her muscles tense under my gaze. Her teeth dig into her bottom lip.

Swallowing, I whisper, "This isn't pain."

A slight shake of her head.

My body grows taut. A single pinprick and I'd snap. My chest rises and falls in rhythm with hers, and a throbbing ache builds low in my stomach.

I blow out a breath. "This is restraint."

She lowers her gaze in confirmation, and her jaw works. "It's torture—keeping my hands from roaming your body, stopping my mouth from exploring what you taste like. I try so hard to be respectful, but I've dreamt of what sweet, breathless noises you'd make for me." She pins me with a stare. "Please, Briar, tell me what you need me to be, and I'll be it."

My breath hitches. The retreats, the long looks, the concern. Words bubble to the surface, but they're too thick and gnarled to escape. Nothing tumbles out but, "You did this for me."

"All of it."

I drop my dagger. My fingers gather the hem of my nightdress, and I ease it up, dragging it over my upper thigh. Kressa tracks my every motion as the thin silk glides over my head and drops to the ground.

Her pupils blot out her irises, and her chest heaves. At her sides, her hands flex with barely restrained control.

"You'll be my ruin," she whispers.

She's wrong.

She'll be mine.

I take a tentative step forward, and the moment my foot hits the ground, she closes the space between us. Our chests press together, and her lips crash to mine as if she's been starved of me her entire life.

In some ways, so have I. Her skin, her soft lips against mine, the way her body feels under my hands—it sweeps a warmth over me unlike I've ever known before. An ache I haven't felt until now.

A low rumble comes from deep within her chest, and she tightens her grip on my lower back, fingers digging in.

Her other hand threads into my hair, and with a gentle press, she parts my lips. Each stroke of her tongue fans the flames building in my core, and I melt into her, my fingers scouring every inch of her body.

I've dreamt of this. Her words come through as pants, breathless. *Every night, I've dreamt of this. And every night, when my need for you becomes unbearable, I have to stop myself from going to you.*

Her hands drag down my hips and hesitate at the band of my underwear, barely dipping underneath. My power untethers from its chains and swirls through my body, dampening the flames.

A sigh comes through her thoughts. *I've endured torture, my love, but nothing has compared to keeping myself away from you.*

I break the kiss and cup her face, staring into her depthless eyes. "Show me what exactly has haunted your dreams so profoundly, Kressa."

Her hands freeze, and she shudders. "Do you have an eternity?"

My heart somersaults around my ribs. "Pretend like we do."

If tonight is all we have, I'll make it last a lifetime in my mind. If after this we part ways, I'll ink her touch into my skin, bottle her breath in my chest.

She lowers me onto the mattress and climbs over me, bracing her forearms on either side of my head. My entire world, enveloped by her. Her leg weaves between mine, pressing against me, and a shiver shoots up my spine, tracing a path over every inch where our bodies meet. She lowers her lips to my collarbone and presses slow kisses along the delicate skin.

I trace my fingertips over her back and smile against the crown of her head as goosebumps follow in the wake of my touch. This woman—so fearless, so deadly—undone by a single touch.

Her hips churn, so thorough my breath comes out ragged.

I reach a hand to the space between us and drag my finger directly over her center, over the shred of fabric separating my hand from her.

"Fuck," she breathes into my ear, chest heaving against mine.

Her hand dives down to meet mine, stopping me mid stroke. She lifts my hand and pins it above my head, her honeyed eyes churning.

You want me to show you exactly what my dreams consist of?

I nod, and a whimper breaks from me as she rolls her hips again. My thighs tighten around her hips, and I press my eyes shut, throwing my head back into the pillow. Her lips resume their place at the arch of my neck, each kiss twisting the growing knot in my stomach.

She lifts her head, and our gazes meet. Her eyes soften as she studies my face, beholding me like I'm a wonder. She huffs, shaking her head.

"What?" I say.

She cups my jaw. "I'd dismantle the night sky for you."

My chest tightens, my heart expanding past its confines—reaching and stretching toward her. I blink, and before I respond, she dips her mouth to my breast. She captures my nipple in her mouth, and my breath catches, fingers pressing into her nape as a low whimper escapes me.

Heat builds in my core as her tongue traces over the sensitive skin, then continues a path over my stomach. She trails farther, pausing at my underwear. Her fingertips dip beneath the band and slide across in a slow, torturous line.

She skims her hand up my thigh and cradles the space behind my knee, propping up my leg. Lowering her lips to my inner thigh, she nips at the skin. Heat spears into me, and I arch my back, body begging for relief.

She lifts her head, and our eyes meet as she gives me a lopsided grin.

"Please," I whisper.

She holds my gaze as she weaves her hands beneath my underwear, easing them off. I lift my hips in silent invitation, and she smirks, dragging a finger through me, circling it over my clit. My eyes roll back, and I fist the sheets.

Unravel for me, Briar.

She dips her head between my thighs and drags her tongue over my center. I arch into her mouth, and a muffled moan escapes from her, vibrating against me. Heat wrenches around my body, and I sink my fingers into her hair, rocking against every stroke of her tongue.

My power melds with the heat, and she slides a finger in, angling it in a way that singes each of my nerve-endings. A second joins it, and I cry out, gripping her hair tighter. Her fingers pump in rhythm to her tongue as she guides my legs over her shoulders.

Hold nothing back.

The knot low in my stomach pulls taught and I thrust my hips against her, wave after wave of pleasure washing over my skin. She grips my outer hip and pulls me closer.

My resolve snaps.

Euphoria crests, weaving with my power beneath my skin. I cry out as her tongue drags over me, and her fingers slow, but each thrust sends a fresh shudder through me. My breaths come out as pants, my heart thrashing against my ribcage.

She presses a kiss to my hipbone. "Even better than I could have imagined."

A drunken, lazy smile spreads over my face, and I map every dip of her body as she crawls over me. The freckles that trail up her waist, a splatter on her shoulders. The way her muscles shift beneath her.

"Kressa—"

She covers my mouth with hers, parts my lips, gently drags her fingertips over my nipples. I inhale a sharp breath and melt against her, my body liquid.

Her hands roam my body, memorizing every inch of my skin the way I did hers, mapping it out. She pulls away, and I blink my eyes open.

She trails her gaze up my body, over my breasts, my lips, my eyes. Silence hangs between us, and the blue light in her chest grows, casting the room in swirling shades of cobalt and sapphire. Like we're underwater.

She runs her thumb along my jaw, and her eyes soften. "How did I find you?"

The knot bound in my chest—guarding me from anyone who could get too close, loosens. Unspools for her. I breathe her in, and the glow in my chest brightens. I have nothing to offer—nothing but a small gift. A sacrifice.

I trust you, I say.

She searches my eyes, tracing her fingertips down my arm. Shivers follow in its path, and her gaze remains pinned on mine.

"I trust you, too."

My lips part, and unsaid words tumble in my throat, scrambling in my mouth. Heat blooms in my chest, and on a whisper lighter than air, I say, "For eternity."

I press a gentle kiss to the corner of her mouth. Her fingers tangle in my hair, and as she presses her forehead to mine, our breaths still heaving, my soul teeters on the edge, threatening to fall into her forever.

Her arm finds a home around my waist. "Eternity wouldn't be long enough."

"No, it wouldn't."

I tilt my head and trace her scar with the pad of my finger—from the dip of her chin into her hairline. "Who did this to you?"

Her lips form a tight line and she absentmindedly cups my hand, like it's the most familiar thing in the world. Like my touch grounds her.

She presses a kiss to my palm. "You know, you weren't the first woman to hold a blade to my throat."

I blink. "Did you deserve it?"

She shakes her head.

I study the scar. Based on the angle, the woman stood behind her and wielded with her left hand. That narrows down the pool of women I'll scour until I find the one responsible for this.

"It happened the night Sarenia fell."

I prop myself on my elbow. "In the castle?"

She nods, and my stomach twists. One of my crew members could have very well done this, and if they did—are they still alive? Did she kill them? A swallow slowly makes its way down my throat.

"It was foolish, but he was nowhere to be found." She runs a hand over the scar, as if reliving that night. "My brother, Elias, was meant to be married that night."

I stop breathing.

"I was glamoured as him."

48

My fingers halt their aimless path along her stomach, and a ringing fills my ears. "Married? To who?"

Her eyes glaze over. "We had been secretly gathering our forces, training them to take down Caelus's air armada. Elias didn't want to marry her, and that's why he fled. But we needed the alliance, so I pretended to take his place, but..."

Her voice trails off, and my heart pounds, thumping against each rib so hard it might break bone. I can't breathe, can't do anything but stop my fingers from digging into her skin.

My voice lowers to a whisper. "Who was he meant to marry, Kressa?"

Her gaze meets mine. "The Princess of the Sea."

I bolt upright and clutch the sheets against my chest, my bare skin suddenly too vulnerable. "You aren't just friends with Barren."

She shakes her head. "He goes by Elias, to close friends and family. But Elias—Prince Barren I should say, is my brother."

My throat tightens. "And you?"

The answer sours on my tongue, but I don't dare say it out

loud. As if keeping it in my mouth means it can't exist. I back off the edge of the bed and stand, my legs unsteady.

She reaches for me, but I flinch back.

"This changes nothing, Briar."

"It changes everything. Now, answer my question."

She glamoured herself and nearly conned not only me, but her brother into a marriage neither of us wanted.

Her face goes slack, and she pushes from the bed, taking a step toward me.

I retreat and snatch my dagger, holding it out. "Golan didn't have any female heirs. I'll ask one last time. Who are you?"

My voice almost cracks, but I grit my teeth and hold it together. It feels sacrilegious, holding out a blade after falling into her arms. Sharing her bed. Coming undone for her.

I scoop my nightdress from the floor, fingers trembling as I slide it on.

"Please, Briar." She stands, and her shirt falls past her hips. "Let me explain. My father didn't want anyone to know about me. I've been kept a secret my entire life. Every movement I've made, every choice I've been given, has been controlled by him for the good of the kingdom. Please, believe me, I lo—"

"Do not finish that sentence."

She freezes.

My knuckles blanch on the hilt of my blade. Behind the betrayal and rage, I'm nothing but a fool, falling for the sister of the man I was given to against my will. The one I failed to kill. I swallow, and a stone settles in my gut.

I shared my power with her.

Ten years ago, I tried to kill her.

I shift. "So, you're a princess."

She nods. "Princess Cordelia. Next in line to the throne."

"So when your father dies, that makes you—"

"Queen," she finishes.

A wrench twists at my chest, and I retreat another step.

That was her blood I watched pool across the stone floor, not Barren's. *Her* throat I slit. I watched the life blink out of her eyes—her chest halt its breathing. "How did you survive?"

She shrugs. "One moment, she dragged a blade across my throat, and the next I woke up on a ship to Ignata. The healers called it a miracle. Maybe she didn't hit an artery."

I most certainly hit an artery. I severed it. She shouldn't have survived the blow or the blood loss.

A strangled huff comes from my throat, and I point the tip of my dagger at her chest. "Give my power back, or I'll carve it from your chest myself."

"No."

I angle the dagger. "It wasn't a question, Cordelia."

"Don't call me that." Her words are thick, hurt. "I'm Kressa."

"Would liar be better? Or do you prefer I resort to formalities and call you Queen? Your Highness, perhaps?"

She steps closer, pressing her chest to the tip of my blade. "You won't hurt me."

A dare.

"The hundreds I've killed beg to differ."

Her chest moves a breath closer, and the tip of my blade pierces skin, drawing a bead of crimson onto the metal. Something in me softens, and my traitorous arm snaps to my side.

I avert my gaze and turn to the door. "Never speak to me again, and stay out of my fucking head."

She flinches back, and my hands ache to comfort her, but I grip the doorknob. She's spent weeks telling me how much she loathes the Princess of the Sea. And now it all makes sense.

Her brother was almost my husband.

And my refusal to marry was the downfall of her kingdom.

Before she has a chance to stop me, I throw the door open and retreat to Harriet's room. I toss my nightgown to the floor and rip a pair of leggings and tunic from the armoire. Empty of Kressa's heat, the cold air in the room bites at my skin.

Kneeling at the bed, I yank the bag of jewels from under the mattress and secure it to my waist. Raindrops roll down the windowpane as I cross to the servant's door and trace the path to Gemma's room in my head.

The only person capable of hiding an identity.

49

———

I wind through the abandoned hallway leading to Gemma's room, greeted by nothing but silence and flickering lanterns.

I jog past rows of closed doors and steady my hand over the hilt of my dagger. My thoughts churn, uncontrollable like a riptide. I should have known when Gemma stiffened the first time she saw Kressa, or when I found out she worked in the castle.

They knew each other, and I was too blind to see the truth.

My shoulders tense, and I grit my teeth until my jaw aches. If she's known Kressa her entire life, what has Gemma said about me? Does she know I'm Harriet?

Footsteps come from around the corner, followed by a shout of orders.

I freeze and press myself against the stone wall, my heart a drum in my ears.

"Keep up!" a guard shouts, the metal of his sword clanging against his belt with each footfall. "The castle is surrounded. She's not getting out."

I scan the other end of the hall, but I'd never make it before they turned the corner. A door stands to my left, and I try the knob. Locked.

I flatten against the door. The handle bites into my back and I hold my breath, willing my body still.

Shadows dance on the wall, growing larger and more defined. Closer. The first guard appears and darts onward without looking in my direction. Four others follow suit, but the one at the end pauses at the crossroads. He stiffens, and his head turns toward me.

Our gazes catch.

Julian.

My eyes widen, and I clutch my blade. If he calls for the guards, I'll have no choice but to fight my way out. And against six men in close quarters, with only a dagger? I swallow.

At least Thea is safe. And Kressa—well, Kressa doesn't exist anymore. Not for me. I've painted Cordelia's features over the idea of her.

I risk a step and flash my blade, holding it steady at my side.

Julian's lips quirk, and he glances toward the guards down the hallway. But he doesn't advance on me or call for them. His smirk spreads into a smile, and he tips his head.

He follows after the guards, and their footsteps fade away.

I stand, frozen for a heartbeat, until it comes together. Him and the servant who tainted Caelus's wine during the ball—working for Kressa. How long has she been infiltrating Sarenia? How many at her disposal?

Pushing from the wall, I creep to the mouth of the hallway and quiet my breaths. I'm met only with the drip of water and scuttling mice.

I bank left and stop at Gemma's door, giving it a single knock. The door cracks open, and Marianne's blue eyes stare at me through the slit.

They go wide. "Briar? What are you doing here?"

I force my way into the room. "Where's Gemma?"

In the armchair before the fireplace, Gemma looks over her shoulder, her face giving nothing away. I stride to her, but she doesn't rise. Fear doesn't flicker in her brown, unforgiving eyes.

I come to a stop, fingers flexing on my dagger. "You knew who she was this entire time."

"Who?"

"Does Princess Cordelia ring a bell?"

She doesn't blink. All the confirmation I need that she's the one who glamoured Kressa that night—knew that the Earth Court's heir has been risking her life in these deadly trials.

Gemma's gaze trails down the length of my arm to the tip of my dagger. Unbothered. "Her real name is Kressa. Cordelia was only a pseudonym Golan forced her to take on when her mother died at a young age."

"I don't care what name she goes by," I snarl. "You're working for her."

Marianne toes the edge of the hearth. "What's going on?"

Gemma gnaws on her lip and ignores Marianne. "I swore my life to serving her, and I didn't know she came to Sarenia until I saw her in the courtyard before The Gales. If I had known she entered, I never would have helped you."

I stop between her and the fireplace. "Have you told her that I'm Harriet?"

"No, but maybe I should. Or perhaps I should go to Caelus?"

Lunging forward, I pin her throat against the back of the chair. "Convince me why I shouldn't kill you."

She claws at my hand, but the scrapes don't register, even as blood blooms on my skin.

Her eyes darken, and on a rasp, she manages, "Who do you think glamoured all those women so Kressa could sneak them through the castle?"

My grip on her falters.

She winces, but her expression remains cold. "And what

would Kressa say if she finds out her bonded threatened her oldest friend?"

The nerves in my brain misfire, my ribcage cleaving in two. "Bonded?"

Marianne shifts.

"Don't come any closer," I snarl.

The blood drains from her face, body rigid. "Gem, what are you talking about?"

Gemma's eyes soften. "Let go of me, and I'll explain everything."

I hesitate, but loosen my grip and step away, my blade trained on her.

"I'm not saying a word until you hand over your dagger." She nods toward Marianne.

I begrudgingly pass it over, and Marianne tucks it into the top drawer of the dresser. Gnawing my lip, I calculate how long it would take me to retrieve it. Three seconds, tops.

"Sit," Gemma says.

I sink into the armchair across from her. Wincing, she rubs at the red finger marks on her neck, sure to leave a mark.

Marianne settles between us and pinches the bridge of her nose. "Kressa is our queen?"

Gemma presses her tongue to the inside of her cheek and nods. "I wanted to tell you, but you were so young at the time, and—"

"No." Marianne holds up a hand. Her fiery hair bristles over her collarbones. "You've lied to me my entire life. You can apologize later, but for now, leave me alone."

I rub my lips together, the flames at my back suddenly too stifling. The air thickens, pressing in.

Gemma blinks and takes a deep breath, settling her gaze on me. "You didn't know you and Kressa were bonded?"

I shake my head.

Gemma blows out a long breath. "Bonding was extremely

rare occurrence. Before she passed, Golan was bonded to Kressa's mother, and could wield her power alongside his. And hers was infinitely stronger."

"How have I never heard of this?" I say, wringing my hands in my lap.

"Like I said, it's rare, and can only happen with souls that are intimately compatible. Familiar, from another lifetime." Gemma shrugs. "Since then, instances of forced bonds have surfaced, where someone is brought to the brink of death and filled with power. But they're called—"

"Binding." A swallow shoves down my throat. "Caelus wanted to do that with me."

Marianne's face pales. "You wouldn't survive. No one has."

My gaze darts to Gemma, and she nods, solemn. "Caelus believes he is higher than the laws of nature. Or he's discovered a way to make it possible."

"But that isn't what I did to Cordelia, is it?" I say. "She was on the brink of death, but I didn't bind her, right?"

"No, you didn't. But bonds don't exist anymore. Or at least they shouldn't be possible." Gemma chews on her lip and shakes her head. "After Golan tried to resurrect his bonded, Terra stripped the ability to bond. Which means—"

"We've bypassed Terra," I finish.

She nods. "Somehow. And even before bonds were stripped, they were incredibly rare. In its most simple form, this is true love."

"I don't love Cordelia."

She shrugs. "Perhaps not, but bonds are predetermined by fate, selecting people who are mirrors of each other. Two halves of one soul."

"I don't believe in fate."

Yet as the words leave my mouth, my lips tingle with the remnants of Kressa's. My fingers ache for her touch, and my very being yearns for her. But I cannot love her. If I did, the lives lost over the past decade would be in vain. My mother's death would bear no purpose.

"It doesn't matter what you believe," Gemma says. "You can hear each other's thoughts, can't you? Communicate with your minds? Unable to kill each other?"

Blood drains from my face and pools in my feet. My vision tunnels on Gemma's porcelain skin. How many times has Kressa told me I can't kill her? Not that I won't, but *can't*.

This is why my assassination attempt failed.

"Cordelia knows we're bonded, doesn't she?"

Gemma and Marianne share a requited look, and the former nods. "She does."

I bite down on my cheek. Hard. She knew what sharing our power meant, and she *lied* about it.

"I don't want it," I say, my voice sharp. "Can I return her power? Deny the bond?"

Marianne shakes her head. "Holding back or refusing what fate decides would be a pain worse than death—it would be all consuming torture."

The flames Kressa endures. Swallowing, I stand and cross to the window. I part the curtain a sliver and far below, guards swarm every exit and sweep the streets.

I lean my shoulder against the wall. "I assume that since I'm bonded to your future queen, you'll glamour me for the final trial?"

Gemma's jaw tics, and she gives me a look that screams she'd rather drop dead, but Marianne replies with a simple, "Yes."

"Very well. I'll get going then."

As I walk past, Marianne grabs my hand. "Where are you going?"

"Harriet's room, to sleep in the closet."

She stands and blocks the servant door. "You're staying."

"I appreciate the offer, but I'm not welcome here, and the guards will be searching your room any minute."

"They already did. Long before you got here," Marianne adds. "And if Kressa finds out we turned away her bonded, she'd never forgive us." She looks over my shoulder. "Right, Gemma?"

Gemma grinds her teeth and stares into the fireplace. "You're safe here, Briar. On the couch."

I worry my lip. If I return to Harriet's room, I risk being caught. And if I spend the night in my room, I might as well hand myself over to Caelus.

"Fine," I say, easing my wrist from Marianne's grip. "I'll stay."

She smiles, but it doesn't quite reach her eyes. "I'll gather a pillow and blankets. And I have a spare change of clothes."

I nod and retreat to the small bathroom. A stream of ice-cold water pours out of the faucet, and I splash it over my face. I grab a towel from the wooden shelf and scrub at my skin, rubbing off the last traces of Kressa.

But the light flickers in my chest, a nagging reminder of her power lingering beneath—tethering me to her.

If she can't die by my hand, I should have let her die in the second trial.

50

———

I wake with a start, and my body jackknifes, the couch groaning under the sudden movement. The sheets tumble to the floor, and at the opposite end, no farther than five feet away, a shadow shifts.

My heart thrashes in my throat. "Who's there?" I reach for my dagger, but my hand comes back empty, and my blood chills. It's still in the dresser.

"Answer me," I say, my voice wavering

I strain my eyes, but heavy curtains block the moonlight coming through the window. The embers crawling through the logs in the fireplace offer no help, but they glint off the fire poker leaning against the hearth.

The shadow takes a step closer.

Throwing myself from the couch, I reach for the poker, but a sudden blast of air tosses it into the fireplace and out of reach. My knees smack into the hearth as smoke billows into my face and down my lungs.

Scrambling back, I gasp for air, rubbing soot from my eyes.

A hand covers my mouth. "Briar, stop. It's me."

I freeze. "Isolde?"

She pulls her hand away from my mouth. My eyes adjust, and Isolde sinks down across from me—my back against the hearth, hers against the couch.

I lower my voice and glance at the bedroom doors at the opposite end of the room. "What are you doing here?"

"We need to talk."

A bruised purple ring circles her wrist, and my stomach clenches. It's from Caelus, no doubt, but it doesn't erase the anger brewing deep within my core—doesn't negate her betrayal.

"How did you find me?" I say.

She pulls her knees to her chest and rests her arms across them. "I asked the staff."

I was seen, then, roaming the corridors. Bumps roll over my skin. If they told Isolde where I am, someone might be willing enough to tell Caelus or the guards.

Narrowing my eyes on Isolde, I push away the thought. "What do you want from me?"

She sighs, and the light from the dying fire casts a glow across her face, emphasizing her cheekbones and the red rimming her eyes. "My forces are ready. I'm here to bring you with me, like we discussed."

I scoff. "I'm not going anywhere with you."

"What are you talking about?" A desperation fills her tone, her words coming out faster—rushed. "You promised."

Flames coil in my stomach, anger begging to be set free. Uncaged. "You told Caelus about my thievery, knowing he would order my arrest."

"I knew you'd get away."

I push to my feet and shake my head. "I almost didn't. The guards were firing arrows at me, Isolde. If it weren't storming, or if I was inches to the right, it would have pierced my throat." My tone grows cold, eyes narrowed. "I heard what you said to

Kressa. How you spoke of me, like I'm nothing to you but an object. How could you?"

"How could *you*?" She jerks to her feet, her nose inches away from my face. Cold radiates from her in waves, ice coating her eyelashes. "How do you expect me to act, after I find you kissing her every chance you get? She comes into your life, and suddenly there's no room for me."

"I was *assigned* to get close to her."

"But you weren't assigned to fall in love with her."

I stiffen. "I am not in love with her."

She scoffs, pressing her tongue into her cheek as she shakes her head. "I've known you for a decade, Briar, and never once have you looked at me the way you do her."

"It means nothing."

"Is that so?" Her breath fogs the air between us, and she crosses her arms. "I've sacrificed myself to protect you, so I know what it looks like to withhold knowledge to safeguard someone. The information about Kressa that Caelus wants? I know you already have it. If she means nothing to you like you claim, then tell me what she's hiding."

The words sputter on my tongue. Kressa would have me hung if she knew who I really was, but despite everything, I can't turn her in. And if I were to tell Isolde what I've discovered, she'll use that information against me. She'd force me to go with her, or tell Caelus. If I were to go with her now, I'd die the moment the third trial began.

I lose either way.

I shake my head. "I can't."

Buried beneath it all, there's a truth I'm unwilling to face. The foreign power that's made a home in my heart. One I can't seem to shake loose.

She grits her teeth. "Can't, or won't?"

I'm unwilling to meet her eyes. Instead, I stare at the space over her shoulder, her curls filling my periphery as I swallow back the angry tears climbing my throat. When this is all settled and The Gales have ended, Kressa will never agree to help me, but I need Isolde's alliance if we want to take down Caelus.

I can't do that if she won't forgive me.

"I'm done waiting, Briar. Perhaps Caelus is right about you, and maybe all you're good for is being a courtesan." She scoffs, heading toward the door. "Perhaps that's all I was to you, too. An object to pass the time."

The tone in her voice is so unfamiliar, it jerks my attention to her. It's laced with anger—not the kind that billows in my core, hot and fiery. No, this is an icy rage. And the look nestled in her eyes? Betrayal.

"Isolde, wait."

She shakes her head, and the embers reflect off a single tear trailing down her cheek. "You've made your choice. I can only hope that you'll be able to live with the consequences."

"Please." I can't tell her who I really am, but I can tell her a similar truth. That I'm Harriet. Closing the space between us, I grab her hand and pull her to a stop just before the door, turning her to face me. My heart thrashes in my throat. "I'm—"

She flicks her hand. A blast of air throws me back and slams me into the ground. The air shoots from my lungs and I gasp, unable to pull a full breath. I writhe, grasping at my stomach, willing the words to leave my lips, but she's choking me, pulling the oxygen from my lungs.

"You promised you'd always come." She twists the knob and pulls it open. "I thought you were someone I could trust. Someone I could rely on. Unfortunately Briar, it seems you're just like the rest."

The door clicks shut behind her, and I swallow a mouthful of air.

51

I wake before the sun crests over the horizon. Peeling from the couch, I silently pad to the dresser and slide out my dagger, careful not to wake Marianne and Gemma, fast asleep in their bedroom.

Dagger strapped to my thigh, I tie the pouch of jewels to my waist and sneak to the window. Through the bleak dark, the side door sits unguarded.

A handful of guards walk the perimeter, but if I time it right, I can sneak by.

I snatch a cloak off the hook—Gemma's, based on its shorter length—and slide through the servant's door.

At this hour, I weave through the empty corridors unnoticed and emerge into the twilight. Silencing the jewels at my waist, I search for guards, met only with a rabbit scurrying under a stone wall. I tighten the hood around my neck and take off toward the safe house.

Brisk air carries the salty brine of the sea as I make my way down the cobblestoned alley. I breathe it in, inhaling every bit of home I can, and when I exhale, I send a silent promise.

The queen will return.

Entering the alley, I make a tight turn up the short set of stairs to the back door. I rap my fist against the wood. Three swift taps, a long pause, then one more.

Voices come from the other side, and I press my ear against the door, but they halt. The skin on the back of my neck crawls.

Those weren't women's voices.

The door swings open, and Rita's eyes meet mine, wild and wide, her glasses askew on the bridge of her nose. She leans closer. "Briar, run. Leave—"

A hand shoves her, and two royal guards fill the doorway. I gasp and reach for the dagger at my thigh, but one of the guards knocks it out of my grip. It plummets to the ground, and the second guards clamps a pair of shackles around my wrists.

Rhodium.

"Let me go!" I buck and throw out my legs, making contact with one of the guard's shins.

He shouts, mutters something under his breath, and throws a punch into my side. My ribs crack and I crash into the doorframe, falling to my knees. Before I can right myself, the guards drag me into the foyer and slam the door.

Rita stands against the wall, pale. Ropes bind her wrists behind her back.

"Rita," I whisper, tears stinging my eyes.

"Bring her in here," a familiar voice says.

My blood cools to ice, and I thrash harder, but it's no use against the guards flanking me, their arms looped beneath mine. The rhodium digs into my flesh, siphoning whatever power of mine isn't bound in chains.

They drag me through the hallway, the wooden planks snagging my leggings and piercing my calves with splinters. In the kitchen, a handful of women sit on the tiled floor, hands bound behind their backs. A guard stands watch over them, and I scream, flailing my arms. A boot meets my middle, and my shouts dissolve into a fit of coughs.

The guards drop me on the living room floor. I flip onto my stomach and press to my knees, but halt at the eyes staring back at me.

Honey eyes.

The world spins, and my vision blurs.

Daylight spears through the gauzy curtains behind Kressa.

She bows her head. *I'm sorry.*

A gust of wind forces me upright and slams me against the wall. Ropes woven of air pin me to place at the waist, the thigh, the throat. Caelus ambles over, hands calmly clasped behind his back.

Kressa struggles behind him, but a guard punches her in the stomach, and she doubles over, wrists secured at her back with matching cuffs.

I jerk toward him, but Caelus's power nails me tighter in place.

Footsteps come from the doorway leading to the kitchen, and Isolde strides into the room.

My muscles go numb, and I stare at her, gaping. Yet the woman who stares back is unrecognizable. Not in her weakness, or the power that's drained from her blood, but there's an unknowing to her.

As if we haven't traded whispers in the dark—our bodies in secret. Made promises to fight Caelus together.

A smirk crawls over her mouth. "I should've known when Kressa led us here, you'd be the one to follow."

I struggle against the rhodium cuffs and the invisible bindings, but it's no use. Isolde's fingers skim the drawstring pouch at my waist, and I would fight, but my stomach hollows out. My breaths turn weak and panicked.

My gaze jerks to Kressa. *Where is Thea?*

I don't know.

Panic seizes my throat and paralyzes my limbs. If Thea isn't here, where is she? Isolde unhooks the pouch and pulls it open, smiling at the contents.

I told you never to return, I say to Kressa, my thoughts thick and accusatory. *Do you know what Caelus will do to these women? What he'll do to us?*

I was looking for you.

My hands ball into fists. "This is all your fault."

Kressa flinches. Good. She knows the words were aimed at her.

"Oh no, Briar. It's all your fault," Isolde says, handing the sack to a guard. "I told you there would be consequences."

I grit my teeth. "Where is Thea?"

"Ah, yes," Isolde says. "You thought I was too busy watching you kiss Kressa to notice Thea slip out of the ballroom."

My nails claw at the wall. "What did you do with her?"

She scoffs. "*I* have done nothing."

My gaze swings to Caelus, and I don't bother trying to hide the plea in my voice. "Where is she?"

He shrugs. "I have grand plans for her in the third trial, but don't worry. You won't be there to witness her death."

"No." I shake my head, and a tear rolls down my cheek. "Please. I'll do anything. Just don't hurt her."

He dips his mouth to my ear, breath hot against my cheek. "Anything?"

I swallow a sob and nod. My legs go limp, no longer searching for footing.

Caelus pulls away and nods at the guard restraining Kressa. "Bring her here."

Two guards lock their arms beneath Kressa and drag her forward. Their fingers dig into her skin, and her jaw clenches against the pain, her legs uselessly thrashing. I grind my teeth.

They release her to the floor.

"You lied to me," I hiss.

"I never meant to."

We're bonded.

Her eyes widen.

Why didn't you tell me? I say.

Caelus shoves her in the back, and without her hands to brace herself, Kressa splays to the floor. He turns to me. "I'll spare Thea if you tell me why Kressa joined the competition."

Kressa pushes herself to her knees, and the barrier between us falls—crumbles like ancient, sea battered stone. *I spent my life knowing I'd one day rule the earth—a life I never asked for. I'd never force you to accept the same fate. To have no other option. I kept this from you because I wanted to give you freedom, even if it killed me.*

My chest constricts and turns my breaths to ragged gasps. That's what she told Harriet—she wished she could give me freedom.

But she's only chained me.

Caelus tightens the cord around my throat. "Have you suddenly forgotten how to speak?"

I narrow my eyes at Kressa. She blackmailed me, threatened me, lied to and manipulated me. But the worst is, she made me *trust* her. She took advantage of my vulnerability.

And I'll do anything for Thea.

My tongue turns to cotton, and as I nod, the wind loosens around my throat. I suck in a breath. "She's looking for a man named Elias."

"Briar, no."

Kressa's voice is no more than a rasp, eyes pleading. I throw up my mental barriers and shield the waves of anguish and betrayal roiling from her. I swallow the guilt—hot and barbed as it slides down my throat.

The accusation isn't anything illegal, but I could take it farther—expose her brother as Prince Barren, her as the future queen. But that would ensure her execution, and a soft part in my chest can't bear the possibility.

Caelus sneers. "Thank you, courtesan." He tilts his chin to the guards. "Take Kressa to her room and chain her to her bed until tomorrow's trial. And take Briar to the dungeon. My dungeon."

The wind pinning me to the wall disappears, and I push off, my boot aimed for Caelus, but two guards slam into me.

I fight their hold and flick my hair out of my face. "I gave you the information you want. Now take me to Thea."

Caelus grips my chin and yanks it up. "Oh Briar, you should know better than to trust me. She will die tomorrow." He lowers his mouth to my ear. "And so will Kressa."

A tremor wracks my jaw, the entire fabric of my being unraveling like a strand of thread. My hands thrash against the rhodium cuffs, and I lunge forward, but the guards tighten their grip.

"Hold her straight." Caelus says.

The guards tilt my shoulders until my bones screams in their sockets, threatening to dislocate. I grit my teeth and bite back the pain. "Too worried you wouldn't stand a chance if I were unbound?"

Caelus reels his fist back and strikes my cheekbone.

Kressa screams and lunges, throwing the guards off of her. But one lands a punch to her jaw and knocks her to the ground.

"Kressa!" I shriek.

For a heartbeat or a lifetime, our gazes lock. A thousand words pass between us—none spoken aloud or across the bond.

But in the silence, my heart crumples. I did what I promised I wouldn't do.

My eyes water, and an apology balances on the tip of my tongue. I form the thought into words and crack open my mind, ready to send it to her.

The hilt of a dagger slams into my head, and the world goes black.

52

———

sh fills my mouth. A throb beats in my head, loud and relentless.

I groan and force my eyes open, pushing to a seat on the stone floor. My vision swims, and I prod the tender spot at my temple. I wince, and bile rises up my throat. Pulling my legs to my chest, I hang my head between my knees and breathe away the nausea.

A breeze brushes over me, carrying a fine mist on tendrils of air. It teases my cheeks, weaves through my hair, and settles at the nape of my neck, grounding me.

No, *burning* me.

My head jerks up, and I take in my surroundings. The last rays of sunlight cast a glow over three walls of solid black granite. To my right, a metal door interrupts the wall. A small, latched window sits at the top, only large enough for a pair of eyes to peer in.

And to my left.

I scramble back, feet sliding against the damp floor.

Where a fourth wall should be, there's nothing but open air.

I steady my heart and lower to my stomach, sliding to the edge. Digging my nails into the black stone, I peer over.

A breath catches in my throat. Far, far below, the ocean roils, and waves crash against the side of the cliff face. Jagged rock formations jut from the surf like teeth, waiting to spear whoever falls over the edge.

This dungeon must be embedded in the mountains along the castle—a part I've never explored.

Sliding my hand over the edge of the cell, my fingers meet nothing but rock worn smooth from the unforgiving sea winds. Risking the drop, I reach further, but there are no breaks in the stone for handholds. I won't be climbing, then.

I crane my neck out of the cell. The mountain curves, and a few feet away, there's another opening. Wind batters sideways and whips my hair around my head as I scoot to the corner.

I cup my mouth. "Hello?"

Silence.

"Is anyone there?"

The wind carries away my voice.

"Thea? Elias? Are you there?"

My breathing stops, as if it could will them into existence. But I wait a full minute, and no one responds. I push back and lean against the side wall. My fists clench into my thin tunic, wringing the fabric.

A bang comes from the door, and I shoot to my feet as the small window slides open.

Blue eyes peer through. "You're awake."

I stride to the door and slam my hands against it. "Let me out, Caelus."

"You know, it was very convenient that Isolde turned you in as the thief, and we found the evidence directly on you. I had planned to lock you away in here anyway, but you gave me the perfect excuse."

My blood freezes over, and my palms dampen. "What are you talking about?"

The corners of his eyes crinkle. "If you would have bound yourself to me when I asked, you wouldn't be in this cell. But instead, you'll be doing it against your will."

I wrap my hands around the ledge of the small window and grit my teeth. "I will *never* bind to you."

A low laugh. "Briar, you have no choice. This cell has been constructed with power meant to break even the strongest minds. It's very effective. But don't worry, the pain of binding will pale compared to what you'll endure in these confines. You'll be begging for it before long."

My jaw clenches, and my fingernails drag over the door, metal screeching. "Where is Thea? Is she in this dungeon?"

He shrugs. "If she was, it wouldn't matter. Maybe you'll see her, or perhaps you'll only hear her scream."

Fire blazes through my veins. "I'll kill you."

He backs away from the door, into the dark hall, and looks at me down the bridge of his nose. "No, Briar. You will bow at my feet. And when I free my power from Terra's shackles, you will worship me. I'll keep your life hanging by a thread, just so you can bear witness to my power."

The window slams, echoing through the cell. I smack my palms against the door. I throw my body into it and scream until my lungs ache and my voice grows hoarse, but it's no use. The door doesn't so much as shift in its frame.

Pressing my forehead to the damp metal, I close my eyes.

"Briar?"

I freeze at the voice, and the hair on the back of my neck stands on edge. My throat seizes up, and a thick sensation burns at the back of my throat.

"Briar, honey?"

I turn, and the air rushes out of my lungs. The wind ceases, and my knees give out from under me. "Mother?"

She smiles, piercing my heart and shattering it into a million pieces. Her hair floats around her head as if she's underwater. But her voice is as clear as the sun in the sky, as crisp as the sea mist. And her ruby eyes—like swimming through coral reefs.

She holds out a hand. "I've missed you so much, Briar."

A sob wracks my body, and I stand, stumbling to her. I fall into her arms, and her embrace envelopes me—warms through my chest and eases the years that separated us. I cry into her shoulder as she combs her fingers through my hair, like she did when I was young.

"I'm sorry," I stammer. "I'm sorry for everything."

A choked sound comes from her, and her fingers halt. I lean back and tip my head. "Mother?"

But her eyes aren't focused on me. Her mouth widens into a silent scream, and her hands clutch her heart where blood pools beneath her white tunic. She stumbles back and slips, falling off the edge of the cell.

I throw myself forward and reach out an arm, but it's too late. Her body tumbles down and disappears into the waves. Gripping the edge, I will her to reappear—to swim safely through the waters we've called home forever. But she doesn't resurface.

My tears stream between the cracks in the stone, and I press my forehead to the floor as a scream rips from my throat.

"Briar?"

I stiffen, and a sour taste fills my mouth.

"Briar, honey."

My mother stands in the center of the cell, a hand outstretched. It isn't until now that I spot the haunting, blank look in her eyes—seeing but unseeing. Here, but not really. I don't move, and blood spreads down her tunic. She staggers backward and plummets to the sea.

I scramble away from the edge, digging my fingers into the stone as hot tears stream down my cheeks.

A tap comes from the metal door, and the window slides open. Unfamiliar eyes stare into my cell—not Caelus's, but equally as sharp. He turns, as if speaking to someone else. "I give it a day, tops."

The window shuts.

"Briar, honey."

Stomach acid burns my throat, and I crawl to the cobwebbed corner of the cell. I lean my head against the wall and cover my ears, but nothing stops my mother's pleading voice from seeping through. Her scream as she falls.

Twilight takes over evening, and the cell silences. Splashes from my mother's lifeless body halt. My muscles relax at the reprieve, and I open my eyes, dropping my palms from my ears.

A palm rests on my shoulder.

"Captain?"

My stomach plummets. I bury my face into the crook of my elbow and choke back a sob. She kneels beside me, her braids swishing around her waist, and I risk a glance.

Her face twists into a sneer, her nostrils flaring. "It's all your fault."

I bite a bloody hole into my cheek and sob, my throat tight.

"You took Celia away from me. And my power. My life is gone—all gone, because of you."

"Thea," I whisper, my voice grating.

But she doesn't answer. A high pitched, soul cleaving scream cuts through the air. I wrap my arms around my legs and press myself further into the corner as her shrieks echo through the chamber.

Their faces flash through my mind. Thea hanging from the mast with Celia at her side. Odette standing at the bow, wide eyed and fearless. Elayne, Collin, and Ivy—raising and lowering sails like extensions of their own arms. Katrina in the crow's nest. Astrid and Leigh at the stern. And Inez, eyes peeled over the water, searching for danger.

The Twelfth Night—the ship who never led me astray. A member in her own right. Without her, we're nothing.

Without them, I'm nothing.

Thea's wails shake the walls and etch into my mind. A reminder that I tore us all apart. I fall to my side and curl into a ball, staring ahead as stars twinkle into the night sky.

Her shrieks stop, and Thea disappears as quickly as my mother.

And somehow, the silence is worse than the pain of her company.

The ocean blends into the horizon, indistinguishable under the starry sky. Only the whitecaps reflect the moonlight.

A huff escapes my dry, cracked lips.

I'm a queen, gazing at my court. Yet touching it would mean death.

I close my eyes and burrow into my chest, searching for a shred of my power to cling to. A sign that I'm still me. But all that's left are monochromatic tendrils of what was once unlimited ribbons of power. I'm nothing but a husk.

A hand brushes through my hair, and a finger tucks a strand behind my ear. I shut my eyes, but even behind my eyelids, I know who it is. I'd know her touch anywhere.

"My love."

The fingers—her fingers—trail over my face and trace the curve of my jaw, the swell of my trembling lip. A stone settles in the back of my throat, and I'd do anything, give anything, to stop this torment.

Lips hover over my ear. "Even before I tasted your power, I knew we were bonded. When I looked into your eyes for the first time, I saw a future—fated to be yours. I've loved you from the moment I saw you."

A fresh wave of tears burns my cheeks, but I keep my eyes shut and whisper, "I'm sorry."

Her arms, so strong and so *real,* gather me to her chest. I cling to her and nestle my face into her shirt, giving myself a moment to pretend this is real. Fresh rain and white oak fill my nose. Her heartbeat thrums beneath my ear, and I let it envelop me, as if it generates my own.

"There's nothing you could do—in any lifetime—that I wouldn't forgive you for. I'm eternally yours, Briar."

I risk opening my eyes and tilt my head up.

A smile spreads over her face, her eyes shimmering in the starlight, and my heart rattles against my ribs. The light in my chest flares to life and bathes her in emerald. It's her. It's really her.

She's not dying, not falling over the edge. Not disappearing. Real.

"Kressa," I breathe.

"I'm getting you out of here." She presses a kiss to the top of my head. "Then we're going to find Thea and go far, far away."

I sink into her, and the tension leaves my body like a wave retreating from shore. "How did you get—"

My shoulder slams into the stone, and I press to my palms, frantically scanning the cell. But it's empty of everything but me and my heaving sobs. My throat constricts.

"No," I rasp.

She's gone.

A fresh wave of nausea sweeps over me, and I crawl to the edge of the cell, retching over the side. When the bile eases, I rest my chin on the jagged stone and stare into the abyss below. It beckons me—promises a swift death. I'd smash into the piercing rock formations, or plunge into the water. Either would be instant.

Far less painful than the endless torture of this chamber.

"My love."

My stomach tightens, but there's nothing left to be emptied. Teardrops fall like rain. Footsteps pad to me, and the ghost of her fingers caress my face.

I shake my head and push back from the edge. I can't allow myself to break—not tonight, at least. Tucking my knees into my chest, I curl into a ball. Kressa's warmth envelops me, and I don't fight her off. Better to let myself imagine the comfort is real.

She whispers tender words into my ear, and sleep overcomes me, interrupted every few minutes by a soft caress from the ghost of her.

My only tether to reality.

53

A cramp in my stomach stirs me, but I seal my eyes shut. Anything to avoid seeing another person I care about disappearing or falling to the jagged rocks below.

But no voices float to my ears. Kressa's fingers don't comb my hair. No screams rattle the cell. And somehow, the empty pit in my stomach grows.

The ocean swells, and early dawn paints the whitecaps in pastel hues of pale pink and tangerine.

My last sunrise. And if Caelus keeps his promise, the last for Thea and Kressa, too. My eyes are swollen and dry, yet fresh tears fall down my face. Because of me, Kressa will never see her brother again, and Thea will never reunite with Celia.

The third trial begins in a few short hours, if not sooner. When it does, the power binding me to the competition will kill me.

I peer over the edge, and the jagged formations beckon me. At least mother was killed in battle, protecting our court. I'll simply perish in this cell, staring at the home I've done nothing but harm.

Queen, indeed.

I rest my cheek on my forearm, and the rough obsidian floor digs into my ribs. But I don't shift. I deserve the pain piercing my skin, aching my muscles. A penance.

A sweet song fills the air.

My body tenses, stomach churning at whoever the cell will torment me with next. Marianne? Rita? The remainder of my crew? Perhaps I'll see *The Twelfth Night* floating in the distance, engulfed in flames.

But no touch appears—no bodily manifestation. The notes grow louder, floating over the ocean. I untangle my arms and legs and press into a seat, training my focus on the song.

A grin spreads across my face.

I jump to my feet and cup my hands around my mouth. "Louder!"

My words aren't more than a hoarse croak, but the voice grows, joined by another, and another.

Sirens.

I throw my weight into the door and beat my fists against the metal. My skin splits over my knuckles, but I don't relent. The song continues, sweet and melodic. Irresistible.

The small window unlatches and swings open, revealing a pair of beady eyes. "I'm surprised you haven't jumped. You screamed all—"

His pupils dilate, blotting out the blue of his unblinking eyes. They hone in on the ocean.

I smile. "You were saying?"

The heavy bolt slides, and the door opens into the cell. The guard enters, his arms and legs swinging as the languid notes pull him closer to the ocean. As if I'm not in the cell, he strides off the edge and doesn't make a sound until his body slaps the water.

Sunlight spills over the waves and illuminates three heads

bobbing in the distance. I nod and sink into a deep bow. A tug pulls in my mind, and I open the bridge.

We bow to you, Your Majesty.

The space behind my eyes stings, but I don't have time to cry—not when the final trial will start any minute. Holding my breath, I lean out of the cell and peer down the corridor. Empty.

I slide into the dark hall, and my hand reaches for my dagger, but it closes into a fist and I grimace. Caelus's guards knocked it out of my grasp at the safe house. The blade I've had for my entire life, gone.

The hall curves on itself, and no windows line the space, yet natural light streams through—

"No."

Cells hang open, as if a group of prisoners were escorted out. I count them. Eight—one for each competitor left. My stomach plummets, and I break into a sprint, my boots sliding along the slick, uneven stones.

I grip the rail of a steep flight of stairs, going down two at a time, and come to a landing with a narrow door. Light seeps from the crack at the bottom, and voices filter through. I ease it open, and my blood freezes over.

Two alabaster thrones sit on the dais, facing away from me. I slip into the ballroom, and the door disappears into the marble wall, the seams hardly visible—like the servant's door in Harriet's room.

I swallow. Kressa didn't know about this dungeon. Her father either kept it hidden, or Caelus had it constructed when he invaded Sarenia. I can only hope it's the latter.

Voices echo, and I peer around the throne where a servant crosses the entryway, her arms laden with a basket of bread. I throw myself from the dais and run across the room.

"Wait!"

She backtracks and furrows her brows. "Briar?"

"Have you seen Gemma?"

Her gaze drags over me. My hair hangs limp around my shoulders, clothes damp from the constant sea mist, eyes red and swollen.

She bites her lip. "She left for the final trial with everyone else about twenty minutes ago. The kitchen staff were asked to stay behind and prepare lunch."

My vision blurs, fingers trembling at my side. "When does the trial start?"

She glances at a clock above our heads and shrugs. "About fifteen minutes."

My stomach sinks through the floor, and my pulse races in my ears. I'll never make it. "Where?"

"Behind the gardens." She reaches a hand to my shoulder and squeezes it. "Is everything okay?"

"Fine."

I slip from her grip and take off through the castle. Servants stare as I fly past, and my heart thunders in my chest, my body aching from where Caelus and the guards hit me. My lungs beg for air—for a break—but I can't stop. I have to get to the final trial with or without glamour.

I stumble into my quarters and dart for the dressing room, yanking out the pirate's clothing from my armoire.

Shedding my clothes, I slide the pants on and haphazardly tuck in the shirt. My fingers shake as I wrestle with the laces on my boots, tying them as tight as possible. I stand before the mirror.

A vise squeezes my windpipe.

Our frames are entirely different—Harriet's stature taller than my own. But only someone looking close enough would notice the difference in our shoulders and the length of our legs.

It's my face and hair that's a dead giveaway.

But I have no other choice.

I snatch the wide brimmed hat and sprint to the vanity. Rummaging through the drawers, I pull out a pair of shears and wrap my hair around my fist. In a single slice, I cut it off. The blunt ends fall to my shoulders, and I shake it out. It's not the same ashy blonde as Harriet's, but it'll have to do.

I gather it into a bun at my nape and press the hat low over my face, hiding the majority of my hair and shadowing my eyes.

Seconds tick by on the clock. Five minutes until the trial. I don't have time to consider how, if someone gets too close, they'll recognize me.

Either I die here when the competition begins, or I die trying to save Thea.

The dagger's absence weighs at my thigh, but I bolt through the door and bank to the ballroom, my heart slamming against my ribs. I clear the balcony and sprint down the curving double set of stairs.

Nobles mill about the garden, sipping on champagne in suits and elaborate gowns. A newly constructed staircase sweeps up the face of the mountain, leading to a grandstand perched at the top rim. A cluster of dark clouds hang over the arena, promising rain.

A hesitant smile crosses my face. The clouds cast shadows over the arena, just dark enough to hide my main features.

I shove through the crowd and anchor the hat over my face as I climb the stairs, my legs shaking by the time I reach the top. Weaving through the bodies, I skirt around the side and lower myself into the arena.

The grandstands form a half circle around the arena, where the seven other competitors stand in a single line, staring at the rocky plateau in the distance. At the other end, metal cages hang off the cliff.

My stomach hollows out, and a cold pang slices down my spine.

In the center cage—Thea.

54

———————

I scan the crowd from lowered eyes. Caelus and Isolde sit at the top, flanked by royal guards, and a sliver of tension releases from my shoulders. They're too far away to recognize me.

A flash of red catches my eye from the opposite end. Marianne stands and taps Gemma's shoulder, pointing at me. Our gazes lock, and the color drains from Gemma's face.

She holds out her hands and mouths, "I can't."

I nod. "I know."

Her hands drop, and Marianne sinks into her seat. I tip my hat. If I don't make it out of this trial, I hope they know how much their help meant to me.

In the distance, Thea clings to the rungs of her cage. And beside her—I squint my eyes. A man sits on the metal floor with his knees tucked into his chest, and on his lowered head— a black helmet.

Elias.

As if he senses my stare, he lifts his head and turns in my direction.

A body shoves me from behind.

"Where have you been?"

I stiffen at the familiar voice and yank the hat farther down, dipping into a shadow. Closing off my mind, I clear my throat. "I slept in."

Her boots crunch over loose rock. "You haven't been in your bedroom for days, and I haven't seen you since the night of the ball." Another menacing step. "I'll ask one time, *pirate*, did you tip off Caelus? Did you tell him where I was going?"

"What?"

Frost sparkles over the stands and silences the crowd, tearing Kressa's attention away, enough for me to widen the distance between us.

Caelus rises, and a grin pulls at his lips. "Welcome to the final trial. Competitors, you may have noticed there is someone important to you at the other end of the arena, hanging off the cliff. The cages are charmed in such a way that the person inside cannot free themselves."

The cages swing in the distance, the hinges squealing.

"When the cannon blasts, you have thirty minutes to make it to the other side and free your loved one before he or she falls to the ocean below. If you are still in the arena when the final cannon blasts, you will die, and your target will be dropped."

I scan the plateau and furrow my brows. Nothing separates us from the cages but a craggy expanse. If I hurried, it would take no longer than five minutes to get to Thea.

Guards roll a massive hourglass into the arena.

The tip of Kressa's boots comes into view. "Answer me. Now."

"I didn't tip off anyone." I shove my hands into my pockets and stare at the ground. "I'll answer all of your questions later."

She takes a step closer. I retreat one.

Her hand rests on the hilt of a dagger I've learned she keeps hidden at her waistline, and her voice lowers to a growl.

"Where were you when Briar left the castle? Did you hand Thea over?"

I flinch. "Of course not."

"Then why won't you look at me? What are you hiding, Harriet?"

She reaches for my hat, but I throw my hand on top of it. My heart leaps to my throat, and I duck farther into the shadows, but she only follows.

There's only one thing I can do.

I open my mind.

Cordelia?

Her entire body stiffens, and she stumbles back. I peek out from under the brim of my hat. Shielding her eyes with a hand, she searches the stadium.

I swallow a gasp at the deep bruises peppering her jaw, and the swelling at her brow. A swollen eye. My hands ball into fists. Caelus couldn't kill her, but that didn't stop him from coming close. I don't need to see the rest of Kressa's body to know bruises cover her ribs, her legs.

Her hand falls from the dagger. *Briar? Where are you?*

My throat aches. After everything I've done, her voice still softens for me. And that voice—the same one that whispered into my ear in the cell—is the only things that kept me from rolling off the edge. I bite my cheek and stave off the tears gathering behind my eyes.

I caress her mind. *Does Caelus know who you really are?*

Her gaze rakes over the crowd, the far edges, the rocky mountains cradling either side of the arena. *No, they think I'm Elias's lover. Not illegal enough to execute me apparently.*

A lump rises in my throat. *I'm sorry.*

We both made mistakes. Are you in the stands?

My mouth pinches into a half smile. *No.*

Then where are you? Are you okay?

My fingers brush the pendant beneath my shirt. *Don't worry about me. I need your word that no matter what you may discover about me, you'll never look at me any different. I need to know you won't hate me.*

She runs her hand over the back of her neck. I commit her to memory—the breadth of her shoulders, the way the ends of her hair curl slightly, her soft, comforting hands. The way my soul calls to hers. If I die today, I want to die with the memory of her fingertips trailing a line of fire down my skin. I want the ghost of her lips to live on mine forever.

Warmth sweeps into my mind, and I lean into it.

A swallow bobs her throat. *Nothing could change what I feel for you, Briar.*

And Cordelia?

Her lip quirks. *I'm Kressa to you. I always have been and always will be.*

I watch her, but I don't see Cordelia. I see Kressa—my bonded. The other half of my soul. Would she see me the same, if she knew who I really was?

I shove the thought away. *Don't harm Harriet. She had nothing to do with this.*

Kressa glances sidelong at me. *I don't trust her.*

But I do.

Her tongue prods the inside of her cheek. *Fine. I won't harm her. On one condition.*

What's that?

Your forgiveness. If it means I drop to my knees at your feet and beg, so be it. I will crawl to you if I must—if it means you'll forgive me for lying to you. If what you truly want is to never see me again, so be it. But I cannot bear my existence knowing I hurt you.

Silence stretches between us—each beat of her heart echoing as if it's my own. I could lose her in this trial, and nothing would hurt like that. I need her to live.

Survive, Cordelia. And I'll find you.

The cannon blasts.

55

———

A competitor takes off and scrambles over the jagged rocks of the slight incline. A woman inside a cage slams her hands against the metal bars, screaming something inaudible over the roaring crowd. She falls to her knees and cups her face with her hands.

The man freezes, and the ground sinks beneath his right foot.

He throws out his arms and stares down, his eyes widening. The crowd silences, and the air thickens with anticipation. He lifts his foot, and an arrow shoots from an opening along the mountainside, toward him.

It pierces his chest.

Before his body hits the ground, the metal arm holding the cage releases, and the woman plummets to the water, screaming until a splash silences her.

The breath rushes from my lungs. Sand streams through the middle of the hourglass. Too fast.

"It's laced with traps," Kressa whispers.

I sink into a crouch and survey the arena. With the rugged landscape, there's no way to predict where the traps are.

Standing, I angle my body away from her. "We only have thirty minutes."

A strong gust of wind blasts us, tossing up loose rocks and gravel. I throw a hand over the hat as we're shoved deeper into the arena. The other pirate—Mahone—trips over his feet and slams to the ground. It sinks beneath him, and he scrambles, but a spear shoots from the rocks and skewers him to the spot.

A cage drops.

Bile rises in the back of my throat.

The wind disappears, and the heavy clouds floating above dump a sheet of rain, obscuring my sight and slickening the rocks under my feet. Over my shoulder, the stands are completely dry.

Caelus wants us all dead.

A cannon fires, vibrating the ground. Five minutes have already passed, and I haven't budged. I'm no closer to saving Thea. My pulse races faster than the sand draining through the hourglass.

Through the rain, movement catches my eye, and the cages swing farther from the edge. Thea drops to the floor of her enclosure, gripping the bars.

"They go farther out every five minutes," I breathe. "By the time we get there, it'll be nearly impossible to reach."

Kressa risks a step. "Then what are we waiting for?"

She tests the ground with the edge of her boot, and when it doesn't give way, she puts her full weight on it. I hold my breath and study the mountain walls. No arrows shoot out, and no spears fly from the ground.

Her lips press into a thin line. "Any day now, pirate."

I follow her lead, testing each step before advancing another. The cannon fires—twice this time. Ten minutes. The cages slide out again, swinging precariously over the drop. A third of the time has passed, and the cages are still small in the distance.

"We won't make it going this slow," I say.

She nods, staring at her brother, sitting calmly in his cage while the others tremble. After a decade in confinement, I suppose this death is a merciful one.

A gasp comes from nearby, and no more than a dozen feet away, Eric freezes on all fours with his hand sunken into the ground. His eyes widen, and he mouths an apology toward the cages. A young girl—no older than ten—presses her face against the bars.

"Wait!" I scream.

Scrambling over the rocky terrain, I disregard where my feet fall and throw myself to his side.

His tear-stained eyes meet mine, and his brows furrow. "You're not Harriet."

"If you say anything," I hiss, fixing the hat over my eyes, "I will kill you before the trap does."

He swallows and nods.

I lift a small boulder and brace it against my body, testing its weight. "This might hurt, but you can't move."

Slowly, I lower it onto his hand. He winces, but doesn't pull away as his fingers are crushed beneath it.

"I'm going to lift the edge, and when I do, slide out your hand."

He nods. I heave the very edge of the stone, and his mangled fingertips clear the space. Blood drips onto the ground. I release the rock and hold my breath, but no arrows fly toward us.

"Thank you," he whispers.

"I didn't do it for you." I nod toward the cages, rain spilling over the brim of my hat. "I did it for her."

He rubs at his mangled hand. "Consider me in your debt."

Ice climbs up the incline behind us, and the rain morphs into hail. It pelts against my shoulders and chest, hard enough to leave welts.

Caelus's voice rumbles. "Cheating will not be tolerated."

Lightning spears the top of the neighboring peak over and over in blasts of blinding white, until a layer of rock becomes loose. The ground shakes, and boulders bounce down the mountainside. A rock the size of my torso sails through the air, and I dive out of its way, throwing my hands over my face as the earth shudders and debris burrows into my skin.

Jumping to my feet, I throw Eric ahead of me. "Run!"

I search for Kressa, but falling stones and hail block any visibility. A scream rips through the air, followed by a splash, and my stomach clenches. I slip on ice and fall to my knees, rocks digging into my palms, but force myself upright.

The cannon blasts, and the cages swing out, groaning on their hinges. I've lost track of time. I narrow my eyes and make out Thea's cage. And beside her—Elias. A breath rushes out of my lungs. Kressa is okay.

The rockslide eases, and boulders settle into a heap, covering half the arena. The hail halts and silence falls.

"Get down!" Kressa screams.

I drop, and an arrow skims my hat. It sinks into the side of the competitor beside me, and he falls the same moment a cage does.

Three remain.

A hand appears in front of me, the lines running her palm so familiar it aches. I refuse it and straighten, angling my head away.

"Thanks," I murmur.

She turns toward the cages, prodding each step with her boot. The fabric of her shirt is torn at the shoulder, exposing a wide, bleeding gash. I reach out, but close my hand into a fist before my fingers brush her. Harriet wouldn't do that.

The cannon blasts.

Kressa quickens her pace. "We only have fifteen minutes."

Eric reaches his cage and leans over the edge, pulling it

closer and turning the handle. The young girl jumps out and wraps him in a hug, sobbing into his shoulder. A path appears along the edge of the arena—a safe route back.

I test each step until I stop feet in front of Thea's enclosure. Our gazes meet, and the blood drains from her face.

"You're not—" Her voice levels off in a tremor, knuckles blanched around the cage bars.

Bringing my finger to my mouth, I whisper, "I couldn't get to Gemma in time."

A dozen feet away, Elias turns his head, and his eerie gaze pierces me like he's solving a puzzle. I angle away and shake off his stare as I toe the edge of the cliff. I lean out, reaching for the bars of the cage, but the cannon blasts, and the cage swings out of reach.

Thea yelps, clinging the bars.

My heart catches in my throat. "It's okay. I'll get you."

Her chest shudders, but she nods. I retrace my steps and wait for the cage to stop swinging.

"Keep still," I order.

I take off at a sprint, feet pounding against the rocky mountaintop. My hat, heavy from rain, weighs my head down. I reach the edge and jump. My arms windmill as the safety of ground disappears beneath me, and I slam into the cage. It lurches, and I wrap my fingers around the rungs.

There's nothing below but the raging, open ocean.

I shoot Thea a wild smile. "To the ends of the earth?"

She doesn't laugh. "Get me out of this fucking cage."

I hone my focus on the bars instead of the thrashing waves and make my way to the door. A gust of wind rattles the metal, and I reach out, twisting the handle. The door bursts open.

She hesitates.

"Go," I pant. "I'm right behind you."

With a nod, she steps to the back of the cage and pins her

focus on the plateau. She breaks into a run, and I hold my breath as she jumps from the edge.

Her dress catches the wind and billows out behind her, slowing her down, but her feet meet the edge of the cliff, and she stumbles forward to safety.

I release a breath and climb into the cage, navigating to the back. The cage steadies itself and I turn, ready to make the leap.

But I halt, and bile rises in my throat.

At the edge of the mountain, Kressa stands frozen, her right foot sunken into the earth.

56

Elias rises, his knuckles white on the bars of his cage.

I can't breathe, can't form a rational thought as I clamber out of Thea's cage and scale to the top. Wind batters me, and I crouch low on the edge, hands trembling.

Don't move a muscle, I say through the bond.

Kressa flinches, and her gaze lands on me, eyes narrowed. *Briar?*

"Thea!"

She stands at attention. "Yes?"

A smile coats my lips despite the drop below me. The way she stands, with her hands pinned to her side, eyes rapt—my first mate. "Find a boulder heavy enough to replace Kressa's foot."

She nods and takes off toward a pile of boulders. Elias's eyes brighten and, following my thought process, he centers himself in the cage, leveling it out.

Kressa's eyes shoot wide. *This whole time, you've been—*

I grip the final rung and bring my knees beneath me. *I told you. I need that ship.*

Her gaze flicks between me and the top of Elias's cage. *Don't do whatever you're about to do. You can join Thea and win the competition. I—I can't lose you.*

I made you a promise.

I leap. My stomach bottoms out as I catch a glimpse of the ocean below. A gust of wind flips my hat off, and my hair comes loose from its tie. Gasps explode from the stands as I slam into the side of Elias's cage and grapple for the bars.

Putting one hand over the other, I circle the edge of the cage to the door. My hands sting, raw and bloodied from the abrasive metal.

Through the rhodium helmet, his brown eyes blink. "You're her bonded."

My fingers freeze around the handle as I study the man I was meant to marry. "How do you know?"

The helmet hides his mouth, but his eyes crinkle around the edges. "I see it on her face. The way she looked at you when you leapt from the cage—love doesn't come close."

I throw the door open, and it clatters into the bars. "We can discuss your sister's feelings when we're on land."

An amused huff comes from the helmet, and he backs into the cage, holding his arms out for balance. He inhales a deep breath and runs, leaping through the air to the mountaintop.

Thea appears with a large boulder between her hands, but a layer of ice appears under her feet. She slams to the ground, and her head bashes against the rock. She goes limp, and my scream echoes off the mountains.

Scrambling into the cage, I throw myself to the back and turn.

I take a step, ready to run, but the cannon blasts. The cage shoots away from the edge and I grip the bars as it swings wildly, threatening to throw me out the open door.

"Briar!" Kressa screams.

Ice inches closer to her, and a group of guards stride up the side of the arena. A knot forms in my throat. Caelus, flanked by royal guards, and Isolde following at the rear.

"Swing the cage!" Kressa calls, voice trembling.

I step forward and brace myself on the bars, shifting my weight forward and backward. The cage swings, but no matter how hard I throw myself around, it doesn't get close enough to clear the jump.

Listen to me, Briar.

I pause at the defeat in her voice. The intent in her eyes as she studies the hook holding the cage.

She returns her gaze to me. *Jump on my count. There's a dagger in my boot. Take it and fight your way out.*

My limbs go cold, and I shake my head. *No. Don't you dare.*

It's the only way.

If you lift your foot, Kressa, I will never forgive you. I cannot lose you.

A smile crosses her face, pure and genuine. *Losing me is impossible, my love. I've always been yours. And forever will be.*

"Three."

Tears stream down my face. "No!"

"Two."

My lungs seize up. "Kressa, no!"

Caelus's narrowed glare comes into view, and lightning crackles in the storm clouds.

The cage swings, cresting closer to the edge, and Kressa smiles.

I love you, Briar.

"One."

She lifts her foot.

An arrow shoots from the mountain and plunges into her heart.

A scream wracks my throat, my lungs. Blood blooms beneath her shirt, and she falls to her knees, slumping to the side. My soul cleaves into two as the life pours from her.

The cage reaches its peak, and I fling myself toward the mountain. There's nothing but the open sea beneath me as solid land shoots closer. I grapple for loose rocks on the edge, and my hands find purchase on a root, holding tight. Grimacing, I heave myself up and throw myself onto the plateau.

I lunge to Kressa and fall to her side, running my hands over her body. I trace the arrow where it meets skin, but it's burrowed too deep to pull out. My breaths come out in rasps, and my throat constricts. Her chest rises and falls, but her heartbeat slows, chest stutters.

Then it halts.

A scream rips from my throat and reaches the heavens, severs the ocean.

Diving into myself, I scrounge every wisp of power I can and press my hands to Kressa's chest, willing it into her. It saved her once, and if I have to drain every last drop of my power to do it again, so be it. A blue glow radiates through my chest, down my arms, and straight into Kressa.

Her power flickers in my chest, as if it can sense her fading. I hold my breath until my lungs burn.

She doesn't move.

"Briar, you are under arrest for treason."

My hands still on Kressa's unmoving chest, and my fingers curl into fists. I inch my fingers down her body and slide the dagger from her ankle. My breath catches.

It's my dagger.

I force myself up and suck in air through my nose, lips pressed into thin line. My eyes harden, and a boiling swell churns within me. Pure, unadulterated rage ripples from me in waves, my hand a vise on the dagger.

Caelus smirks. "Arrest her."

The pair of royal guards draw their swords and advance. I lunge at the first and dodge his sword. Spinning behind him, I drag the blade across his throat.

He drops, sword clattering to the ground.

The other hesitates, and I slam my boot into his chest. He lands on his back, and I lunge, plunging the dagger into his chest.

"Treason, you say?" I glare at Caelus. "Or perhaps you're simply embarrassed I fooled you."

A chunk of ice slams into me and throws me away from the guard. The dagger flies out of my hand and lands out of reach as another blast hits me across the face. My vision swims. Rocks dig into my palms, and I come to my knees. I lift a leg, but before I can stand, a layer of ice freezes me to the ground.

I fight against the ice, bashing it with my fists, but it holds steady. It crawls up my legs, over my hips, and roots me to the spot.

Caelus looms over me. "Do you have any final words?"

"I do, in fact." My lip curls away from my teeth. "You are many things, Caelus. A murderer, a false king, a tyrant. But there's one thing you'll never be—a god. You will never have power of your own."

He draws his sword. It whines against the scabbard, and he lifts it over his shoulder, early morning sun glinting off the metal.

My limbs grow heavy, and exhaustion overcomes me. This is it. I've failed. With no heir to the sea, it will forever be ruled by Caelus. Thea will never see Celia again. And Kressa—

Perhaps I'd rather die than live without her.

A tear splashes to the ground, and I lower my head, waiting for the final blow.

"No!"

A body tackles Caelus to the ground, and they roll in a blur, shards of ice piercing the air.

Kressa.

She wrestles the sword out of Caelus's hand and flicks it to his chest. The ice melts around my waist, turns to slush, and I rise, my pants soaked with freezing water.

I take a step toward Kressa, my breath catching. "You're alive."

I scan her—the hole in her shirt bloodied from where she pulled out the arrow. The open gash now a healed, light pink.

"Impossible," Caelus breathes.

An arm wraps around my throat from behind, and a dagger presses deep into my skin, right above the artery.

"Drop the sword, or I'll slit her throat," Isolde says.

My eyes shoot wide, jaw trembling against the hands that once held me so gently.

Kressa's hand falters on the sword.

Don't! I shout through the bond.

I wrap my fingers around Isolde's forearm and dig my nails into skin. She yanks me against her chest, shoving the blade deeper.

A bead of blood trails down my throat.

She lowers her mouth to my ear. "Or perhaps I'll slit it anyway."

I squirm, but she anticipates every move, holding me tight.

A tremor shakes the ground, and the blade drops from my throat. Isolde grunts, and her body disappears from mine. She falls to her knees and clutches at her chest as a blue cloud pours from her.

Her power.

I pluck my dagger from the ground and swallow mouthfuls of air. A shimmer appears at the cliff, thickening, and a woman manifests. Where her feet land, grass grows and flowers bloom. A warm breeze rustles her long, silver hair, and at her fingertips —water.

Terra.

I fall to my knees, and Kressa rolls from Caelus.

The goddess disregards us, turning instead to him.

"Caelus." Her voice is sweet as honey, yet hard as stone. "You know the rules. All who survive the third trial shall be judged."

Isolde writhes, and the cloud of power around her billows.

"But she disguised herself to enter," he says.

Terra drags her gaze over me. Her eyes oscillate between shades of blue and hazel and black. She tilts her head. "Interesting."

A warm breeze sweeps over me, carrying notes of lavender and salty brine. It sinks beneath my skin, and Terra stiffens.

She returns her attention to Caelus. "You will hold a fourth trial for her."

Elias appears with his arm slung around Thea's waist, helping her walk, and I swallow a sob. She's alive. Bloody, but alive.

Terra nods at Elias. "His freedom has been won. Release him."

Caelus stands. "But his power is too dangerous."

Isolde screams, and her face loses blood as her power drains.

"Fine," Caelus bites, digging a thin skeleton key from his pocket.

He approaches Elias, but Terra holds up a hand. "No, not you." Her head turns to me. "She saved him, she releases him."

I nod and rise on shaky legs, swallowing as I stride to Caelus. Hesitating, I pull the key from his hands and turn it over. Despite its small size, it's heavy, and a delicate filigree runs along its base. Elias settles Thea against a boulder and crosses to me.

The man I tried to kill.

"I owe you my life," he says. Cords of green are woven in his brown irises, the opposite of Kressa's.

"You don't owe me anything," I whisper.

He turns, and I slot the key into the base of the helmet. With a twist, it fractures into two. He reaches behind his head and separates it. Oily blonde hair spills out, falling to his shoulders in ratted curls.

The rhodium helmet drops to the ground.

He turns to me and roams his hands over his face. A smile tugs at his mouth, but when our gazes lock, it disappears.

The green swims in his eyes, and his voice lowers to a whisper. "You're the Princess of the Sea."

I flinch back. "I don't know what you're talking about."

"We were meant to marry." His head tilts, and he hums. "Ah, I see. Kressa has no idea who you are. That you tried to kill her, thinking she was me."

I swallow. "You're wrong."

"I'm never wrong." He clicks his tongue. "Don't worry, I have no reason to tell my sister who you are. Not yet, at least."

Terra steps to my side and lifts a weightless hand to my cheek. "Time for your final trial."

My vision goes black.

57

Midday sun beats down on my back, my arms bound at the wrist. Seagulls cry overhead. I lift onto my knees and blink my eyes open.

The ocean stretches into the distance, and a sandbar peeks through the low tide. Waves crash into wooden posts and spray sea mist through the cracks in the planks.

I swallow and twist, looking over my shoulder.

The wide docks form a maze back to the shore, punctuated by ships belonging to both pirates and the Sky Court. A crowd gathers at the harbor, shielding their eyes from the sun.

But between the safety of land and me, Caelus and Isolde stand surrounded by royal guards. Eric and Kressa linger behind, and the latter watches me, inspecting my every move. I search the crowd in the distance, but Thea is nowhere to be found.

Venom shoots through Caelus's glare. "In an unprecedented turn of events, we will be holding a fourth trial. On the sandbar in the distance, there is a small item. Retrieve it, and you'll be included in the final judgement. Fail, and you succumb to the creature in these depths."

I stand, clenching every muscle against the imbalance of having my wrists bound. Wincing against the rope, I peer over the edge. There could be any number of creatures in the water, but that isn't what I have to worry about.

Kressa taps on my mind, and I ease it open.

Do you still trust me? she says.

The hole in her shirt reveals the pale pink scar over her heart. The heart I brought back to life.

I nod. *Yes.*

Then trust I'll keep you safe.

Caelus brandishes a short knife. "Hold out your arms."

He cuts through the rope, and I rub at my wrists—angry and red from being bound so tight. I glance at the ocean and snarl. "No one would survive this."

"That's exactly the point. A shame for such beauty to go to waste. You could have allowed me to bind you, and you'd be living a peaceful life by my side. But then you escaped from the dungeon." He tips the blade toward my throat. "How did you do that?"

I bare my teeth. "Go ahead, slice my throat open. We'll see how long it takes Terra to return. If I was a betting woman, I'd say before the first drop of my blood hits the deck."

He snarls and tosses the rope into the sea. It floats at the surface, and a ripple cascades around it.

Caelus smirks. "No need to dirty my hands when there's something that can kill you much quicker."

A shadow lurks beneath the strip of rope, then grows larger. Wider. A fang-tipped jaw shoots from the murky depths, and a snakelike body twists out of the water. Scales larger than my hand spear from its skin.

A sea serpent.

It releases an ear-piercing screech and closes its maw around the rope. I scramble back as it curves in on itself and the cloudy film coating its eyes parts. A yellow eye stares at me, the pupil nothing but a vertical black slit.

It dives into the ocean and disappears.

My knees tremble, and I search for a way out, but there's nothing. Nothing but a dock at my back and a splintered sea at my front.

Raise your head, my love. Do not let him see you balk.

"If you don't begin," Caelus says, "it'll count as a forfeit, and you will lose your life."

My gaze finds Kressa. The world beyond the two of us blurs and time slows, as if this space between us was granted by the heavens itself. With her, a thousand lifetimes would never be enough.

And here we are, without even one.

Sucking in a breath, I run a calming hand down her mind. *When I fall into the water, I'll die. And it's not death that scares me, but fear that wherever I go, you won't be there.*

Briar, that's something you never need to worry about.

But—

Her eyes harden. *I'd find you anywhere.*

A blue light shines beneath her shirt, dim enough to go unnoticed, and warmth blankets me.

"Enough already."

Caelus shoves me over the edge of the dock. I scramble for the planks, but my fingers slide off the edge of the rotted wood.

I fall.

Waves churn beneath me, waiting to swallow me whole, and my stomach bottoms out. I force my eyes open. If the ocean welcomes me home by stealing my final breath, I want to see it.

I slam into solid ground.

The air knocks from my lungs, and sand envelops my fingers. A small island, not much bigger than me.

Briar, run!

Shadows bounce between the planks above, and boots

pound against the wood, edging closer. I scramble to my feet and rub my shoulder where it slammed into the earth.

Earth.

Kressa's power.

You need to move, now!

Her thoughts come through panicked, and I whip my head up as the serpent breaks the surface. My heart rises into my throat. The creature arcs through the air toward me, fangs preparing to tear flesh.

Run!

I break into a sprint. The serpent lands on the small island, and its sharp fin catches my pant leg, slicing a clean cut through my calf. I scream, pumping my arms, and under each footfall, earth appears.

A low hiss vibrates from the serpent, and it slinks back into the water.

The sandbank grows nearer, and sweat drips down my face, the sun blinding me.

On your right!

The serpent shoots up, mouth open wide, fangs dripping with a poisonous green liquid. Filmed eyes flash across my vision, and it slams into me.

I crest through the air, the water inches below me. A grunt echoes in my mind, and I crash into sand, sliding to a stop. The serpent arcs, its tongue tasting the air as a hiss reverberates through my bones. It rears back, and I dart out of the way as its fangs sink into the sand. It thrashes, but its jaw is stuck. Leaping to my feet, I take off toward the sandbank.

I pump my arms as the ground rises beneath me, as if Kressa can predict my every move.

Almost there, she says.

Exhaustion seeps through her thoughts, and her words are heavy as my feet reach the sandbank. A small drawstring pouch sits at the peak, and I sprint to it, my chest heaving.

I fall to my knees and spare a glance over my shoulder, where the people on the dock aren't more than specks. Turning back to the pouch, I pull the strings open.

My brow furrows. It's a large, clear marble. Inside, waves of light and dark blue twist together like a vortex. I close my fingers around the sphere, and a blinding, blue light shoots into the sky.

Applause travels from the harbor and over the water.

The light disappears as quickly as it came, and I shove the marble into the bag, tying the drawstrings around my belt loop. Scanning the waves, I search for any disturbance in the water, but it's calm. No sign of the serpent.

I tread to the edge of the sandbank, where Kressa's path leads back to the dock. But the ocean ripples, the earth itself shaking. And in a single breath, the path back sinks into the water.

My heart thuds against my ribcage, and my throat constricts. *Kressa?*

Her thoughts come through muffled, as if it's an effort to communicate. But two words break through the static. *Rhodium cuffs.*

I retreat a step. Another. I fall to my knees.

My damp hair plasters to my forehead and hot sand dumps into my boots. The waves pull out and crash back in, stretching higher than before. Foam nearly reaches my knees.

High tide.

I run a finger over the damp sand, and ignore the searing pain as it burns my skin. I bite my lip and consider. An instant of blinding agony, then it would be over. Death would be my choice—at the hand of my home rather than Caelus.

Rising, I step closer to the surf.

Don't you dare.

My gaze drifts to the sun-beaten dock, and the bond pulls my focus directly to Kressa.

Panic flows from her, as well as the bite of rhodium as she strains against the cuffs.

Please, she begs.

Tears stain my cheeks, and a wave arcs, crashing against the sandbar.

Goodbye, Kressa.

I take the final step.

58

The serpent slams into me and throws me to the sand. Its weight slithers across my middle, razor sharp fins ripping through my shirt and slicing into flesh. I scream and thrash, beating my fists against its scales.

Its body lifts, and I jump to my feet, blood streaming down my shirt. The serpent slides along the sand and turns, blinking open the film coating its eyes. It hisses and arches its front half from the sand, like a whip ready to strike.

I back up, my legs trembling. Without a blade and nowhere to run, I don't stand a chance.

Its eyes glaze over, and a forked tongue samples the air.

Then it strikes.

I throw myself to the side as its fangs sink into the sand. Its gaze lands on me, and the pupils dilate. His head dislodges, and he rears back, hissing as poison drips from his fangs and burns holes into the sand.

I back up, the waves inches from my heels.

Its yellow eyes widen, and its breath coats my skin in a thick wave. A screech shakes the sand at my feet.

It attacks.

A roar comes from the ocean, and tentacle shoots from the water, slamming into the serpent and knocking it into the sea. I stumble forward, away from the rising tide, and fall to my hands. My vision swims.

Hello, princess.

The air in my lungs wheezes out, and I nearly sink to the scalding sand. A guttural laugh rasps out of me. *It's Queen now, kraken.*

His clubbed head breaks the surface, and deep-set eyes crinkle at the edges. A tentacle extends from the sandbar, its tip poised to the dock. A bridge.

I eye him. *You won't drown me?*

A life for a life. He blinks, as if considering his words. *The sea needs you, Your Majesty.*

Despite the sand biting my wounds, my lips tilt. *Aw, it does have a heart.*

I can go if you'd rather take your chances with the oversized worm.

Waves rise. I have minutes before the ocean swallows the sandbar. I double check the bag tied to my waist and risk a step onto his outstretched tentacle. Holding out my arms, I test the grip of my boots on the smooth grey skin. I take another step. And another.

Then I sprint. Wind whips through my hair, and the waves sing to me, crashing against the rounded edges of the kraken's tentacle.

As I reach the dock, his tentacle rises, and he delivers me to the planks on the dock. Behind me, the kraken fans his tentacles high into the air and sways them back and forth. A threat.

I bite back a smirk. *Thank you.*

Screams come from the harbor as people retreat, some scrambling for safety. The figures on the dock step back, eyes wide at the sea creature. But Kressa—Kressa stares at me, jaw slack, mouth parted.

"You're incredible," she whispers.

I pin Caelus with a cold, hard stare and untie the pouch from my waist. I shove it into his chest. "You can keep this."

I shoulder my way to Kressa. Bruises from the past day stand stark against her skin and blood trickles down her chin from a fresh cut. I reach up and gingerly wipe it away.

The rhodium hinders our connection, but I push through and say, *Do they suspect who you are?*

She shakes her head.

The knot in my chest unravels, and I look over my shoulder. "Get these cuffs off her. It's not illegal to have power."

"You know," Caelus says, coming up behind me, "you look just like your mother."

My mouth goes dry.

"The look of terror on your face when Kressa stepped into that trap—I saw that look before. When I sank my blade into your mother's chest."

He killed my mother.

My hands ball into fists, but I loosen them and cast my gaze away from Kressa. "I don't know what you're talking about."

His breath is hot on my neck. "You don't? What about that aunt and uncle you were so fond of? What were their names again?" He makes a low humming noise and glances at Isolde.

"Lydia and Malcolm Lockett," she says.

Caelus nods. "Ah, that's right. Both of which do not exist. And your name—Briar Rielle—also fake."

My chest heaves, and I try to swallow around the growing lump in my throat, but it only widens and traps the air in my lungs.

"There has always been something peculiar about you, and this trial proved that," he continues.

"This trial proved nothing," I snarl.

"Ah, but the item you retrieved was charged with power. The light that speared the sky would only flare if touched by someone with Terra's original power running through their veins."

A tempest swells in my stomach and roars in my chest, clawing against my skin, unable to escape.

Kressa brushes her fingers against mine. "What is he talking about?"

Caelus chuckles and turns to her. "Have you ever wondered why Briar can't touch the sea? Why she has sea court power she can't wield?"

"Stop," I plead.

"She's told you she once captained a ship, I presume? Did she ever share its name?"

Kressa flicks her gaze to me.

"And I assume she never shared anything about the marriage she refused a decade ago?"

The world sharpens to a pinprick, and the bond between Kressa and I snaps taut as she stares at me and whispers my name.

Tears sting my eyes. "I was going to tell you."

Caelus smirks. "Tell her what? That your real name is Briar Calisdana? Otherwise known as the forgotten Princess of the Sea."

Kressa's jaw slackens, and she stumbles back a step.

My heart pounds in my throat, and I stretch over the bond, reaching for a hint of the heat between us. Anything to anchor myself to her. But she throws up a wall and locks me out. A mask slips over her face, and I hardly recognize the look in her eyes.

Her head tilts. "Is this true?"

A single tear trails down my cheek, but I knuckle it away and square my shoulders. "Yes."

Her face smooths into cool indifference. She nods to Caelus. "Then I believe these cuffs belong on her."

I gasp. A cord of wind wraps around my body and pins my arms down.

"You promised!" I cry. "You promised nothing could change how you feel."

Kressa doesn't acknowledge me.

"You promised," I whisper on a sob.

Caelus steps around Kressa and unlocks the rhodium cuffs. I don't struggle as his wind drags me closer, and he clamps the shackles tight around my wrists.

He dips his mouth to my ear. "It's fair to say you have indeed broken the law, but I have no plan to execute you. No, binding a princess will be the greatest pleasure of my life."

"Queen," I snarl.

Kressa rubs at her wrists and lifts her head, but nothing shines for me behind her eyes.

Our bond stretches and thins out to a weak, fragile strand. The dregs of power swirling through me deflate, and the world beneath me seems to divide into two.

"Kressa," I breathe.

She turns her back to me. "Let's get this over with."

The group gathers at the edge of the dock. Caelus grabs my upper arm and shoves me forward, stopping in front of a row of guards.

He hands the keys to the guard behind me. "After the judgement, take her to the mirror."

"Yes, Your Highness."

My mouth sours, and I thrash against the cuffs, but they only burn into my skin. Yet this is nothing compared to the torture of a lifetime in that rhodium cell.

I focus on Kressa. I know pain—endured it when I lost my crew. My power. My mother. But this sort of soul shredding agony is gnawing, unbearable.

I would do anything to reach out and brush her hand, say anything to feel her touch. I swallow a choked sob. I need her more than I need salt air in my lungs, more than I need the deck of a ship beneath my feet.

Clenching my jaw, I shed every ounce of pride and expose every raw and unfamiliar vulnerability. I shove myself against her mental barrier and show her the things I don't like about myself, the guilt I've carried for the past decade, the feelings for her I've kept so carefully buried.

If she sees me like this—emotions laid bare—and still refuses our bond, there's nothing more I can do.

I hold my breath.

A muscle tics in her jaw, and she blinks. But she doesn't turn, doesn't respond.

My chest hollows, Kressa's power slowly pulsing like a beating heart. The only piece I'll keep of her.

At the edge of the dock, a shimmering cloud manifests, and Terra steps out. Porcelain skin blinds me, and lavender fills the air. Her polychromatic gaze sweeps to me, and she arches a brow at the shackles behind my back. A smirk tips her lip, and she dismisses me.

Life blooms beneath her feet as she saunters to Kressa and Eric.

"Only two remain," she drawls, voice warm as a summer breeze. "And only one of you will receive a wish. You have my regards, Caelus."

Venom tips her tone, and she spares a serpentine smile at the king, one that promises she can remove his power as swiftly as she granted it.

"It's an honor," Caelus says.

Beside him, Isolde's hands clench into fists.

Terra rakes her gaze over me, and her nostrils flare ever so slightly. "Now, to choose the victor." She shakes out her hair and tilts her head to the heavens. The waves pause their lapping against the wooden posts, ships stilling at the dock. The breeze ceases, and time comes to a halt.

The sky explodes into a rainbow of color, and the moon passes by, followed by a flurry of shooting stars, dizzying me.

It disappears, and the sky returns.

Her head jerks down, eyes glowing shades of blue and black and green.

"Kressa."

59

"What is your wish, Kressa?" Terra says.

Her gaze flicks to me, unreadable, and returns to Terra. Leaning in, she whispers something beneath her breath.

Terra hums. "Are you sure?"

"Yes."

I hold my breath, and the rhodium cuffs hang heavy on my wrists. Kressa never entered the competition to win—only to search for Elias. What could she wish for? To sever our bond? End my life?

The world rumbles, and Terra's lithe form fades. "It is done."

Caelus rolls his shoulders, and his chest expands on an inhale, Isolde's power restoring to its full strength. He leans to the guard at his right, and says something under his breath. The guard nods and relays orders to those further along the dock. They spread across the wooden planks, hands resting on the hilt of their swords.

An uneasy feeling clenches my stomach.

"What is it then, Kressa?" Caelus says. "What did you wish for?"

She turns and drags her fingertips over a rope mooring a ship to the dock, a pirate flag waving from its mast. "You know, Caelus, I've imagined this moment for the last decade." She strides up the gangplank and boards the ship, resting an elbow on the worn railing. "At first, I thought it would be best to storm the castle and take you by surprise."

Caelus stiffens, and frost bites his fingertips.

"But that would be too similar to how you invaded Sarenia. Too cowardly. So instead, I bided my time and infiltrated your court. The Gales was the perfect way to get myself in unchecked, so I thank you for that. It's amazing how sloppy someone gets when they're greedy."

Kressa straightens and tilts her chin, eyes hardening. The look of someone accustomed to royalty. Fierce. Unforgiving.

Powerful.

Guards shift, their sheaths bumping against their thighs.

Kressa's gaze meets mine. "I have to admit, not everything went to plan."

I look away, but not before I catch her nod at someone over my shoulder. A key slips into the cuffs and twists, freeing my hands.

Julian.

"That's why I, Queen Cordelia of the Earth Court, name Briar, Queen of the Sea, captain of this ship."

My attention shoots to Kressa.

Your freedom, my love.

The surface of the ocean rattles. Salt stings my eyes, and waves churn into riptides—growing in anger. For those lost. For those loved. For those robbed from the depths that call it home.

For *me*.

The waves buckle and smash over the dock. An iridescent sheen wraps around me, caressing my skin and lapping at the wounds left behind by the last ten years. It heats my chest and boils to a sizzling rage. Red clouds my vision.

And like a dam, the cage around my power shatters. It bursts free. Salt water swirls with my blood, and briny air infiltrates my lungs.

I inhale a breath through my nose—the air sweeter, colors more vibrant. Lifting a hand, I will the ocean into submission and collect a puddle of salt water into my palm. I meet my reflection in the small pool and smile, allowing the water to fall through the cracks in my fingers.

The ocean. My power.

Me.

Lips parted, Kressa's gaze is trained on me, as if looking away would pain her. The bond between us braids and strengthens, and an overwhelming warmth sweeps over me.

Her nails dig into the rail. *Do you feel that?*

I nod. Whatever was between us amplifies tenfold. Like she rose the sun for me, and I sprinkled the stars in the night sky for her. The world exists for us.

"Kill them!"

The world slams into focus, and a row of guards charge toward me, swords drawn. I stagger back as a wave of soldiers crests from the harbor onto the docks, each armed with blades and arrows. And behind them—

"Wielders," I whisper, the power within me shuddering.

Diamond crested battle armor glitters in the sun, and potent sky power swells at their fingertips, crackling like whips. My mouth goes dry.

Nobles and servants and courtesans alike scatter from the harbor. All but two figures not running away, but sprinting toward us.

Elias and Thea.

"Briar!"

A glint of metal slices through the air and arcs toward my

chest. A blast of flames cuts across the dock and singes the guard to nothing but ash. I stagger back and whip my head to the bow of the ship.

Kressa blinks at her palms.

I stiffen. *You have power from the Fire Court?*

Her gaze roams over me, and she swallows. *I do.*

Storm clouds gather overhead, and the temperature plummets.

Caelus turns to me, ice coating his hands. "Do you want to know what your mother said before I killed her?"

The ocean roils at my back, and I breathe it in. Bend it to my will. The hair brushing my shoulders rises and floats as if I'm underwater. I narrow my eyes. "I'm sure you'll tell me either way."

He smirks. "She dropped to her knees and begged me to spare her."

I snarl, and a wave snaps the dock behind me, spilling over my boots. "You're lying."

"And before I sank my sword into her chest, I promised I'd find her daughter and kill her, too." He lifts his hands and draws icicles from the ocean. They slide between the planks, razor sharp, and each blade points at my heart. "I don't intend to go back on that promise."

They shoot toward me, and I duck, rolling to the side as they hit the ground and shatter. Another spear aims for my head, and I lunge, but it drags across my shoulder and pain blooms in its path.

I snarl and clench my hands into fists, blasting him with a wave. But before it crests, he throws up his hand and turns it to ice.

He chuckles. "A little out of practice, I see."

A chunk of ice slams into me and throws me off the dock. I plunge beneath the dark waves, twirling and spinning in the thrashing water.

Pressing my eyes shut, I allow her to consume me—to reacquaint herself. It's been a decade, and while the waves remain as ancient as ever, I've changed. Evolved.

My power thrums through my body and stretches from its slumber. I float until my lungs beg for air. Opening my eyes, I swim toward the surface.

And slam into a sheet of ice.

I bash my fists against the wall and blast it with water, but it only thickens. Air bubbles from my mouth and my lungs scream.

Kressa!

I claw at the ice, and my thoughts fog, air threatening to expire in my lungs. Flames blot out the sky and a hole appears through the ice, warming the water. I grip the edges and heave myself over the top, gasping for air.

Caelus smiles down from the dock. "Your mother would be ashamed."

I drag myself onto the ice and stand despite my waterlogged clothes. My fingertips tingle at my sides, ready to command the sea, but can't quite remember how.

It's been too long.

Flames lick the skies, shooting from Kressa's hands, but it's not enough to stave off the soldiers storming the docks. It's only a matter of time before she burns out, and the wielders are still at the harbor, waiting for Caelus's orders.

Kressa blasts fire at Caelus, distracting him while I skirt the edge of the ice and climb a rope to the dock. I right myself, and sea water drips down my face, puddling at my feet.

Farther down the dock, Thea and Elias twist around each other, each brandishing a sword as they slice through soldiers. Julian fights beside them, though blood seeps through his clothing, and he winces with each movement.

Marianne and Gemma take up the back, each holding a blade as guards close in on them.

The sky sparks with lightning, and a gust of wind slams into the ship, throwing Kressa onto the deck. Her exhaustion seeps down our bond, and I swallow. She's burning out too fast.

I glance at the shore, where the remaining soldiers and wielders wait. An entire army.

My stomach clenches. There are too many.

We can't take all of them.

"Thea!" I scream, voice carrying over the clash of swords.

Caelus hurls a shard of ice at me, and I throw myself down as it skims the top of my head.

Thea appears a heartbeat later. "Yes, captain?"

I swallow a sob, but we don't have time for a reunion. "Get everyone off the dock and take them to shore."

Her gaze searches me. "And you?"

"I'm staying here."

She hesitates, but nods and hands me her sword. "You need this more than I do."

"Thank you." I wrap my hand around the leather hilt, testing its weight as frost gathers on the planks.

Without another word, Thea takes a step and vanishes.

She reappears in front of Elias, wraps her arms around him, and they disappear. I bite my cheek. If her power is as weak as mine, it'll take her longer than usual to get everyone to shore.

I suck in my cheek. *Kressa?*

Yes?

Her voice comes through with a grunt, and her fatigue seeps into my bones. A pair of guards dart for me, and I lunge, slicing my blade through them. As their bodies fall, more advance.

Can you raise the earth on dry land like you did in the water?

Yes.

How high?

Her gaze meets mine from the bow of the ship, where wave

after wave of guards smash into her. Nicks cover her face, shirt torn along her arms.

Tell me how high, and I'll raise it for you.

A high-pitched scream rips through the air, and I turn as a sword pierces Marianne through the chest. Her body goes limp, a flash of red as she falls to the dock.

Isolde watches me as she yanks the blade from Marianne.

Gemma screeches, falling to her knees over her sister as Isolde mumbles something low enough for only Gemma to hear. Her shoulders stiffen, and she glances at me, her eyes swollen with tears.

"What have you done," I snarl, as water climbs over my skin and coats me in a thin layer of liquid. Waves thrash against the dock, and red floods my vision as I swing my blade through the bodies blocking my path.

The water against my skin heats, nearly scalding.

Let it consume you.

I slam a boiling wave into Isolde, knocking her sideways across the dock. She grapples at her face, skin red and blistering as steam wafts from her.

A guard swings his sword over his head, aimed for Gemma's neck, and I blast a boiling wave into him. He screams and stumbles off the dock, into the water. Behind him, the wielders file down the dock, closing the distance far too quickly.

I scan the space. Where is Thea?

At the ship, Kressa staggers back, hand clamped over her shoulder. Blood seeps through her fingers, and a group of soldiers advance on her.

Kressa, get down!

She drops to the deck, and I cool the temperature, crashing a wave over the ship. A handful of soldiers tumble over the edge, but not nearly enough.

Wielders reach the gangplank and pause, whispering as

they toe the edge. The one closest lifts his hands, and a buzz fills the air, lightning dancing in the clouds overhead.

The water on the deck hasn't drained. My power stutters.

They're going to electrocute her.

Thea appears in front of me, panting. Her chest heaves, and sweat coats her brow.

"Get Gemma to the harbor!" I scream, voice scratching my throat.

She nods and falls to her knees, reaching for Gemma's shoulders.

Gemma grapples for Marianne's lifeless body. "I'm not leaving her!"

"I promise I'll come back for her," Thea whispers, lifting a knowing gaze to me. A lie.

In the next heartbeat, they're gone.

I sprint to the ship, wildly swinging my blade through soldiers. My heart beats in time with the waves roiling beneath the dock, and I throw myself into the wielder at the gangplank.

A flash pierces the sky, and lightning smashes into a rear mast, sending wood fragments flying in all directions. But it didn't strike the water. I sink my blade into him, shoving the body over the edge of the dock.

Thea will be here any second, I say. *When you reach shore, you need to raise a wall around the entire city.*

She heaves herself to the rail. *And you'll meet us there? You can wield the sea from the harbor?*

I quiet my thoughts and will my face to remain blank. *Yes.*

The lie slides out too easy. She would never leave if she knew I was staying here, but my power is too volatile right now. And if she isn't behind the wall to protect the city from my power, I'll drown all of Sarenia.

Kressa blasts a sheet of flames over the wielders, but they shield themselves and ready their hands for another strike. I glance to the skies, dancing with lightning.

Swinging my blade, I dart to the edge of the dock and sever the ropes tied to the ship. Thea materializes at the bow and retches over the side. She wipes her sleeve across her mouth and turns to Kressa.

"Kressa?" I say.

She looks down at me from the ship. "Yes?"

I exhale and relinquish every wall I've built, every shred I've hidden from her. "I'll find you anywhere."

She furrows her brows. I nod at Thea, and she swallows, her face grim.

They disappear.

"Very brave of you, this suicide mission."

Flanked by wielders, Caelus steps closer.

At his shoulder, covered in burns, Isolde bores her gaze into me. "Enough, Briar."

I smile and retreat a step. "It's *Your Highness* to you."

I dive into the ocean.

60

The ocean embraces me, singing me a song only I know. I plunge deeper and let her guide me to the hull of the ship drifting away from the dock. This far down, I can't see past my hands, but the ocean reads my mind, and knows exactly where to send me.

I surface on the other side of the ship, out of sight from the dock. Climbing up the side, I throw myself over the rail and onto the deck.

Sea mist blows against my cheek. I don't have the time to indulge, but I lower myself to the worn planks and revel in the sway of the ship. I inhale the wood, and my fingers trail over the knots in the planks. They don't have the familiar grooves of *The Twelfth Night,* but if I shut my eyes and tune out the world, it's almost like I'm on my ship.

If I pretend enough, it almost feels like home.

The bond tugs at my chest. *You lied to me.*

My mouth sours, but no regret settles in me. *Protect your court, and I'll protect mine. I need you to ground my power and keep me from drowning Sarenia.*

I could have helped you.

I rise and stride to the main mast, unfurling the rope. The sail snaps open. *You will, more than you know. And if I die, someone has to stop Caelus.*

It isn't anger that comes through the bond, but fear. And acceptance. She knows as well as I do the burden we bear. We can't afford to be selfish.

Her thoughts pause, then, *When this is over, I'll find you.*

The temperature plunges, and a layer of ice stretches across the water. Wind whips the sail and the ship rotates. I sprint to the helm and grab hold of the wheel, but it spins out of my grip.

I lunge to the foremast and ease it open. The ship lurches, throwing me against the rail, and as I look over the side, ice traps the ship.

Digging into my power, I smash wave after wave onto it. It splinters at the edges, but doesn't budge, circling the hull. At the dock, a soldier lowers himself to the ice. Then another.

Heat gathers at my palms.

I delve into Kressa's power and flood my thoughts with my mother, with Marianne—all the innocent men and women who lost their lives in The Gales. Rage burns through my veins, searing my blood and boiling the water beneath my skin.

I bottle it up, and just as I'm about to explode, I release it.

At first, nothing happens. Then a crack echoes through the air and shakes the ship. It races across the glacier, and steam rises through the fissure. The water around the ice boils, and soldiers scurry back to the dock. I clench my fist and throw a wave into them. They stumble into the bubbling water.

And don't resurface.

The ice around the hull melts, and at the harbor, a wall of earth rises from the ground, surrounding the outskirts of Sarenia. I push from the rail and run to the wheel, aiming the bow due west, farther out into the ocean.

I close my eyes and will the waves to carry me out. Clouds

billow overhead, crackling, and lightning spears the deck. Smoke billows from the plank and I throw a wave over it before a fire breaks out.

Wind whips at the sails, and a gust slams from the other direction. My heart climbs into my throat as the ship pitches sideways and tilts, the mast tapping the surface of the water.

I'm going to capsize.

I slide across the deck as the pirate flag dips underwater. I find purchase on a rail and cling to it, splinters digging into my palms. I grimace but hold tight as my feet swing airborne. I reverse the direction of the water, and the ship sways back, slamming into the waves.

My forehead smacks against the deck, but I stand and brace myself against the wheel, wiping wet hair out of my face. Between Caelus's wind and the constant change of the current, the ship has hardly moved. Without another pair of hands, I can't shift the masts and steer at the same time.

Screeches fill the air, followed by a steady beat of flapping wings. My throat constricts. A flock of massive falcons blot out the sun, each topped with an archer.

Caelus's air armada.

They inch close enough to make out the snapping beaks of the giant birds. Without full control of my power, I stand no chance against them. And the wall is not nearly high enough yet. My heart thrashes against my ribcage, fingers trembling.

We're out of time.

An arrow nicks my cheek and burrows into the deck. A warning shot.

"Surrender," Caelus yells, "and we'll spare the others."

I lift a hand to my face, and my fingers come back bloody. Silence hangs in the air, interrupted only by wings growing closer with every second. A decade ago, I would have laughed in his face and sent him to the seafloor.

But a decade ago, I was selfish. I didn't know what I had to lose. And now—now I have Thea. I have Kressa. The sea.

I've run out of options.

My hand drops to my side. The waves calm, barely lapping against the hull, and I let out a slow, resigned breath. If my surrender gives Thea and Kressa a chance at survival, I'll take it.

A battle cry sounds from the harbor. One I know deep in my bones.

I sprint to the bow as Thea's feet hit the wooden planks, a sword sheathed at her back. She vanishes, and reappears farther along the dock with a wild grin on her face. She pulls out her blade and swings it in a wide arc. Soldiers fall in her wake, and she disappears again.

Holding my breath, I search for her as the guards and wielders ready themselves. In a flash, she appears at the very end of the dock, her gaze pinned to me as she sprints, faster and faster toward the edge.

Her feet push off the final plank and she leaps into the air, disappearing over the water.

Seconds tick by, and my heart stills as I frantically scan the surface, searching for any trace of her. She's never crossed a distance this far, and with how weak her power is—

"Looking for someone, captain?"

I gasp and spin around. My knees almost buckle. "Thea."

Throwing myself from the rail, I wrap my arms around her. My first mate. My other half. Tears climb my throat and burrow into my eyes.

She throws her arms around me. "You did it, Briar. You broke the curse."

A sob escapes me. I pull back and take in her blue eyes, lit from within. "I told you not to come back."

"I swore my loyalty to you years ago, and today is no different." She dips her head into a bow. "Queen Briar, I will stand by your side to the ends of the earth."

I smile through tears. "And I will stand by your side, to the ends of the earth."

She strides to the main mast and collects the rope in her hands. "And anyway, you look like you forgot how to sail a ship."

"I'm going to pretend you didn't say that."

She smirks, and the wind whips up, throwing my hair around my face. I jump to the helm and grab the wheel. As if she hasn't skipped a beat, Thea maneuvers the sails with the changing wind and guides us out to open ocean.

She twists, and her braids fly in the wind, a smile lighting her face. "Are you ready, captain?"

I nod. I've waited a decade for this.

Hands firmly on the spokes, I press into my power and send it into the ocean. It weaves with the current, dances with the waves. And with half a thought, we gain speed, nearly flying over the whitecaps. The bow skips over each crest, shooting mist over the deck.

Thea leans into it and laughs.

An arrow whizzes past her head.

A dozen falcons dive toward the ship, and panic seizes my throat.

"Hold on to something!"

Thea scrambles for the main mast and throws her arms around it.

I inhale through my nose and release my hands from the wheel. The sails snap and the ship pitches, spinning out of control. I burrow my power into the sea and sweep a wave over the ship, into the air armada. Sunlight filters through the cover of water and time slows as rainbows fracture over the deck. Falcons screech, and the water throws the riders from their backs, into the ocean.

I part the wave, and the world comes back into view. A handful of riders rear back, falcon wings heavy, sodden.

Caelus's foot army scrambles from the dock, but they're met with the growing stone wall—impossible to penetrate or climb. I scan the top, where the tallest buildings in Sarenia still peek through. It's not high enough yet, but if I wait any longer, I risk an arrow to the chest.

I inhale a breath and still my thoughts. "Thea, tie yourself in."

She nods, lips pressed tight as she winds a rope around her waist and secures the other end to the main mast.

I blow out the breath.

Calming the waves smashing against the hull, I steady my feet and lean into the tune of the ocean. I cast my power down into the farthest depths and sweep the water from the shore, tugging it to me.

A tsunami.

Shells, small fish, and coral of all colors lie bare on the exposed seafloor, searching for water. My fingers tremble and my chest grows heavy with the mounting weight at my fingertips. The ship rises higher and higher on the waves, pitching back and forth in the wind. I grit my teeth, my entire body taut as I bend the sea.

Under this water, Caelus won't survive. And neither will Isolde.

A falcon dives toward the ship, its shadow sweeping across the outstretched mast. It emerges from the other side, and the archer releases an arrow. I duck, and it burrows into the wood beside my head.

My power slips, and the ship plummets. We go airborne, and my feet lift from the deck, but I clench my fists and reel it back in. The hull smacks into a wave, and I slam onto the deck as Thea clings to the mast.

The ship groans, and I peer over the edge at the world far

below. Eye to eye with the mountaintops, high above the tallest turrets of the castle, this wave could sink the kingdom.

And we sit at the crest.

The falcon soars off, joining the rest of the armada darting toward the group stranded on the dock.

"Briar." Thea comes to my side, her tone unsteady. The rope around her waist pulls taut.

Below, they load Caelus and Isolde onto the backs of falcons.

"You need to do it, now," she says.

I glance at the wall in the distance that isn't quite high enough, and swallow. "I know."

My fingers tremble, and a searing pain blooms behind my eyes from the pressure of my power. Any longer like this, and I'll burn out.

I turn my head to Thea, the movement making my vision swim. I brace myself against the wheel. "Are you ready?"

She searches my face and nods.

Inhaling a slow, steady breath, I close my eyes and surround myself in a vortex of power. My hair lifts from my shoulders and floats around my head. Pin pricks cover my skin, and my clothes billow in a phantom wind. The ocean rages, splashing onto the deck with each surge of the ship. I tune it all out and hone my focus on the mountain of power beneath me.

My eyes bolt open, and I release it.

Nothing happens.

The waves climb higher, grow more frantic. The sails buck in the wind, ripping against their tethers.

"Captain, what's going on?"

I stare down at my shaking hands—the pressure in my head increasing with every passing second. My breathing rattles. "I—I don't know. It's stuck."

"You have about five seconds to get it unstuck before—"

A grunt severs her words. An arrow protrudes from her

chest, and blood pools from the wound. The ship jolts, and she slides toward the stairs at the helm. Her body slams into the wood, motionless.

"Thea!"

A falcon screeches overhead and dips, its feathers brushing the sails. I scramble from the wheel and crouch beside Thea. She lies still, unconscious. Her chest rattles on an inhale, but barely, her braids dipping into the blood pooling beneath her.

The falcon banks and turns around on itself. Red fills my vision and I bare my teeth, straightening. Unsheathing my sword, I sprint to the bow, toward the arrow pointed at my chest.

The ship pitches, and I leap, arcing my blade through the air. It slices through muscle on the falcon's wing and the beast shrieks, slamming against the rail. The rider loses his grip on the reigns, and they both tumble into the water.

Sheathing the sword, I sprint back to Thea and fall to my knees. Crimson spreads over the planks, and her breathing grows heavier, serrated.

I grab her hand. "Thea. Thea, wake up. I need you."

She doesn't stir.

The space between my ribs hollows out. I hang my head over my shoulders, and tears splash onto the wood.

Falcons screech in the distance, mocking.

I rise in one fluid motion. My eyes narrow, face settling into a cool, concentrated calm. But beneath the facade, a sea rages in my veins and thrashes against my bones. The planks of the deck singe beneath my footsteps, steam rising as I climb to the bow. I stand still at the very edge, my hands loose at my sides.

Far below, where I've sucked the water dry from the seabed, a flock of falcons take off, each seat filled with a rider. I scan the group and find a pair of icy eyes.

Caelus.

I've spent the last decade under his thumb, doing his work.

I stood complacent, unable to do anything while he attacks my court, kills my people. Shames my name.

Not anymore.

I channel every last ounce of power into my fingertips, straining against the burnout. Kressa's power melds with mine, and with anger boiling in my veins, I seize the ocean.

And let it go.

I release an earth-shattering scream and my hold on the waves shatters like glass. The entire world shifts, pitches, and the deck beneath my feet tips down. It gains speed, skimming the waves.

With a tug, I sink the hull into the wave and level out the deck.

Wings fill my vision and arrows arc through the air. I shield the ship with a wave, snapping the arrows in half. A falcon pierces the veil and lands on the deck, beak snapping as the archer pulls back his arm and readies an arrow.

I throw out my hand.

Flames burst from my palm. I gasp, and the falcon and his rider tumble back into the waves.

I stare wide-eyed at my open hand. Turn it over.

Kressa's power.

I throw back the wave shielding the ship. The tsunami roils closer to the wall, its lowest reaches swallowing the soldiers on the dock. Falcons swarm overhead with their beady gazes pinned on me. I restrain the fire and twist a nearby wave into a swirling vortex. Before it funnels, I throw it into a tornado. It grows, towering as it spins across the waves and swallows every falcon in its path.

Then it freezes over and shatters into a million pieces of hail.

I dodge a sheet of ice, and on the back of a falcon, Caelus swoops between the masts. He leaps from his bird, landing on the deck between Thea and me.

A layer of ice coats the wood, the planks groaning under the pressure.

His gaze snakes over me. "Did your mother ever tell you why she promised you to marry?"

"Do not speak of her," I snarl, but the fire raging in my chest falters.

He stalks closer, smirking as frost freezes Thea's blood. "She didn't, did she? She never told you about the deal she made with Terra." A low chuckle rumbles from his chest. "Your mother—Marina—promised you to marry if Terra made her the ruler of the sea."

I stagger back, bracing a hand on the rail. "You're lying."

His lip curls. "I wish I was. Before you were born, your mother killed the original queen and stole the throne."

"No, she didn't." My fingertips tingle, power begging to be released. "The sea was gifted to her when my grandmother was murdered."

"A convenient lie constructed with Terra's help." He takes a step.

My hold on the ocean nearly collapses, and a breath catches in my throat.

I unravel a hand and stare at my palm. The ocean sings in my veins, calls to my soul. Bends to my will. I shake my head. "You're a liar."

"You can ask your mother when I send you to Serinos."

He snarls and lunges forward, swinging his daggers through the air. One slices a gash through my shoulder, but I dodge the second, and his blade shatters on the rail. Another forms in his hand, and I twist, putting myself between him and Thea.

Warm blood trails down my arm, and I swing my blade. It slices across his forearm, and I slam my foot into his stomach, throwing him to the deck. I shove my boot to his chest and angle my sword to the vein pulsing over his throat.

I tilt my head and smile. "For the last decade, I've dreamt of the day I get to take your life."

An icicle forms in his hand, and he buries it into my calf. I scream, but the fire swirling through my veins melts the ice before it sinks any further. His eyes widen, and ice rises from the boards, forming along the whitecaps of nearby waves. But I melt it with half a thought.

Flames build in my chest, and I welcome it. I let it consume me until my vision clouds over and my bones singe. The water under my skin boils, morphing to steam.

"You—" he stammers.

Pushing my blade deeper into his skin, I draw a bead of blood. I will a wave of heat through my arm and down the blade, heating it to a brand. The very tip burns into his skin.

We rush closer and closer to the wall, and an arrow burrows into the wood at my feet. I don't flinch. With a flick of my wrist, I throw a shield of water over the ship.

The sea tunnels around us. "I am Briar, Queen of the Sea, captain of this ship. And you, Caelus, are trespassing on my court. I find you guilty of murdering my mother, the former queen. An act punishable by death."

Raising my blade, I grip it with both hands and spear it through his chest. He coughs blood, and I let it gather on the planks, not bothering to wash it away with a wave. No. I want the memory of his death to stain this deck. I sink down to a knee and clench his jaw in my hand, forcing him to look at me.

"You don't deserve a dignified death," I snarl.

I drop his face and yank my blade free. Releasing my hold on the shield, water rains down on us. I toss him from the deck on a wave and throw him into the air, higher than the falcons— higher than the wall growing closer, so any onlooker, any person he has wronged, can watch him die.

He floats midair for a moment, and I raise my palm to the sky.

Fire blasts from my hand into the heavens, turning Caelus into nothing but a cloud of ash. The waves carry me forward, and whatever remains of him floats down onto the sea, deep into the depths, where his soul will know no peace.

I don't spot the wall until we slam into it and the ship splinters into a thousand pieces.

61

———

A gentle sway stirs me from sleep. I groan and turn my head as a throb pulses behind my eyes. Light filters through my eyelids, and I blink them open. Waves lap against a set of sweeping windows, and blinding light reflects off water. Deep cracks sting my dry lips, but a smile pulls at my mouth.

The ocean.

Yet I can't taste her salt or hear her song.

I shift, and my shoulder stings where tape secures a wide strip of bloodied gauze. Wincing, I go to rub my eyes, but my hands don't cooperate, as if they're weighed down. An ache spreads through my chest, hollow and gnawing. With how much power I expelled, it's a miracle I didn't burn out completely.

"She's awake."

I swivel my head to the voice, and my vision tunnels on a generous captain's quarters, about the size as *The Twelfth Night*. Yet there's nothing familiar about the crest on the wall—a sprawling tree with intertwined limbs.

A table takes up the majority of the space, its edges adorned with deep green emeralds. On the far wall, two portraits frame a detailed map, yet no sign of Delterran's whereabouts.

Kressa sits on a padded armchair, knuckles white against the arms. Our gazes lock, and she looks away, her grip tightening. Resting against the open doorway, Elias presses his lips into a thin line.

A sea breeze floats in from outside, carrying wisps of brine, and sways the ends of Kressa's hair. Sunlight beats down on the wooden deck, and a crew chatters.

I go to swallow, but my mouth is too dry. "Where am I?"

Neither of them answer.

I open my mind. *Kressa?*

She doesn't so much as flinch, as if my words didn't register.

"Can you hear me?" I ask.

Elias straightens, sending a final glance to his sister. "I should go check on Thea."

I gasp and jolt from the mattress, but my arms jerk back and metal bites into the skin at my wrists. My gaze trails down my arm and past the crook of my elbow. I shrug off the thin sheet.

My stomach hollows out at the metal wrapped around my wrists.

Rhodium.

"Where's Thea!" I scream, jerking against the bed frame bolted to the wall.

Pain sears up my side, where skin pulls taut against a row of stitches. I bite back the sting and thrash harder, but the rhodium only siphons more of my power and energy.

Elias lowers his gaze and backtracks out of the room, pulling the door shut behind him. The quarters dim and cast Kressa's face in shadows, but she hasn't muttered a word—hasn't even looked at me.

I freeze and pin her with a glare. "Explain. Now. Where is she?"

She doesn't raise her head. "In the brig. Recovering, like you."

"*Brig?*" I snarl.

She doesn't pause. "Caelus is dead, but Isolde escaped on the back of a falcon. And you, my"—her hands clench, and she clears her throat—"We're crossing to Ignata."

"Why am I in rhodium cuffs?"

Finally, she stands. A sliver of sunlight washes over her face, and I resist the urge to flinch. The soft look in her eyes she spared only for me has disappeared. Rather, they're hard as stone, her jaw set like granite.

I search the recesses of my mind and grapple for the door leading to hers, but it's nowhere to be found. The cord tethering me to her—our bond—gone. My heart races, and I press myself to a shallow seat as she stops before me.

"You are in rhodium cuffs, Briar Calisdana, because you are a prisoner of the Earth Court."

THE END

ACKNOWLEDGMENTS

Where do I begin? The process of writing a book is akin to scooping your heart out and handing it to a room full of people, hoping they'll love it. I have infinite gratitude for the people who saw my heart, turned it over, and held it gently along the way.

To my agent, Cathie Hedrick-Armstrong. This book came into the world in a different way than we imagined, but your enthusiasm for the story and commitment to my career never waned. I am so, so lucky to have you in my corner.

Kelsey—you've been here from the very beginning. I wouldn't be the writer I am without you and your never-ending support. Thank you for naming roaches after people who hurt my feelings, having a spare pocket for my grudges, and making me laugh until I cry. I can't wait to see all the good coming your way.

Lindsay—you feel like the brightest star in the sky. I wish I could siphon your talent and ability to make such compelling stories. Thank you for always offering to read my books and tarot cards, and for being someone I can always turn to.

Aleshka—we've been friends in every timeline. You are the most genuine person I know, and I'd trust all of my books in your hands. Thank you for being a voice of reason and for being someone I can always lean on.

Cara—you inspire me to no end. Your writing and ability to craft characters that break my heart is so impressive. Thank you for paving the way for me and answering all of my questions.

To the Train—Alice, Allissa, Brenna, Katie G, Katie J, Liz, Emily, Isabelle, Lex, Makayla, and Megan. I adore every single one of you. Thank you for your endless support of this book and for loving the kraken as much as I do. I couldn't do it without you all.

Maggie Eckersley, you were one of the first to read the original version of this book, and your support for it means the world to me.

To the indie authors who gave me priceless advice—Cara Calloway, Emilia Finn, Alexis Maragold, Tee Harlowe, and Margaret Rose. Thank you so much for your wisdom and patience with my onslaught of questions.

A huge thank you to all the authors in the Mid-List Discord. You all are a wealth of knowledge, and I am consistently blown away by the talent in that group.

Editë, Shelbie, and Marissa—what started out as a book club has become such a wonderful group of friends. Thank you for filling my cup every month and never being mad when I don't finish the book.

Kate, Tiffany, and Margaret—our monthly writer meetups are my favorite. I am so grateful to have such a wonderful and talented group of local writers I get to call friends.

Alex—thank you for your support in all the early days of my writing career. James and Ellie are so lucky to have you.

Taylor Holland—you have seen me through so many phases of life and loved me in each of them. It's crazy to think it's been over a decade since we shared a bunk in college, and even crazier to think we haven't known each other our entire lives. Thanks for being like a sister to me.

Maddie, Katie, and Mikayla—you bring so much color and joy into my life. Thank you for being true and constant friends.

Riley and Brooklyn—thank you for your themed parties, endless laughter, and support for my writing. They say you can't pick your family, but I'd pick you two anyway.

James and Eleanor—seeing the world through your eyes is my greatest joy in life.

Madisson—you make me believe in the love I write about. Thank you for fiercely believing in my dreams and cheering me on every step of the way. I love you, endlessly.

To the queer community. Your enthusiasm for this book proves how important it is to have representation in literature. As long as I am writing, my books will always be a safe place for you.

And finally, to every reader who gave this book a chance. My heart is in your hands now.

ABOUT THE AUTHOR

Haley J Munroe writes emotionally devastating sapphic romance. When she's not writing (rare), she can be found daydreaming, diving down a rabbit hole, or photosynthesizing. You can find her across social media @haleyjmunroe.